Since her first book was published in January 1996, **Lori Foster** has become a *New York Times, USA TODAY* and *Publishers Weekly* bestselling author. She lives in Central Ohio, where coffee helps her keep up with her cats and grandkids between writing books. For more about Lori, visit her website at lorifoster.com, like her on Facebook or find her on Twitter, @lorilfoster.

Brenda Jackson is a *New York Times* bestselling author of more than one hundred romance titles. Brenda lives in Jacksonville, Florida, and divides her time between family, writing and traveling. Email Brenda at authorbrendajackson@gmail.com or visit her on her website at brendajackson.net.

New York Times Bestselling Author

LORI FOSTER

IMPETUOUS

**HARLEQUIN
BESTSELLING
AUTHOR
COLLECTION**

**HARLEQUIN®
BESTSELLING
AUTHOR
COLLECTION**

Recycling programs
for this product may
not exist in your area.

ISBN-13: 978-1-335-54263-2

Impetuous
First published in 1995. This edition published in 2020.
Copyright © 1995 by Lori Foster

The Proposal
First published in 2011. This edition published in 2020.
Copyright © 2011 by Brenda Streater Jackson

This edition published by arrangement with Harlequin Books S.A.

For questions and comments about the quality of this book, please contact us at CustomerService@Harlequin.com.

Harlequin Enterprises ULC
22 Adelaide St. West, 40th Floor
Toronto, Ontario M5H 4E3, Canada
www.Harlequin.com

Printed in U.S.A.

CONTENTS

**Also available from Lori Foster
and HQN**

Road to Love

Driven to Distraction
Slow Ride
All Fired Up

The Summer Resort

Cooper's Charm
Sisters of Summer's End

Other must-reads

Jax (ebook novella)
Boone (ebook novella)
Tucker (ebook novella)
A Buckhorn Baby
Built for Love (ebook novella)

Don't miss *The Somerset Girls* from HQN,
available June 2020!

Visit the Author Profile page at Harlequin.com,
or lorifoster.com, for more titles.

IMPETUOUS

Lori Foster

Chapter 1

"You can't be a coward forever."

Carlie chuckled, despite her nervousness. "Quit pushing, Bren. You're not going to provoke me into rushing out into the party dressed like this."

"Rushing? You're already ten minutes late." She had parked in the back of the house, away from the main flow of human traffic entering the party. Small, twinkling lights surrounded the pool and pool house, even though the weather was too brisk for swimming.

"And that's *your* fault. What were you thinking, to pick me a costume that was so...so..." Carlie couldn't quite find the words to describe the skimpy harem outfit her best friend had chosen for her. If she had to go to Brenda's stupid Halloween party at all, she would have preferred to be a pumpkin or a witch. Anything that was less revealing.

"So…what? You look fantastic. What's wrong with that? I want you to have fun tonight. I want you to loosen up a little and try socializing. Talk to people."

"You mean men, don't you?" Carlie shook her head. "I'm not a hermit, Bren. I have my students and more than enough school activities to keep me busy." Then she glanced down at herself. "What *were* you thinking?"

"You said you didn't have time to pick out an outfit yourself." Brenda lifted one shoulder in a halfhearted shrug. "Besides, you make a very sexy harem girl. All the single men here tonight will drool. It'll do you good to realize how attractive you can be when you aren't hiding behind those hideous suits."

Carlie winced. She was feeling far from attractive. Exhibited, displayed and downright exposed was more accurate. She was pretty certain she looked ridiculous more than anything else. "Which single men, exactly, did you invite?"

Brenda waved her hand in dismissal. "You've met almost everyone, I think. Some of Jason's associates, a few neighbors, friends… Tyler."

Carlie went perfectly still for a heartbeat, then frowned at Brenda. "Tyler Ramsey at a costume party? I didn't think your notorious brother-in-law would bother with something so—"

"Don't make fun of my party, Carlie."

"I wasn't. I just thought fancy banquets were more his speed." Carlie couldn't imagine Tyler dressed in a costume. He always seemed so…suave. And he always had a very sophisticated, very elegant woman on his arm.

"Tyler came because Jason asked him, and he would

never let his brother down. You know how close they are." Brenda shook her head and added, "You know, you and Tyler actually have a few things in common."

Carlie turned away. "You're dreaming, Bren. We live in different worlds."

"You just don't understand Tyler. He had it pretty rough growing up, too." Then she touched Carlie's arm. "But at least Jason was always there for him."

"My brother had his own life," Carlie said. "And he was right, my problems were my own."

"Jason would never turn Tyler away if he needed help."

"Jason's a terrific guy. But he and Tyler are nothing alike."

"Not now, maybe, but they used to be," Brenda said with a grin. "But then, Jason met me. I think Tyler will be the same. When he finds someone he cares about…"

Carlie narrowed her eyes and stiffened her shoulders. "That will be a little hard for him to do when his relationships rarely last long enough to get to know a woman."

Brenda stared at Carlie, her eyebrows raised. "You seem to be keeping pretty close track of my young brother-in-law."

"He's not that young." But Carlie flushed at being caught. "I mean, he's a grown man. He must be in his early thirties…oh, never mind."

"Tyler's a good guy, Carlie. He may change dates a lot, but that's because the women he usually hooks up with are only impressed by his status in the community and his expanding financial portfolio. Tyler *thinks* he wants a no-strings attachment, but he's never satisfied with it."

Carlie had a feeling it was Tyler's looks and outrageous charm that really attracted women, but she kept her mouth shut. She certainly didn't want Brenda to get the idea she had a crush on Tyler Ramsey.

Good grief. A *crush*! No, she didn't. Certainly not.

Carlie was shaking her head at her errant thoughts, even as she said, "You don't have to defend Tyler to me, Bren. What he does is no concern of mine."

"Fine. Then if you're done stalling, can we get back to the party now? I think it's about to rain."

Carlie glanced up at the dark sky and smelled the moisture thick in the air. "You go on, Bren. I think I'll just wait a few more minutes."

Brenda hesitated, then she nodded. "Don't be too long."

Too long? Carlie wondered if another hour or so would be too long. She truly didn't relish the idea of going inside, not that anyone would recognize her. Dressed so differently, no one would see her as Carlie McDaniels, grade-school teacher and spinster extraordinaire. Her persona this evening was as far from her usual self as a woman could get. Even her hair and eyes were different, thanks to the wig that came with the costume, and the colored contacts she was wearing.

She was a coward, true, but it had been two long years since her divorce, and though that had been enough time for her to gain her independence and put some order to her life, it hadn't been time enough to repair her confidence in herself as a woman. Brenda claimed Carlie was attractive and appealing. Carlie's ex had made an entirely different claim.

Shivering, she forced her mind away from the disturbing memories, mustered her courage and started toward the door. She could make Brenda happy by mingling for an hour or so, then she could make her escape. The thought of her small, tidy, *empty* house seemed very nice all of a sudden.

Tyler Ramsey hated parties.

Looking around in mild amusement, he tried not to appear bored. Everything was the same—the ritual, the games. There were several women, alone and obviously on the hunt, who had been eyeing him since he'd entered. A Cleopatra, an elf, a disco dancer—they all were playing their phoney roles to the hilt. They were drawn to his reputation, he knew. The funny part was, most of it wasn't even true.

Turning away, he wondered why he'd allowed Brenda to talk him into coming. True, he'd been bored for a while, at loose ends with himself. He needed a spark; he needed someone who could make him laugh.

His brother laughed a lot these days.

Not that Tyler wanted to settle down. He hadn't met a woman yet with whom he could consider spending the rest of his life. Jason was lucky to have found Brenda; she was the best. But women like her were rare. Glancing around the room again, Tyler realized just what a find Brenda was. The house was filled with females, but none of them held his attention. They were all…the same. Laughing, flirting, drinking. They stood poised to best advantage, their gestures predictable.

He'd been told more than once now how dashing he looked in his pirate costume. Everyone knew it was him. He wasn't wearing makeup as some of the other guests did. His only concession was an eye patch, worn rakishly over his left eye. A billowing white shirt that he found extremely comfortable, and tight black trousers completed the costume. His belt—wide, with a huge brass buckle— held a scabbard, with a sword resting inside it. His black boots came to his knees.

He sat in a chair, observing the crowd dispassionately. Immediately, a blond Valkyrie, brass breastplate shining in the glow of party lights, came to perch on his knee, and gave him a sly smile. He recognized that smile. It belonged to his ex-companion, Valerie. It was a smile that signaled her intent, and he used to respond to it appropriately. All he felt now was irritation. She leaned close, and he forced a polite expression to his features. They'd shared something brief, and by her insistence, with no strings attached. The outcome had been predictable.

She'd wanted a man who knew the score, who could afford the best, who moved in certain circles—her circles. She liked his sports car, his professional connections, and sex. In that order.

And he'd needed someone to help him fill his time, to give him something to think about other than his legal cases and the fact that his personal life was basically…empty. But it was over.

He knew it. Why didn't she?

"Don't you recognize me, Tyler?"

There was no place to put his hands, so he rested one on her back, the other on her naked thigh. "Of course. You're a beautiful Norse goddess." His legendary innate charm surfaced through his impatience.

Valerie chuckled throatily. "You make a very believable pirate. Have you made any plans to plunder the party and steal away with female captives?"

He didn't feel like playing, so he conjured the lie without hesitation. "Actually, sweetheart, I have."

She pouted, and ran her fingers through his hair. "You look so dashing, Tyler."

He barely restrained himself from rolling his eyes. He thought of going home to his empty house—and the thought no longer seemed so unappealing.

He glanced up, and saw his sister-in-law, Brenda, standing by the kitchen door, talking with a man dressed as a Roman general. Tyler was just deciding to go home and nurse his discontent in the privacy of his own home, when Brenda turned toward the kitchen with an expectant look on her face. She gave a wide smile, and the Roman nearly dropped his glass of liquor.

Tyler felt anticipation for the first time that night. He stared, waiting. Brenda suddenly appeared to be very delighted, and he wondered why. She seemed every bit as impish as the fairy she was dressed to be.

Slowly disengaging himself from Valerie's clinging hold, Tyler stood, his curiosity swelling. He was so intent on watching Brenda, he didn't hear Valerie's complaints. His eyes were glued to the kitchen doorway.

And then he saw her.

His knees locked and he felt his thighs tense. The woman stood uncertainly by Brenda, apparently oblivious to the stares she was drawing. She was magnificent.

Long, dark curly hair fell to her shoulders, and her costume left little to the imagination. Lush, was the first thought to come to mind.

She wasn't slim, but her curves were in all the right places. Her long legs were beautifully shaped, lightly muscled, teasingly displayed in the wispy, transparent harem pants. Her waist was trim, her navel a soft shadow in the gentle swell of her belly. Her shoulders, straight and broad for a woman, were held proudly, despite her obvious reluctance, and her pale breasts were very full, firm and high. She was wearing an ornate mask, that covered her face from her nose to her hairline. He didn't care.

She bent and whispered something in Brenda's ear. Brenda lost her smile, and looked around the room as if seeking encouragement. Her eyes passed over Tyler, then seeing his rapt stare, she turned to the harem girl. *Her eyes* soon followed.

He caught her gaze, literally. Even from the distance that separated them, Tyler could feel her nervousness. She seemed startled by his awareness, and displeased. She was poised for flight.

He didn't smile. He pulled off his eye patch and started toward her. She seemed unable to move, her eyes widening. As he came closer, he saw that she was very pale and that her eyes were a startling, unnatural shade of vivid blue. Contacts? As part of her costume?

He was intrigued.

With only a few feet separating them, he was pulled to an abrupt stop by Valerie.

He glanced at Valerie with stark impatience. "I have to go."

"Tyler, wait! I wanted to talk to you." Her hand slid up his arm to grip his shirt. Her voice lowered to a purr. "I need a date tomorrow. For a banquet. It will be...fun."

He didn't have time for this. Valerie always came around when she wanted something from him. He had no doubt she needed him to gain entrée into the charity banquet. With plates going at a thousand dollars apiece, she knew there would be influential people there.

He wasn't interested.

Shaking his head, he turned back toward the woman in the harem costume…but she was gone. He moved to the kitchen in time to see her ducking out the back door. A hundred thoughts flew through his mind.

She was exquisite, exciting, and she was evidently running. From him?

He didn't want to lose sight of her, didn't want to take the chance that he wouldn't be able to find her again later. It was ridiculous, really, the urgency he felt, but he acted on it, anyway.

Brenda caught his arm as he tried to go past her.

"Tyler!" Her grip was firm, effectively stopping him. "Aren't you going to say hi?"

"What?" His question was a bark, filled with impatience.

Brenda stared at him. "What's the matter with you?"

"Who was she?"

Her eyebrows arching, Brenda looked behind her. "Oh…just one of the guests."

Tyler narrowed his eyes. "She's leaving already?"

"No, she…" Brenda shook her head. "She's a little shy. I had to talk her into coming tonight and now she's having second thoughts."

"I think I'll go get some fresh air."

Her smile slipping, Brenda seemed startled by his abrupt statement. "It's starting to rain, Tyler. Why would you…?"

Starting to walk away, but at a more reasonable pace, he said, "Don't worry about it, Brenda. I prom-

ise not to track in any mud." Then he stepped out the
back door and peered through the cloudy night, trying to catch sight of her. A lighted path led to the pool
house, and more lights, in an array of party colors,
circled the small building. Through the smattering of
raindrops falling on his face, Tyler was able to see
a flash of movement. Ignoring the rain, he followed.

His heart was hammering heavily, his stride rapid
on the wet flagstone walk. His muscles were so tight,
his movements seemed rough and jerky. He couldn't
remember the last time he'd felt so anxious to meet a
woman.

Impatience and anticipation were riding him, and
he forced himself to stop outside the door of the small
house. He tilted his head back, letting the rain cool
his face. He was overreacting. She was only a woman,
after all, he told himself.

But then he remembered her wide, startled eyes and
felt his stomach clench.

He put his hand on the doorknob, half expecting
it to be locked. It opened silently, allowing the muted
sounds of the party to intrude.

Colored light filtered through the windows in diminished shades, elongating shadows and playing over
various forms and furnishings. He gave his eyes a moment to adjust to the dim interior, and then he saw her.

She had been standing turned away from him, one
hand pressed to her forehead, the other knotted at her
side. But when the door closed with a soft click behind
him, she jerked, then swung around to face him. Her
hand fluttered to her chest and she took a hasty step
backward, then halted, staring.

Tyler swallowed heavily. He could feel her nervousness, her uncertainty, and something very basic, very male, erupted inside him. He'd never known a woman to be this way, had never before felt the overwhelming urge to offer comfort, to ease a woman with assurances. He wanted—right this minute—to hold her, to touch her...to make love to her. He sucked in a deep breath, leaned back against the closed door and forced a gentle smile. "Hello."

Carlie felt frozen in place. She could feel his eyes drifting over her body, could hear every breath he took. She didn't know what to do. He couldn't have recognized her, yet he obviously liked what he saw. She'd never seen a man react that way—not to her. She couldn't speak, her voice was trapped in her throat.

He whispered softly, "You're beautiful."

Her eyes shifted nervously with the racing of her heart. Brenda had said men would find her attractive, but... She hadn't believed her, not really. Usually, Tyler never looked at her twice, but then, he'd never seen her dressed like this.

The costume was definitely a mistake.

Tyler was still watching her, and she inhaled. She had to say something. "You look...dangerous."

His teeth flashed in a quick grin. "Not dashing?"

Confused, she shook her head. In an even lower tone, sounding of accusation and anticipation, she asked, "What happened to your date?"

He tipped his head, as if he was straining to hear her, then carefully stepped away from the door. "She wasn't my date."

Liar, she thought. A man like him wouldn't come to a party alone. He attracted beautiful women without

even trying. And Valerie Rush was certainly that—
beautiful, chic, sophisticated and very sure of her own
appeal. She was everything Carlie was not.

So why was Tyler here now? She'd always been
aware of him; he was impossible to ignore. Dark,
charming, a devastating man. But completely unat-
tainable. At least for her.

Of course, after her disastrous marriage, she didn't
want any man, not even Tyler Ramsey.

He took another step forward when she remained
silent, and she went back one, bumping into the wall.

He was watching her so very closely, almost stalking
her, and she could feel her chest shuddering, straining
for air. She trembled inside, feeling light-headed and
so conscious of him as a male. She didn't dare take
her eyes off him.

He took another step.

The rain was coming down more heavily now, tapping against the windows and the wind had begun to
whistle. Carlie was glad for the darkness. She didn't
want reality to intrude too quickly. She didn't want
him to recognize her. Not yet.

Maybe not ever.

He started to reach for her, then dropped his hand.
"Do you know who I am?"

She shook her head. "No." She didn't know this man
at all, so intense and attentive, exuding raw sexuality.
The air was filled with his scent, his purpose.

His eyes drifted over her body again, then he stared
intently into hers.

She didn't dare say anything. What was there to say?
He wasn't reacting to Carlie McDaniels. He was reacting to the night; to the atmosphere and the mystery of

a masquerade. If he knew who she was, he'd lose interest quickly enough. He'd give her that same polite nod she'd always received from him, then go on his way.

Tyler stepped toward her and she balked, feeling her back against the wall. It would be mortifying for him to realize her identity now, with her acting like such a ninny. She was a professional woman, a teacher, mature and capable. And here she was, behaving like a coward. A virgin coward.

She knew in that instant, she wouldn't tell him. He would never find out who she was. She had to leave, had to…

His hand caught her arm. "Wait. Please."

She trembled, trying to pull loose, stunned by the strength of his grasp.

He released her instantly. Holding his hands out to the sides, he tried to softly reassure her. "It's okay. I'm sorry." She trembled again, and he said, "You're cold."

Swamped with uncertainty, wanting to do one thing, but knowing she should do another, Carlie turned away. Then Tyler was behind her, not touching her, but the warmth of his body surrounded her. She felt a pulse beat of heat run through her, swirling in her belly. The feeling was unfamiliar…and exciting. As his breath brushed her nape, she shivered with growing sensation.

His palms grazed her shoulders, smoothing away the chills and the dampness from the rain, warming her. She was surrounded by him, by his scent.

His touch was tentative, careful, and when she didn't move, he leaned closer, his chest barely touching her back, his thighs brushing her own. She shuddered.

His fingers continued to stroke, feather-light, up and down her arms. He drew in a slow, rough breath, then molded his hands over her shoulders, holding her. She felt his suspended breathing, his hesitation. And when he finally spoke, his voice was low and unsteady.

"*I want you.* I think I wanted you the moment I saw you."

She stilled as his lips very lightly touched the side of her neck. Slowly, he drew her toward him, her back against his chest, then waited, keeping her pressed close to his solid length.

"I want you," he repeated. *"Stay with me."*

Only in her wildest imaginings had she ever considered Tyler saying such a thing to her. It was unbelievable. It was outrageous.

It was her own private fantasy.

She swallowed hard, squeezed her eyes shut, then whispered, "I want you, too."

Chapter 2

Tilting his head back, Tyler exhaled slowly, then tried to relax. It was unbelievable how much her answer meant to him. *She was staying*.

He didn't understand his own reaction, or hers, for that matter. He only knew he needed to get closer to her. She'd stood there in the doorway earlier, looking feminine, yet so unsure. Unlike the other women in the room, she hadn't flaunted her assets; she hadn't even seemed aware of them, despite the provocative harem costume that left her more bare than not. Even now, she seemed so vulnerable, so wary.

He leaned down, inhaling her fragrance, then touched his open palm to her soft belly. She jerked and pulled away.

He was surprised by her reaction, and forced himself to go perfectly still. He squeezed her shoulders again. "Shh. I'm not going to hurt you." She remained strangely quiet, her body trembling, and then it hit him just how innocent she truly was. Suddenly, it made sense—the way she'd reacted to his interest. She was wary, and with good reason. He felt confusion first, then the unfamiliar stirring of protectiveness. He didn't want to frighten her, didn't want her to be uncomfortable with him. He closed his eyes and wrapped his arms around her, hugging her carefully.

"I would never hurt you."

Her hands came up to clasp his arms where they crossed her chest, giving him her silent trust.

His chest squeezed tight. It was remarkable how she affected him. Smiling, he rubbed his chin against her temple, then turned her to face him.

He cupped her jaw, tilting her chin toward him. He could see the scant light reflected in her wide eyes. Slowly, tentatively, he bent and put his lips to hers. It wasn't a devouring kiss, but tender and sweet. She seemed unsure of where to put her hands, then laid them lightly on his chest.

He groaned quietly, tugging her closer. "Open your mouth," he urged, continuing to nibble at her lips.

She did, gasping, and he teased her, stroking her mouth, licking carefully at her lips, touching her tongue with his own.

After a few moments, he pulled back. Her fingers had curled tight against him, and she was panting softly. Instinctively, he pressed his arousal, full and hard, against her belly. She seemed stunned by his blatant need, and he relished her reaction to it, watching her eyes slowly close. Nothing had ever made him feel so wild or urgent, so alive with sensation, as her innocent acceptance.

Her mask was in the way and he touched his fingers to it. Instantly, she jerked back, her hand coming up to cover her mouth.

His muscles grew taut. "I didn't…" Tyler hesitated, then shook his head. "I'm sorry. I just…it seems so…right."

She shook her head. "You can't take off my mask."

His eyebrows shot up.

"I don't want you to know…who I am."

He stepped closer to her, feeling the heat build under his skin. She was the most fascinating woman he'd ever met. He tried to get her to look at him, but she turned away. It was unbelievably erotic, a woman appearing so demure, but wearing such an enticing costume. He touched her chin, bringing her face back toward him. "What do you want?"

Swallowing hard, she whispered, "You. This." And she leaned toward him.

Tyler caught his breath, and then he was kissing her again. He stroked his tongue deep in her mouth, drawing her closer, feeling his urgency swell. He was no longer thinking of his own consuming desire, not entirely. Now he was driven by a need to give her everything she asked for, everything she could possibly hope for. He didn't want her to regret trusting him.

He didn't want her to regret anything.

When he lifted his head, she was breathless and trembling, her small hands clasping his shirt in a death grip. Moving slowly, he touched the buttons on her skimpy jacket, for the moment ignoring her mask. "A mystery lady."

His words were deep and husky and she trembled as he undid the first button. As soon as it slid free, he raised his gaze to her face, judging her reaction.

She flattened her hands on the wall beside her hips, but she didn't protest. Tyler smiled, then looked down to watch the slow unveiling of her breasts.

The second button was undone, and still he didn't touch her in any other way. He was only using one hand, being careful not to startle her. The third button was straining at the material. With one finger, he traced her cleavage, over the swell of each breast, then up her throat. He looked at her lips, then traced the fullness of her mouth, pressing slightly to glide over the inside of her bottom lip.

Her lips parted and she instinctively curled her tongue around the tip of his finger. His eyes closed and he drew a slow, painful breath. When he looked at her again, she was watching him cautiously, her eyes dark in the dim shadows. He leaned forward and kissed her very gently, tenderly, his lips moving over her chin, to her collarbone, then her breasts.

The third button held, and Tyler found her nipple through the cloth. She moaned. Even through the material he could feel the heat of her body as he drew upon her, his teeth carefully nipping.

The last button opened, and he covered each breast with a warm palm, cradling her lush weight, shaping her with his hands. He pressed her breasts together and nuzzled her cleavage before moving his mouth to a nipple, licking and plucking with his lips, then finally taking her inside, suckling strongly. A sound of raw hunger escaped her, and he felt the impact of that small sound deep in his belly.

Her fingers sank into his hair, pulling him away. But he didn't leave her. Instead, he slipped to his knees, his mouth against her ribs. Closing his eyes and locking his arms around her hips, he rubbed his face against her skin, breathing in her heated scent, tasting her.

He savored her, taking his time to explore each facet of his senses; touch and taste and smell. And sight. He enjoyed looking at her; he enjoyed her pleasure and her surprise as he found a particularly sensitive spot.

His hands cupped her buttocks, startling her. Then slowly, he removed her slippers, his fingers lingering on her slim ankles. His palms coasted up her calves, over her thighs, and to her buttocks again, squeezing and cuddling. Then his fingers hooked in the waistband of her harem pants and, still watching her, he started sliding them down.

Tyler saw her embarrassment, and he leaned forward, kissing her navel, dipping his tongue teasingly inside. He wanted to reassure her, wanted her to understand how unique this was for him. But at the moment, words escaped him.

She stepped out of the pants as he directed, then remained silent while he looked his fill.

Oh God, what she did to him.

Gazing at her from his position on his knees, he had to call upon all his restraint to keep from rushing her. He wasn't himself. Feelings he hadn't known existed washed over him in hot, insistent waves.

The small jacket hung from her shoulders, serving more as ornamentation than covering since her breasts were freed. The shadowy room only enhanced her curves and made the moment more intimate. He could see the darkness of her nipples, her navel, the soft feminine curls between her thighs. He lightly brushed his fingers over her, finding her wet and hot. He delved deeper, stroking her, his breaths coming fast and low.

She gasped, and her hand clasped his wrist.

He turned his palm so he was holding hers, then took her other hand also, pinning her arms gently to her sides. He leaned forward, and this time it was his tongue that stroked her. She reacted immediately, pulling away, staring at him in appalled fascination.

Again, he felt that possessiveness, that need to protect her.

Tyler came slowly to his feet, his face flushed, his chest rising and falling quickly. He kept his tone gentle and quiet. "What's wrong?"

Her voice emerged as a dry croak. "It's…you can't."

Since he now understood her innocence, Tyler didn't press her. But he wanted her to realize the depth of her own allure. "I understand, but honey, I want to kiss you there. I want to kiss you everywhere." He held her eyes, refusing to let her look away, then added in a husky whisper, "You taste like a woman should, very sweet and sexy."

She shivered, then pressed her right hand over his chest, near where his heart was thundering. He covered her hand with his own, then began unbuttoning his shirt. He felt her nails as she flexed her fingers into his flesh. He'd never had a woman watch him with such intent curiosity. His body reacted to her interest, tightening and swelling. His gaze never left her face.

He removed his trousers quickly, hearing her low, fast breathing. He found a condom in his wallet, then tossed his pants aside. He laid the protection on the table.

When he turned to her again, he saw her uncertainty, and pulled her close, relishing the feel of her naked skin. Kissing her throat and shoulder, his hands curved around her body, his fingers splayed warm and firm on her sensitive belly.

He was patient and gently persuasive, but he was also very aroused. Deliberately, he nestled his fullness against her buttocks. He needed her to know the effect she had on him.

He kissed her for a few moments, and when he finally slid his fingers down her belly and into the soft curls between her legs, she didn't draw away. His fingers delved deeper, and she moaned.

His heart thundered at the small sound. "That's it. Relax, sweetheart." He slid a finger inside her, and she quivered, letting out a short cry. "You're wet," he said, softly stroking her, bringing his other hand up to hold a heavy breast, idly plying the nipple with his thumb. She leaned back on him, gasping, and he smiled.

She clutched at his hard thighs, her fingers biting deep into his muscles. Her legs stiffened, and soft, hungry sounds escaped her throat.

Close to losing what was left of his control, Tyler lifted her into his arms and carried her quickly to the narrow couch. He laid her down, coming over her and pulling her close.

She moaned as his mouth closed over her nipple, then moaned again when he smoothed his hand over her soft belly and into her feminine curls. His fingers stroked, dipped, plucked lightly, making her squirm. He lowered his mouth to her nipple and toyed with it, teasing her with his tongue and teeth.

Her climax took him by surprise. It gripped her

body, forcing her to arch wildly, her eyes closed, her mouth open as she gasped and gave low, throaty moans. Enthralled, Tyler watched her, feeling her pleasure and her loss of control. Seeing her shock.

And when the rushing sensations would have ended, Tyler bent to taste her, crushing down on her with renewed urgency, his hand holding her face still for his kiss. She was crying, unable to help herself, and he kissed her jaw, undone by her soft, breathy sighs.

"It's all right now. Shh."

She shook her head. With tears clogging her throat and reflecting in her voice, she whispered brokenly, "I've never..."

"Shh. I know." His mouth skimmed hers, his eyes alight with satisfaction and possession.

He couldn't wait any longer.

Lifting slightly away from her, he reached for the condom and slid it on. She didn't watch him, but he didn't think it was embarrassment now, so much as repletion. Her breasts, heaving still, showed soft and white, reflecting the scant light. Her belly still quivered. But there was a small, awed smile on her lips, a look of wonder that filled him.

Thunder clapped loudly outside, and the storm picked up tempo, mirroring his explosive emotions.

He began kissing her again, light, biting kisses that made her smile and open her eyes. His muscles were taut, straining for release. She laid her palm to his cheek.

He sat back to look at her, running his fingers through her hair. It was then he realized she was wearing a wig. The hair was too coarse, too dense to be real.

The fact that she had taken such pains to conceal herself only added to her intrigue. His mystery woman.

She pulled him closer in silent demand.

He reached down and parted her with his fingers, then gently pushed inside. His groan was long and ragged. Gasping, she twisted against him, her arms tightening, her hips lifting to his. He pressed her knees wider, giving himself more access to her body, then clenched his jaw as he sank deeper. "There we go. All the way."

She shuddered as her body adjusted to his length and thickness. It was pure fantasy, he thought, wishing he could stay like this forever. She squirmed beneath him in delicious sensation.

Tyler shuddered, pressing his hips to hers to still her movements, trying to maintain his barely leashed control, but it was too late. He reared up, his arms stiffened on either side of her, his eyes hot and probing, holding her gaze. Then he began to move.

The friction was exquisite, and she lifted her hips toward him, taking more, her legs wrapping around him. His gaze dropped to her breasts, to her tightened nipples. He was enthralled, watching her full breasts sway as each of his thrusts rocked her body.

He threw his head back, biting off a groan. His jaw was tense, his words a growled whisper. "I don't believe this!"

He felt her tighten around him, felt the pulsing of her climax. He groaned heavily, and his body went rigid as he climaxed. Then he stilled.

His weight was now fully upon her and his heartbeat rocked his body with its uneven cadence. He stroked her idly, without thought, without even knowing what he was doing. She smelled so good, and he *felt* so good.

She stirred beneath him, and he obligingly raised himself to his elbows. Her mask was askew, and he smiled at the picture she made, tousled innocence, sensual lure. He didn't want the night to end.

"Do you have to go anytime soon?"

That surprised her.

Smiling, Tyler stroked her cheek. "Will you stay with me for a while longer?"

Her smile was shaky, a bit uncertain, but it was a smile.

Laughing, feeling incredibly lighthearted, he held her tight as he turned on the couch, putting her on top of him. She came up on her elbows, her heavy breasts swaying over his chest.

"Now, this is nice." His hands cupped her, his thumbs flicking over her soft, dusky nipples until they drew tight.

"Can you scoot up just a bit?" he growled. "I want you in my mouth."

Her lips parted, but she complied, her breath already thickening. Tyler swept his hands down her back and spread them wide over the buttocks, pressing her close.

"I'm going to make love to you all night, honey. I want to show you all the different ways to enjoy yourself. I'm going to see to it that you're so overwhelmed with pleasure, you won't be able to resist seeing me again." He said the words quietly just before he took her nipple in his mouth, licking and teasing and making her shudder. His hands moved over her bottom to the back of her thighs, then parted her legs so she was draped over him. "You'll wake up at night and think of me touching you." His finger slid inside her and she tensed, her hips pressing hard against him.

"I want you to think of me," he explained, loving her with his fingers until she trembled uncontrollably, "because I know I'll be thinking of you."

Tyler held to his promise, exhausting both himself and Carlie with pleasure.

Hours later, long after midnight, he slept, still holding her close. Carlie was stunned by all that had happened, never having imagined that such complete satisfaction was possible.

Tyler lay relaxed beside her, one heavy muscled arm circling her belly, his hand splayed over her hip. He was even beautiful when he slept, she thought, when the lines of his face softened, making him look almost vulnerable.

Of course, he could never know the truth. She would be mortified if Tyler ever discovered he'd made love with his sister-in-law's dumpy best friend. Tyler didn't even *look* at women like her, let alone sleep with them.

Not that she wanted it any other way. She was dumpy by design, choosing her clothes with an eye for concealment, rather than enticement. She didn't want a man, any man—not now, not ever.

Relationships hurt. She'd learned that lesson after her marriage failed. And she'd also learned she could rely on no one but herself. Not on the grandfather who'd raised her after her parents' death, treating her more like a burden than a grandchild, nor on her brother, who'd made it clear she was to deal with her mistakes on her own.

But marriage had been her biggest mistake. One she wasn't likely to forget.

She could never tell Tyler the truth, but at least she'd learned something valuable; she wasn't frigid. Her husband had been wrong, his accusations unjust. Probably, it had just been another of his attempts to destroy her self-confidence. But now she knew the truth, and for that, if nothing else, she was glad she'd stayed with Tyler.

He shifted in his sleep, and she stilled, watching him closely, but he didn't awaken. She leaned down and very gently kissed him on the corner of his mouth, then slipped from the couch.

By the time Tyler woke, a smile of anticipation on his face, Carlie was gone.

Chapter 3

"You can't tell anyone I was at the party."

Brenda tugged Carlie through the kitchen door and then quickly shut it. "I wondered all night what happened to you. Where did you go? Why did you leave so soon? I thought for sure you were going to enjoy yourself."

Wincing, Carlie gave Brenda an apologetic look. She had enjoyed herself, all right, just not the way Brenda had expected. She pulled out a chair at the round wooden table and slumped into it. "I didn't mean to worry you. I'm sorry."

"So what happened? Why did you run off?"

Hesitating, Carlie tried to decide how much to tell her friend. It wouldn't be the whole truth, that was for certain. Somehow, the night seemed…magical, something she could tuck away and keep to herself. She couldn't share it, not even with Brenda. But she had to tell her something...

"Brenda... I felt really foolish...in the costume. Maybe if I hadn't been wearing something so..."

"Sexy?"

Carlie spared her friend a quick look, and saw Brenda was smiling. "Yeah, well, maybe. I just couldn't face all those people looking like that."

"I'm sorry I pushed, Carlie. I just wanted you to realize how attractive you are. Those damn baggy suits you wear make you look fat." Brenda pursed her lips, then idly traced the wood grain in the table with a fingertip. "Tyler noticed you."

Carlie felt her heartbeat race. "I... Did he say something to you?"

"He asked who you were."

"You didn't tell him!" Carlie nearly choked on her embarrassment, waiting for Brenda's reply.

"No. I just told him you were a guest." Then she patted Carlie's arm. "Hey, calm down. It wouldn't be the end of the world if Tyler took a liking to you. You have to admit, he's gorgeous."

Oh, yeah, he was gorgeous. Carlie licked her lips, then said carefully, "He, ah, approached me."

"He did?"

"Yes." Carlie cleared her throat, then immediately launched into her rehearsed story. "We talked for a while. In, ah, the pool house."

When Brenda's eyes widened, Carlie reminded her, "It was raining, remember? And we went inside to stay dry. He, well, he was attracted to me."

"No kidding?"

Carlie hated the note of fascination in her friend's

tone. She also hated lying to her, but she didn't see any way around it. Brenda leaned forward. "So, what happened?"

Carlie shrugged. "He didn't recognize me."

"Well, of course he didn't! He's used to seeing you looking like this!" Brenda indicated Carlie's dark, frumpy suit. With her honey blond hair in a tight braid and a pair of glasses perched on her nose, she looked nothing like the harem girl of the night before.

"This isn't funny, Brenda!" Carlie felt like strangling her. "And you can't ever tell him, either. I don't want him to know it was me he was...flirting with."

Brenda looked skeptical. "Ah, Carlie, don't you think—"

Whatever Brenda was going to say was cut off by a loud voice from the living room. Seconds later, Jason and Tyler strode into the kitchen. Carlie stiffened, all her defenses jerking into place. But her face remained impassive. Almost painfully so. There was absolutely no way she would let Tyler know she was the woman he'd spent the night with. She didn't even want to think about how mortifying that would be.

Brenda didn't miss a beat after shooting Carlie an I'm-not-responsible-for-this look. "I thought you fellas were going fishing. What happened?"

Tyler reached Brenda first. He leaned down and lifted her from her chair, giving her a tight bear hug and a kiss on the cheek.

Brenda's face turned pink. "What did I do to deserve that?"

Tyler's smile was so warm and sincere, Carlie had to look away. "You invited me to your party." Then he added softly, "Thanks."

Jason shook his head, and Carlie had the horrifying suspicion that Tyler had confided to him what had happened. *Don't blush, don't blush!* She glanced at Jason, but he was looking at his wife.

Leaning down, he kissed Brenda, then nodded briefly to Carlie. "The fish weren't biting and it's damned cold out there. Besides, Tyler can't seem to sit still today."

Tyler pulled out a chair and straddled it, crossing his arms over the chair back. "Could I have some coffee, Bren? Then I need to talk to you." He glanced at Carlie, and smiled. "Hi. Ah, Carlie, isn't it?"

"Hello." Carlie mentally applauded her calm response. She was more than a little surprised Tyler remembered her name. She prayed it was all he remembered. And then she looked at him, and despite herself, she remembered lying beside him in the pool house, remembered that magnificent body of his leaning toward her... She looked away, trying to collect her thoughts. Good looks only took a person so far, and from what she knew of Tyler, his had taken him around the block more than a few times. Last night had been a milestone in her life; to Tyler, it had probably been no more than a good time.

Carlie breathed a sigh of relief when she realized he hadn't connected her to the party. His expression had been friendly, nothing more. Already he was ignoring her, dismissing her easily.

"I'll have the coffee ready in just a minute." Brenda was grinning affectionately at Tyler, obviously more than pleased to cater to him.

Tyler tapped his fingers on the table with an excess of energy. His gaze took a turn around the room, then settled on Carlie again. "So. What are you ladies up to today?"

She felt her heart flutter and color rise to her cheeks. Carlie wanted to smack herself. Enough was enough. She would not be an idiot around this man. She composed her features and met his look squarely. "We were talking about the new sports program I'm working on for the school." She paused, then decided to elaborate. "It's a way to help the kids who have trouble socializing. They're not bad kids but they just aren't sure how to conduct themselves with their peers. They need guidance and a chance to interact, with supervision. If they're playing a sport, they'll be getting exercise, burning off energy and learning to work together. I think the program will go over pretty good. I thought I'd try basketball first. The kids have to play together, but since it's not really a contact sport, tussles ought to be kept to a minimum. Brenda and I were just discussing how great it is that Jason has agreed to be an instructor."

Tyler listened, his eyes intent on Carlie's face, watching her so closely she felt herself near to blushing again. "Sounds like you really care about these kids."

His tone was soft, almost disbelieving, and Carlie stiffened. "Of course I do. I care very much about all my students."

Tyler rubbed his chin, still watching her. "And you really think you can make a difference?"

Carlie leaned back in her chair, forgetting her embarrassment, forgetting last night. The gall of the man, to question her like this! With her hands in fists, she replied, "I'll certainly do my best to. At least *I'm* trying to do something to help."

Jason looked at Carlie, then Tyler. A smile appeared. "I, ah, suppose I should tell you something, Carlie. I won't be able to help you, after all. Some things came up at the office." His grin widened, and he shrugged. "I talked to Tyler this morning, and he agreed to do the project with you, instead."

Carlie closed her eyes for a heartbeat, praying she hadn't heard that. But when she opened her eyes, Tyler was still watching her, his smile now smug.

She cleared her throat and shoved her glasses needlessly up the bridge of her nose. "I don't know, Jason." What excuse could she use after practically challenging the man to help? "Maybe that wouldn't be a good idea."

It was Tyler who answered her. "Why not?"

Floundering, she racked her brain, but couldn't come up with a valid reason. "You understand, it will be three or four nights a week? And we need someone who will set a good example for the kids. Someone patient."

Tyler raised his eyebrow, looking affronted. "I'd be a good example. Hell, I'm a lawyer, same as Jason. I've been to college. I'm articulate."

"You're even housebroken," Brenda added, seeming to enjoy the situation.

He nodded. "Damn right." Then to Carlie, "You see? I'll be perfect for the job."

"But..." The truth was, she simply didn't want to work with Tyler. Not now, not after last night. "I don't know. Have you ever worked with kids? And remember, these kids can be a little...difficult."

Jason interrupted. "Tyler should understand them on a gut level, because he was always damned difficult, too."

Tyler laughed. "So it's settled. When do we start?"

Carlie stood with as much aplomb as she could muster. Tyler's eyes drifted over her body, almost out of habit, it seemed, but there was no sign of recognition in his expression. It rankled, even while she prayed he wouldn't make the connection. She tugged at the bottom of her tailored suit coat, smoothing it over her slacks. Then she used a tactic that had worked with many rebellious students. She deliberately looked down her nose at him. "I'll have to let you know."

Tyler merely nodded. "You do that."

Brenda rushed forward to give Carlie a hug. "Give me a call later. Promise?"

"Of course. And thanks for the company, Bren. See ya' later, Jason." She ignored Tyler, not feeling the least bit guilty about it, and exited the room, her back stiff, her tight braid pulling at her temples. She wasn't entirely out of the house when she heard Tyler say, "That has to be the prickliest woman I've ever met. I got the distinct impression she didn't like me. Can you imagine?"

Jason's laugh was sharp. "Unheard of, isn't it?"

There was a shrug in his tone when Tyler replied, "There's just no figuring some women."

Carlie allowed the door to slam just a bit too hard behind her.

It was a very neat, utilitarian office. Carlie was surprised at how functional each piece of furniture was, with only a modicum of necessary decorations. The walls were beige, the carpet a swirling mixture of blues and creams. The sofa and two chairs were upholstered in a rough nubby fabric of a deep blue, and the wooden end tables were light oak. It was a comfortable room, without any indication of Tyler's personal style, which she'd assumed to be rather flamboyant.

The office door opened and Tyler stepped out, accompanied by the secretary who had first greeted Carlie. His smile was warm, a natural smile that Carlie knew he bestowed on almost every female he encountered. Beyond him, she could see into his office, and noticed his desk strewn with papers and files. Suddenly, she realized how disruptive, and presumptuous, her visit was, but she also knew if she hadn't come today, she wouldn't have come at all. Brenda had told her he'd been asking about the harem girl from the party. He wanted to know who she was.

Carlie hoped he would eventually give up and forget about that night…but then, she also knew how badly it would hurt her if he was able to do just that.

Lately, she felt awfully confused.

"I'm sorry I kept you waiting, Carlie. I didn't realize it was you. I'm not familiar with the name McDaniels."

Of course, he wouldn't be. Carlie took his hand. Very briefly. "I hope I'm not interrupting. I can see you're busy. I just wanted to stop by and tell you I'd like to accept your offer of assistance for our new sports program." She was rushing through her words, but she couldn't seem to stop herself. She'd spent three days stewing over what to do, and finally decided that her personal embarrassment had to take a back seat to the kids' problems. She was the only one who knew she had reason to be embarrassed, and since no one else had agreed to help, Tyler was her only option.

"We hope to start next week, so I wanted to drop

off the material I've put together. You might want to look it over before meeting the children."

Tyler accepted the papers she thrust toward him, then motioned her into his office. "Come on in and have a seat."

"I don't want to take up too much of your time." And she wanted to get away from him as quickly as possible.

He lifted one shoulder in an exaggerated shrug. "I needed a break, anyway."

Carlie followed him into his office and sat on the edge of a straight-back, narrow leather chair. Tyler went behind his desk, seating himself with all the officious attitude of any good lawyer.

After skimming through the papers she'd given him, he looked at her again. "You're very thorough."

She blushed and she hated herself for it. "It's just a basic overview of the children who will begin in the program. I thought it would help if you knew what kind of problem each child was having and what their backgrounds were like. The idea is that any child who collects more than three after-school detentions or in-school suspensions will have the choice of joining the team or having their misconduct shown in their grades. Of course, if they choose to join the team, they'll have to contribute wholeheartedly and follow instructions to the letter. In other words, they'll have to work together and get along. They'll have to accept that rules have a purpose, and everyone has to follow them. The program had been used in several schools. So far, it's been very promising."

Tyler nodded, then gave her another of his intent,

probing stares. "How many children will we be starting with?"

Carlie cleared her throat and looked away. She let her eyes roam around his office while she spoke, pretending an interest in his bookshelves, but really trying to avoid his stare. "The list I've given you has nine kids. Of course, that number can change daily. And the children will be released from their obligation whenever they show an improved attitude toward school. But no child will ever be forced to quit the team."

"Will we get to compete against other teams?"

Carlie didn't answer right away. Tyler's genuine interest amazed and confused her. She had half expected him to give only a show of concern. But he was studying the list, all signs of the womanizer gone while he perused her notes. She was looking at the top of his head, at how thick and dark his hair was, how it curled just the tiniest bit. He glanced up and caught her staring. At his *hair* for crying out loud.

He ran his fingers through it negligently. "What's the matter? Have I sprung a streak of gray?"

Carlie folded her arms defensively. "No, I…no. I was just thinking."

Tyler laid the file down, once again giving her his full attention. "About what?"

"About…whether or not we'd be playing other schools, of course," she said quickly. Then, taking a deep breath, she continued. "I don't believe so, at least not at first. If after a time the team shapes up, that would be entirely your decision how far to carry it." Carlie forced herself to stare at him directly, though she felt a faint blush on her cheeks.

Tyler smiled at her again, leaning back in his chair

and folding his hands across his stomach. "You have the most unusual eyes. Very intense. Especially now, while we're talking about the children. I don't believe I've ever seen that exact shade of hazel."

She stiffened. "Thank you, but I don't think the color of my eyes has any bearing on this program."

"It was just an observation."

He was still leaning back in his chair, his posture relaxed, his gaze lazy, and Carlie realized he was deliberately provoking her. She decided not to oblige him. She came to her feet, still holding his gaze, and stared down at him. "Personal observations aside, do you have anything else you'd like to discuss?"

Carlie watched as he struggled to stifle his amusement. He stood behind his desk, his dark eyes warm and smiling. Then, leisurely, he began looking her over. She tolerated his perusal, trying to keep her expression blank, even while her pulse raced and her palms grew damp. She was well aware of what she looked like. Her suit was a deep, dark green, almost brown, and it was cut in straight lines, effectively hiding any signs of her figure.

"You're tall for a woman."

What an inane comment. But true. Carlie's head was just about even with his nose, and she was wearing flats. She glanced down at her shoes when he did. They were ugly, round-toed, and extremely comfortable.

She drew on disdain to hide her sudden discomfort. "If you don't have any other questions about the program, I'll be on my way. I wouldn't want to keep you from anything…important." She turned, and headed for the door without another word.

Tyler came around his desk and stepped in front

of her, blocking her exit. He wasn't grinning now, but she could still see the humor in his eyes. "Forgive me, Carlie. I didn't mean to be rude." Before she could reply, he lifted the folder in his hand. "May I keep this?"

She watched him warily. His apology sounded genuine, but she still felt he was laughing at her. She gritted her teeth, wishing she could rid her mind of intimate thoughts concerning Tyler Ramsey. She hadn't thought of a man that way in a very long time.

She was determined to stop right now. She didn't return his smile, or acknowledge his apology. "Of course. I have my own copy."

Tyler gave her an amused, mischievous grin, almost as if he'd read her thoughts. "Excellent. When do we start?"

"How soon can you start? I'll send home the notices to the parents as soon as you give me a schedule that suits you."

"Tell you what. Let me check things over and I'll get back to you tomorrow. What time do you leave the school?"

Carlie hesitated. "Around four."

"I'll come by then. Maybe we could go somewhere and work out a schedule that will suit us both." He indicated his cluttered desk. "Unfortunately, I don't have the time right now to take care of it."

"I…" Carlie mentally scurried for excuses. She did not want to go anywhere with Tyler Ramsey. The man had a chaotic effect on her senses. He had only to smile at her, and memories came rushing back, so intense, so powerful, that her stomach clenched and her nerve endings rioted. She hoped her thoughts of him would fade with time; she hoped she could eventually forget him completely.

It wouldn't happen today. Though she hated to admit it, even to herself, he rattled her as few people could. But she refused to be a coward about the situation. The best way to deal with a problem was to face it head-on, she reminded herself. Summoning a bland smile, she nodded. "That would be fine, Tyler. Thank you."

She was standing at her desk, stacking papers, when Tyler walked in. Her door was open, so he took a moment to simply look at her. Dressed in another of her prim, spinsterish outfits, her hair pulled back in a braid, she looked like the epitome of the perfect schoolmarm. And she was humming softly.

He felt something shift inside him. Never in his own school days could he remember a teacher like her, someone who actually wanted to help. He'd always thought of Carlie as simply Brenda's friend, a little odd, a lot frumpy, but nice enough.

Now he had to look at her with new respect.

Raising a hand, he gave two sharp knocks on the open door. She jerked, looking up with wide eyes and peering at him through the lenses of her glasses.

"They told me at the office where I could find you." He stepped in, looking around the room with interest. "Very nice."

She smiled with an obvious touch of pride. "Thank you. I try to make the classroom nice. It should be a comfortable place to be, an *easy* place to be. Do you know what I mean?"

Strangely enough, he did. The room was decorated in bright colors with plenty of the children's artwork hanging on the walls. It was a thought-provoking room. He walked toward a workstation that was filled with hands-on activities. There were dominoes, rubber stamps and numerous math games. The room gave an overall appearance of bustling activity. He smiled at her, seeing that she was watching him cautiously. "You like to teach."

She straightened. "Yes. And I'm good at it. Children respond well to me."

She could be so damned bristly, with no real provocation. "I'm sure you are. You're authoritative, but gently so. Children wouldn't be afraid of you."

Lowering her eyebrows, she gave him a ferocious look, as if she didn't trust the sincerity of his words. He smiled back, and waited.

Finally, she nodded. "No child should ever be afraid. Certainly not of their teacher. I do my best to make sure they're at ease, to let them know they can talk to me if they need to."

Tyler turned away. He didn't want her to see how she affected him. He could still remember being a kid himself, feeling defensive and hurt because his dad wasn't around, and his mother couldn't be bothered. His teachers hadn't cared about a kid with problems. Their idea of understanding was to send him to the office whenever he upset their lessons.

He certainly hadn't had a teacher like Carlie.

"What is it, Tyler? What's wrong?"

Her perception was uncanny. He realized he was holding a math paper one student had left on a desk, and he slowly laid it down and turned to her. "I have the greatest respect for teachers. For anyone having a gift with children. There are too many people out there who don't care about kids, even their own."

He knew he shouldn't have said so much the minute the words were out of his mouth. Carlie was scrutinizing him carefully. He shook his head and wandered around the room, surveying all the desks, laughing when he saw one that was overflowing with old papers. He straightened a chair, centered a book, replaced a pencil that had fallen on the floor.

Carlie began helping him tidy up. "The children may like me, but they're always in a hurry to leave when the bell rings." She indicated the disheveled desks. "They tend to be a little sloppy at times."

Tyler refocused on her. "Do you have children of your own?" He discovered he was suddenly very interested in her.

"No."

Just that one curt word. He crossed his arms over his chest. "You're not married?"

"Mr. Ramsey..."

He smiled. "Do you want children of your own someday?"

Lowering her gaze, she ignored his question and pulled her purse from beneath her desk. "We'd better be going. I have tests to grade tonight and lessons to prepare for the morning."

He accepted her change of subject without comment, and motioned for her to lead the way. They'd be spending a lot of time together, several nights a week. He'd get to know her better, and she would eventually warm up to him.

That thought brought with it images of another woman, a woman who had warmed up to him, only to leave him. He still felt irritated when he thought of how he'd woken up alone, a stupid smile on his face.

But even then, he hadn't considered that was the end of it. He'd assumed he'd find out who she was from Brenda, then have the pleasure of getting to know his harem girl better.

But Brenda said the woman didn't want to be identified, and short of telling her *why* he wanted to know, he couldn't very well demand the mystery woman's name. But he hated the thought he might never see her again, and he hated even more that the night had evidently meant so little to her. It had been special to him, a night to cherish.

And the woman didn't want anything to do with him.

Carlie was halfway to the door when Tyler caught up with her, automatically taking her arm. "Let's take my car, and I'll bring you back here when we're finished."

"I'd prefer to drive."

Bristly. She was stiff, her arm rigid in his grasp. He had the distinct notion she resented his touch, though he hadn't a clue why. He was getting a little disgruntled with female rejection, and the question came out a little sharper than he'd intended. "Why?"

She didn't look at him, but he saw her pull her bottom lip between her teeth. She had a nice profile, he realized, and the lip she was punishing was soft and full. Then she nodded. "Very well. You may drive."

Chapter 4

Tyler had very large hands.

Carlie stared, without meaning to, as he cut into a piece of peach pie, then put the bite in his mouth and chewed. His jaw was strong, lean and hard, with only a slight shadow of dark beard stubble. His nose, straight and high-bridged, would appear aristocratic but for the lump where he had broken it in a fight when he was younger. Bren had told her the story, about how Jason had joined in and the two brothers had ended up defeating four other kids.

His eyebrows were straight and dark. His lashes thick and long. His cheekbones high and sculpted. There was a healthy color to his skin, not a dark-baked tan, but definitely the added color of outdoor activities.

Carlie sipped her coffee, her gaze going again to his hands. She remembered those hands so well, the way they had touched her, their strength, their gentleness. The memory gave her an odd tingle.

"Aren't you going to eat your pie?" he asked.

Carlie pulled her eyes away from his hands. She nodded and took a large mouthful to give her something to do, namely chew, while Tyler filled the silence with questions.

"I could come to the school Friday, around four again, if you want me to do some sort of sign-up, or make a roster. What about you? Can you make it, or is that too soon?"

"Friday would be terrific. I'll put out a few calls tomorrow during lunch to see who can stay over. The ones who can't make it can have a schedule Monday."

Tyler pulled a piece of paper from his pocket. "These are my best times to get together. I tried to make them as regular as possible, so the kids can know what to expect. You can look that over then let me know if you'll have a problem with any of those dates."

She tucked the paper into her purse. "It'll be fine."

"You didn't even look at it. How do you know it won't interrupt your plans?"

Carlie gave him a quick smile. "We're glad to have your help. Whatever works for you is fine with me."

Tyler laid his fork by his plate and shook his head. "You know the saying about all work and no play? You have to take time for a social life, too."

"Why don't you let me worry about my social life, all right?" she said, annoyed with his persistence.

"What social life? It doesn't sound to me as if you have one."

That was entirely too close to the truth, and rubbed Carlie the wrong way. "Look, Mr. Ramsey. You may be the authority on having a good time, but I take my commitments seriously."

She watched Tyler's face go rigid, and then he leaned toward her. "And I don't?"

"Not from what I hear."

Leaning back, Tyler observed Carlie thoughtfully. "You know, if we're going to work together, you'll have to get over your attitude. I don't know why you dislike me so much, but it's not something I'm used to. Nor do I intend to get used to it." He waited a heartbeat, and Carlie felt his annoyance wash over her before he added, "I'd really like to work with you and the kids. But if you would rather find someone else to help you with your project, I'll drop out."

It was plain, by his tone and expression, he didn't want to do that. He wanted to be involved, for whatever reasons, and Carlie *did* need him. She hated to admit the truth, but it was her own personal conflict that was causing the problems. What she needed was an emotional compromise.

After adjusting her glasses, she straightened. "I think we can manage to get along if we keep it on a business level."

Tyler shook his head. "No go. I don't have a 'business level.' You're going to have to get your little nose out of the air and be friendly."

Her compromise exploded into oblivion. Did everything have to be his way? "You're an extremely arrogant person!"

His chuckle was warm and husky. "Bren says the same thing regularly. Funny, it sounds almost affectionate coming from her."

"She's too softhearted."

"Yes, she is. It's amazing you two are friends."

Uh-oh. Dangerous territory. Carlie held his gaze with an effort, the implied insult overlooked entirely. "We've known each other for a long time."

Tyler considered that. "Do you know many of her other friends?"

"A few."

"Who?"

Ah, so that was it. He didn't for one minute suspect her as the mystery woman from the other night; she was too unlikely to even be considered. But he was fishing to find out who the woman was. She hesitated just long enough, pretending deep thought, until he cleared his throat.

Several names came to mind, most of the women quite attractive, and Carlie named them, watching as he pondered each one. She was ready to laugh, when a familiar voice interrupted them.

"Ms. McDaniels! How nice to see you here. And how is my boy doing?"

Carlie smiled, and turned in her seat to face Mr. Briant.

She was totally at ease as a teacher dealing with a parent, and invited him to join their table. She reassured the anxious father, taking a few minutes to go over things he could do at home that would help his son improve his skills even more. She was specific, but very patient with the man's concerns. She was also aware that Tyler was watching her, sipping his coffee and listening to their conversation intently. He looked almost…impressed by her.

When the father finally left, Tyler lifted his coffee cup in a salute to her. "Does that happen often?"

"Yes. This is a small town, and thankfully the parents are, for the most part, very involved with their children's education."

"Your Mr. Briant seemed to hang on your every word."

Carlie smiled crookedly. "We had a misunderstanding of sorts with the first failing grade I sent home with his son. You see, he decided it was my fault, and came to the school to tell me so."

"Let me guess. You chewed him up and spit him out, right?"

Carlie's smile froze. "I'm not an ogre. He was upset, so I tried to explain. I pulled out all the papers I had been keeping on his son, Brady, and showed them to him. I went over the procedure we used with new materials, and I told him his son was distracted and not paying attention in class."

"Carlie, I didn't mean—"

She shook her head. "It's all right. I know what you meant." Idly stirring her coffee, she whispered, "It was such a sad situation. Mr. Briant had just lost his wife. He was very withdrawn and angry. He hadn't been able to concentrate on his son yet, who was having his own problems adjusting." She sighed, remembering how difficult it had been to see the father and son together, each struggling with his loss. "We spent a lot of time together after class. Sometimes we worked on lessons, but a lot of the time we just talked. I… I lost my parents when I was young, so I knew how Brady must have felt. At a time like that, school work kind of takes a backseat to trying to survive the emotional pain."

Tyler was studying his coffee cup. "It must have been rough for you."

His quiet words, filled with understanding and sympathy surprised her.

She nodded. "Everything worked out, though. After Brady started catching up, Mr. Briant joined us in our after-school lessons. I think he was lonely, too, and looking for some direction. He wanted to learn how to help his son study, so for a few weeks I helped him do that. Now they're on their own, and Brady Briant is earning A's."

Tyler stared at her, and Carlie could feel him looking beneath her calm control, trying to read her thoughts. "You're very dedicated," he said quietly.

"You have to be dedicated, to any job, if you want to do it well." Then she smiled, curious over Tyler's distracted expression. "That's no reason to be so solemn, though."

"I was just wondering how dedicated I am to my job, to handling the small load of petty cases that land on my desk each month."

"And?"

"Oh, I'd say...not very."

"That can't be true. Jason says you do a wonderful job."

"I'm a good lawyer." It was a statement of fact, with no fringe of lace to pretty it up. Abruptly, he reached across the table and took her hand.

Carlie tried to pull away, but he held her firm. "I'm sorry if I inadvertently insulted you. I only meant that you're very sure of yourself and you appear to be able to handle any situation. Including irascible fathers."

It was more difficult than she'd expected, because Tyler wasn't what she'd expected. At least, not completely. There were too many facets to his personality, and now he seemed genuinely thoughtful, interested in the children and concerned that he might have hurt her feelings. And he'd been very patient while she'd talked to Mr. Briant.

His hand was warm and strong, feeling exactly as she remembered. But her reaction wasn't dulled by familiarity.

"I'm not invincible, Mr. Ramsey. I simply don't believe in allowing myself to be trod upon."

"You've done that before, you know. Called me mister when you're agitated. I think we know each other well enough to dispense with mister and Ms., don't you?"

She managed to slip her hand free, but only because Tyler allowed it. She needed to regather her defenses; Tyler was a devastating man when he was being the seducer. But as a caring, considerate man, he was downright potent. "I don't really know you at all, but I think I know your type, and I'm not all that impressed by it. That's one of the reasons I hesitated to involve you in this program. But I'll be honest with you... Tyler. There was no one else to take Jason's place, and—"

He interrupted her long enough to say facetiously, "Stop, Carlie. You'll swell my ego with all this praise."

Carlie heaved a disgruntled sigh, and saw Tyler's eyes go automatically to her breasts as she inhaled. He wouldn't be able to tell a damned thing, though, other than the fact that she did have them. Her shirt was buttoned to the throat and her suit coat was bulky, concealing any dimensions or shape. Carlie glared at him.

Still not looking at her face, he said, "You've made

quite a few assumptions about me, haven't you? Did you ever consider you might be wrong?"

"No. I hadn't considered that."

"Well maybe you should."

When he finally looked up, appearing totally unrepentant, she frowned at him in exasperation. "I think it would be better if you kept your hands to yourself."

Tyler did a double take. "All I did was hold your hand. I didn't make an indecent proposal."

His blunt speech could easily rattle her, but still her tone was brisk and confident. "This is a very small town," she said. "People love to gossip. I don't want to give anyone reason to speculate."

Tyler blinked, completely incredulous, a small, uncertain smile playing about his mouth. Then the smile broke, and he indulged in unrestrained laughter. Carlie immediately felt like a fool. Her remark had been totally asinine. No one would ever assume Tyler Ramsey was romantically involved with her. Secret rendezvous in disguise aside, the idea was too absurd.

Tyler shook his head, still chuckling and watching Carlie with an air of expectation, as if he was waiting for another joke. She knew her face was red, and she hated it. She reached into her purse, blindly searching for her wallet, then threw a couple of bills on the table and stood. She slipped her purse over her shoulder and walked away.

"Carlie! Wait a minute."

She ignored him.

Tyler cursed as she walked out the door. When Carlie glanced back, he was hurrying after her.

It was a beautiful autumn day outside, with only a hint of chill in the air to suggest that winter was approaching. The sun was a hazy tangerine glow dipping low on the horizon. And beneath it, her sturdy shoes clapping loudly on the pavement, stomped Carlie. She was intent on marching back to the school to retrieve her car.

She heard Tyler jogging after her.

"Leave me alone," she said succinctly as he reached her side and tried to grasp her arm.

"Be reasonable, Carlie. You can't walk all the way back to the school."

"Of course I can. We didn't go that far."

"I'd rather drive you."

"*I'd* rather walk."

Growling, Tyler grabbed her arms, despite her resistance, then shook her gently. "Will you stop being so contrary? You were worried about causing speculation? Well, what do you think it will do if I carry you back to my car?"

"You wouldn't dare."

"Take one more step and you'll find out what I dare."

It was a standoff, and they glared at each other until finally Carlie did an about-face and, without a word to Tyler, stalked over to his car. She stood by the passenger door, impatiently waiting for him to unlock it. But before he opened the door, he caught her shoulders again.

"Carlie, I didn't mean to…that is… Oh, hell, I'm sorry, all right?"

Carlie faced him, hard as that was to do. She felt thoroughly humiliated and had no problem blaming Tyler for her discomfort. She may have memories to cherish, but Tyler would obviously be appalled to learn the true identity of his mystery woman.

Straightening her shoulders to hide her hurt, she stared at him with cold indifference. "Do a good job with the children. That's all I ask. Beyond that, you don't concern me."

Tyler nodded stiffly, then walked to his own side of the car. His hands flexed on the wheel twice before he started the engine.

"Doesn't anything rattle that damned calm reserve of yours?"

Carlie stared out her window. "Is that what your insult was meant to do? Rattle me?"

"Actually, I didn't mean to insult you at all."

Carlie snorted. "I'm not an idiot, Tyler. I understand how ridiculous I must have sounded. Certainly no one would ever think… I mean, the idea of me and you…"

"That's not why I laughed, Carlie."

She snorted again, and he grinned. "There, you see?" he said. "You just never say or do what I expect. You were sitting back there all prim and proper, your pretty hazel eyes all disapproving, and it just struck me funny. You seem too much of a modern woman to be so prudish."

Carlie felt mortified. "I'm not prudish," she mumbled, memories of a few nights ago tumbling about in her mind. Then she told the necessary lie. "Just circumspect."

They stopped at a red light, and he turned toward her, scrutinizing her. She stubbornly ignored him, only briefly glancing his way. But it was enough to see his smile. She had the vague suspicion that he felt challenged. And an even worse suspicion that if it came to a battle of wills, she'd lose. Hands down.

Tyler certainly had more experience sparring words. A thrill of trepidation ran down her spine, and then her reason for that trepidation was verified.

"Your lips are nice. Full and soft, but not a hint of a smile. And I like your small, stubborn chin."

He was teasing, she could tell. And she almost grinned at his underhanded tactics. Almost.

"Does it hurt?"

That gained her reluctant attention, and a quizzical frown. "What?"

"Wearing your hair so tight. It gives me a headache just to look at it."

She should never have looked at him. His dark eyes were shining and his firm lips were tilted in a boyish grin. He appeared totally harmless. But she wasn't buying it.

"How long is it?" Tyler moved when the traffic light turned green and drove smoothly down the uncrowded street. "Shoulder-length? Longer?"

"I can't see where my hair could possibly interest you, Tyler. But to end your juvenile tactics to annoy me, I'll tell you. It reaches my shoulder blades, is a very mousy brownish blond, and I wear it this way because I don't have time to fuss with fancy hairdos. As long as a person's hair is clean, what should it matter to anyone else how it's worn?"

Very softly, but with devastating sincerity, he said, "I don't think your hair is mousy."

Her head swiveled so sharply to look at him, she winced.

"I think it's a nice color, especially with the sun on it. I see shades of red—which suits you—but also blond and dark brown. It's very nice. You should wear it loose."

"I don't know what game you're playing, but I'm not interested. I'm not a teenager to be flattered by comments on my hair or eyes. I want to do a job here, Tyler. I'm very serious about it, even if you aren't."

"You are so damned defensive."

With reason, she wanted to scream. If he found out… She sucked in a calming breath and stared at his profile. Her voice was patience personified, and filled with sane reasoning. "I'm not defensive. Just realistic. As you already made clear, there's very little about me that would ever entice you. I'm not naive. I'm aware of how I look. Why don't we talk about something important now? Like the students."

"I was only being honest with you, Carlie."

She gave him her patented teacher's look, reserved for students who had pushed her past the line. He shrugged, then returned his attention to the road.

She felt oddly deflated.

As he pulled into the school parking lot a few minutes later, he asked, "Were you at Bren's Halloween party?"

Coming out of left field like that, the question left her temporarily routed. Then she gathered her wits, opened the door and stepped out. Tyler left the car also, the consummate gentleman, and walked her to her own car, opening her door.

Carlie wasn't certain if it was just an innocent question, or if he was guessing at the identity of the masked lady again. She hesitated.

"Carlie?"

She saw no way around the lie. "No, I didn't go.

There's always a lot happening at school this time of year. We had our own class party, you know. For the students, I mean. And we've already started practicing for the Thanksgiving play. And then, with the new project I've been working on…" Carlie came to a fast stop, appalled at her rambling. She looked into his eyes as she added truthfully, "I don't go to parties very often."

"Why not? You don't have a steady date?"

Carlie rolled her eyes, leaning back on the car. She adjusted her glasses carefully on the bridge of her nose. "I most certainly don't need a man to take me to a party if I wish to go."

"Of course not. I was only going to say that I didn't have a date, either, but I…well, I had a…terrific time. You should have come. I think you would have enjoyed yourself." He grinned. "I went as a pirate."

"How appropriate. Did you rape and pillage your way through the party?"

It was a lousy jest, and Tyler made certain she instantly regretted it.

"I wouldn't do something as reprehensible as rape, Carlie. As for pillaging, I would never steal from my brother. Now, if it was at your house…do you own anything worth stealing?"

She should have known better than to throw that verbal punch, but she hadn't been able to resist. She didn't have an answer to his facetious question, so she settled for a look of disdain. Tyler only smiled.

Carlie turned away and climbed into her car. She needed to get away. She couldn't remember the last time she'd felt so emotionally drained. Or so invigorated.

That personal acknowledgment angered her even

more, and she tried to slam her car door. But Tyler got in her way, gripping the window frame and holding the door open.

"You should go out more, Carlie. It might do you some good to socialize, I think."

"Then you probably shouldn't think. You might damage something vital, and then what would the female population do?" She smiled with false sweetness, slammed the door and immediately pulled away.

She glanced in her rearview mirror and saw Tyler still standing there, watching after her. Even from a distance, she could see he was smiling. And then Carlie realized she was smiling also. She shook her head, bemused. She couldn't recall the last time she'd actually had fun with a man. Even arguing with Tyler was somehow fun.

Maybe she had been missing out and didn't even know it.

On her drive home, she thought about seeing Tyler again. She was actually anticipating it. He didn't seem to be at all deterred by the cold shoulder she was giving him. In fact, she believed it amused him. He smiled often enough to give her that impression.

The very last thing she wanted to do was amuse Tyler. She had to maintain an emotional distance; she had to keep herself safe. It certainly wouldn't be easy, but she'd just have to try harder not to react to his little provocations. The only problem was, Tyler could be very provoking even when he wasn't trying. All the man had to do was stand there, and women fawned all over him.

But Carlie wouldn't be like other women. He'd find that out soon enough. She'd see to it.

Tyler bounced the basketball, feeling impatient. Where was Carlie? He was anxious to see her again, which surprised him to no end. He'd decided he must be a glutton for punishment, because as much as she seemed to look down on him and his life-style, he still enjoyed every minute he spent with her. Even when they were arguing.

The woman had a real flair for putting him in what she considered his place. She was fun.

He heard a sudden squeaking of gym shoes and looked up, a huge grin spreading across his face when he saw her. Carlie was waltzing onto the gym floor, looking as if she wore the comfortable, baggy sweat-pants and thigh-length sweatshirt every day. She couldn't quite stop her nervous hands, however, from tugging on the hem of the shirt, trying to pull it far-ther over her thighs.

He couldn't resist teasing her. "Well, Ms. McDan-iels! You have very long legs. I hadn't realized."

She held his steady gaze and Tyler found himself anticipating what she might say. She never reacted as he expected her to. She never reacted as most other women would.

She was definitely unique.

"There was no need, nor will there ever be a need, for you to notice my legs, Tyler."

His grin never slipped. He enjoyed baiting her, watching her struggle with her temper. "Is every damned thing you own the same shade of mud? Don't you have anything blue or yellow?" He smacked his forehead, as if struck by a thought. "Red! You might look…nice, in red."

Her teeth snapped together in a loud click. "Watch your language. There are children present, and no, I have no desire…"

"None at all?"

"…*to wear red!* We're only playing basketball, for goodness' sake, and I hardly think the occasion warrants dressing up."

"It doesn't warrant dressing down, either. Is your body actually in there somewhere?" He leaned back, his gaze ranging slowly over her. "There's enough extra material there to clothe three women."

"Not that it's necessary for me to explain myself to you," she told him, starting to lose that steady, rock-solid calm, "but I thought I should wear clothes that were loose to allow for freedom of movement. I always wore something similar when I was a child and played basketball. I believe in being comfortable."

Tyler paused with interest. "You have some experience with the game then?"

"A little."

He chuckled. Knowing Carlie, and he *was* getting to know her, despite her efforts to remain aloof, "a little" probably meant she was very proficient at the game. "Excellent. We'll start by outlining the rules to the children, then we'll choose sides. I'll lead one team, you can lead the other."

Carlie nodded, but put in, "After warm-ups. I don't want to take a chance on anybody getting hurt."

"Whatever you say. But you'll have to lead those. I don't know any, other than sit-ups and such, and I'm not certain what kids this age are used to."

Tyler watched Carlie as she rounded up the kids and introduced them to him. As he spoke with each child, taking the time to joke and put them at ease, he caught Carlie staring. He winked at her, and she favored him with a genuine smile.

He wasn't used to her doing that, and for a second there, it threw him. Then he realized she was merely pleased that he was taking the time to really *talk* with the children. What had she thought he'd do? Bark at them?

The exercises she'd chosen were simple, but she challenged the children to keep up, to do each individual stretch properly. Throughout it all, Tyler watched her, and he grew increasingly curious.

Her breasts bounced. He'd never really noticed how amply endowed she was until now, but Mother Nature had treated her generously. And from what he could tell, she was totally unaware of it.

Unfortunately, he wasn't.

After helping a little girl catch the rhythm of the exercise, he wandered between all the children, checking to see if anyone else needed help. But even as he did that, he kept his gaze on Carlie, watching her every move.

When they finally broke up into teams, Carlie taking four girls and the biggest boy, Tyler with four boys, he announced they would play "shirts and skins." He led the boys in stripping off their shirts, then noticed Carlie staring. She tightened her mouth and blushed bright red when he caught her eye. He was amused, but he also liked the idea of her liking his body. Walking toward her, seeing her back up a step before she could stop herself, Tyler grinned. When he reached her, he slipped a fingertip over her lips, then chucked her chin, all without a single word. She closed her mouth with a snap, stomping to the other side of the hoop. But still, she looked her fill.

Later, after each of the children had taken a few practice shots, Tyler pulled Carlie aside. "They're well-behaved. Only a few of them are a little rambunctious." He laughed. "I heard one of the boys daring another to do a few…indiscreet things. They saw me looking and changed their minds."

"Just remember that when the novelty wears off and they get used to you. They can become a little more than rambunctious."

There were several occasions to point out misconduct, ranging from offensive language to shoving. Once, Tyler had to break up a skirmish between two of the boys. By the time six o'clock rolled around, Tyler was beat and Carlie looked exhausted.

But still, she took the time to make certain each child was bundled up properly. She helped with tying shoes, answered numerous questions and convinced one little boy that he didn't really want to hit another, just because the child had sneezed on him.

Then she gave the sneezer a tissue.

"I'm impressed," Tyler told her, his eyes on her flushed face. "You're really good with kids. You never once lost your temper."

She shrugged off his compliment. "I enjoy them. They're fun, and honest to a fault."

Tyler felt a tug on his hand, and looked down at a little girl named Lucy. She was smiling at him, showing him the stuck zipper on her coat. He helped her get her coat closed, then tweaked her nose. As he started to stand, she threw her skinny arms around his neck and squeezed him tight. "Thank you, Mr. Ramsey. I had fun."

Surprised, he looked toward Carlie, then ruffled the girl's tangled hair. "I did too, Lucy." She giggled, and Tyler grinned at her. "You'll be here Monday?"

"Yes, sir." She skipped away, leaving Tyler to stare after her.

"Whatever could that little girl have done to deserve detention? She's a doll."

Carlie waved goodbye to the last little boy, watching as he climbed into his parent's car, before allowing the heavy gym door to close. She turned to Tyler, chuckling softly. "Lucy has a problem with her language. She could make a sailor blush when she puts her mind to it. Personally, I think she just wants attention. Her father took off about a year ago, and her mother has her hands full trying to take care of five kids, all under the age of fifteen. Lucy sort of falls into the middle of the group."

Tyler turned away, his left hand rubbing the muscles of his neck. "I hate hearing stories like that. They make me want to strangle somebody." He began idly bouncing the ball, just to give his hands something to do and his mind something to focus on other than the problems of innocent children. But it didn't work. The issue was a sensitive one with him. "Why is it the kids who have to get hurt?"

"It's always the ones who are most vulnerable. That's simply human nature." She shrugged philosophically, then took him by surprise, snatching the basketball out of his hands and dribbling it across the court.

Tyler watched her antics, knowing she was trying to

distract him, and appreciating her efforts. Being with the children today reminded him of his own childhood. It had been rough for him and Jason, and when they'd become teenagers it had only gotten worse. Tyler had always pretended with his friends, bragging about the freedom he and Jason had, making it sound as if raising themselves had been a lark. And he had refused to admit to the embarrassment of having a mother who was the town "lightskirt."

God, it had been hard. Luckily, he'd had Jason. But it wasn't the same. Children needed an adult to look up to, someone they respected and who cared about them.

These kids had Carlie, but he wanted to help, too, wanted to make a difference.

"All right, Tyler," she said, breaking into his thoughts. "Enough moping over things you can't change. I hereby challenge you to a little one-on-one. The first to make ten baskets wins."

His grin was slow and filled with wicked delight. He put his hands on his hips, watching Carlie as she continued to expertly dribble the ball. "What are we betting?"

"That I can beat the pants off you." Her tone was smug and taunting. And then she understood exactly what she'd said. She flushed scarlet.

"My pants? Well, Ms. McDaniels! It wasn't enough to ogle me without my shirt? You want to strip me of all modesty?"

"That would be impossible." Her face was still hot, but she began dribbling the ball again. "You don't possess any modesty and probably never have."

His grin widened. He approached her slowly, his eyes never leaving her face. "I'm ready when you are, sweetheart. But the stakes have to be worthwhile. Say…dinner? At the winner's choice of place?"

Carlie gave him a confident smile. She did a fancy little feat of bouncing the ball behind her back, then between her knees, before shouting suddenly, "You're on." She raced down the court, scoring the first basket before he realized the game had started.

"Oh, ho! Getting tricky on me, huh? I like a woman who can take me by surprise." Carlie faltered at his words, nearly losing the ball. Tyler lunged, staying right on her, his body looming over hers, his arms outreaching her, his legs able to cover the same amount of ground more quickly. Carlie claimed it was an even match.

She was good, real good. She dunked the ball three times before he had a chance to score. Then he got serious. But all the while, he grinned. He felt better than he had in a very long time.

They were both sweaty by the time the score was evened up, eight all. Tendrils of hair had come loose around Carlie's face, sticking to her forehead and flushed cheeks. She looked done in, but still very determined to win. And she was laughing, obviously enjoying herself.

Then Tyler accidentally hit her. He made to jump for the ball, and his elbow smacked against her temple. Stumbling backward, she landed on her butt, her glasses slipping off her nose and dropping into her lap.

Tyler was horrified. "Oh, God, Carlie. I'm sorry!" He knelt beside her, taking her face in his hands, staring into her dazed eyes. Wide, hazel eyes. "Are you all right?"

She managed a slight, shaky smile. "I'm okay." Then she looked up at him.

His eyes locked with hers, and his fingers moved an almost imperceptible amount. As he studied her, something seemed familiar, some memory tickling at the back of his mind. Those wide eyes...

Then Carlie broke the contact, pulling away from his hands.

"You knew you were about to lose, right? That's why you belted me?" Her voice shook, and she tried another grin, but it was a weak attempt. Tyler wondered how badly she was hurt.

He was too busy trying to analyze the situation to answer right away. Carlie stuck her glasses firmly back on her nose, then called, "Yoo-hoo? Anybody home? Tyler?"

Finally, he shook his head, chasing away the errant confusion. "Sorry. Here, let me help you up."

"I'm fine, Tyler. I don't need any help." He helped, anyway, giving Carlie no choice in the matter.

He turned her, holding her chin in his palm. "Let me look at you. I think you have a lump coming up already."

She jerked away. "I told you, I'm fine. Quit fussing."

Tyler propped his hands on his hips, worried and filled with guilt. "I'll concede the game. Dinner is on me."

Carlie looked down at herself, then shook her head. "Dressed like this? I don't think so, but thanks, anyway."

Her refusal didn't surprise him, but it did annoy him. "You have to eat. It's been a long day."

"I have stew in the Crock-Pot at home. You're free and clear."

He picked up his shirt, drying the sweat from his chest and arms with it. He didn't particularly want to be free. "Stew sounds good. We bachelors don't get a home-cooked meal all that often."

Carlie raised her eyes to his, a look of disbelief mirroring her thoughts.

As hints went, his was blatantly clear and he held his breath while waiting to see what she would say.

"*You* are wrangling *me* for an invite?"

He shrugged, but the movement felt stiff. "I figure anyone who can play basketball as good as you, must surely be able to cook, too."

"Your logic escapes me, and besides, I don't think I made enough."

It was almost as if she was challenging him. He wanted to spend more time with her, but she was determined to put him off. He didn't like it, not one little bit. They *would* spend the evening together, despite the woman's ridiculous reservations. "I'll stop at the bakery and pick up some sourdough bread to go with it."

Carlie narrowed her eyes at his persistence. "Don't you have some female somewhere waiting for you to call and check in?"

"Nope. And I'm hopelessly lonely. Be kind, Carlie. Take me home."

"Like a stray dog? If I feed you once, will I have trouble getting rid of you?"

He managed to look hurt. Shrugging his bare shoulders, he said, "Never mind. I didn't mean to intrude. I just thought since we were both going home alone, we could share a meal. I had fun today. I don't get to goof off all that often anymore, regardless of what you think."

Carlie froze. He knew she wouldn't be able to handle hurting his feelings. Carlie was, despite her efforts to prove otherwise, a real softie. He watched her out of the corner of his eye and knew the moment she relented.

"I had fun, too, Tyler. And I suppose it would be nice to have someone to chat with over dinner."

Tyler raised his head, all remnants of self-pity disappearing. "Terrific! I knew you could be reasonable."

"Why, you big fraud!"

He simply laughed, not the least bit concerned with his deception. "Go get your things. I'll follow you to your house."

He watched Carlie stomp away. He could see her silently fuming. Damn, but he enjoyed her company. She was prickly, independent, determined to do things her way. She didn't pout, didn't treat him to the silent bit. No, when Carlie had something to say—and she usually did—she said it. She was so unpredictable, so *unexpected*, she chased boredom right out the door.

Chapter 5

Tyler drove behind Carlie, noting the slow, careful way she maneuvered her car. He was on the verge of laughing out loud. He shook his head, bemused. He couldn't recall ever having such verbal skirmishes with a woman. Women didn't react to him that way. But damned if he didn't like it. It was fun.

For that matter, Carlie was fun.

And he'd never thought of a woman that way before. She appeared totally immune to his flirting, but it wasn't because she was shy or withdrawn.

On the contrary. She was one of the most outspoken women he'd ever met. And intelligent. He enjoyed her company.

It was like having a pal, someone he could exchange mild insults with and still smile. But it was so utterly different with her being female. It was as if a whole new facet had been added to the relationship. It went a long way toward relieving his distraction over the mysterious—and missing—masked lady. And that in itself was a major feat.

Carlie pulled into her driveway and parked beneath a carport. Tyler pulled up to the curb out front, then he stared. He wasn't sure what he'd expected, probably a mud-colored house with a barren expanse of lawn and not a single speck of color. She took him by surprise. Again.

Her house was a small Cape Cod cottage nestled at the end of a narrow side street. A farmer's fields were on the right side of the house, a heavily wooded area to the left. Behind and in front of the white-and-yellow wooden structure was a well-tended lawn. Daisies were blooming everywhere, and her mailbox was designed to look like a small, colorful barn.

Tyler looked around, captivated. There was a tire swing hanging from the gnarled branch of an ancient oak off the back corner of the house. A curving porch circling to the right of the front door had a rattan porch swing attached to the overhang.

"A real swinger, aren't you?"

Carlie shrugged as she dug her key from her purse. "I'm not an idle person. I don't like to be still, even when I'm relaxing."

Tyler tried to imagine the classic picture of a woman superimposed with Carlie in a flowery dress, her hair loose, swaying in the breeze and humming softly while her bare feet maintained the gentle motion of the swing.

He wasn't quite that imaginative.

The inside of her house was also a contrast, so different from the woman he was getting to know. There was little furniture, only the basic necessities. It was an eclectic mix of modern and antique, light oak and glass, chintz material and delicate doilies. There were no photographs, but there were framed prints of the most outrageous things. Each room appeared to have a theme.

The living room was spring, with a large, brass-framed picture of a bee, busily collecting pollen from a daisy. Porcelain flowers decorated each tabletop and filled one curio cabinet.

The dining room, which was minuscule, was decorated with birds. A border of them circled the room, a dainty, delicate figure sat looking over every corner, and in each plant, one peeked from between the leaves.

The kitchen was whales.

He raised his eyebrows at her in question. "How did you choose whales, may I ask?"

Carlie had been busily putting their jackets on the coat tree and checking the stew. She looked at him over her shoulder as she lifted the Crock-Pot lid. "One of the children at school gave me one, once. I said I liked it, and…" She smiled.

"They all decided to give you one?"

"Each class seems to take it into their head that I need a new collection of something. But I don't mind. It makes for consistent Christmas presents. There are bunnies in the bathroom and cats in my bedroom."

"What are you going to do when you run out of rooms?"

She tilted her head. "Mix and match?"

He smiled at her wit. "Can I help you set the table or something?"

"No. You can turn on the television if you like. I'm just going to heat the bread and set the table."

Tyler wandered into the living room again. His attention was drawn to the television set and an array of DVDs sitting on top. He looked through them, and stopped when he spotted a "Work Out With the Oldies," video. He carried it with him into the kitchen. "Whose is this?"

Carlie paused in the process of serving the stew. "Mine. Who else would it belong to?"

"You work out to the oldies?"

"I like older music. It's more fun than this new stuff kids listen to."

"So do you hop and jostle around in a pair of tights?"

She smirked at his expression. "You're looking at my workout clothes." She spread her arms in the air. The shirt raised a bit and he caught a glimpse of the pale flesh of her belly.

To his disbelief, and annoyance, he felt a brief spurt of interest. It had only been a flash, an instant of white skin, gone too quickly to really appreciate, if indeed, there had been anything there to appreciate.

With the clothes she favored, it was hard to tell for certain. But she definitely had a large bosom. He'd established that today when she was exercising, her body bouncing in all the right places. And from that prominent point, her clothes fell almost straight down, giving no hint of curves or dips and hollows.

But her arms had felt slim when he'd shaken her the other day. And when she'd come into the house, she'd kicked off her shoes, showing narrow feet and trim ankles.

It was simple curiosity, he decided, that was making

him react to her. Not that he would ever consider doing anything about it. She was a schoolteacher, which was bad enough as far as dalliance went, but on top of that she was too damn prickly, and was his sister-in-law's best friend, to boot. She was so far off the scale of available females, he knew he didn't have to concern himself. But he did, anyway.

He'd never met a woman so dedicated to a cause, so at ease with children and so giving. She was totally disinterested in his supposed prowess, in his community standing, in his reputation. All she wanted from him was his help in achieving a worthwhile goal.

Disgruntled with his thoughts, and his overactive imagination that kept him guessing at her elusive figure, he stalked toward her and asked bluntly, "How much do you weigh?"

Carlie halted in the middle of opening a package of butter. "That's none of your business!"

"You're working out, so you must feel you need to lose some weight, right?"

"Wrong. I work out to keep in shape. Everybody should." She poked him in the middle. "Don't you?"

"Of course. But that's different."

"Why?"

"I go to a gym. I'm a man."

"Well, I can't afford to go to some fancy gym. And no one ever told me being a man was synonymous with being outrageously snoopy and impertinent. I would have thought a man your age would have learned some manners by now."

It was her teacher's voice again, and Tyler saw that he'd made her truly angry, though she was trying to hide it. He watched as she slammed bowls onto the table, then practically threw the spoons next to them.

"What are you drinking?" he asked cautiously, waiting to see if she would end up throwing something at him.

"I'm drinking milk. You can find yourself something in the refrigerator."

He did. Milk.

After sitting down to eat in perfect, strained silence, he ventured, "I'm sorry…?"

"You're not sure?"

"Of course I'm sure. I just didn't know if you would want me to speak to you. I, ah, seemed to have hit a nerve."

Carlie sighed, dropping her face into her hands.

Tyler had the awful suspicion she was going to cry. In a near whisper, he asked, "Carlie?"

Her shoulders shook, and Tyler's heart stopped. "Aw, Carlie don't. Sometimes I just stick my foot in it. You shouldn't pay any attention to me. Really. Carlie?"

She slowly raised her head. A wicked grin spread across her features. One look at Tyler and she broke into peals of laughter. He fell back against his chair, glaring at her.

"Oh, Tyler. You didn't hit a nerve, honestly." She chuckled again, then removed her glasses to wipe her eyes. "Actually," she put in, obviously intent on controlling her hilarity and not entirely succeeding, "you're finally acting exactly as I thought you would."

"Is that right?"

"Yes, it is."

He felt the sting of her insult, deliberate, he was

certain. "So, you assumed all along that I was a jerk? Is that it?"

"Not a jerk. Not really. You're an okay guy. But you think you can make up your own rules and everyone, especially females, will abide by them. You deliberately provoke me, and you're purposely outrageous. You don't even try to follow normal codes of manners or behavior. And why should you? Women relentlessly fall at your feet, despite your attitude, so why should you change to accommodate polite society?"

He didn't like having her categorize and analyze his faults as if he fell into an expected mode of "male behavior." "All this lecturing simply because I commented on your weight?"

"Because you felt it didn't matter if you were rude. After all, I'm not a woman you'd aspire to sleep with. You have no personal, sexual interest in me, so why go out of your way to be charming? There wouldn't be any benefit, now, would there?"

He studied her, his eyes probing. Damned if he wasn't letting her get the best of him, again. So far, that was how it had been. She consistently sliced him up, verbally at least, while he was sitting there admiring her. Laughing with him was one thing, but Carlie was actually laughing *at* him. It was intolerable. "I'll be honest with you. For some inexplicable reason, I'm intrigued by you."

Her eyes widened enormously, and she choked on a breath. Her amusement was instantly, and completely, gone.

He waited impassively until she'd regained her breath. "I've decided it's because you're so damned mysterious."

She sent him a wary look, then shook her head, refusing to meet his eyes. "No. No, I'm not. I'm an open book. You simply refuse to accept there's a woman who isn't bowled over by your charm."

He pretended she hadn't spoken. "What does your body look like? That's what I'm wondering. How plump are you? How big are your breasts, how bountiful is your bottom? I'm used to looking at a woman and seeing what's there, be it attractive or not, not this infuriating guessing game, trying to see beneath layers of ugly clothing."

Very slowly, Carlie laid her spoon by her bowl. She stared at him, then tightened her mouth. "You're terribly spoiled. You think nothing of going for the jugular just so you can win. All right. So I'm overweight." She lifted one shoulder in a stiff shrug, holding his gaze. "It runs in my family. And flaunting my body would be a bigger crime than hiding it. But so what? I don't need a man's approval to feel good about myself. I'm a very nice person, and I do a very good job, and I *care*. About this community, about the children, about people in general. Can you say the same, Tyler? So you're handsome. So what? What real contribution have you ever made to your own small part of the world?"

He spooned up a bite of stew, saluting her with it before putting it in his mouth. He chewed thoughtfully, feeling her simmer beside him, her anger growing with his nonchalance. Finally, knowing he'd pushed her far enough and sensing that she was ready to throw her stew at his head, he said, "You do a good job of going for the jugular, as well. I can't think of a single important thing I've ever done in my life. But I don't do bad things, either, discounting my comment on your weight, of course. I pay my taxes on time, I don't drink and drive, I donate to charities—although, only when they actually catch me. I'm a gentleman and I'm kind to older people. Surely all that counts for something?"

"Not much."

"Come on, Carlie. Can't you forgive me? I was only curious, after all, not being deliberately insulting. If I was too nosy, well it's only because I think you could be very attractive. No, don't make rude noises at me again. You are intelligent, very intelligent. That's something to be admired. If you made a little effort with your appearance, you might have plenty of equally intelligent men knocking your door down. You would probably have a very busy social schedule."

"I don't have time for a...busy social schedule."

"It's not a disease, you know. You're a fun person to be with. You should be involved with someone special."

Carlie tilted her head back to survey the ceiling. Without looking at him, she asked, "Why do you care, Tyler? I'm not some bird with a broken wing you need to teach to fly. I don't want to fly. Walking is much more my speed."

"I have an idea," he announced, very pleased with himself.

"Oh, no. Now we're in it deep."

He laid his palms flat on the table, and raised himself out of his chair to loom toward her. "Date me."

Carlie eyed him as if he'd grown a second head. As she kept him waiting, he reseated himself, tapping his fingers on the table. "Well?"

"I'm waiting for the punch line."

"All right. Here it is. You might like it. You might enjoy my company."

She made a show of stifling her laughter. "You should get paid. You're a professional."

"Professional what? Or should I ask?"

"Comedian, of course."

"I'm being serious here. The least you could do is listen to me."

"No, the least I could do is make you go home and take your insanity with you." She seemed almost angry—and flustered. Her cheeks were a warm, rosy pink, and her hands trembled just the tiniest bit. Then she widened her eyes comically, gasping. "You don't think it's catching, do you?" She shoved her chair back, holding her hands up in a defensive gesture.

Tyler slowly rose from his seat. "All right, you. I think I ought to take you in hand. Talk about *my* manners!" As he advanced on her, circling the table with a menacing stride, Carlie shrieked and jumped to her feet, moving quickly to keep the table between them.

"All right! All right! Tell me what you have to say."

Tyler advanced. "Too late. You've challenged my masculinity. And with my ego as enormous as you claim, that must surely be grounds for assault. Now you'll have to pay."

She was trying not to laugh. He watched the grin grow on her face, and felt satisfaction. Chuckles emerged from between her tightly drawn lips. She clapped a hand over her mouth, still moving cautiously. He followed.

Then Tyler lunged across the table, grabbing for her. She screeched in surprise, but it was already too late. He had her.

Hauling her body across the table, his grip firm on her upper arms, Tyler grinned at her. She was laughing, her glasses were askew, her chest heaving. And he had the insane, almost overwhelming urge to kiss her.

What the hell? he thought, and leaned closer, his eyes on her soft, slightly parted lips. He was filled with an anticipation that even surpassed what he'd felt at the pool house with the masked lady, and that had been shocking in its intensity. What he felt now was so alien to his jaded senses, he actually jerked when she spoke.

Her voice wasn't breathless. It was low and menacing. "Back off."

He did. Slowly regaining his wits, mortified by what he had almost done—to *Carlie*, for Pete's sake—Tyler managed an unconcerned shrug. "I've never really... played with a woman before. I was only going to—"

"Oh, please. Spare me. I know what you were doing."

"Uh, what?" Maybe she could tell him, for he certainly hadn't a clue what had been in his mind. *Carlie?* Good grief.

Carlie fussed with her glasses. "You're playing games. I already told you, I won't have it."

That sounded plausible, though not entirely true. But it helped him to regain his aplomb. "Of course I was playing. And so were you. That's why you should date me. Ah-ah, just hear me out." He waited until she sat down again. "Now, don't storm out on me. I think we could enjoy each other's company, at least, as long as we keep it platonic. I hope you didn't think I meant—"

"Why?" she interrupted, her tone sharp, her look suspicious. "Why would you want to spend more time with me?"

"I like you. *Really* like you. You make me laugh." Then he added, "And you keep me humble."

She snorted, then ignored his chastising look at the rude noise.

"It would be good for us both. You would learn to relax a little, to concentrate on something other than your obligation to the school, and like I said, I enjoy your company."

"Surely there are other women whose company you would enjoy more?"

"Perhaps. But for different reasons." She opened her mouth, and he raised a hand in surrender. "I know. Uncalled for. Acquit me. But I've been really bored lately and…"

He frowned at her bubble of laughter. "I'm perfectly serious, I'll have you know. Here I am, laying my heart out to you, and you're rudely stomping all over it."

"You know what, Tyler?"

He didn't trust her grin. "Probably not."

"It has been fun at odd and varying moments, which if you're being sincere, is surprising to us both."

He grabbed his chest, feigning a heart attack. "What? You admit to enjoying my company? I'm not totally without redemption? I'm not totally cast down? Carlie McDaniels likes my company! What more encouragement could a man ask for?"

"At odd and varying moments," she clarified. "Okay, so where would we go and what would we do on these experimental, platonic dates?"

"Then you'll do it?"

"Absolutely not. Not until you answer my question."

"I don't know." He hadn't really thought things through. "The usual stuff?"

"Such as?"

"Dinner? Dancing?" He grinned, ready to elaborate

and add to his list. "Roller skating? Bungee jumping? Body surfing?"

"I could maybe handle a movie. It's dark there and nobody would have to know I was out with a maniac."

He beamed at her. "Excellent choice. Tomorrow?"

"Tomorrow is Saturday. Don't you have a real date?"

"Carlie, Carlie, Carlie. This *will* be a real date. Up to, but excluding, the good-night kiss."

Carlie twisted her mouth in apparent thought, chewed the corner of her bottom lip and studied her short, neat nails.

"You're not contemplating death, you know," he said dryly. "I'll even let you choose the movie." He watched the fleeting expressions on her face, and saw her indecision, her...nervousness? Damned unaccountable female. He couldn't remember the last time he'd had to actually beg for a date. It was a rather disturbing experience.

"I can choose what we'll see?"

His heartbeat picked up speed. "Absolutely."

"A true concession. All right. I'll go."

Tyler felt his muscles ease, and only then realized how stiff he'd been. He felt as if he'd accomplished something major. Carlie was no easy nut to crack. But he was determined to help her loosen up. He could help her with the children, easing some of her obligation, and also show her how to have a good time.

He suddenly realized that things were starting to pick up. Boredom was a thing of the past. First there was that night with the mysterious, timid masked lady, whose identity Brenda refused to reveal, no matter how he cajoled. His curiosity over that little episode was still extreme; he'd never met a woman like her before. Sooner or later, he *would* find out who she was.

Of course, he'd never met a woman like Carlie, either. She was as unique as any woman could be. He smiled, thinking of her again. Prickly, independent, outspoken Carlie. He surely had enough excitement to keep boredom at bay for some time to come.

"I can't believe you chose this movie."

Carlie smiled in the dim theater, very aware of Tyler sitting beside her. He was dressed in jeans and a dark sweater. She could smell his after-shave, and his own natural, masculine scent. It was comforting, stimulating and very distracting. "I love Mel Gibson."

"Now, why does that surprise me? Oh, yeah. You've made it clear to me on several occasions that macho, sexy men are low on your list."

"No. I made it clear that men who *thought* they were macho, sexy men were low on my list."

"Don't look at me like that! I never claimed to be macho."

"Are you claiming to be sensitive, instead?"

"Certainly. Especially in specific areas. Like low on my stomach, the top of my spine…"

Carlie's breath caught and her skin suffused with heat. He wasn't lying. She remembered all too well just how sensitive he was in those particular areas. Throughout that one special night, he'd shown her how to give as well as take, and she'd thoroughly enjoyed each lesson.

She elbowed him roughly to cover her reaction. "You're impossible."

"Naw." He waited a heartbeat. "Just *very* sensitive."

"Hush, the movie is starting." Carlie knew she sounded rude, but she didn't care. Tyler's flirting was just that, flirting. He did it with every woman he came into contact with, be she nine or ninety. It shouldn't mean anything, and likely wouldn't if she wasn't the mystery woman. But she was, and his words affected her in numerous ways. Her head knew he wasn't serious, but her heart jumped into a wild cadence of excitement every time he teased.

"Lesson number one, Carlie. You don't rudely tell your date to hush."

She shifted her gaze, peering at him in the growing darkness. "Not even when the movie is starting and he's yakking on about his sexuality and very personal preferences?"

"That's right. You should have told me where you're sensitive, too."

"Oh. Well, let's see. My feet?"

"You're not trying to get in the mood here, are you?"

She chuckled, feeling some of her tension ebb at his dry expression. Leaning slightly toward him, she nudged him affectionately with her shoulder. The action surprised them both, and Tyler whispered, "That's better," then boldly put his arm around her.

It felt good. Comforting and exciting at the same time. But she had to remind herself this was only a game to him. And she was only a distraction.

"You shouldn't stiffen up so, either," he added. "I'm not getting fresh. Just relax."

The words had been whispered gently in her ear. She could have added it as another sensitive spot, yes, indeed. He was being so careful with her, lightly teasing and so solicitous. She wanted to lean against him, to feel more of his heat against her side. Instead, she stared straight ahead. "Shh. Don't make me miss the movie."

It would be okay, Carlie thought, once she managed to relax a little. Tyler would never connect her with the pool house. And he wasn't attempting to fondle her; his hand wasn't moving from her shoulder and he wasn't drawing her nearer to his body. He was just…there. Firm. Nice. Male.

They shared a huge bucket of extra-buttery popcorn and a large cola. Carlie felt Tyler's eyes on her when she unconsciously licked the butter from her fingers, but when she turned to him, he didn't say a word. He looked perplexed, annoyed and exasperated. Carlie frowned at him, but he shook his head and looked away. She couldn't begin to decipher his thoughts, and a few seconds later he excused himself to go buy candy. He returned with a box of chocolates.

"After all that popcorn, you have room for candy?"

Her tone had been whisper-soft, and he answered in kind. "You're doing it again. You don't talk to your date as if he's a glutton. You should say, 'Oh, candy!' and thank him for it."

She contrived a blank expression. "Oh, candy! Thank you."

He laughed out loud, prompting the people behind him to grumble a complaint.

Carlie whispered, "I gather by your display of humor, I didn't do it right?"

"You are amusing, Carlie. You really are. Thank you for coming with me tonight."

Her throat felt tight when she tried to smile. She dropped her gaze to her lap for a moment, then raised it to look at him. "I'm having a good time, too. Thank you for asking me."

He held her eyes a moment longer, tightened his arm around her in an affectionate squeeze, then turned his attention back to the screen. Carlie silently studied his profile. He wasn't the puffed-up, conceited ego-maniac she'd accused him of being. At least, not now, not with her.

Probably because he was with her; he wasn't trying to impress or seduce her. He'd claimed boredom, but she wasn't at all certain that was possible, given his reputation. There was no doubt Tyler Ramsey could have a different date every night of the week, without resorting to asking her out.

But it was nice being with him, knowing he didn't really see her as a woman, but rather as a companion, someone to spend a few hours with. She thought of the party and trembled.

Tyler accepted that she was heavy, plain and greatly lacking in good taste. He'd made no bones about de-testing her choice in clothing. But it had taken only a few small modifications—a wig, colored contacts—and he hadn't recognized her at all.

With each passing hour, she found herself growing more attracted to him. It had started out being strictly physical. After all, Tyler Ramsey was the kind of man girls dreamed about and women fantasized over. And Carlie had recently lived a few of those fantasies. But now, she realized how easily she could lose her heart.

Carlie thought about the woman she used to be, so frivolous, so anxious to attract her husband's atten-tion, wanting and needing his approval. She'd failed dismally then, and eventually had learned a valuable lesson. Not that she blamed her husband entirely, for she had failed him in numerous ways. But he hadn't even tried to be patient with her. He'd thrown out accusations without remorse or consideration to her age and inexperience. At first, she'd been crushed that she wasn't a sexual person, that she'd failed in the most basic female concepts.

She was older now, wiser, no longer taken in by men and their obscure promises. Her husband hadn't wasted any time in finding someone who suited his sexual tastes better than she did. It didn't hurt anymore to remember, nor did it fill her with disappointment and self-reproach. She'd vowed never again to be that vulnerable. And she'd never been tempted to waver from that pledge.

Until Tyler. Now she had a night to herself, a special night to remember when she felt the loneliness that would surely come one day.

Gaining Tyler's friendship was fun, but knowing him as a man, for that one special night, was a memory she would repeatedly indulge in recalling. Without even trying, he'd made her feel things she'd never felt before, things she'd thought herself incapable of feeling. He'd proven her husband had been wrong about her. That would have to be enough.

She would have to be very careful that he never became suspicious. Any more friendly, casual dates would have to be forgotten. She couldn't risk it. The possibility of emotional hurt was too great. But the program? Could she distance herself, even while working with him for hours on end?

It wouldn't be easy, but she had no choice.

* * *

"Tell me about Carlie."

Brenda paused in her efforts to finish folding her laundry. "Carlie? What do you want to know about her?"

Tyler shrugged. "I don't know. How long have you known her? Why isn't she married?"

Brenda swallowed, then looked away. "She was married. When she was very young. But it didn't work out. And since then…she just hasn't found the right man. She's intelligent, bright and funny and caring. She's very special."

Tyler was frowning slightly, then waved away Brenda's defense of Carlie. "You don't need to convince me. I've been with her a lot lately, and I like her, too." He was silent a moment, then shook his head. "I didn't know she'd been married. It was rough, huh?"

"I…ah, Carlie is very private, Tyler. I don't feel comfortable talking about her."

"I didn't mean to pry. I just think it's a shame she doesn't have anyone special."

Brenda turned and looked at him. "She told me you two went to the movies."

"Yeah. It was really fun. I enjoyed it. It's nice to be out with someone without having to worry about how the night will end. It was actually better than being with the guys. I didn't have to listen to, and return, all the raunchy jokes about sex and who had enjoyed the latest conquest. It was comfortable. Do you know what I mean?"

Very gently, Brenda smiled at him. "Don't look so confused, Tyler. I know exactly what you mean. Jason says he felt the same way after he met me. With other women and with his male friends, there was always a certain face he had to wear, a certain way he was expected to act. Around me, he could just be himself."

"There's a major difference here, Bren. Jason couldn't keep his hands off you."

Her sudden burst of laughter was quickly cut off. "That's true enough, thank heavens. I don't suppose you suffered the same thing with Carlie?"

"Carlie? That woman gives new meaning to *bad taste*. Her clothes alone are enough to keep my stomach churning. And there were several times I would have dearly loved to yank those damned glasses off her nose and stomp on them."

"I've had the same thought myself, Tyler. But Carlie won't ever change. She won't dress to suit other people. And she's comfortable with herself and the style she's chosen."

"What style? There is no style to her." He grinned suddenly and admitted, "I've wondered what she would look like buck-naked, without her hair being tortured behind her head in that braid."

Brenda's mouth dropped open, then she sputtered. "Tyler Ramsey! Don't you dare seduce my friend out of idle curiosity. I'd never forgive you!"

Tyler stood, glancing at his watch. He sighed philosophically. "You don't want me to have any fun, Bren."

"Have *fun* with some other woman. But you leave Carlie alone."

"Carlie is safe enough." Then he added, "You sure you won't tell me who the harem girl is?"

"I can't. I promised her I wouldn't."

"But why? What is she hiding?"

"She…she knows your reputation. And…and I

guess she just doesn't want to get involved." Brenda shrugged. "I'm sorry."

Tyler worked his jaw in frustration. "She doesn't trust me?"

"Well…no."

He exploded. "What is it with you women? I am not some overcharged male bimbo! Doesn't anyone allot me the benefit of having scruples?"

"You women?" Brenda grinned at him. "This sounds like a Carlie lecture. Has she been rough on you?"

"One minute, yes. I get the feeling she doesn't think very highly of me. But then she'll laugh and be outrageously funny." He paced a few feet away. "She keeps me guessing."

Brenda walked him to the door. "I know you have scruples, Tyler. And I think you're a very nice man, despite everything." She skipped away when he turned, grabbing playfully for her. Laughing, she continued, "But Carlie's different. I don't want to see her hurt."

"Hurt? Carlie's about as vulnerable as a porcupine. But if you're worrying I'll make her promises I can't keep, don't. I've told her I like her friendship, that's all. I admire her, despite her atrocious clothing, but I doubt I'd be even tempted to go beyond platonic with her. She's safe enough."

Even as he said the words, Tyler thought what an adept liar he was. He was tempted, more than tempted. It was just that the temptation had come in a different package. As often as not, he wanted to simply touch her, on the hand, on her smooth cheek. Holding her would be nice.

"Thank you, Tyler. I'm glad you've befriended

Carlie. She needs some fun and excitement with men other than those stuffed shirts on the school board."

Tyler had been in the process of walking out, but he halted abruptly. "I didn't get the impression she was dating anyone in particular."

"Carlie doesn't consider going anywhere with them a date, because she works with them. She thinks that their interest is purely work-related. But I don't think so. I think they're as curious as you are, but probably don't have the conscience you have." She looked up at him, frowning. "So far, Carlie hasn't allowed them the chance to appease their curiosity."

"What about Carlie? Doesn't she get curious?"

"Carlie?" Brenda fidgeted with her hair, looking away from Tyler. "Naw. She just isn't interested anymore. Like her clothes, she thinks spending a lot of time on a social life is a waste of perfectly good brain waves."

Tyler grinned. "I can hear her saying that." He glanced at his watch again, then asked quickly, "So you knew her in school?"

"Carlie and I have known each other for years. Without her help, I'd never have made it through college."

Tyler was silent a moment, acknowledging Brenda's words. "Carlie's like a mother hen, isn't she? She *likes* helping people."

"Yeah. That's Carlie, all right."

Nodding in satisfaction, Tyler left, late for his appointment. His trip to his sister-in-law's had been spontaneous. Carlie had refused to see him again except at practice, claiming she had too many papers to grade and a big test to prepare. He'd missed her.

Carlie seemed to have an innate rapport with children. When he was younger, he'd thought it was only his mother who didn't like and understand kids. Women, in general, were supposed to be maternal, he'd thought. But as he'd matured, he'd learned exactly how wrong he could be.

His mother hadn't wanted him or Jason because they hampered her life-style, which basically meant they curtailed her sexual freedom. At least she claimed they did. Tyler could never recall his presence slowing her down.

From a very young age, he'd known what women did with men. He'd *seen* what women did with men. His mother hadn't been circumspect. His mother hadn't been much of a mother.

And since then, he'd met too many women who seemed to share her sentiments. Life was for enjoying; as long as you had money and looks and prestige. It was a life-style most women sought, with no place for kids. Children interfered with careers or ruined otherwise perfect figures.

He would probably never have any children of his own. His life wasn't conducive to raising kids. And he would never cheat a child of the warmth and love they deserved. Children should enrich life; they should be cherished and protected, not considered a burden to be tolerated.

An image of Carlie, married and cradling a baby of her own, flitted through his mind. It left behind conflicting emotions; tenderness, because he knew she would be an excellent mother. But also possessiveness, which made no sense at all. He refused to dwell on that sentiment, and put the image firmly from his mind.

It disturbed him, how much she occupied his

thoughts. Especially when he had other things to think about. He wouldn't give up on the mystery woman—he wasn't a man to leave a puzzle unsolved. But time and again, he found his thoughts veering to Carlie and her unusual wit, the gentleness and patience she gave her students.

Anyone who took the time to really know Carlie, would realize there was nothing plain about her, despite the horrendous clothing she wore. She was about as complex and complicated as any female could be. He hadn't exaggerated when he said she intrigued him.

Though he knew she'd had a good time with him, she had refused any future dates. She didn't return his calls, either. He would almost swear she was avoiding him, but why?

He would take his time, and sooner or later he would figure her out.

He intended to enjoy every minute.

Chapter 6

Carlie saw Tyler's car pull up to the curb in front of Brenda's. His arrival was unexpected, and she went perfectly still. He jerked the car into Park, then jumped out, appearing determined—more than determined, if the look on his face was any indication. He disappeared past the window, then came to the kitchen door.

He knocked sharply, once, then stepped inside without waiting for an answer. Brenda met him there, her hands on her hips, blocking his vision of the kitchen table where Carlie sat.

"Tyler! What are you doing here?"

"I insist you tell me who she is."

"Who?"

He gave her a look of impatience. "Enough, Brenda. You know who I mean. The harem girl. Who is she?"

Brenda rolled her eyes. "For the last time, Tyler. No!"

Carlie wanted to disappear. It was a miserable Sunday morning, aptly suiting her mood. She'd come to Brenda's for solace, her emotions in turmoil. Nothing was as it had been only days before. She didn't know what to think, what to do. She'd learned so much lately. Too much.

One thing was certain: she couldn't just look at her experience with Tyler as a sexual lesson. Her one "date" with him had proven that. Tyler had touched more than her body. He'd thrown away the misconceptions she'd had about herself, stolen her fears and her disappointments.

And now that she saw him nearly every day, she feared he might very well steal her heart.

She couldn't let that happen. She needed time to think, to reason out her reactions. But here was Tyler, wanting to know who she really was. It was too ironic to bear.

"Your friends are something else, Bren. They're driving me crazy." He ran his hands roughly through his hair, the gesture filled with frustration.

"Friends?"

"Don't sound so innocent. First the harem girl refuses to tell me who she is. Then Carlie refuses to return my calls. I ask her out, and all she can say is no. I swear, that woman is totally—"

Brenda interrupted him then, clearing her throat loudly and gesturing with her eyes to draw his attention to the kitchen table. He looked, and Carlie saw his beautiful eyes narrow slightly.

His annoyance seemed to disappear; he became almost cheerful. "What the hell's the matter with you? You look awful."

After shooting him a disgusted frown, she turned away. "I have a cold," Carlie said. She sincerely hoped he wouldn't question her further, because her swollen, sleepy eyes had little to do with illness.

"And that made your hair all frizzy?"

"No, that didn't make my hair all frizzy." She mimicked him perfectly. "I jogged over here in the rain, and the rain makes my hair go frizzy."

Tyler scrutinized her. "You just said you had a cold! Why the hell were you out in the rain?"

"I jog every Sunday. Why should today be any different? A little rain never killed anyone." She knew she was being more waspish than usual, but she hadn't planned on having to face him this morning. Her heart ached, and her head followed suit.

"No. Rain doesn't kill, it just makes some people's hair go frizzy." Tyler grinned. "At least a few strands found the excuse to escape that infernal braid. It's probably a hair rebellion."

He laughed at his own jest, and Carlie stiffened at the sound. She pushed her glasses up, then lifted her chin. "Maybe I should go now, Bren. Tyler obviously has something he wants to discuss with you. And I'd hate to get stuck in the downpour, anyway."

Brenda smacked Tyler, then hurried to Carlie. "Don't go, yet. We haven't finished...talking."

"Yeah, Carlie." Tyler pulled out a chair and straddled it, facing Carlie with a huge grin. "I probably won't get any information out of Brenda, anyway. She's looking very stubborn, don't you think?" Then he turned to Brenda. "But you and I will talk later."

"It won't do you any good. I already told you I'm sworn to secrecy."

Exasperated, he looked at Carlie pointedly. "Do you really want to discuss my personal life in front of company?"

Brenda scoffed. "Carlie isn't company."

"Gee, thanks, Bren," Carlie said.

"You know what I mean, Carlie. Besides, I'm sure you couldn't care less about Tyler's love life. Right?"

Carlie tightened her mouth, feeling caught in a nightmare. Brenda was trying to tease; she still wanted Carlie to tell Tyler the truth. Only Brenda didn't know what the truth was, and Carlie had no doubt she'd be shocked if she did. For that matter, Tyler would be shocked, too. And probably disappointed. Carlie couldn't bear that. "You're right. I don't care to sit through any details. So—" she stood "—I'm off."

Tyler caught her wrist. "You can't walk home, now. It's raining."

"Believe me, it won't bother me a bit."

"Now, Carlie, don't be obstinate."

"Tyler, I'm dangerously close to laying you low." She had to get away from him. Now.

"Violence? My, my, your cold is making you surly."

She tugged, but he didn't release her. "Tyler, what did you intend to do today, before you came here and decided to harass me?"

"I was going to harass Brenda, but you'll do better."

She could feel the warmth of his hand on her arm, feel the probing intensity of his eyes. "Let go. I want to leave."

Tyler looked down at his hand, still wrapped around Carlie's wrist. She saw what he saw. His fingers entirely encircled her. She had slim, fine-boned wrists. He said, "You've been avoiding me."

Her breath caught somewhere in her diaphragm, causing her chest to ache. It took a great deal of effort to banter with him. "I've been busy. And why are you calling me on a weekend, anyway? Surely your social calendar is fully penciled in."

He flashed her a grin. "No, and there were numerous disappointed ladies, I can tell you."

She knew him well enough now to know he was only baiting her. He wasn't nearly the egomaniac he pretended to be. A reluctant smile curved her lips. "Tyler, quit fooling around. Let go."

"Not until you promise to help entertain me. Let's do something, go someplace. I'm bored and despondent. I need company."

"Despondent?" He was charm personified, and much too appealing. It was strange, but not only had she played the part of two different women, she *felt* like two different women. Tyler was managing to lighten her mood, even though he was the cause of her foul disposition in the first place.

"That's right. And with good reason." He grinned at Brenda. "I got shunned by someone at Bren's party the other night, and now she won't tell me who the woman is."

With a theatrical gasp meant to cover her uneasiness with the topic, Carlie stared. "No! It can't be true."

"Sadly, it is. I fell in love, and the wench dumped me."

The words had obviously been said as a jest, but still Carlie jerked. Brenda said quickly, "He…he met a friend of mine during the party. They seemed to hit

it off, but…she doesn't want to see him again. Ever."
She ended with a shrug.

"Just tell me who she is, Bren. I can handle the
rest."

Wanting to play her part properly, Carlie asked with
laudable suspicion, "You don't know who she is?"

"Absurd, isn't it? But she refused to remove her
mask, just so I wouldn't know who she was."

Carlie struggled to relax her tense muscles. "Smart
girl."

"Oh, she wasn't a girl." He gave her a taunting
smile, obviously irritated with her snide comment.
"She was very much a woman. A damned sexy
woman." He turned to Brenda, a mocking plea in his
eyes. "Please! Tell me who she is. I promise you, she'll
thank you later."

Brenda grinned at his woeful expression. "I don't
know. What do you think, Carlie?"

Carlie would certainly strangle Brenda later. She
cleared her throat. "I think if a woman had enough
sense to avoid getting involved with Tyler, you should
respect her wishes."

Tyler lost his smile, then said, his words deliberately precise, "There you go again, casting aspersions
on my character. What makes you think you know so
much about me, Carlie?" She tried to tug free, but he
tightened his hold. "I've never coerced a woman into
a relationship—other than you, of course, but that's
a different matter, isn't it? Usually, the women are
trying to coerce me. And they're up-front about it.
They say what *they* want, what *they* need out of a relationship, and undying devotion isn't on top of their

list. Now, that would make me the used, not the user, wouldn't you say?"

"No, I wouldn't. I have no interest in commenting on your exploits one way or the other."

"But you do often enough."

"Then I apologize." She stared down at his hand, still grasping her wrist. Her heart was thundering so rapidly, she could barely breathe. She'd never seen Tyler so intense, so direct about his private life. Maybe she had been misjudging him. It was something she needed to think about in the quiet of her own home. "Now, if you'll turn me loose, I'll get out of your hair."

His mood seemed to switch mercury quick. "But I want you in my hair today. Haven't you been paying attention? Even though you're wearing the most disgusting outfit I've even seen on man, woman or beast, I still want your company." He hesitated, then asked reluctantly, "Where did you find that, anyway? Surely there isn't a store that actually sold you that thing?"

Carlie looked down at her khaki green nylon jogging suit. It was lined and very warm. She was wearing a gray sweatshirt underneath.

"I wasn't trying to be fashionable, Tyler. I was jogging. In the rain, not on a runway. What does it matter how I look?" She gave one final yank and freed her arm, then headed for the kitchen door. "I'll call you later, Bren."

Carlie hurried out the door, then jogged away in a loose-limbed stride, feeling the rain immediately soak her hair and drip down her face. She was nearly a block away, when Tyler caught up with her.

He pulled his car up to the curb and rolled down his window. "Hello, Carlie."

Without looking his way, she said plainly, "Go away."

He drove slowly, keeping pace with her. She ignored him. "You know, Brenda said I hurt your feelings."

That effectively stopped her. "Not on your best day, with your best shot."

"Then why are you so ill-tempered today?"

"Me! What about you?"

"I asked first."

Carlie briefly considered her options, then decided on one truth she could share. "I'm concerned about one of the children at school. His father's in the hospital, and it doesn't look good. When I called yesterday, their phone had been shut off."

They had both stopped. Tyler lowered his head. "That's rough."

"Yes, it is. I wish I knew some way to help."

"Maybe I can help."

"How?"

"I don't know. Let me think about it, all right?"

Carlie started off again. "Fine. And while you're doing that, leave me alone."

He shook his head sadly. "Can't. I told you. I'm despondent." Then in a clear pleading tone, he added, "I need you, Carlie."

Water dripped down her nose. She blinked at him, feeling her heart jump several beats and her throat go dry. He was a cad, a beautiful cad, but still, she couldn't give herself away. So she laughed. Hard.

"You're a cold, cruel woman."

She laughed again for good measure.

"Come on, Carlie. Get in before you get too wet. I don't want you to ruin my seat covers."

"I'm already soaked to the bone, Tyler. And you have leather seats. I would surely ruin them."

"I'll forgive you. I promise."

She could feel herself weakening against his insistence. "You really want company so badly?"

"No. I really want *your* company. You're good for my ego."

"Then I must be slipping."

Tyler got out and went to the passenger door. He opened it with a flourish, bowing for her to enter.

Carlie gave in gracefully. She realized that she didn't have it in her to deny him. She wanted his company too much. Already, she felt more buoyant, more alive. He didn't treat her like any other man she knew. He was honest with her. She knew where he was coming from and what he was thinking. She could trust him.

Tyler hurried back around the car and slid in behind the wheel. He sighed, then turned to grin at Carlie. "I'll take you home to change before we go to a movie."

"When did I agree to see a movie?"

"You will, won't you?"

Carlie waited a moment, then asked with a degree of curiosity and disbelief, "You're really bothered that this woman walked out on you?"

He didn't answer right away, and she prompted, "Tyler?"

"I liked her. So, yeah, it bothers me. We…well, things just really clicked. It was like I knew her already, you know?"

"But you see a lot of women."

He didn't dispute that, but he didn't confirm it, either. Again, she wondered if she'd misjudged him.

"What about you, Carlie? Have you ever met anyone that really felt *right* from the very beginning?"

"Brenda and I were instant friends, even though we're so different."

"That's not exactly what I meant, and you know it."

No, she knew what he meant, but she couldn't very well confide in him about her lack of a love life, about a lack of love, period. Until that night in the pool house, she hadn't believed she would ever enjoy the sexual side of a relationship. "I was married once. But things didn't work out."

She jumped when Tyler reached across the seat and took her hand. "Tell me what happened."

"No. Let it suffice to say, I was young and foolish and made some dumb mistakes. End of story."

"You must have been hurt."

A nervous laugh escaped her, and she covered her mouth with her hand. He'd said similar words at the pool house. She was playing a dangerous game, and it was wearing on her.

Tyler frowned at her. "Was that funny? I think I missed the punch line."

She shook her head. "No, I'm sorry. It's just…yes, I felt bad about it at the time. But as you can see, I got over it. Don't worry about it, okay?"

His hand tightened on hers, and he appeared disgruntled. "You know, you should probably be really careful about hooking up with anyone again. I mean, guys can really take advantage. You deserve to be treated special."

Carlie looked at him questioningly, seeing that he was agitated, but not understanding why. He smiled.

"You want to go home first to change and get dried off?" he asked.

"Yes. But you should know right now, Tyler, you won't like my change of clothes any better than you like this outfit. I refuse to dress up on Sundays. It's my day off, a day for comfort." And besides, the sloppier she looked, the less likely Tyler was to recognize her. Not that he had the slightest suspicion now.

"Fair enough. But can I at least request you avoid shades of green? It makes my stomach churn."

Carlie flashed a crooked grin. "I'll see what I can do."

"Ah, just what I like. A submissive woman."

That comment earned him a playful smack.

After they reached Carlie's house, she disappeared into her bedroom to change and Tyler nosed around her living room. Carlie emerged minutes later, her hair only slightly damp and combed into place, her wet jogging suit replaced with a dry one. It was blue, and hopefully less objectionable, at least in color; the fit was still very loose and concealing.

A short while later, they were back in the car, on their way to Tyler's house. The storm intensified, covering the streets with debris and filling the car with a steady drone of raindrops hitting the roof, interspersed with rumbling thunder. Carlie was relaxed in her seat, unconcerned with the weather.

"The storm doesn't bother you?"

She lazily swiveled her head toward Tyler, not raising it from the back of the seat. She was exhausted from too little sleep, and mind-weary from fretting about things she had no control over. "I love storms."

He grinned. "I should have known better than to think they would frighten you."

She smiled, her eyes still on his profile. "When I was a little girl, I used to sit on the porch and listen. The rain would blow under the overhang, wetting my legs and sometimes my face. But the smells...so clean and fresh. I've always thought of storms as being peaceful, despite their noise."

Tyler glanced at her, his eyes drifting over her face. He grinned teasingly. "I've always thought storms were sexy."

Carlie's heart jerked, memories of the storm the night they'd spent at the pool house flooding into her memory. She cleared her throat, but still her words emerged as a dry croak. "Is that right?"

He laughed. "Hmm. They have one hell of an effect on me."

"Good grief." Carlie had to joke to cover the heat that surged through her. A vivid mental picture had surfaced with his words, and she had to rely on wit to hide her feelings. "You won't embarrass me by attacking some poor, unsuspecting female at the movies, will you?"

His grin was wicked. "You're not concerned for your own safety?"

She snorted.

"You do that really well, you know? I don't think I've ever heard another female snort with quite your flair. It's very descriptive."

"Thank you."

Tyler laughed at her dry tone, then shot her a narrow-eyed look. "Have you ever made love during a storm?"

Forcing herself to breathe normally, Carlie peeked at him, then quickly looked away. She felt hot from the inside out, her skin tingling, her stomach coiling tight. *She had to lie.* She shook her head, then realizing he was watching the road, she whispered, "No."

That should have ended it, but she couldn't stop herself from asking, still in a whisper, "Have you?"

Tyler glanced at her again, his look unreadable. His words were quiet and carefully measured. "I thought you didn't want any details on my exploits."

She felt disgruntled by his evasion after she'd summoned up the nerve to ask. "No details. Just a statement. Yes or no?"

He stared straight ahead. "Yeah." He sighed. "Yeah, I have."

Carlie turned away. His husky tone nearly melted her, and she said without thinking, "It would probably be nice."

Tyler's eyes skipped quickly to Carlie and then back to the road again. "Carlie?"

"Hmm?"

Her head was laid back against the seat, her eyes closed. She could never have another sexual interlude with Tyler, but just being with him was nice, too. Maybe she should let that be enough, she thought. Maybe she should try to relax and enjoy her time with him, even though it was risky.

She didn't see his incredulous expression, or the way he was watching her.

"Carlie, did you mean you thought it would be 'nice' to make love to *me* during a storm?"

Her eyes shot wide open, her relaxed position shot to hell. She felt tense from her toes to her eyebrows, her heart going into spasms. She peered at Tyler, totally speechless.

They stopped at a traffic light and he turned to face her, bracing one arm on the back of the seat. "Well?"

Her laugh sounded a bit forced. "I didn't mean you specifically. I meant…the storm in general. Someone who really enjoyed sex would like it in this kind of weather." She was babbling, but she couldn't seem to stop.

His gaze was disturbingly intent. "You don't enjoy lovemaking?"

"I never said that!" She was flustered and had to struggle to keep from looking away. "I just meant there are a lot of people who don't. But someone like you, someone who appears, by all accounts, to like it very much, probably would enjoy it during a storm. I… I think I would, just because I love storms, I mean."

Carlie ground to a painful halt, her rambling finally at an end. Tyler stared at her, and Carlie didn't want to know what he was thinking.

He cleared his throat, but the words came out sounding husky. "You should definitely try it sometime."

Conversation, after that bit of advice, was nil. When they arrived at the video-rental store, Carlie gaped. "What are we doing?"

"Renting a movie."

Uh-oh. "Renting a movie, to watch…where?"

Tyler shot her a grin. "My place. You said you didn't want to dress up, so I thought you'd be more comfortable at home."

Her home, maybe. Not this. She didn't want to go to his...

"Wait here, and I'll run in and get it. No reason for both of us to get soaked."

Carlie sat in his car, stupefied. How could she refuse without looking ridiculous? How could she explain the difference between being in a crowded theater and being *alone* with Tyler?

She was still pondering that problem when he returned, the DVD tucked inside his jacket, his dark hair glistening from the rain. "All set." He took his seat and started the car. "You're gonna love this movie."

She had her doubts.

There was an underground garage at Tyler's building, so they didn't get wet going in. Carlie walked slowly, hesitant to enter his private domain. But, like his office, Tyler's home was fairly generic. It was large, with a fantastic view, and very tastefully decorated. But everything looked...cold and impersonal. He explained it was a furnished apartment, and a cleaning crew came in weekly.

Carlie thought that was a sad way to live.

Tyler must have picked up on her sentiments, because he said, "Not exactly 'home sweet home,' is it?"

"If you don't like it, why did you move here?"

He shrugged, looking around the apartment. "When I was a kid, we lived in a dirty little hellhole with ratty furniture and peeling paint. I decided that when I picked a place of my own, I'd make sure it was nice." He shook his head. "At the time, I suppose I thought this place was nice." He winked at Carlie. "But I like your house much better."

She grinned. "Thank you. I like my house, too. I

picked it because it's small. Grandfather had a huge old farmhouse. It was always cold and empty. I hated it."

"You said your parents died when you were young. Your grandfather raised you?"

Carlie nodded, but looked away. "My brother was already old enough to be on his own, and I didn't see him much. It was just me and Granddad."

"Were you lonely?"

"I suppose." Then she changed the subject. Talk of her childhood always made her melancholy. "So, are we going to start this movie or not?"

Tyler took her hand, gave it a soft squeeze, then left the room. After fetching colas and pretzels from a sterile kitchen, he turned off most of the lights. "A scary movie has to be watched in the dark…for effect."

Carlie relaxed, settling herself into the soft leather sofa. "I know why you wanted to come here to watch the movie." She waved a finger at him. "You didn't want witnesses when you get scared and start screaming."

"Perceptive girl." After putting in the DVD, Tyler took his seat next to Carlie. He sat very close, his damp hair pushed back from his face, his long legs stretched out.

Unexpectedly, Carlie leaned toward him and nudged him with her shoulder. "You're all right, Tyler."

He stared at her, grinning crookedly and looking very pleased by her offhand compliment.

He gently touched her cheek. "I'm glad you think so."

It was such an easy and natural thing to do. She leaned into his hand, and his fingers found a stray wisp of hair escaped over her temple. He toyed with it, running it through his fingers, then giving her a gentle tug.

He could make her stomach flip with just a word or a look, but he also made her feel accepted, made her a part of things in a way she'd never been. Being raised by her grandfather had left her sheltered but alone. Brenda had been her first real friend.

Now she had Tyler, too.

"I like you, Tyler. I'm…really glad we're friends."

"I am, too. Though I'll admit, I've never been just friends with a woman before." He tucked her hair behind her ear. "And by the way, this is another date. Try to remember the rules."

She immediately put on her best vacant expression, removed her glasses and batted her eyelashes. "Tyler," she whined, looking pathetically vulnerable, "I'm scared of the dark. Hold me."

He grinned and reached for her. She promptly shoved him back into his seat. "You've got the basics down right, but you're supposed to be clinging to me right about now."

"You big coward." She shook her head at him. "You better control yourself during this movie, Tyler. I mean it. Date or no date, I don't want you crawling all over me just because you chose a movie you couldn't handle."

He smiled slyly, apparently enjoying himself. "Did I tell you, I've seen this movie before? I'd be willing to wager that about halfway through, *you'll* be crawling all over *me*."

"I'll take that bet." She grabbed his hand and pumped it. "What will you give me when you lose?"

"I won't lose. You will. Then you'll invite me over for another home-cooked meal. Agreed?"

"Fine. But when *I* win? What do I get?"

"A kiss?"

"Ha! Why play if the stakes aren't worth much?"

"You're saying my kisses aren't to be devoutly sought?"

"Not by Carlie McDaniels."

"Carlie, Carlie. You've already forgotten that this is a date. You should have been more determined to win, with a kiss as the prize."

Carlie twisted her lips into a wry smile. "How about you help me grade tests next Friday night when you lose? You're college-educated. You could probably handle third-grade math."

"I would, of course, endeavor to do my best—if I lost, which I won't. Now, hush, the movie is about to start."

The picture began with a bloodcurdling scream, then continued with screams for quite some time. Ten minutes into the movie, Carlie was glaring at Tyler. "This is awful!"

"I know. Don't you love it?"

"Oh, I don't believe this! They almost die at the hands of a monstrous alien, and now, while hiding in a dark, dank hole, they're getting aroused?"

Tyler put his arm around her, reacting with world-weary logic. "These things happen."

"Good grief!" Her eyes were glued to the picture. "From blood and guts to pornography! It's obscene."

Halfway through the movie, Carlie was watching through her fingers, her hands covering her face. She was leaning toward Tyler, or he was pulling her close, she wasn't sure which.

But she liked it. Tyler kept smoothing his hand over her shoulder, not paying the least attention to the movie. When she gasped and moved close to him again, his arm tightened, instinctively offering her comfort.

He was unbelievably hard and warm. And he smelled good, like the storm outside, fresh and alive and very male. She wanted to cuddle closer, to turn her nose into his chest and breathe deeply of his unique scent.

Instead, she forced herself to pull away slightly.

Tyler refused to let her move too far. He turned her chin toward him. "You about ready to give up and crawl into my lap?"

"Very nearly," she whispered back, seeing the glimmer of his dark eyes in the dim light. She could feel the firm, unyielding muscles of his upper arm pressing into her breast, and there was a strange tension in the air. Carlie wondered if Tyler felt it, too. Probably not.

She was beginning to accept how easily he could make her react to him. She'd never had the problem with any other man, and in fact, had been repulsed when they'd tried to become romantic. But not so with Tyler. He could easily infuriate her one minute, make her laugh the next, then fill her with sensual heat with only his smile.

But he didn't want her. He wanted a masked harem girl.

Suddenly, there was a particularly grotesque scene, accompanied by a blast of startling noise. Carlie launched herself against Tyler in reflex, and he pressed her face into his throat. Just as she turned her gaze back to the screen, she felt Tyler's lips skim her temple.

She went perfectly still, unable to believe what had just happened, wondering if she'd imagined the fleeting touch. But then she felt his breath, warm and gentle on her cheek, and the feel of his lips on her skin again, tentative and soft. He sighed quietly into her ear, sending ripples of sensation over her skin.

Oblivious to the movie, Carlie shuddered with the shock of the erotic kiss. He lightly circled the rim of her ear with the tip of his tongue, then delicately slipped his tongue inside, teasing her with a leisurely attentiveness to detail.

Softly, with consternation, she asked, "Tyler?"

"Hmm?" He was laving her ear, tracing the swirls, his breath warm and moist.

"What…exactly…are you doing?"

"Exactly?" He asked the question against her temple, his voice husky and low. "Putting my tongue in your ear."

Carlie pulled back, incredulous at the easy way he made that confession. "You're putting your tongue in *my* ear?"

Tyler stared at her, his dark eyes appearing almost black in the dim shadows. "Well…yes."

"Whatever for?"

"You, ah, didn't like it?"

Carlie searched his face, unable to tell if he was being serious or clowning around again. She thought it must surely be another of his jokes, like the lessons in dating. "I don't know. I suppose you took me by surprise. I thought this was to be strictly platonic."

He shrugged, totally unconcerned. "I love women's ears. Yours are very nice."

Carlie opened her mouth, but then closed it again. He was playing with her, and she didn't like it. "I'm not at all certain you should be doing this, Tyler."

He ignored her vague protest. "I want to know if you liked it, Carlie."

"Why?"

"Most women have sensitive ears. I just—"

"No. I mean, why me? Why should you care if I liked it?"

"Curiosity?"

She frowned at him a moment, struggling to hide her disappointment. She shouldn't have asked, and now she wished she hadn't. Turning back to the movie, she pushed on her glasses. "I think it would be best if we forgot the idle curiosity."

"Aren't you just a little curious, too, Carlie?"

His insistence annoyed her. "I'm curious about a lot of things, Tyler. But sometimes curiosity is better left unappeased." She refused to look at him again, overwhelmed with uncertainty.

"I didn't mean to upset you."

"You didn't."

"You provoked me, you know."

She slanted him a quick look of exasperation, pretending a great interest in the movie. "I did no such thing."

"Sure you did. You crawled, just as I said you would, into my lap. I'm only a man, Carlie."

She gave him her full attention. He was behaving exactly like the cad she'd accused him of being, flirting with her simply because she was female and available. What other reason could there be? "Were you this pushy with your lady friend from the party?"

Tyler rubbed a hand over his face, then stared at Carlie in chagrin. "You know, as incredible as it seems, I'd all but forgotten about that little incident. I don't think I'll thank you for reminding me." He looked away from her, then said, "I knew you'd help me forget the mystery woman's desertion, but I didn't think you'd deliberately bring it up again."

"This morning, you acted as if you had to know who she was. How could you forget about her so easily, anyway?" As soon as she'd asked the question, Carlie wondered if she was losing it. She was purposely treading on very dangerous ground.

"You don't want to hear about my conquests, remember?"

"Ah, so it was a conquest. Not that I'd ever doubted otherwise, given your reputation. But it is unfortunate the lady was masked, don't you think? Otherwise, it might have been her here now, and I'm sure she'd be more appreciative of your charms than I am."

Tyler caught Carlie's hand, demanding her attention. "It isn't like that, Carlie. I—"

His innocent look of confusion infuriated her. "Isn't like what? I like you, Tyler, I really do. But I don't appreciate being treated like a fool. Does it make you feel macho to come on to every woman you meet, even those you don't really want?"

Tyler looked startled by her anger. He visibly collected himself. "I like you as a friend, too. More than I've ever liked a woman. I feel completely at ease with you. And I'm not 'playing' with you, Carlie.

You're a woman. That's an irrevocable fact. I can't help being—"

"Don't you dare tell me again that you're *curious*!"

His hand came up to cradle her cheek. Smiling slightly, he said simply, "Then you'll have to stop being so unique, so intelligent and witty and fun to be with."

"So." Carlie tightened her mouth, and moved out of his reach. "What about your masked lady? Have you given up on finding her?"

She could see the frustration that replaced his smile. "I don't know." He gave her another smile and shrugged. "You know, I'd never met a woman who could so easily confuse me, and now I've met two. Not really sporting, is it?"

"Tyler…"

"Shh. Stop fending me off and just relax, okay? I promise not to attack you again. I won't lose my head and have my wicked way with you."

He was back to normal, or what she accepted as normal. When he talked complete nonsense, she was comfortable with his attention. Carlie finally smiled, then playfully slugged Tyler in the arm before giving her attention back to the movie. "You're impossible."

Carlie wanted to linger once the movie ended, but Tyler didn't invite her to stay, and she didn't know how to ask. It didn't feel as though he was tired of her company, but rather that he was tired of his apartment.

He said, "I'm not here all that often. I only come home to sleep." Then he laughed. "I've probably only used that television a handful of times. But it was fun today, with you."

She berated him all the way home for showing her

such an outrageous movie. And then he reminded her she owed him dinner.

"All right, though I don't think you played fair. You'd already seen the movie and knew what to expect."

Tyler grinned. It was still storming, and the driving was slow. The inside of the car was warm and humid and Carlie's hair had once again rebelled. She tried to get the damp tendrils back into place, but gave up after Tyler shook his head at her. He reached across the seat and took her hand with easy familiarity. "I suppose I did have the advantage. So how about I help you grade your papers, anyway? I wouldn't mind."

Carlie smiled. It would probably be best to refuse, but he gave her fingers a gentle squeeze, and she found herself agreeing. "Very sporting of you, Tyler. Thank you."

"You're welcome. And I'll bring dinner. Pizza or something. Okay?"

"Why are you so conciliatory all of a sudden? You're making me very suspicious."

They pulled up in front of Carlie's house. Tyler put the car into Park and turned off the engine, then shifted in his seat to face her. The air, sealed by the heavy rain outside, smelled of damp flesh and wet hair and Tyler, masculine and seductive.

"I meant what I said today, Carlie. I can't recall ever enjoying another person's company as much as I enjoy yours. I like helping the kids and I like the exercise. But I think I like arguing with you most of all. You get riled so easily."

"Arguing with you is my pleasure. And as to the rest, the children and I should thank you. You're making a difference, and we appreciate it." Tyler looked embarrassed by her praise. She knew she shouldn't, even debated with herself for several moments, but she couldn't resist inviting him in. "I don't have anything pressing to do. We could play cards or something."

"I thought that if I sat here in the rain, looking forlorn long enough, you would finally ask."

Carlie indicated the rain lashing the windows. "Are you ready then? We'll have to make a run for it."

Tyler grinned at her. "I'll race you."

They each dashed from the car as the rain pounded them with stinging force. They huddled together, Tyler protectively putting his arm around Carlie, trying to cover her as best he could. Laughing, they nearly tripped each other in their race for the house.

Stumbling onto the front stoop and under the tiny roof, they collapsed against the door. Gasping and winded, with rain dripping from their bodies, they shivered from the chill October air and tried to stifle their laughter.

Carlie pulled off her glasses and swiped at her eyes. She looked at Tyler, then burst out laughing again, falling against his shoulder. "Oh, Tyler, you're soaked!" She reached up and pushed a wet strand of dark hair from his forehead.

Tyler didn't move. She was huddled under his arm, her hair plastered to her skull, her glasses in her hand. He raised a finger and brushed gently against her eyelashes, spiked from the rain. Carlie smiled up at him.

Then his eyes dropped to her lips, and she parted them, without speaking, without even breathing. The tension was back, nearly choking her now. She ached so badly...

"Carlie?"

His voice was husky. Carlie tried to lean away, but he held her firm. His eyes drifted over her face and she blinked at the tenderness there.

And then he kissed her.

Chapter 7

Carlie gasped and squirmed against him. The sound of Tyler's breathing was even louder than the rain pelting the roof of the overhang. Carlie felt his tongue touch the seam of her lips, and without conscious decision, she parted them. He groaned low in his throat, held her face between his hands and slanted his mouth over hers, stroking deep inside, imitating the lovemaking she was only recently familiar with. It made her body tingle with remembered heat.

He released her mouth, his lips traveling over her cheek and temple and the bridge of her nose. "Carlie…" He murmured her name wonderingly, over and over again. His hands slid down her shoulders, and one palm ventured forward to cover her breast, rubbing over her nipple with tantalizing expertise.

It was that expertise that brought her to her senses.

Shoving him away, Carlie covered herself with her hands. Tyler stood staring at her, apparently dazed. "Carlie…?"

"You…you…" She couldn't believe what she had almost let happen. Her thoughts were in turmoil, her emotions sensitized, and it was all his fault. "How dare you!"

He frowned, his eyes black with a mixture of passion and frustration. He shook his head the tiniest bit, then growled, "I don't know. I…hell." He turned his back, his hands flexing, but when Carlie began struggling with her keys to unlock the door, he jerked around to face her.

She flinched from the hand he reached toward her. She felt so confused and angry at Tyler for complicating things further, for apparently wanting his mystery woman, but willing to toy with her, as well. She concentrated on the anger, unreasonable as it seemed. "Don't you touch me! You lied!"

"About what?" His shout matched the volume of her words.

"You said you wouldn't attack me!"

"I didn't attack you, dammit! I kissed you. There's a big difference."

"You…you pawed me."

He loomed over her. "I touched your breast. That's all. Your nipples were hard and I saw that and—"

She gasped loudly at his audacity, feeling her face pulse with heat. "It's cold out here, you ass! My…my…"

"Nipples," he supplied, smirking at her.

His attitude infuriated her. "It's because of the cold, certainly not because of you."

"I know that. I'm not stupid to women's bodies. But

the sight made me lose my head a little." He suddenly looked solemn, and a little confused himself. "You have very nice breasts, Carlie."

Her heart raced in her chest. "My…my…"

"Breasts!" He stared at her irritably. "They're called breasts, dammit."

"Well, they're none of your business! Keep your opinions to yourself."

"You're repressed," he accused, sounding disgusted with her. "It was no big deal. Forget about it."

No big deal. The words crushed her. And to call her repressed…that was the same label her husband had applied, though she now knew it wasn't true. She had the same feelings as any other woman, but right now, she wished she didn't. Maybe it wouldn't hurt so bad if the accusation was true. She swallowed, staring at Tyler and his dark expression of irritation. "I'd sooner forget you, Tyler Ramsey." And she meant it. "Go home and leave me alone."

Carlie turned, finally unlocking her door. She tried to enter, but Tyler stopped her. "You invited me in."

"I changed my mind."

"We need to talk, Carlie. This isn't going to go away."

"Of course it is. Just as soon as you do."

"No, it's not." He took her arm and forced his way into her house.

Carlie refused to close the door. She was trembling inside and felt ready to snap. She was furious, with herself, with Tyler, with the circumstances. "Get out."

"No. I want to talk to you."

She snorted. "You have a funny way of talking."

"Look, Carlie…" He tried to sound reasonable, but

his eyes dropped to her breasts again, almost unintentionally, it seemed. "Let's get dried off. Then we can
sort this out."

"There's nothing to sort out. You crossed the line
and I don't want you to ever do that again."

"Well, I'm damn well going to do it again, and
real soon if you don't get your butt in the other room
and find something dry to wear that isn't showing off
your…"

She fled the room, and purposely slammed her bedroom door. Hard.

Odious man! Carlie yanked off her sodden clothing,
repeatedly shoving her glasses up on the bridge of her
nose. And all the while she rained silent curses on Tyler's head. Talk about fickle! First, he claims to be depressed because he's without a date; then, he wants to
see the mystery woman again and can't; and then, he
makes a move on her, Carlie. She stopped in the process of pulling a thick terry-cloth, floor-length shift
over her head.

He'd actually done that—made a pass at her. And
he couldn't have been completely toying with her. He'd
been affected also, she could see that. Slowly, she sat
on the edge of her bed.

Tyler Ramsey wanted Carlie McDaniels? Good
grief.

But, her thinking continued, he also wanted her alter
ego, the mystery woman, and had already slept with
her. *She* knew they were one and the same, but Tyler
didn't. Was he only biding his time with her until he
could discover the identity of the masked harem girl?

It was equal parts ridiculous and unreasonable, but
she was feeling jealous of herself.

She finished dressing, then left the bedroom. Tyler was pacing the living room, his shirt discarded, a towel in his hands as he tried to dry himself off. He'd removed his shoes and socks and had left them by the front door. His jeans were dark, soaked from rain and molded to his thighs and buttocks. Carlie cleared her throat.

Turning, Tyler stared at her. She was nervous, she couldn't help that. Everything had suddenly shifted again, so many changes converging on her all at once. She was at a loss as to how to deal with it all.

His eyes swept over her, from her still-wet hair to her naked feet. He didn't say a word, but held her eyes, his hands hanging from his sides.

"I apologize if I overreacted," she said. "You took me by surprise. I never once suspected you might…"

A reluctant smile curved his mouth. "You acted as if I'd defiled you in some way. Was it really so bad, honey?"

"No." She shook her head, her heavy braid swinging behind her. "But I really don't think getting physical is a good idea. I like being friends with you too much to complicate things. And it wouldn't have the same effect on you—our being…involved—I mean, as it would on me."

He approached her slowly, then stopped in front of her. She lowered her eyes, unable to meet his probing gaze. He crouched slightly to look her in the face. "Carlie. Don't sell yourself short. You can't know how I might react to you."

But she could, because she knew how he'd reacted to the mysterious and provocative harem girl. She was simply Carlie. Plain and boring. "You're used to beautiful women. Tons of them."

"Tons, huh? Well, that's not true." He wrapped the towel around his neck, holding the ends. "I haven't had an ounce of experience with any real relationships. In fact, the only relationship I've ever had that was worth a damn was with my brother. And now Brenda. But that's not what we're talking about, is it? So give me a break here, okay?"

She stared up at him helplessly, and then he cupped her cheek, his thumb stroking her temple. "I like the way we are together, Carlie. We could have a good relationship."

She needed some space. With Tyler standing so close, she could see the water drops still clinging to the dark swirls of hair on his chest. His body was moist from the rain, his muscles slick and smooth. Her nipples tightened again and she stepped away. Space. She definitely needed space.

"Why don't you tell me what you really want, Tyler." She walked into the kitchen as casually as possible and pulled two mugs from the cabinet.

She was filling the glass coffeepot with water, when she felt Tyler behind her. His hands lifted to her upper arms and he pulled her back against his chest. He murmured against her temple, "I'm not sure. I know I like spending time with you. And I know I'm going to want to kiss you again."

Carlie closed her eyes. "What about other women?"

"What other women?"

"Your masked lady, for one. Are you only wanting to spend time with me until you can convince Bren to give you her name? And if your harem girl wants to see you again, what then?"

She could feel the added tension in the way Tyler's hands gripped her. "You're jumping the gun, Carlie. Hell, I didn't ask you to marry me. I'm not asking for a lifetime commitment."

She pulled away, embarrassment vying with the anger rising within her. He made her sound desperate! "That isn't what I meant, Tyler. I certainly don't aspire to tie you down. I don't aspire to do anything with you. It's just that I know how you are about commitments, and I'm trying to point out that you would only be using me until something better came along. Right now, I like you as a friend. I'm grateful for the time you donate to helping the children. But if you... that is...if we..."

Tyler rolled his eyes in exasperation. "If I made love to you. That *is* what you're trying to say, isn't it?"

"Yes. If we...did that. I'm honest enough to admit my heart might get involved, and then my pride would suffer when you decided to toss me aside. I don't think I could forgive you, and our friendship, which I count more important than a bit of hanky-panky, would be ruined."

She couldn't look at him after that little speech. Instead, she went about setting out cookies and preparing some coffee. She felt like a fraud.

Tyler narrowed his eyes in disbelief. "You're amazing, you know that? I'm surprised you didn't carry your predictions through to the end of Time. And you forgot to cover a few scenarios. I mean, what if that jerk you told me you used to love suddenly reappeared? Or what if one of your teacher buddies caught your eye?

You could ditch me!" He stormed around the kitchen, his hands on his hips, his dark eyebrows lowered in a fierce frown. "I wasn't talking about some time in the distant future, dammit. I was talking about now."

Carlie choked on the sip of coffee she'd just taken. Tyler grumbled and proceeded to pound on her back.

"All right, all right! Don't beat me to death." She sucked in several desperate breaths, then glowered at him incredulously. "You're wanting to…to…"

He rolled his eyes again, and sighed loud enough to rattle the windowpanes. "Make love. It's called making love, Carlie. People have been doing it since the beginning of Time. They'll continue doing it until the end of Time. It's a necessary and enjoyable part of life, you know."

She gave him her patented snort. "I'm not as cavalier as you, Tyler. *I* certainly haven't been doing it." She realized her slip immediately. Tyler was looking at her curiously, and she stammered an explanation. "It isn't necessary. Enjoyable, maybe. But not necessary."

"God save us from liberated women." He advanced on her, and Carlie held her coffee cup between them like an insubstantial shield. Tyler took it from her. "Do you care about me, Carlie?"

"I care about a lot of men. That doesn't mean I want to sleep with them."

He stiffened, and his eyes grew hard. "Who? Who do you care about?"

"Jason, for one."

"My brother?"

"Yes. And several teachers who I've been friends with since I started teaching here. I care about some of the parents I've gotten to know, and a few of my neighbors…"

"Carlie." Tyler laid his finger against her lips. "There's caring, and then there's *caring*."

She nodded. Tyler removed his hand from her mouth, then stroked her cheek. "Tell me you care about me."

"This sounds suspiciously like a seduction routine you've practiced to perfection."

Tyler stepped back, shoving his hands into his pockets. "Obviously, I haven't practiced it enough."

Carlie smiled, her first real smile since he'd kissed her. He looked every bit as confused as she felt. "Tyler, be reasonable. I'm not going to jump into bed with you, just because you suddenly find me strange and interesting."

"I never said—"

"I'm different from other women you know, and the main difference is that I'm *not* trying to wend my way into your bed. You're just stymied, not really aroused. Go home and take a warm bath and you'll feel better in the morning."

He shook his head, being very precise. "I won't."

Carlie chuckled. "Don't pout, Tyler. Surely some woman somewhere has told you no before."

"Not that I would admit to. And just because you're not interested right now, doesn't mean I'll stop being interested. When you get used to the idea and accept it as a fact, you'll see that I was right."

She looked at him suspiciously. "About what?"

Quickly, before she could move away, Tyler bent down and kissed her, hard and fast. "We'll be good together. I'm sure of it. Very good."

That was an already proven fact, but Tyler couldn't know it. She mustered a shaky smile. "Bragging, Mr. Ramsey?"

"No." He stared intently into her eyes. "Making a promise."

Carlie felt the heat building in her stomach. But then Tyler pulled out a seat at the table and sprawled in it. "In the meantime…" He raised his arms and clasped his hands behind his head. "No pressure. You're the best friend I ever recall having. I suppose I can be content with that. For a time."

Carlie felt relief, and quelling disappointment. "Good. Then we can stop all this nonsense and play some cards." She pulled a deck from a drawer and sat across from Tyler.

"What would you like to play?" She looked at Tyler.

"Strip poker?"

Carlie started to rise, her mouth drawn in annoyance, but Tyler stopped her. He was laughing. "Okay, okay. Bad jest. Sorry."

She nodded grudgingly. "So. What should we play?"

With a twinkle in his eyes, he asked innocently, "Old maid?"

She threw the cards at him, then sat there glaring.

"Well, I suppose that decides it." He grinned wryly, a card sitting on top of his head, the rest scattered in his lap and on the floor. "Fifty-two pickup it is."

Tyler tried to keep his mind on the basketball game they were playing, but he couldn't keep his eyes off Carlie. She was trying to treat him the same as always, but he wasn't going to let her get away with it. Everything was different now, the way he felt when he was around her, the effect her smile had on him. She was doing her best to ignore his attention, but there was only ten more minutes before practice was over. Then he'd be going home with her again. That fact had his stomach in knots.

When was the last time he'd so anticipated spending time with a woman?

But Carlie wasn't just any woman. She wasn't impressed by monetary things. In fact, she almost seemed disdainful of them. And she wanted nothing from him, other than companionship and help with a group of children who deserved someone better than him.

He'd thought about that, too, about ways he could help. He'd never given much of himself—money didn't count, because that wasn't him. But for Carlie, for the kids...for himself, he was going to try to make a difference. And he had a plan he hoped would work.

Practice ended, and Tyler found the little boy whose family's phone had been disconnected. He walked him out to his mother's car. After discreetly questioning the woman, Tyler discovered that she used to be a secretary. He casually mentioned that he always had papers that had to be transcribed, and would be glad to have her assistance. When he mentioned what he was willing to pay, and that she could do the work at home, she readily accepted. He arranged to start sending her documents next week.

And in the meantime, he explained a scholarship of sorts he was setting up that would enable her to enroll her children in the extracurricular activities that they'd been forced to drop out of due to lack of funds.

By the time Tyler finished convincing her to take advantage of his offer, he was feeling pretty good. It was a damned nice thing to know you'd been some small help. But when he came back into the gym, he realized instantly that Carlie was disgruntled with him for having excluded her.

Well, that was just too bad. He intended to surprise her when things were settled, and not a moment sooner.

She was ready to leave, her keys in her hand. He realized he hadn't even changed out of his sweaty shirt yet.

"I'll just be a minute," he said, and started toward the change-room door. She didn't answer, just stood there, tapping her foot. He chuckled. "I know what you're thinking. Curiosity is written all over your face."

She gave him a haughty look, and he prepared himself, knowing he was going to get an earful. "Actually," she said, a slight blush on her cheeks, "I was thinking how…sexy you look right now."

That stopped him. "Is that so?" He advanced slowly, seeing her struggle to stand her ground. "Enough to warrant a kiss?"

She leaned toward him, her expression smug. "Nope."

Tyler reached for her, but she ducked away. "You're a terrible tease, McDaniels!" Then he grinned. "I think I like it."

She was waiting for him to tell her why he'd been outside so long. He knew, and deliberately kept silent. Her mouth pursed, then she asked, "Are you still coming over?"

"Only if you'll give me a kiss. You can't tell a man he's sexy, then just walk away."

She shrugged. "Sure I can."

He grabbed her arm, grinning. "*No.* You can't. Besides, you want to kiss me. You know you do. What are you afraid of?"

Her lips parted, then she drew in a shaky breath, her gaze going to his mouth. "I'm not afraid of anything."

Tyler leaned back, bending his knees so he was looking directly into her eyes. Carlie squirmed, and he knew she was feeling much the same thing he was, even if she denied it. Finally, satisfied by what he saw, Tyler held out his arms. "Okay, if you're not afraid, then give me one kiss. My hands won't move, I promise."

It was a challenge, and he was willing to bet she wouldn't be able to resist. When she placed her hands on his shoulders, he felt his breath catch. When her gaze dropped to his mouth, his muscles clenched.

Going up on tiptoe, she lightly, quickly, brushed her lips over his, then settled back for his reaction.

His mouth twitched with humor. He left his arms outstretched. "Well? Are you going to kiss me or not, honey? Oh, you mean that little wisp of air that blew over my mouth was your kiss? How disappointing. I thought you could do better than that."

She blinked at him. "You didn't…like it?"

"I have no idea. It was over with before I could decide. Hell, Brenda kisses me better than that. In *front* of Jason."

Her eyebrows lowered and she shoved her glasses higher on the bridge of her nose. Tyler could practically see her mentally hitching up her pants, and he had to fight a smile.

She tightened her hands on his shoulders, and came up again, this time pressing her mouth more firmly to his. Tyler lightly licked her lips, moving his mouth against hers. She went still for a single heartbeat, then accepted his challenge, and returned the gesture. But once her tongue touched him, he drew her inside, and the kiss became ravenous.

He heard her soft moan and instantly grew hard. The game was over. He pressed against her, forcing her to step backward until they reached the wall, then he trapped her there with his body. His hips settled against her groin, rubbing insistently. His mouth now took over, eating at hers, his tongue plunging inside, feeling her own tongue move in a way that made him tremble.

He had to stop. He groaned and raised his mouth. "Damn." His head dropped onto her shoulder, his face turned inward so he could inhale her scent.

He could feel her shaking. His body was laid against the length of her own from shoulders to knees. Her legs were open, accommodating his hips.

His chuckle was wry and filled with wonder. "I asked for that, I suppose." He lifted away from her shoulder, but kept his body close to her. His voice dropped to a whisper. "I want you, Carlie."

She shook her head.

He pressed his hips closer, holding her gaze. "You can feel how much I want you, sweetheart."

She snorted, then pushed him away. "This isn't the eighth grade, Tyler. So you're aroused. So what? It's the same reaction you'd have to any woman you were kissing."

He propped his hands on his hips, feeling his lips twitch with amusement again, despite the ache in his body. "Not quite."

Carlie waved away his rebuttal. "Are you also going to tell me you're in pain? That's next, isn't it?"

"I am in pain." He started toward her. "Your screeching denials are giving me a headache."

"I wasn't screeching! I was only pointing out... Tyler, don't you touch me again!"

He took her by the shoulders, and pulled her body roughly against his. With his nose touching her own, he gently demanded, "Admit you want me, too, Carlie. Now."

She hesitated only a second. "*I do.* It's just that..."

He released her. "I'm willing to give you all the time you need, honey, but..."

She snorted, louder than usual.

Tyler grinned. "Okay, so I've been pushing. I'm having a hard time keeping my hands off you. But you know you can trust me, Carlie. I would never try to force you to do anything you didn't want to do."

He waited, all shreds of humor gone, and finally Carlie nodded. "I know that."

"Good. Then don't keep denying everything I feel. Believe it or not, I want you. You, Carlie, not some other woman, not because you're handy, not because I can't get somebody else." He stroked her cheek. "You're special, sweetheart. And what I feel for you is special."

Her eyes searched his, and she asked, "And what is it you feel, Tyler?"

He should have known she'd ask. "I'm not sure, yet—and don't snort at me!" He grinned again. "I'm trying to be honest here, Carlie. Be patient with me."

Carlie swiped up her gym bag from the bleachers and headed for the door. Tyler trotted after her. "Am I still invited for dinner?"

She didn't slow her pace. "If that's all you want. Because dinner is all you'll get."

"I promise not to do anything...that you don't want me to do."

He felt smug when her step faltered. But he also felt determined not to rush her. Carlie was worth waiting for, and she evidently needed a lot of reassurance. He could give her time. He could behave himself. It wouldn't be easy, but... He'd never known women could be so different. He'd never known a woman could be like Carlie.

And he no longer cared if he found out who the mystery woman was. Carlie, with her bristly independence and concealing wardrobe, was mystery enough to keep his attention for a long, long time. Maybe even forever.

"Hello?"

"Tyler?"

There was a pause, then, "Who's this?"

"We...ah, *met* at the party..."

Another pause. Carlie waited breathlessly, her hand gripping the receiver so tightly her fingers ached. She had deliberately disguised her voice, but it was shaking so badly, it had probably been an unnecessary measure.

"I didn't expect to hear from you again. Brenda refused to tell me how to reach you."

"I know. I...it has to be that way."

"I'll admit I'm curious to know why."

Traitor, Carlie thought. She was huddled in the middle of her bed, her nightgown twisted around her up-drawn knees. Her hair was loose, hanging down to shield her face, which, even though Tyler couldn't see, was burning. "I'm sorry."

"You have no reason to be afraid of me."

"I know. But..."

"You ran out on me."

"Yes." Carlie squeezed her eyes shut. This wasn't going the way she'd planned. She'd convinced herself to call him, hopefully to find out how determined he was to meet the mystery woman or if he even still cared. He claimed to want her…"her" meaning Carlie. But could that be true if he was still intent on meeting another woman? Even if the other woman was herself? But he didn't know that…so… It was just too confusing. Her brain felt muddled, and she was willing to try anything that might give her some real insight as to how Tyler truly felt about her.

But Tyler wasn't giving her a chance to question him. He was too busy pressing her.

"Tell me who you are." He sounded more annoyed than ever.

"No! I just…wanted to talk to you. To ask…"

"Ask me what?"

Surprised, Carlie accused softly, "You're angry."

"No, I'm frustrated. I don't like games. You're a grown woman. I understand what happened between us was unexpected. You couldn't have been any more surprised than I was. But it's too late to change things now." Then, very persuasively, "Tell me who you are."

Carlie shook her head, as tears gathered in her eyes. If only she could. "No."

"Dammit!"

She squeezed her eyes shut. "Please. Don't be angry." There was a tremor in her voice, and Tyler reacted to it.

"I'm sorry." He sounded almost weary. "We can talk. That's why you called, isn't it?"

Carlie was afraid to speak again. This was a stupid

idea. She should hang up now before he figured out who she was.

He said again, "Do you want to talk about it?"

"Maybe you should just forget…"

"Not without knowing."

Those words, said so sincerely, washed over her. Her heart ached. If he wouldn't forget, then she would have to stay away from him entirely. She drew a deep breath, calming herself. "Why?"

It was Tyler's turn to be thoughtfully silent. "It was different. You were different. More intense. It didn't seem like just sex."

"No." It had been more, at least for her.

"You felt it, too?" he asked.

"I did."

"I want to meet you. I want to know who you are. Stop playing games."

"It's…it's not a game," she said. "You would be angry…"

"I'm angry now! This isn't the eighth grade, dammit!"

Carlie jumped at his raised voice. He'd unconsciously repeated her defense. It seemed like a betrayal. "Aren't you seeing anyone else?"

She hadn't meant to ask that. This wasn't a test he had to pass. She'd only wanted to understand why he was so determined to find her. But it was too late to call back the words.

She could feel his frustration, it was so keen. His reply, when it came, was carefully modulated, the words exact. "I'm not intimate with anyone right now, if that's what you mean."

"I see."

"How could you, when I don't? I hate this!" He growled in frustration. "I don't want anything from you! But I hate knowing you might pass me on the street, and I wouldn't even know it. I hate that you have intimate knowledge of me, but I don't even know your name."

Carlie trembled. She hadn't thought of it that way, how it would be for him. She was very sorry. "Tyler, please…"

"You'll see me somewhere and remember. While I'm saying hello, how do you do, you'll be thinking of how it feels to climax with me deep inside you."

His words were harsh now, deliberately taunting, baiting her. He was being ugly, and even while she understood his frustration, she hated it. "*Stop.* Please."

"Tell me who you are, dammit."

"I can't." The words were rushed, husky with need. Carlie had to get them out before she did or said something she'd later regret. "It's impossible. I'm so sorry." Then she added in a tiny whisper, "You were wonderful, Tyler."

"Don't hang up…!"

Very gently, Carlie laid the receiver in the cradle, then curled onto her side. It had been a mistake to call him. She had to stop torturing herself and Tyler. Her heart ached with her decision.

He was right. She was behaving like a teenager with a sorry crush on the captain of the football team. She was leaving him to wonder about a woman who didn't exist. On Friday, when he came over again, she'd tell him. She wouldn't take the coward's way out by sending him a letter or giving her explanation and then running. It would be face-to-face, and she would accept his anger, for he would surely be enraged.

Carlie found sleep impossible that night. She pondered a thousand different ways Tyler might react. But it all came down to one final, irrevocable conclusion.

She had lost him, when she'd never really had him in the first place. And until now, she hadn't fully realized how badly she wanted him.

Chapter 8

Tyler set the pizza on the table, then turned to Carlie. She'd been quiet, too damned quiet, all day. He caught her as she walked by to set the table.

He pulled her into his arms. She was more rigid than usual. "I missed you, Carlie. How about a hug?"

Her arms remained at her sides, and she looked beyond him. He was stymied. "What is it? Are you mad at me about something?"

"No, I'm not mad."

"Then what is it?" He bent to look into her eyes. "You can at least give me a hug, can't you?"

She did as he asked, but it was a measly effort at best. Tyler let his hands drift down her back, and realized suddenly that it was the first time he'd ever done so. Her back was narrow, her flesh firm, and her waist tapered in. His hands started to explore there, but she pulled away. He touched her chin, seeking her eyes again. "What is it?"

"We need to talk." She peered up at him, her eyebrows lowered in a nervous frown, and shook her head. "But later, after we eat."

"Ah, intrigue. You don't have to work at keeping my interest, you know. I'm already caught."

Carlie slapped a huge piece of pizza onto his plate, splattering tomato sauce over the table.

Tyler raised his eyebrows. "You are entertaining, Carlie. When we don't have practice, I have nothing to look forward to at the end of the day. I think of you, though."

Carlie stopped in the middle of pouring the wine. She turned to Tyler, her expression serious. "Why?"

"What do you mean, 'why?' I like you."

"But *why*, Tyler? What is it about me that you like?"

He considered her question with grave seriousness. She was being very sober. His answer obviously mattered a great deal to her. The first thing that came to his mind was her honesty. "I can trust you. You don't play games, and I don't think you would ever lie to me. You're straightforward and genuine, blunt to a fault. I've never known a woman like you before."

Carlie looked stricken, which wasn't the reaction he had expected. She crossed her arms over her chest and turned away. He walked up behind her and wrapped her in his arms, holding her close despite her stiffness. He still felt frustrated and angry over his mysterious phone call, and now, with Carlie seeming so intent on separating herself from him, he actually felt needy. It wasn't a feeling he enjoyed.

"Carlie, talk to me. I don't like this. I'm used to you

giving me hell and making me laugh and then making me so hot I can't breathe. I'm not used to this silence, sweetheart."

She turned abruptly, throwing her arms tight around him and he groaned in relief. His arms were around her middle, and it registered, rather abruptly, that she was actually slim. She was wearing her usual basketball clothes that consisted of baggy sweats, and since the day was cooler, she was layered under several pieces. But his hands were stroking up and down her ribs, and it amazed him how tiny her waist was. He pulled back, shocked.

Carlie was watching him. "Don't even say it."

He was amused by her fierce expression. "What?"

"Whatever you were thinking. I'm not stupid."

"No, you're not stupid. But you are a big faker." His mouth tilted in a quizzical smile. "There's not an ounce of extra fat on you, is there?"

Carlie propped one hand on her hip in an arrogant stance. She glanced down meaningfully at her chest, the implied message very clear.

Tyler choked back his laugh. "That's not fat, sweetheart. That's a bonus from Mother Nature." Then his eyes slid over her, and his amusement slowly disappeared. "I want to see you."

"You're looking right at me."

"You know what I mean."

Warm color bloomed in her cheeks. "Oh? You want me to strip naked and dance on the table perhaps?"

"Damn! You're not as unreasonable as I thought." He pulled out a chair and made a big production of seating himself. "Go ahead. I think I'm ready. Wait!

Do you have smelling salts available? I'm not sure my heart can take this."

Carlie stared back at him blandly. Then she pulled out her own chair and sat down. She shoved a glass of wine toward him. "Eat. You need something to occupy that mouth of yours."

"True. But I could think of other…mmm!"

Carlie had jammed the piece of pizza into his mouth without concern for his clean face. He ended up laughing, and wiping pizza sauce from his nose and cheeks.

They ate in near silence but for the music Carlie had playing in the background. Tyler watched her, simply enjoying her nearness. After a moment, the quiet began to bother him. "I meant what I said earlier. About your being different. Until I met you, I thought all women were the same."

"That's an asinine comment unworthy of recognition."

"I know it sounds cynical, but it's true. Most of the women I've known were users. They would lie or mislead, even jump into my bed, just to get what they wanted."

Carlie looked slightly dazed. "What did they want?"

"Marriage, usually. You may not believe this, but I'm considered a prime catch. I'm single, and Jason and I run a successful law practice. I'm financially secure, and I drive a flashy car. That's all the criteria most women require. It wouldn't matter *who* I really was."

"I can't believe that."

"That's because you're just a little naive, honey." He studied her affectionately. "Other than Brenda, no woman has taken the time to really get to know me. Except you."

She searched his face, her eyes bright with curiosity. "What about your mother? Or other relatives?"

"I don't have other relatives. And all my mother ever wanted was for me and Jason to get out of her hair. Most times we did. It didn't matter where we went, as long as we weren't around to interfere in her affairs." He didn't quite meet her gaze, feeling her empathy, and not entirely comfortable with it. Discussing his past was not something he was familiar with.

"Jason was the one who convinced me I could get a degree. And at the time, that was no easy feat. I was so busy indulging in my bad-boy popularity, I'll admit I was something of a punk."

Carlie touched the bridge of his nose. "Brenda told me you broke your nose in a fight."

He sent her a small, brief smile. "Yeah. I did a lot of fighting back then. Mom loved it when I kicked ass. It was the only time she ever gave me any recognition." Tyler was amazed the words were coming so easily. But then, it was always easy to talk to Carlie. "You see, it really didn't matter who I was. It was what I did that was important."

"It always matters, Tyler. If not to someone else, then to yourself."

He was filled with satisfaction. "There, you see? You know that, but no other woman I've ever met has thought so. When Mom took off, and that was some time ago, she couldn't have cared less who I was or what I might become."

Carlie looked down at the remains of her pizza, then tightened her fingers around his hand. "You can't categorize all women based on one, Tyler. That isn't fair."

Tyler laughed wryly. "Don't go getting psychological on me. My mother and her many faults didn't form any lasting impression on me. It's the dozens of women since who've done that. All but you." He lifted her fingers and kissed them. "You, I'm convinced, are incapable of guile."

Carlie jumped to her feet, picked up the plates and carried them to the sink. "I'm just your basic female, Tyler, subject to the same flaws as anyone else. I can make mistakes, I—"

Tyler stood, going to Carlie and taking her face between his hands. She stared up at him, her body taut with apprehension. "You would never hurt me, Carlie. I know you wouldn't."

"You sound so positive."

He smiled as his thumbs stroked her cheeks. "That's because I know you care about me. You grouse and grumble and complain, but you do care, don't you?"

Her gaze was direct and fiercely earnest. "Yes, I do."

He hesitated, his smile disappearing. "A little?"

"A lot, Tyler. A lot."

He ached. She made him feel important to her. And most of all, he believed her. She truly cared for him.

His kiss wasn't meant to seduce, but rather to show tenderness and understanding. "Thank you, Carlie. For caring."

He was still cradling her face, but their bodies weren't touching. Carlie bit her lower lip, then hugged herself to him. Tyler had the awful suspicion she could look into his soul and see his vulnerability. It shook him, and he sought casual conversation to break the mood.

"It was the same for Jason, until he met Brenda. You should have seen him in action. He had women throw-

Lori Foster *151*

ing themselves at him, and he seldom ducked to get out of the way. After we opened the law practice, it only got worse. It seemed every client who came in knew someone or was related to someone, or *was* someone, who they thought Jason should get to know intimately. It grew old real quick. He started sending the younger female clients to me."

"And now look how incorrigible you are."

He chuckled. "That's right, honey. Put the blame where it's deserved. I'm just a product of circumstance."

"You're a product of indulgence." Carlie leaned back to smile up at him. "I remember when Brenda went to work for Jason. She said he was gorgeous, charming and entirely insufferable. He tried giving her a bracelet once, you know."

"I remember. She threw it at him. Damned thing was heavy, too. Left a bruise on his shoulder."

"It was at the Christmas party you two had, where she kissed him under the mistletoe. She seemed to float for two days."

"Yeah. I got the load of the cases because Jason was too busy wooing Brenda to bother with anything as trivial as work. She really ran him ragged." And, Tyler thought, he now had a much better understanding of what his brother had gone through. Carlie could tie him up in knots with just a look.

But there was one major difference. Jason loved Brenda, whereas Tyler had no idea exactly what he felt for Carlie.

"She made him chase her until she caught him. But they both enjoyed it, and look how everything turned out." Carlie said the words quietly, with a strange, wistful smile.

"Brenda isn't the type of woman I would have figured Jason to fall for. Don't get me wrong. There's not a better person than Brenda. She's good for Jason, and I love her. But Jason always had a preference for tall, busty sophisticated brunettes. Not short, perky, domesticated redheads."

Carlie darted him a quick look. "I guess you never can tell."

"No." Tyler tilted his head, studying her, and then he agreed. "You never can tell."

Tugging her closer, he watched as her thick lashes lowered behind the lenses of her glasses. She gave a feeble protest when he reached up and removed them from her nose, laying them carefully on the table. "Tyler…"

"You're very pretty, Carlie." He toyed with her braid, dragging his curled fingers over the length of it. He reached the end, felt the cloth-covered rubber band holding the braid secure, and pulled it free. Carlie's eyes widened, but he didn't give her time to stop him.

His fingers sifted through the strands, separating them, then pulling her hair over her shoulders. It rippled with waves, a dozen different colors highlighted by the overhead light. It was beautiful—she was beautiful—and Tyler never felt so needful of anyone in his life.

Bunching her hair into his fists on either side of her head, he pulled her face up to his. "I want you, Carlie."

The kiss was devastating in its intensity, powerfully erotic, and sensually sweet. Her body leaned into him. Tyler walked her backward to the counter, then pressed himself hard against her. He swallowed her gasp and gave his groan in return.

And still he kissed her. He was in no hurry to speed things along. No one had ever tasted so good, so right and so perfect.

His hands moved down her body languidly, exploring, excited by the feel of what he'd never expected, never imagined. She was all full, soft curves, lush. Fine-boned, her arms were slim, her wrists and elbows tiny. Her waist was slight, her soft belly only a marginal curve, very feminine, utterly seductive. His palm lingered there. He heard her shuddered breathing as he stroked her, feeling her muscles quiver.

He palmed her bottom, finding it exquisitely soft and equally firm. He pulled her against his aroused body, rubbing and stroking. Carlie clung to him, and he loved it. He couldn't get enough of her or her response.

"I want to see you, honey."

"No." Her face dipped down and she pressed her lips into his throat. "Please…"

He kissed her again, his tongue thrusting, his breath coming in harsh pants.

"Take me to your bedroom, Carlie." He held her face until she opened her eyes and looked at him. "I'm going to make love to you."

It was inevitable. "Yes."

He threw back his head and closed his eyes for an instant. Then he pulled her from the counter and turned her toward the hallway. "Your bedroom."

She slowed as she neared her bedroom door. "I haven't showered."

"It doesn't matter." Nothing mattered except making her his, completely.

"But we…the basketball…"

Tyler shoved her gently inside, closing the door behind him. The room was in shadows, dim and close and intimate. It smelled of Carlie, her elusive, feminine scent. He reached for her in the dark. "Believe me, it doesn't matter."

He held her close, one hand caressing her full, lush breasts, finding a stiffened nipple and tugging on it lightly, hearing her groan and then palming her, crushing her soft flesh delicately in his large hand.

"Where's the light?" The question was tinged with his haste, his need.

"No." Carlie threw herself against him. "Not tonight, Tyler. Give me tonight."

He didn't understand her, but he relished her obvious urgency. He forgot the light—there was enough moonlight to illuminate the room with vague, slanted beams of opalescence. The shadows were thick and heavy, but he could see Carlie, could read her expression by the gleam in her beautiful hazel eyes, the wet sheen of her tongue as she flicked it over her lips. Her hands touched his chest tentatively, her fingers kneading the muscles, as inquisitive about his body as he was about hers. They explored each other leisurely, their excitement growing, the air thick with sexual tension. Tyler kept trying to calm himself, to call on his control, but it was nonexistent. He throbbed with need, and he was with Carlie. It was unbelievable.

Carlie kicked out of her sneakers and pulled off her socks as Tyler simultaneously whisked off her sweatshirt. They nearly toppled each other to the floor, but Tyler caught her by the waist and they landed on her bed. The covers billowed around them, soft and fragrant as Tyler's weight pressed Carlie deep into the mattress.

"You feel so good, Carlie." He rubbed against her, but she protested, tugging at his sweatshirt. Going up on his knees, Tyler jerked off the shirt.

An instant later, they were together again, each frantic to touch the other. Carlie raked her nails gently through the dark, curling hair on his chest.

Tyler reared back, unable to control himself with her innocent, curious touch. He stared down at her partial nudity—a stray beam of moonlight slashed across her breasts, showing them to be milky white and smooth, full and firm. His hands covered her, and she arched into him.

"God, Carlie. I can't believe how you hid yourself. Never again, sweetheart, do you hear me? You're mine now. I won't let you hide from me again."

He lowered his head, unable to wait a moment longer, and caught a nipple, nibbling with his lips, lightly flicking with his tongue.

"Tyler, please…"

"Yes, honey. Soon, soon." His sharp teeth closed on her, carefully tugging, and when she groaned, throwing her head back and turning her face away as she gripped the blankets in fierce pleasure, he tugged again, pulling sweetly, taunting her. Her hands settled in his hair, urging him closer toward her. He drew her in, suckling gently, then hard, until her hips were writhing against him.

He hadn't planned his seduction, didn't have premeditated intentions of devastating her with his finesse. It just didn't occur to him to end the pleasure anytime soon. He'd waited so long, a lifetime, it seemed, for

Carlie to be like this with him, and his senses were rioting, his body moving of its own volition.

He was mindless to everything but taking and giving pleasure. And at the moment, hearing Carlie's gasps and soft feminine moans gave him more pleasure than he thought he could endure.

Tyler slid to the side of her, his hand coasting languidly over her midriff and beneath the waistband of her pants to caress her soft belly. Carlie turned to face him. "Tyler, I think I'm going to die."

"No. You won't die, sweetheart." He sat up. "Let me get these other clothes off you."

She was trembling all over, her body taut and aching, and as Tyler slid the pants down her long legs, his fingers touched her, skimming over her soft flesh, teasing the insides of her thighs. He pulled the pants free of her ankles, then sat there at her side, simply looking at her. Restless, her long legs moved in subtle, impatient turns. She looked at him, seeing his gaze so intent on her body, then turned away, her eyes closing, only to look at him again.

"I can see all of you, Carlie, despite the dark." His hand slid down her thigh, stopping at her knees, slowly easing her legs farther apart. She gasped, and he smiled in the moonlight. "I love looking at you, a woman with a woman's body. You have nothing to hide, nothing to be ashamed of."

"I'm… I'm…" Carlie gasped again, not able to get the words out.

His finger sifted through her curls, finding her flesh hot and swollen, wet with need. He wanted to shout with excitement. "You're perfect. Just the way nature intended a woman to be." As he talked, he stroked her, slowly, one finger dipping just inside her, withdrawing when her hips rose sharply.

"Feel how wet you are for me, Carlie." He pressed his finger inside her again, this time deeper, and she groaned, her legs spreading wider without his instruction. Her every move inflamed him, she was so special...yet somehow, it all seemed familiar.

His body rocked with his pounding heartbeat and he bent to press his face into her belly. He could smell her, the spicy scent of her desire filling him, shaking him profoundly.

Sliding off the bed, he went to his knees between her legs. Before she could voice a protest, before he could even think about what he was doing, he'd caught her thighs and tugged her to the very edge of the mattress. Her legs hung over the side, Tyler between them. She raised herself on an elbow, peering down at him in confusion, and he quickly lifted her knees over his shoulders, then pressed his face into her heat.

Her gasp was immediate, her protest loud. He ignored her, locking his arms around her hips, holding her still. "You taste so good, Carlie. So damn good." She fell back with a low cry, lifting herself to his seeking tongue.

Her trembling increased, her body arching from the mattress. He caught her sensitized flesh carefully between his teeth, holding her captive for his hot tongue, intent on her climax now, devastating her, enjoying her, driving her closer with each and every movement he made. She called his name, softly, over and over. He slid his hands against her, abruptly pushing two fingers deep inside her.

Wild, shattering sensations swept through her body,

and Tyler could feel her contractions against his mouth and tongue, pressing closer, relishing every second of her pleasure. It seemed to go on and on, and he pushed her for more.

When Carlie finally went limp, Tyler raised himself, scooting up to lie upon her. "You're beautiful." Her hair was tangled about her head and a fine sheen of moisture glistened on her skin. He kissed her slack mouth, then stood, quickly removing his pants.

Carlie opened her eyes, but she didn't smile. She seemed dazed, her gaze intent on his body. Tyler leaned forward, naked, to brush his fingers through the curls between her thighs. She sucked in a startled breath, her hips pressing into the mattress.

His touch eased, barely skimming her, and she trembled. "Too sensitive?" He watched her nod, seeing the confusion in her bright eyes. He palmed her, his hand still and warm.

Sitting on the bed beside her, he looked over her body. Her legs were still sprawled, her knees bent so her calves hung over the bed. Her arms were limp, lying palm up beside her head. She was watching him closely.

He looked at her breasts, still heaving slightly, and leaned down to gently take a nipple between his teeth. She groaned, her body clenching once again. "Tyler, *please.*"

"Just a minute, sweetheart. I have to protect you."

It took him only a moment, but she was frantic with need, and Tyler closed his eyes in anticipation. He felt her thighs open wider, accommodating him, and with only the subtlest of movement, he was ready to enter her.

Poised on his forearms, he watched every nuance of her expression as he slowly, inexorably, sank into her, giving her his length, stretching her with his hardness.

She moved anxiously against him, and forced him past his control. Thrusting smoothly and deeply, he wound his hands in Carlie's hair, anchoring her head so he could kiss her, swallowing her gasping breaths and soft, broken moans.

When he felt her tightening again, this time around his arousal, squeezing him, giving him unbelievable pleasure, he found his own explosive orgasm. Closing his arms around her, he held her tight until the spasms had faded.

It was several minutes before Tyler found the strength to move away from her warm body. He rolled to his side, but immediately pulled her close. He felt oddly disturbed, and frankly disloyal. He'd never known anything like what he'd just experienced with Carlie—except for that one night in the pool house. He hadn't wanted those memories to interfere. They no longer mattered; he no longer cared.

But thoughts of that night, images and heated memories, had danced through his mind even as his senses filled with Carlie. *His Carlie*. He squeezed her closer, trying to chase away the images, but they didn't budge. Carlie leaned up to look at him.

"Tyler? What's wrong?"

She sounded anxious, and he rushed to reassure her. "What could possibly be wrong? Other than the fact I think you may have killed me with pleasure. I'm certain I no longer have legs. At least, if I do, they're totally useless right now." He cupped her cheek. "You're incredible, do you know that?"

She cuddled back down to his chest, her hands stroking through the dark curls there. "No. It was you. You were wonderful, Tyler."

He froze. The masked lady had said virtually the same thing on the phone. It unnerved him. Especially since the two women were so different. The woman at the party had been reserved, nearly frightened and so timid about each move he made, but Carlie had participated wholeheartedly. She was everything a man could want or hope to have in a mate.

He felt as though he'd somehow tainted the otherwise exquisite experience by envisioning another woman. No matter that the thought had come out of the blue. *How* could another woman, any woman, have intruded when he was with his Carlie? And she *was* his now. Savage possessiveness gripped him; he would never let her go.

Thinking that, he lowered his head to press a kiss to her temple. "You can't ever close me out again, Carlie. I won't let you."

Her reaction was immediate, and again, unexpected. She went perfectly still, almost stunned. He ran his hand over her shoulder. "You're mine, Carlie. I need you."

She looked at him from beneath her lashes. "Tyler, there's something you need to know."

He didn't like the sound of that. She was already trying to escape him, but he wouldn't let her. He kissed her again, then rose from the bed. "*Now*, we need that shower."

Her eyes widened. "I can't…!"

"Of course you can. Come on, I'll wash your back. And anything else that needs my attention."

He could sense her thinking, plotting. She twisted her hands in the sheets. "I'm too tired. You've exhausted me. Please, just come back to bed."

It hit him like a lightning bolt. She didn't want him to see her, really see her, without her clothing hiding her figure, making her look frumpy. He frowned thoughtfully, uncertain how to proceed. If she had a scar or some other reason to be embarrassed…but he'd touched every inch of her; certainly he would have noticed if anything was wrong. Still, her anxiety was very real, almost tangible, and he couldn't push her. Not after all she'd already given him, not after sharing herself so completely.

He touched her cheek. "I'll be right back."

He walked out of the room unconcerned with his own nudity, returning only moments later with a damp cloth. He left the lights off and seated himself beside her, content with the way she followed his progress. "Your eyes are so wide, you must think I'm intending some kind of mayhem."

Carlie shifted fretfully. "What are you intending?"

"Only to wash you. Now lie still and behave."

With a rapid peddling motion of her long legs, she scooted backward until she was pressed against the headboard. "Tyler, no! Good grief, I'm perfectly capable of tending myself."

He caught her foot, stroking the damp cloth up her calf and behind her knee. "But I want to do it. Now relax and stop fighting me."

She remained stiff, but she didn't struggle against him. "You're outrageous, Tyler."

"Don't sound so sulky. Before long, you'll learn to enjoy my outrageousness, I promise."

Tyler was thorough, using the cool cloth to stroke slowly over her body, removing all traces of their love-making. Carlie finally gave up her inhibitions, relaxing and enjoying his ministrations. Tyler chuckled when she moaned softly, then he bent to kiss a soft pink nipple.

"Sleep, Carlie. We need sleep." She frowned at him, and he stroked her one last time. "I'll be right back."

Tyler showered in a hurry, not wanting to take the chance Carlie would recover and send him home. He wanted to hold her in his arms all night.

He wanted to wake in the morning and look at her in the full light of day. And make love to her again.

She was an enigma, but he was slowly coming to understand her, completely and without doubts. She was trustworthy, the only trustworthy woman he'd ever known.

With his hair still damp, a towel wrapped loosely around his hips, he reentered the bedroom. He could see Carlie's huge golden eyes shining at him in the darkness. He hesitated, waiting only a heartbeat, and she leaned forward, throwing back the blankets, silently inviting him into her bed.

He dropped the towel over a chair and slid in beside her. She immediately curled against him, settling her hand on his chest. In the smallest voice he'd ever heard from Carlie, she whispered, "Thank you, Tyler."

"Thank you? That's an unusual sentiment from a woman who just gave herself to a man."

"I didn't. Give myself to you, that is. You gave yourself to me. And you did it perfectly. It was wonderful, you were wonderful, and I thank you."

His chuckle nearly jarred her from her position

against his shoulder. "You're very welcome...and by far the most appreciative woman I've ever made love to."

Her hand moved slowly over his chest, kneading the swell of muscle, teasing her fingers through the fine, dark hair. "We'll talk in the morning, okay?"

She sounded wary, unsure of herself. Tyler kissed the top of her head, then yawned hugely. "We'll talk, but only after I've gotten a chance to enjoy waking up with you."

Carlie was silent, her face turned into his skin, and he felt the sweet, very brief touch of her lips. He wasn't certain what to make of this new mood of hers, but then, it didn't matter. She was his, and nothing was going to change that. He wouldn't let it.

It was the sunlight streaming in that first stirred Tyler. His eyes opened slowly. Remembrance came in a rush of contentment, and he looked down to see Carlie still close to him, but now turned so that her bottom was nestled securely against his groin. His palm rested on her breast. Her skin was warm and silky and smooth.

She was peaceful in her sleep, her body lax, one hand curled beneath her cheek giving the illusion of childlike innocence. But she was no child.

Very quietly, Tyler raised himself onto one elbow, gazing down at her, a strange, stirring mix of emotions swamping him. He wanted to wake her and make love to her; he wanted to lie down and hold her forever.

He forced himself to be considerate and do neither. She was exhausted, and she needed her sleep. She didn't move so much as an eyelash when he carefully slid out of the bed.

The first order of business was a shave. His morning beard was harsh, and he didn't want to scratch her tender skin. And he didn't want to have to avoid kissing her in all the most delectable places because of beard stubble. He smiled at the thought.

Carlie wasn't the straitlaced, narrow-minded prude he'd expected. All her talk of reputations and gossip had been misleading. She was magnificent. Wild and open and honest with her feelings. She'd told him he was wonderful.

The mysterious masked woman had told him the same thing.

That wayward thought had him scowling at himself in the mirror. It was traitorous. Carlie deserved much better. He was a cad to still concern himself with another woman's identity. If he never discovered the truth, it wouldn't matter.

Deliberately, he shoved those disturbing thoughts from his mind. The mystery woman may have been a fantasy come to life, but Carlie was a living fantasy. Her effect on him was unbelievable, and he couldn't seem to get enough of her.

Naked, he stood in the bathroom and looked around. Surely Carlie had a razor somewhere. He checked in the vanity drawers, then the medicine cabinet. He didn't find a a razor, but a small contact case caught his attention.

Smiling, he envisioned Carlie wearing contacts, relegating the ugly glasses to the desk drawer forever. She had beautiful eyes, the hazel clear and unique and pure.

It was idle curiosity that prompted him to open the case. For a moment, he stared stupidly at the colored lenses. They were a very bright, familiar blue. Then his face reddened.

He'd seen that color before. The night of the party.

Reality beat a swift path into his brain.

His guileless, forthright, *honest* Carlie had played him for a fool. He remembered the recent phone call, and his face burned, the heat of humiliation spreading rapidly down his neck. He was filled with fierce blinding anger, and the most devastating disappointment he'd ever known.

He'd thought of Carlie as near-perfect; dedicated to the children and to loftier causes for the common good. He'd thought her stubborn, headstrong and thoroughly independent. But not a liar.

She was still sleeping when he entered the bedroom. He was intent on his course, not about to be swayed by the alluring picture she made. Deliberately, he sat on the side of the bed, promptly waking her.

Her long lashes fluttered and her eyes opened slowly. She looked up into his unsmiling face, and reached for him.

"Tyler." Her hand landed on his naked thigh, and she stroked him. He dropped forward on one elbow so they were nose to nose. "Good morning, sweetheart. I trust you slept well?"

Her hand came up to his cheek, and she nodded. She felt his stubbly chin, then smiled slowly. "You're so very dark."

His look was grim. Pushing away the covers, he surveyed her body. "You're certainly not." His eyes fell to the tight curls between her thighs. "Light brown. Close to the color of your beautiful head. Maybe not as golden. Certainly not black."

She gasped.

"Who are we today, Carlie? Maybe you'd like me to run home and fetch my pirate costume? I could pretend you were a virgin maiden, and 'pillage' you to my heart's content."

He saw her pale throat move as she swallowed, but otherwise she remained still, not even blinking. The hurt in her golden eyes enraged him all the more. He couldn't stop himself from taunting her. "No? You don't like that idea? Then how about I rent a sheikh costume? That role you would surely approve of. After all, you wear the veils so well. Maybe I could convince you to dance for me. I'd like that, I'm sure."

She pulled away without touching him. Her look was distant and wary. "You don't understand, Tyler."

"Now, there's where you're wrong." He reached out to wrap a lock of long hair around his finger, tugging her face closer to his own. "I understand perfectly. You wanted to experiment, and were too much the coward to come out from behind your spinster disguise. But now there's no reason to pretend. Hell, I enjoyed myself last night. What red-blooded male wouldn't have?"

"Tyler…"

"Don't look so concerned, sweetheart. I'm still willing to play. I only wish you'd told me the way of it sooner. Just think of all the time we've wasted. We could have been enjoying ourselves quite a bit." He gazed mockingly down the length of her exposed body. He ignored the way her pulse beat frantically in her slim throat, just as he ignored the horrified expression on her face, the tears starting to glisten in her eyes. He wouldn't be a fool again. Once was more than enough. It was more than he could bear.

He hurt so badly. He had never felt so betrayed in his life, not even when he'd finally realized how little he meant to his mother. He'd expected deception and manipulation from her. But he'd trusted Carlie. *Fool.*

Not for the world would he let her know that. He forced a wicked grin, hiding his hurt. Then he bent to press a hard, possessive kiss to her parted lips. He hadn't completely lost, he thought. He was still with her, and they were both in bed.

He could prove to her it didn't matter, that she meant little to him.

And then maybe he could prove it to himself.

Chapter 9

"No, damn you!" Carlie gave Tyler a shove that nearly knocked him from the bed. She scrambled away from him, quickly rising.

He lounged back, surveying her with a look of arrogant annoyance, his arms behind his head. "Calm down, Carlie."

"Get out! Get out now." She was trembling from head to foot, still completely naked, her hands squeezed together so tight her knuckles ached. Did he actually think he could make love to her while he was angry?

His eyes coasted over her slowly, with deliberate insult. But his words were a contrast, and terribly hurtful. "You're magnificent."

Carlie was speechless for just a moment. Then she narrowed her eyes. "I want you to leave now, Tyler." Her words quavered, but she couldn't help it. Everything had fallen apart. Tyler was acting like a stranger, treating her with the same callous insolence her husband had always employed whenever he'd been angry with her. She couldn't bear it.

Realizing that she was standing there, completely naked, waiting to see what else he would do or say made her throat go dry. She wasn't helpless and she was no longer young and naive. She angled her chin toward him, then forced a semblance of calm into her voice. "I won't let you do this, Tyler."

"Let me do what? You're the one who lied and made a fool of me, Carlie." His gaze pierced her, hot and hard and filled with contempt. She briefly closed her eyes against the pain of it.

"I'm sorry. I never intended it to be this way. I should never have done any of it. You're right to be angry. I knew you would be. That's why I decided to put off telling you until this morning."

"You want me to believe you would have actually confessed? I'm not stupid, Carlie. Look at you. You're shocked that I know. You wouldn't have said a word if I hadn't stumbled across your contacts and found out on my own."

She couldn't deny she was shocked, but it was because of Tyler's reaction, his disdain. She expected anger, but not disgust.

She watched Tyler rise from the bed, unmindful of his nudity as he stalked toward her. She couldn't bear his touch, not now, not with the way he felt about her. She pressed back against the wall.

Tyler glared at her retreat, then roughly ran his hands through his hair. Carlie realized, rather stupidly, that he was even gorgeous in the morning, beard stubble and all. His voice, when he spoke, was practically a sneer. "What's with the timid act, Carlie? I thought that little charade ended at the pool house."

Of course, it hadn't been an act, but she wasn't going to remind him of that. She understood his anger completely; she simply couldn't deal with it at the moment. She scooped up his pants and threw them at him. "Get dressed and go, Tyler."

She pulled a robe from her closet and quickly slipped it on. Tyler watched her, his eyes taking in every minute movement of her body. She hated his scrutiny.

His sweatshirt hit him in the chest when she threw it. He caught the garment, but made no move to put it on. He clutched the clothing in his big hands and started toward her again.

Carlie steeled herself, pushing away her guilt and nervousness, calling on her anger. No man would ever intimidate her again. She held up her hand, and Tyler halted. "I'm sorry for what happened, Tyler. Sorrier than you can know. I take full blame and I understand your anger. But it's over now. I won't bother you again. I promise."

His eyes looked dangerously bright. "Is that right?"

"Yes." She swallowed heavily. "I understand how you feel…"

Tyler threw back his head and laughed harshly. "Lady, you haven't got a clue. How could you understand my feelings when you don't have any of your own? Hell, you're not even real. You're make-believe—and there's too damn many of you for me to keep track of."

"I don't know what you're talking about." She hated

feeling defensive, and she hated lying. Deep down, she knew exactly what he was talking about.

"Who are you now, Carlie? I haven't met this woman before. The harem girl I know intimately, I met that timid little kitten at the pool house. She blew my socks off, wanting my body and very little conversation. A good woman if ever there was one. And then I met the schoolteacher. Prickly woman, with the worst taste in clothing I have ever seen. Of course, she made up for it with her show of honesty and compassion and concern. A born actress. And now you. A woman who offers abject apologies left and right. A woman who lied and manipulated without a single qualm, and now, apparently, is sorry for it. It's a good act, I admit, but somehow I can't quite believe you're all that repentant. You played your little game too damn convincingly."

Carlie's mind went blank. All her barely contained emotions settled into one dull ache that she suppressed deep inside herself. The more emotion she gave him, the more he would mock her. And she couldn't bear it. "You're right. But each of those women had something in common, Tyler. Something you obviously missed. They were each a fool and an idiot. And you can believe me this time—liar that I am—they're gone. You won't see them again. Well, perhaps you'll see the schoolteacher, but that's entirely up to you. If you wish to quit the program at school, I'll understand. I even encourage you to do so. I'll find someone else. It would be for the best if we didn't expose the children to any animosity."

She turned and began pulling clothes from her closet, all but dismissing Tyler. She wasn't going to continue to apologize. He obviously didn't want to hear it, and just as certainly, he didn't believe her regret. She'd learned long ago, if one apology wasn't sufficient, a hundred wouldn't do, either.

Tyler caught her arm, turning her to face him. "You're trying to make me out to be the villain here, Carlie." His eyes were clouded with confusion. "I'm the one who was used, the one who was made to look like a fool."

Carlie jerked her arm free. His touch was still disturbing, regardless of all that had happened. "I've thought you many things, Tyler, but never a fool. And as I recall, you didn't object overly to being used. *You* initiated the…intimacies. And as far as the other…well, you should remember I tried to keep our relationship platonic. You're the one who pushed, not me."

"You called me one night," he accused softly, ignoring her words. "Why would you do that except to taunt me?"

Carlie managed a casual shrug, but it was difficult. Her humiliation was gone, buried with her regret. But he was so large and imposing, she couldn't help being very aware of him, of his maleness in contrast to her femininity. He was naked, he was angry and there was no avoiding a confrontation.

She refused to cower, to lower her eyes from his perceptive stare. "I already admitted to being a fool. Just think of that call as another example of my foolishness." She wasn't about to tell him she'd been searching for some truth behind his attentiveness, some sign that he wasn't just playing with her. She'd already given enough of herself away.

"But why, Carlie? Why the damned charade in the

first place?" He was back to shouting, his face dark with renewed anger.

And he still hadn't put a stitch of clothing on.

Carlie stepped quickly away from him, and headed for the bathroom. She had to get away, had to find a moment's privacy to collect herself and call up her reserve. She had the choking need to break down and cry like a baby. She would never feel a loss as greatly as she felt it now. She had lost Tyler.

Who was she kidding? She'd never had Tyler in the first place. She'd reminded herself of that often enough. But somehow, because they had shared sex— she would no longer consider it lovemaking—she had allowed herself to indulge in a whimsical dream. She was such a fraud.

She turned back to Tyler, and caught him watching her intently, a look closely resembling concern shining in his eyes. She disregarded that possibility. He hated her now. She could feel it. "The charade was unintentional, if you'll remember correctly. I had left the party. *You* followed *me*. But I suppose some part of me was pathetic enough to appreciate the attention you gave me. It surprised me. It…" She swallowed. "I was flattered. But I learn from my mistakes, Tyler. Believe me." She laughed, then, a bubbling, nervous sound. She lowered her head with the force of it.

She felt Tyler move toward her and reach out a hand. "Carlie?"

The single word was sharp, edged with a vague emotion Carlie couldn't begin to fathom. She stepped away from him, still chuckling. "Oh, it's too funny. Tyler Ramsey, the stud of the community, feeling used by Carlie McDaniels! It's too absurd to be real. But don't worry, Tyler. I won't tell a single soul. After all, who would ever believe me?"

He flexed his jaw, his stance deceptively mild. "You think it's funny?"

Her smile twisted into a sneer and her eyes narrowed. "I think it's hilarious. One of those too-strange-to-be-true scenarios better shoved to the back of the closet, never to be thought of again."

Tyler caught her chin, and her grin vanished instantly. "You won't be able to forget, Carlie. At least be honest with yourself now." His thumb teased over her bottom lip, and there was genuine regret in the words he muttered. "You won't ever be able to forget." Then he straightened, all signs of disappointment magically disappearing. "I'd actually thought you were different. And in a way you are. You were able to fool me completely. No other woman has done that. You're to be congratulated."

Carlie nearly cried out at those words. Instead, she bit her lip, whirled and slammed into the bathroom, locking the door behind her. The pain nearly suffocated her, making her knees weak and stealing her resolve. She sank, defeated, to the edge of the tub, her fist in her mouth to stifle her low sobs.

She stayed there, hearing Tyler dress quietly, hearing the sounds of him preparing to leave. And then the closing of the door, so soft, so final, so very, very real.

And she broke, crying with all the energy of someone who knows she's lost something invaluable. Something she's never had but always desperately wanted.

"Tyler! My goodness, you're a sight!"

"Why the hell didn't you tell me, Brenda!" He stuck

his face close to hers. "I'm your brother-in-law! I'm family! I can't believe you would stab me in the back like this!"

Brenda covered her chest with one hand, her eyes wide. "Whatever are you shouting about? What's happened?"

Jason entered the room, took one look at his brother and put himself in front of his wife. "Calm down, Tyler."

"Calm down! Do you know…?"

"Yes." Jason's voice was very quiet in comparison to Tyler's. "I know. But I can't let you yell at my wife. Now settle down."

Tyler was thunderstruck. "You knew, too?"

"Don't look so shocked. No one told me, but I figured it out quickly enough. I have to admit, I was surprised you didn't."

Brenda gasped then, shoving her husband aside. She faced Tyler with the most alarmed expression he'd ever seen on her face. "This is about Carlie? You've found out?"

"Yes, dammit! Your little game is over. Did you two sit down to tea and laugh over watching me make a fool of myself? Did she give you all the juicy details?"

Jason opened his mouth, but Brenda didn't give him time to interject. "Oh, Tyler, it wasn't like that!" Then she bit her lip. "You're angry. You…you didn't hurt her, did you?"

Tyler threw up his hands in a gesture of despair. "I don't believe you asked me that! Since when have I been such a bastard that I'd hurt a woman? I may have felt like strangling you both, but I would never—"

"I don't mean physically. I know you would never

lay a hand on a woman." Then she reached up to touch his cheek. "But she's so fragile, Tyler. She's been hurt so much. Please, tell me you didn't do or say anything to hurt her feelings."

She was looking so anxious, Tyler frowned at her. Reluctantly, he admitted, "I was damned angry."

Brenda searched his face, then turned to Jason, her eyes huge. "I'm going to go check on her."

Jason nodded, then bent to kiss her cheek. "Be careful driving. Don't hurry. I doubt she's going anywhere." He handed Brenda the car keys from a hook by the phone, catching her just before she started out. "Everything will work out."

Brenda glanced quickly at Tyler, who only looked back in exasperation. She sighed. "Don't be so sure of that, Jason. I'm not."

Tyler watched her rush out, then turned to his brother. "Aren't you the least bit irate on my behalf? Do you even know the whole story? I was *lied* to."

Jason sat, crossing his arms on the kitchen table. "No, you weren't. Unfortunately, Carlie's been honest with you from the start. She's been herself, and that's as honest as it gets. Now, I sincerely hope you're going to sit down here and tell me you didn't just manage to ruin the best thing that's ever happened to you."

Tyler sat, but it wasn't a concession as much as he suddenly needed the stability of a chair. He could hardly credit his brother's defection. "A woman who lies to me and plays juvenile games is the best thing that's ever happened to me? What the hell would be the worst?"

Jason gave him a long look, then sighed. "The worst, the way I see it, is if you just did so much damage,

Carlie crawls back into her shell and never gives you a second chance. And that's a very real possibility." Jason looked his brother over, taking in Tyler's still-disheveled hair and unshaven face. "Why don't you tell me what happened?"

Tyler realized how foolish his part sounded in the charade, but he needed to talk. He could barely absorb the reality of what he'd discovered. "I just realized that Carlie and my mystery woman are one and the same." He laughed in self-derision. "Do you know, I was actually feeling guilty because I thought I cared so much for Carlie, and yet I was still curious to know who the other woman was. What a joke."

"What did you do?"

Tyler winced at the suspicion in his brother's words. "I kicked up a fuss, of course. I mean, Carlie knew it was her I had—" Tyler halted. He hadn't told anyone he'd made love to his harem girl—and he was pretty certain Carlie hadn't said anything either. Regardless of what had happened now, that night was special, and he wouldn't ruin it. He stared at his brother, then looked away. "Hell, Bren probably told Carlie I'd been asking about her. It's all so humiliating."

"Yeah. Imagine how Carlie feels."

Tyler's jaw dropped open, but he shut it with a snap. "What about me?"

Jason snorted in disgust. It was a good simulation of Carlie's snort, but without her flair.

"You're a big boy. You've been around. So you were a bit embarrassed? You two could have talked about it, about why Carlie felt so unsure of herself as a woman that she'd have to hide behind a disguise in the first place. Who knows, you may have even been able to laugh about it."

"Fat chance!"

There was silence, and Jason got up to pour Tyler a cup of coffee. After setting the cup on the table, he clasped Tyler's shoulder, giving him a brotherly squeeze.

Tyler shook his head. Jason always did that. He could give Tyler hell about something, but he always let him know he cared, either by a pat on the back, a squeeze to the shoulder or an occasional bear hug. They were closer than most brothers, and Tyler never doubted his loyalty.

He waited another second or two until Jason had reseated himself, then he took the bait. "So why is Carlie so insecure?"

Jason idly traced the edge of his coffee cup with his fingertip. "Don't you think that's a question you ought to ask Carlie?"

Swamped with emotions he couldn't sort out, Tyler chose to go on the defensive. "I shouldn't have to ask. If she has a good reason for doing what she did, she ought to come to me and tell me."

"And if she doesn't do that?"

Tyler stubbornly shook his head. "I don't know."

"I think you better make up your mind fast."

That was impossible to do. God, things could get so tangled. He'd only just decided he loved Carlie… Tyler felt his chest squeeze tight. *Love?* That word had the ability to scare him spitless, but that was probably what it was. Because now that things had soured, he was hurting worse than he'd ever hurt in his life. Surely only love could do that to a man. And what if Carlie did have good reason for doing what she'd done? He hadn't even asked her. He'd let his injured pride guide him, when in his heart, he knew Carlie was incapable of simply using anyone. If she felt she had to resort to deception, she must have had a very good reason.

And he'd probably just ruined whatever trust she'd previously had in him.

Tyler dropped his head onto the table, and it landed with a solid thud.

Jason went on, apparently unmoved by his brother's dejection. "This is going to be really hard for Carlie to take. It's not enough that you know, but now both Bren and I do, as well. I would imagine she's feeling utterly alone right now. She doesn't have anyone, you know. No family, no—"

Tyler raised his head, and pounded it back down on the table. Twice.

"Tyler, quit trying to shake your brains loose and tell me what you're going to do."

He sat back up, his eyes bloodshot and burning, his head aching abominably, feeling totally defeated. "I think I might have blown it, Jason. Some of the things I said…"

"So you're going to try to work it out?"

Tyler covered his face with his hands. "I don't know. Hell, she'll probably never speak to me again."

"Give her a few days. She'll calm down."

"Yeah, maybe." But he didn't believe it. He thought of the look on Carlie's face as he'd hurled accusations… the way she'd backed away from him. Her nearly hysterical laugh.

Tyler closed his eyes, and pinched the bridge of his nose. He was afraid he'd thrown away something precious. All because of his injured pride. "She's incredible, you know. Absolutely incredible."

Jason raised an eyebrow. "Are we talking about in bed?"

Tyler looked up, a frown solidly in place. "No! I mean..." He narrowed his eyes at his brother, then shook his head. "I was talking about other things."

Jason watched him, a slight smile on his face. Tyler didn't even notice. "She's terrific with the kids. So patient and gentle, but boy, do they ever listen to her. They go out of their way to please her. And the parents! They hang on to her every word, as if she speaks the gospel. And she's so intelligent. Loads of common sense—except when it comes to her own worth. She hides behind those damned ugly clothes. I hate that."

Tipping his head back, Tyler stared at the ceiling, feeling hopeless and lost. "We had fun, Jason. Real, genuine fun. I would have sooner spent time with Carlie than anyone I know."

"You love her."

Still staring at the ceiling, Tyler said, "Yeah. I think I do. But love is a damn strange thing. I can't decide if I like it or not."

"I know I hated it when I fell for Brenda. I went through major denial. But then I'd see some clown talking to her, and I'd want to kill him. And I couldn't keep my hands off her. She'd yawn and I'd want her. She'd smile and I'd get hard as a rock."

Tyler scoffed, even though he was suffering the same thing. "I remember. You were warped."

Jason merely grinned. "I still am. It's terrific."

Tyler made a quick decision, and immediately felt better. "I have to go see her."

Jason gave him a cautious look. "Do you think that's wise? Carlie needs time to—"

"I don't mean right this minute. We both need time to think and I'm not sure I can think straight at all when I'm around her." Then he grinned. "Hell, I can hardly think when I'm not around her. At least, not about anything other than her."

Jason clasped Tyler's shoulder, walking with him to the door. "It's love, all right." Then he grew serious. "But you have to be sure, Tyler. You have to be certain of what you want. Get your own thoughts straight before you make matters worse. The way you look now, you'd only go there and end up fighting with her again."

Tyler smiled ruefully. "Don't worry. It's not fighting I have in mind."

Jason slapped him on the back. "Remember that."

What a waste of time crying was.

It never solved anything and it was embarrassing. Brenda was sympathetic, but Carlie didn't want sympathy. She wanted solitude, she wanted time to think, and luckily, Brenda was a good enough friend to realize it.

It had been almost two days since she'd last seen Tyler, since the morning he'd walked out her door with the obvious intent of never coming back. Luckily, there hadn't been any basketball practices scheduled, so she didn't have to worry about seeing him at school.

At least, not yet. She had no idea how Tyler intended to handle that. *She* certainly wouldn't quit. That would smack of cowardice, and she had too much pride to be the first to give up. But the thought of seeing him, of trying to be sociable under the circumstances, was nearly too much. She had to get her act together, and she had to do it now.

A warm shower helped to revive her somewhat, and she tried to concentrate her thoughts on the children, on figuring out some way to help the more financially unfortunate families. She also needed some exercise to rid her of her tension.

She had a plan. It was foolproof, which was necessary, since she'd proven herself several times a fool. Part of the secret of recovering from shame and heartache was to make everyone else believe it didn't matter one whit, and pretty soon, after convincing them, you automatically convinced yourself.

Carlie dressed in several layers of sweats, tied her sneakers neatly, and went out the door. The November air was very brisk, and the sky was overcast and gray. The wind was playful, blowing hard one minute, sending stray wisps of hair slashing across her eyes, and then dying, leaving the air strangely still and silent.

Carlie breathed deeply of the scents of approaching winter. It would snow soon, and before long the holidays would be here. That fact meant nothing to Carlie. She hadn't celebrated a holiday since she'd finally escaped her husband over two years ago. Holidays brought memories, and memories only served to destroy her carefully erected peace of mind.

She ran hard for the first few blocks, and then, winded, her lungs aching, she switched to a slow-paced jog. She usually ran for about three miles. It was what she had always done for peace and contentment. Hopefully, it would work again.

But the hurdles seemed insurmountable today. Every step she took brought back thoughts of Tyler.

And each thought ended with the angry flash of his dark eyes. What he must be thinking of her now...

It was as if she'd conjured him with her worries. She rounded the corner, laboring for breath, her cheeks stinging from the cold, and there he was. He was watching her, sitting on her front step, his hands shoved deep into the pockets of his leather jacket.

Her heart lurched, her throat went dry and her skin felt tight—much too tight. But she smiled, a serene, undisturbed smile. "Hello, Tyler."

He blinked. Obviously, that wasn't what he'd expected to hear. Especially not in such a cordial tone. Carlie was very pleased with herself.

He stood slowly, his eyes drifting over her jogging suit in obvious distaste. "You were out jogging."

"Very astute of you. What gave me away? The suit itself or the fact that I just returned, still huffing?" She was trembling inside and her stomach was tied in knots, but she hid it well, knowing she'd rather die than have him know how badly he'd hurt her.

Tyler tilted his head, studying her warily. "I thought we should talk."

Carlie bent over, placing her hands on her thighs. It looked as though she was trying to catch her breath, but in truth she needed a moment to regain her emotional balance. She hadn't expected to see him again this soon. She wasn't ready. The fact that Tyler was here, so near and looking so handsome made the chore of feigning nonchalance that much more difficult. She drew one last deep breath and straightened.

"I'm sorry, I really can't right now. It's a bad time for me. Papers to grade, lessons to plan. And I have a few phone calls to make." She smiled politely.

"Carlie..."

"Yes?"

He rubbed the bridge of his nose. "Things didn't go exactly as I planned the other day. It took me by surprise—"

"That's putting a pretty face on it, Tyler. It shocked the hell out of you. And enraged you. And I understand completely. I probably would have felt the same. But I've already apologized. There's nothing more I can do. I can't change what's already been done. Believe me, I wish I could."

"What would you change, honey?"

Oh, that tone, so sweet and gentle. Carlie forced herself to stand just a little straighter. "All of it, of course. From the day Brenda invited me to that stupid party, to yesterday. I'd erase it all." She smiled at him serenely, hoping to put him at ease with her declaration. But it cost her. Her stomach felt so tight now, she feared she might throw up.

Tyler had probably come over with some vague notion that she might pursue him. She'd die first.

He touched her cheek briefly. "Then I'll be eternally grateful you don't possess magic powers. Because I wouldn't trade the time I've spent with you for anything." He waited a moment, then added softly, "I don't really believe you would, either, Carlie."

Chapter 10

Oh, god, oh, god. He couldn't know that. Carlie summoned a smile, but her serenity had about run out. "You're wrong."

"I've been wrong about a lot of things."

Her eyes widened behind the lenses of her glasses, and she pressed a hand dramatically to her heart. "No! Not you, Tyler! Say it isn't so, or all my grand delusions will blow away in the wind."

"Dammit, Carlie…"

She chuckled. The sound was just a bit rusty, but convincing, all the same. "Go home, Tyler. It's cold out here, too cold to stand around trading recriminations." She went up the steps, fishing her key out of her pocket.

Carlie went inside and then turned to tell Tyler goodbye. He didn't give her the chance. Pushing his way through, he was over the threshold before Carlie could voice a complaint.

He didn't smile. He closed the door and leaned against it, watching her.

Warily, she faced him. "What are you doing?"

Tyler hesitated, then shrugged. "I can help you grade your papers. I still owe you, don't I?"

"I don't remember. But I'd rather you didn't. I don't have time to be distracted."

He came away from the door. "Do I distract you, Carlie?"

She blinked at him, then laughed. "Turn your hormones off, Tyler. I was referring to your inane chatter."

"You can't be that indifferent to me, Carlie. I was there that night, too, you know. I recall perfectly everything that happened between us."

Carlie moved away from the heat of his gaze. It was almost tangible, covering her in waves, penetrating her flesh. She sauntered as casually as possible to the kitchen, Tyler following.

She pulled out a chair and lowered herself into it, while all the time her mind was working furiously. This time, it wasn't as easy to affect a carefree air. Her feelings were even more deeply involved now than when she'd first got divorced. She wasn't a kid who had been disillusioned. And her feelings for Tyler surpassed infatuation.

When Tyler automatically sat opposite her, she regarded him seriously. "Maybe we should talk."

He seemed relieved. "Yes. I want to explain—"

"Let me go first, Tyler." Her heart was racing, her breath was shallow, but she knew she had to have her say and get it over with as cleanly as possible. Even though it cost her, she leaned forward and placed her hand over his. He couldn't know how hurt she was. Pride was all she had left.

Tyler turned his palm upward, clasping her fingers. "Tyler," she started uncertainly, "what happened between us was nice. I'll grant you that." His eyes narrowed, and she released his hand. "Don't interrupt, please. I want you to understand. It was nice, and I believe I already thanked you. But it won't happen again. Ever."

"I don't believe you."

"Then once again, I'm sorry. But it's true. If you're determined for us to remain friends, that's fine with me. I like you. You're a good person and you're a lot of fun. But I won't sleep with you again. Sex isn't on my agenda. It was an aberration that we got together at all. Call it temporary insanity, and the key word there is 'temporary.'"

"People can't just turn off their emotions, Carlie. You were with me every step of the way that night, and it was a damned sight more than 'nice.' Hell, it was more than sex, more than anything I've ever known before. It won't go away."

"There's where you're wrong, Tyler. I can make it go away. I can turn off my feelings with a snap of my fingers. I can do anything I put my mind to. And right now, I'm sending you home." She stood, but Tyler didn't budge. Carlie couldn't believe he'd thought she would abide a casual affair. Without mutual caring between them, it was impossible. But obviously, Tyler didn't realize that. It was just as obvious he didn't know her at all.

He eyed her speculatively. "Is that what you're trying to do now? Turn off your feelings, close off your heart? That's no way to live, honey."

Carlie definitely didn't want Tyler Ramsey rummaging around in her head, trying to decipher what made her click. She gave him a sardonic smile, reminiscent of the Carlie he met so long ago. "Wait, I think I can unearth some violin music around here somewhere to go with all this melodrama." She shook her head. "It's the only way to live, Tyler. At least, for me."

Tyler looked down at his clasped hands resting on the tabletop. "I don't think you can do it, Carlie. I think we shared something very special. It may not have been what either of us is used to, but it was still wonderful, almost explosive. And erotic." He slowly raised his gaze, locking it with hers. "Someday, I'd like to see you in that harem costume again. I swear, I get aroused just thinking about it."

Carlie's head snapped back as if he'd slapped her. She tried to compose herself, but vivid, humiliating images were suddenly whirling through her mind. Her voice was a croak as she tried to regain control. "I want you to leave now, Tyler. I mean it."

He came slowly to his feet, his eyes on her pale face. "Before I screwed things up, I think you would have laughed if I suggested that. I'll get you to laugh again, Carlie. I'm not going to let you run away from me like this."

Carlie snorted, recovering slightly with his calm, arrogant statement. "I don't run from anyone. Not anymore. But I'll be up-front with you. If you persist in making sexual innuendos, I won't associate with you. I mean it."

Tyler tried that word out on his tongue. "Associate? Hmm. Sounds suspiciously like a business relationship."

"Or a casual friendship. The choice is yours." It took all Carlie's resolve to maintain eye contact. His eyes appeared almost black with emotion. He looked very tired.

Tyler gave her a gentle, sincere smile. "If the choice was mine, we'd be back in bed right now, everything else forgotten."

Carlie went rigid. "You were wrong, Tyler. I detest your outrageousness. Now please leave."

He scrutinized her. "Talk to me about your divorce."

He was changing subjects as she'd wanted, but she didn't like this new direction at all. She stared at him, annoyed. "Why?"

"I want to understand. And despite all your dictums, I care about you. I'm beginning to realize I always will."

Her heart took a giant leap, but she repressed the feeling his statement incited. She looked at him with indifference, hoping she was masking her reaction. She couldn't be that big a fool. Not again.

"Will you tell me about him, Carlie?" Then Tyler shook his head, his look almost apologetic. "Let me put that another way. I'm not leaving until you do."

Hiding her exasperation was no mean feat. But she did, because to try to deny him would only cause him to dig deeper, she knew. Tyler could be very stubborn on occasion. She shrugged and went to the refrigerator to pull out a soda, without offering him one. It was a deliberate act of rudeness, but to her chagrin, Tyler merely fetched his own, then sat, watching her expectantly.

Carlie crossed her legs and propped one elbow on the table. "I met him in college. He was one of the 'popular ones,' if you know what I mean. I was a nobody. I worked my way through college, and there was very little time for a social life. It took most of my time just keeping my grades up and working enough hours to make ends meet. I was flattered that he paid attention to me. We spent my last year there dating off and on.

"In spite of the time I'd been seeing him, I guess I didn't really know him. Things between us were pretty casual, and he dated other women, too, not just me. But when I graduated, he asked me to marry him, and I agreed. You see, my grandfather had already told me not to come home. And my brother…he never kept in touch. I was pretty much…alone." She smiled, feeling somewhat foolish for pointing out so many details in her defense. It didn't matter what Tyler thought. At least it shouldn't. "I wanted a family. I wanted someone to want me. I thought he did. Pretty dumb reason to get married, isn't it?"

"It's a hell of a lot more reasonable than some I've heard. So go on. When did things start to go wrong?"

"About ten minutes after I said, 'I do.' We'd gotten married at a justice of the peace. It was a package deal, one of those that included a night at a honeymoon cabin. We went there directly."

Tyler was starting to get an idea where the story was going, Carlie surmised, when he began to scowl at her. "You were a virgin?"

She gazed down at her soda can, running her finger around the rim. It was tough to get the words out, remembering how naive she'd been. "Yes. So I didn't understand that it wasn't supposed to hurt so much. His lovemaking was…crude. And rough." Her eyes found his. "It wasn't at all like what you showed me. I hated it. But he said it was normal. I was totally ignorant of men and I wanted to be reasonable, so I accepted his explanations. Only it didn't get any better."

Tyler lunged from his chair, nearly overturning it. He paced across the room, keeping his back to Carlie.

She spoke mildly, as if it didn't matter one way or the other. "If you'd rather not hear this now, I'll understand." The truth was, she couldn't believe she was actually telling him. She hadn't shared intimate details of her past with anyone, not even Brenda. But in a way, it felt good to talk about it, to say things out loud. She drew a deep breath, then looked at Tyler again.

He was watching her closely. After a few seconds, he resumed his seat. "Go on."

His expression was rigid and his eyes blazed despite his obvious effort at control. Carlie couldn't help herself. She felt a genuine smile pull at her lips. "So outraged on my behalf?"

"I'd dearly love to get my hands on him."

He said it so levelly, with so much gravity, Carlie believed him. She was shocked. Without thinking, she patted his arm. "Relax. It wasn't all that bad."

Tyler growled at her. "Don't lie to me, Carlie, ever."

"You mean 'ever again,' don't you?"

"I don't consider your little masquerade at the pool house lying."

Her eyes widened, he seemed so sincere. "You don't?"

"No. You would have told me the whole of it soon enough, if I hadn't jumped the gun and been such a jerk. Now quit dodging the topic and finish your story."

"All right. The first time I really complained, he said it was my fault. He blamed me completely, excusing himself by saying I didn't respond the way I should. He said I should act more like a woman, and dress up a little more. I tried. I always tried to do what he told me to do. It…just didn't work. I couldn't be…ready as quickly as he wanted, and he would get angry, and… it was a fiasco."

"It wasn't your fault."

He was so vehement, so sure, Carlie felt comforted, despite herself. She nodded. "I know that. Now. But I believed him when he said I was frigid. And I couldn't see making him abstain just because something was wrong with me. I…tolerated him, which only made matters worse. After a while, we grew so distant, I decided it wasn't worth having a home or family or husband if I had to put up with the sex."

She didn't say another word until Tyler prompted her. "So you asked for a divorce?" He sounded impatient, and she swallowed the hurt that always swamped her whenever she thought of those times.

She shook her head. "I felt so guilty. But then I came home early one day, and I caught him in bed with another woman. *She* didn't appear to be having any difficulty enjoying him. He wasn't overly concerned that I found them, either. In fact, he seemed almost proud. I think he needed to prove to me that it wasn't him. That it was me, and only me, that caused the problem."

"And you believed him."

It was a statement, and Tyler sounded somehow disappointed with her deduction. She sighed. "What was I supposed to think? I certainly didn't have anything to compare with. But I was more than ready for the divorce. The only problem was, he didn't want it. He was very possessive of me, and he fought the divorce for a long time. He hounded me for so long, I had to move to get away from him. Looking back, I think it would have been impossible for him to accept any part of the blame. It would have been a mark against his masculinity. I can almost understand him, now. But then... I just wanted out."

"And when you finally got out, you decided you never wanted in again, is that it?"

Carlie tried to draw forth some of the energy she'd been feeling earlier. She needed it now to get her through the next few minutes. It was emotionally debilitating discussing her past, but even more so discussing it with Tyler. She didn't want him to look at her with pity, to feel sorry for the naive, foolish, young woman she'd been.

She angled her head proudly, refusing to turn away from his probing gaze. Surprisingly, she didn't see pity in his eyes. Just determination. "I'm strong, Tyler. I don't need a man. I'm perfectly capable of taking care of myself. I dress to please myself, and I work at a job I enjoy. What I can't get on my own, I don't really need."

"I understand what you're saying, Carlie. But everyone needs other people. You can't just close yourself off."

She stood again. "I can. I did. I finally got that divorce, finally got my freedom, and I don't intend to ever put myself in that position again. It was difficult and stupid, relying on someone else for my happiness. But I'm intelligent enough to remember the lesson, even if I occasionally have a memory lapse."

Tyler stood also, looking very intent. He took a

small step toward her. "What we have is more than a memory lapse, sweetheart. And I'm going to prove it to you."

Carlie stiffened. "You're going to go home." Her words were firm and unrelenting.

"Yes. But I'll be back." She relaxed slightly at his easy compliance. Then he continued. "You have to accept that I'm not like him, Carlie."

A rush of soft laughter escaped her. "Don't you think I know that? You're nothing like him. But I'm still myself. And I can't change."

A smile twitched on his lips. "You change so often, I can't keep up with you. I'm only beginning to discover who Carlie McDaniels is."

"Don't be ridiculous. I've told you who I am."

He shook his head. "You don't know yourself, honey, so how could you tell me?" Then he cupped her cheeks in his palms, holding her gently captive. Against her lips, he breathed, "We'll find her together, Carlie. I promise."

His kiss was light and filled with tenderness, a mere brushing of his lips. Then he turned to go. Carlie didn't say a word. What was there to say? He'd find out soon enough she was exactly who she seemed to be. And then he'd leave her alone. She was strong enough to wait him out.

At least, she hoped she was.

Tyler would be showing up any minute. She'd spent her morning girding herself for the impact of seeing him again. He hadn't canceled on the school project, so she would have to continue working with him. But she was ready.

He sauntered onto the gym floor with his usual air of confidence, and several of the children ran to greet him. Lucy had taken a particular liking to him, and when she threw her arms around him, he tugged on one of her braids.

Tyler took a few minutes to address the other kids, talking with each one, asking about school, joking and teasing and being teased in return.

Carlie felt herself softening. Whoever would have thought Tyler would show so much understanding with children? And it was innate, she was sure, not something that could be summoned forth at will. Children knew if an adult really liked them. And Tyler truly cared about the children.

It hit Carlie then. Tyler, too, had an alter ego, just as she did. In fact, more than one.

There was Tyler the businessman, the astute lawyer who handled cases with flair and savvy. And there was also Tyler, the ladies' man, with a reputation well known by the female population. In fact, Carlie now realized that reputation had been encouraged more by the ladies than by Tyler himself. The things he valued in a woman, as far as she could tell, were intelligence and laughter, not her measurements and unfailing willingness.

And he was also a very perceptive man, considerate and indulgent, with a gentleness toward all things weaker or smaller. That was why he dealt so well with children.

Tyler looked up and caught her scrutinizing him. He strolled over, dribbling the ball. With a slight smile, he stopped directly in front of her. "I know what I'm thinking. Are your thoughts the same?"

Carlie shrugged, stealing the ball away from him. "I was thinking you should get married and have children of your own. You're very good with them." She glanced at him, saw his shock and smiled with satisfaction. "That's all."

"That's all! Hey, wait a minute."

He was too late. She blew the whistle and the children lined up. For the next two hours, Carlie made certain she kept her distance from Tyler, always making sure she had at least one of the kids close to her. It was an ingenious plan—and it was obviously frustrating Tyler. He scowled at her throughout the last fifteen minutes of the practice.

Tyler walked two of the children out to their parents' cars, talking with the moms and dads a few minutes before coming back to the gym. She wasn't going to bother asking him what the discussions were about this time. He'd never confided in her last time. When he noticed she was still in the gym, he headed toward her, falling into step beside her as she started for the locker room.

"I want to talk to you, Carlie."

"Can't right now. I'm running late as it is." That was an easy truth to give, though Tyler didn't accept it.

"Late for what, dammit?"

She didn't look at him. "Don't curse at me, Tyler."

"Then stop avoiding me!"

"In other words, if I don't, you're going to continue to blast me with your foul language?"

He grabbed her arm, halting her. "Talk to me. Please."

It unnerved her, seeing him so abjectly sincere. "I'm

sorry. Really. But I'm starting some night courses and I'm running late. I should have left ten minutes ago."

He searched her face. "What time will you get home?"

"Late."

"Too late to see me?"

"There's no reason for me to see you. I told you that."

"And I didn't accept it. I guess we're at an impasse."

"*We* aren't anywhere. I'm late and you should be getting home. Goodbye."

"No. I'm not leaving until you tell me what you meant by that crack about children."

"It wasn't a crack." She glanced at her watch, a deliberate show of impatience. "You'd make an excellent father. You should find yourself a woman like Bren, and settle down. It would relieve the boredom you're forever complaining about."

"I haven't complained about being bored since I met you. And I don't want a woman like Bren. I want a woman like you."

It took great willpower not to react to that statement. Her stomach had lurched and her pulse had skipped a beat. But he was only being Tyler, flirting and teasing. She couldn't take him seriously. "You want a woman who doesn't want you back? I don't know, Tyler. That might be kind of hard. Didn't you tell me that all the women want you?"

"No. I don't recall saying that. But I know you do, Carlie. Shall I prove it?"

Carlie flushed, silently cursing him for challenging her, especially when she knew she couldn't win. "I can't deny I enjoyed sex with you, Tyler. That isn't what I meant, and you know it. Why don't you take up a hobby? Collect stamps or something so you can entertain yourself without annoying me."

"I wasn't trying to annoy you! I'm trying to talk to you. I want you to forgive me, I want—"

"You're forgiven."

"That was a little precipitous, wasn't it?" He eyed her suspiciously. "What are you forgiving me for?"

"I have no idea. You're the one who wanted forgiveness." She raised her eyebrows politely. "You tell me."

He took a deep breath. "I'm sorry for yelling at you, for jumping to conclusions and saying hateful, uncalled-for things."

"They were called for. And you were justified." She looked down at her clasped hands and made the necessary effort to relax. "Will you forgive me, also? For deceiving you and using you and causing you embarrassment?"

"Carlie." He pulled her against his chest, despite her stiff, unyielding posture. "There's nothing to forgive, honey. I understand why you didn't tell me."

Carlie slowly stepped away, then started toward the gym door. "It's in the past, Tyler," she called over her shoulder. "Forget about it. We're both obviously very sorry and determined not to make the same mistakes again. That's good enough for me. Now, I have to go. I'll see you Wednesday."

"Carlie…"

She didn't stop, didn't turn to him, didn't slow her pace at all. But she could feel his eyes boring into her and just before the heavy back door swung shut behind her, she heard a bang that sounded suspiciously like a fist hitting a locker.

* * *

"You're going to have to help out here, Bren!" Tyler said as he paced the kitchen, his hands shoved deep into his pockets. Carlie was being entirely unreasonable. She wouldn't see him beyond practices and wouldn't take the time to talk to him when it wasn't absolutely necessary. He'd about run out of ideas. And he was getting desperate.

Brenda and Jason stared at him as he paced. Brenda shook her head. "Carlie would never forgive me if I got in the middle of this."

"Just try talking to her for me. She'll listen to you."

"Not a chance. Carlie won't listen to anything I have to say. Not with things so fouled up."

Tyler glowered at her. "Things are not fouled up! Carlie and I being together is not a mistake."

"Hah! Carlie's more determined than ever to stay away from men. She won't even go out with that old school-board guy, and he's certainly no threat."

Tyler halted, then looked at Brenda. "What are you talking about?"

"There's some old stuffed shirt on the school board—"

"He's only thirty-six, Bren," Jason interrupted.

"Well, he seems old, he's so uppity." She gave her attention back to Tyler. "Anyway, she's gone out with him a couple of times. Mostly to talk over school stuff, or so he says. Personally, I think he's trying to ingratiate himself. Now he wants her to help him head up a new fund-raiser at the school. Carlie said she needs to get together with him this weekend to discuss the particulars."

"Where?"

Jason stood. "Now, Tyler…"

He ignored his brother. The thought of Carlie with another man made him see red. He repeated, "Where?"

Jason cleared his throat to hide his smile. "At her house, I believe."

"The time?"

Jason glanced at Brenda, who was doing her best to look innocent. "I think she said around noon, but I can't be sure," she said.

Tyler turned on his heel and headed out, not bothering to say goodbye. He didn't see the smug grin on his sister-in-law's face.

Jason pursed his lips. "I thought you weren't going to interfere."

"Of course I wouldn't!" Brenda gasped. "I gave Carlie my word."

"Then what was this little scene you just enacted?"

"A slip of the tongue?"

"Clever. Just what I love in a wife!"

On his drive home, Tyler formulated his plan. It was Friday evening—he'd gone to his brother's house, frustrated after another unsatisfying attempt to gain Carlie's attention during the practice. She was getting very good at ignoring him. And after practice, she had to hurry off for her classes. He had no doubt they'd been planned just to thwart him. It annoyed the hell out of him.

But he could be just as devious as Carlie. Since he had no intention of giving up on Carlie, he had to overcome her obstacles.

And he had a secret weapon—his own project he'd been working on for some time. He'd planned to surprise Carlie with it. Now it would prove invaluable. But first he needed to get her alone for a bit. He hadn't missed her response the day he'd held her only briefly. But he had been stymied by the fact that she seemed to find it so easy to walk away. She hadn't even looked back as he'd willed her to do. Stubborn wench.

At least she was never boring. He remembered the way she had held him so tight when he'd entered her, how she told him she cared. Not a little, but a lot. He had to believe that. She still cared, and she would get over her anger. He'd help her. Hell, he'd insist upon it.

Tyler planned his arrival perfectly, even to the point of driving around the block twice, waiting for the strange car to show up in front of Carlie's house. He parked and got out, whistling, a sheath of papers in his hand.

He knocked on the door, then waited, doing his best to hide his smile. Carlie answered, dressed in her usual distasteful clothes. This time, it was a long skirt, hanging below her knees. Her slim calves and ankles were hidden by boots, the skirt topped by a large sweater which had no waist or any other defining lines. It was ugly as sin.

"You look beautiful today, Carlie." He spoke loudly enough for her company to hear. She glared at him, but he knew he had her. She was forced to be polite when a member of the school board was in earshot.

"Hello, Tyler. What brings you here today?"

He quickly shouldered his way inside before she could tell him she was busy. "I have some things to discuss with you about your project."

"The team?"

"That's right. I had some ideas to go over with you."

A man entered, dressed in a business suit and looking every bit as stuffy as Brenda had claimed he was. He didn't so much as glance at Tyler. "Is something wrong, Carlie?"

She looked harassed. "Ah, no." Then she grudgingly made the introductions. "Tyler, this is Brad Shaw. Brad, meet Tyler Ramsey, the man I told you about. He's proving to be a big help with the after-school basketball program."

The men shook hands. Tyler smiled with devious innocence. "I'm sorry, Carlie. I didn't realize you had a date tonight."

She didn't disappoint him with her reaction. He grinned as she turned beet-red. Tyler had the feeling it was mostly due to anger. "Brad is a member of the school board. We were going to discuss a new fundraiser."

"Is that right? Maybe I could help. I'm always willing to help support the schools."

It was obvious he'd gotten Brad's interest. He may have wanted to be alone with Carlie, but apparently he also wanted financial aid. He opted for the money. "Won't you join us, Mr. Ramsey?"

He grinned. "Tyler, please. I'd be delighted." Then he turned to Carlie. "But I do need to discuss a few things with you, also."

"Of course. We have the afternoon free." Brad was being very charming. "Isn't that right, Carlie?"

With a strained, slightly malicious smile, Carlie nodded. "Certainly. Tyler knows how interested I am in doing what I can for the school."

Tyler watched her, satisfied. He made certain she

was aware of his intent in visiting. He wasn't planning to be devious—yet. That would come later. Maybe after he'd lulled her with false confidence.

"Would anyone like anything to drink?" Carlie headed for the kitchen. Tyler watched her, knowing she was only using the excuse to fume in private. He gave her thirty seconds, then left Brad looking around an empty living room so he could "give Carlie some help."

She had her back to him, setting glasses on the counter and filling them with iced tea. Silently, he moved up behind her, then bent and kissed her exposed neck.

Carlie jerked, nearly knocking over one of the glasses. Tyler caught it, set it back on the counter, then met her outraged gaze. "I've missed you so much, sweetheart."

"Don't you *ever* do that—"

Tyler quickly covered her mouth with his own. Her startled gasp was held suspended somewhere between them.

Her lips were soft and moist, and she tasted delicious. Using all his experience, he seduced her mouth, nibbling at her soft lips, licking gently, reclaiming her, urging her closer.

"Carlie." He forgot his purpose. It seemed so long since he'd kissed her. Without really intending to, his hand came up to cup her breast.

Instinct alone saved him. Ducking and catching her open palm just inches from his cheek, Tyler chided her. "Sweetheart, if you hit me, how will you explain it to your date?"

Through set teeth, she growled, "He's not my date, you ass!"

"Shh. Do you want him to know what we're doing?"

"I'm not doing anything! You're the one...!"

He watched with interest as her chest heaved angrily. Then he smiled. "You don't have to *do* anything. I read the morning paper and I want you. My secretary, who must be going on eighty, brings me coffee and I want you. I see you standing at the counter pouring tea and I positively throb."

Carlie closed her eyes in exasperation. "What are you doing here, Tyler?"

"I had to see you."

She turned away, picking up the tray. "Now you've seen me. Will you please go home?"

"And leave you here alone with Casanova? No way."

Carlie started out of the kitchen. Tyler took the tray from her. "He's only an associate," she said.

Tyler sent her a doubtful look. "With higher aspirations."

She snorted.

The sound was beautiful to his ears, so much like his old Carlie. He grinned at her, and to his besotted happiness, she actually grinned back. Then she shook her head and whispered for him to behave. He made no promises.

It quickly became a business meeting, just as Carlie had said. And surprisingly, Tyler enjoyed himself. He offered a lot of helpful input concerning the fund-raiser, legal advice Carlie or Brad wouldn't have thought of, and some suggestions of his own which proved very sound.

Brad was clearly impressed with Tyler, and before they called it quits, he was behaving as if they were old friends. "Could I call on you at your office sometime to discuss any problems that might arise?"

Tyler felt smug, but he hid it behind a facade of graciousness. "Of course. Just tell my secretary I said it was fine. She's a real stickler about keeping out people without appointments."

Brad shook his hand. "I appreciate that. Well, I better be off. I'm sorry I can't stay and help with your project, but I'm running a little late."

"Think nothing of it." Tyler simply wanted him gone. "Carlie and I can muddle through."

"If you're sure, then?"

Carlie stood abruptly and went to the door, obviously tired of playing cat and mouse. "Thank you for coming by, Brad. Let me know if there's anything else I can do to help."

She stood at the door, waiting until Brad had gotten into his car and driven away before closing it and facing Tyler.

He saw immediately that she was incensed. He forestalled her tirade by tossing out his own stack of papers. "I want to start a scholarship fund at your school."

Her mouth, already open to blast him, snapped shut.

"You could use it as you see fit. To pay for sports equipment, to help with school fees or lunches, or even to start special classes. Whatever. I've been giving this some thought for a while now." He gave her a slightly sheepish look. "After our practices, I offered to help out a few of the parents who were having difficulties. It's a tough thing, trying to give assistance without making it look like charity. I sent papers to be typed up at one house, and then gave some plumbing business from our offices to another. But it wasn't enough. I didn't want to offend anyone, so I came up with the idea of a scholarship.

"Jason has agreed to pitch in, too, and I think some of the other businesses in the area will follow suit. It would be great publicity for their services. 'Caring for the community' and all that." He drew to a halt. "What do you think?"

Her expression blank, Carlie walked to the table where Tyler had tossed the documents. She picked up the top sheet and scanned it. She looked staggered by the amount of his donation.

Raising her eyes to his, she whispered, "You're serious?"

"Of course. I have a contract ready. I hope you don't mind, but I left the distribution of my donation in your capable hands. As others come in, you could put them before a board of advisers if you want. But you already know the kids and their families so well, what they need and so forth, I thought you'd be perfect for the job."

Carlie was speechless. She stared at him.

"I think the contributing businesses would also agree to hire a few of the parents on a part-time basis. I know I always need papers transcribed and letters sent out. What do you—" He stopped midsentence. "Carlie? Is everything all right?"

She sat on the edge of the couch, his papers clutched in her hand, looking dumbfounded. "You're amazing, Tyler."

He actually felt himself blush. Gruffly, he said, "I'm just trying to help out. I have the money." He shrugged, dismissing her praise. "I wanted to surprise you."

Carlie laid her hand over his. "Thank you, Tyler. This means so much. I can already think of three families who will really benefit from this."

He grinned in satisfaction, retaining his hold on her hand. "There you go! Use it as you see fit. I'll see what I can do about getting some of the other businesses in on it. But in the meantime, if you need more money, let me know."

That did it. She looked near tears, overwhelmed with his generosity and goodness of spirit. And he felt not a single moment's guilt.

After all, he reasoned, he had donated the money. If the timing of his surprise seemed just a bit suspicious, it didn't matter. He needed all the help he could get.

Seeing her so obviously softened toward him, Tyler eased her into his arms. "You're not going to cry, are you? I can't abide watery women."

Pulling away as far as his arms would allow, Carlie gazed at him with a small smile. "I promise not to cry." But no sooner had she made that promise than she broke it, choking on a low sob.

Tyler shook his head. "So you really think I'm amazing?"

"I do."

The words were whispered with such sincerity, Tyler caught his breath. And then he smiled. "Excellent." His thoughts slowed to concentrate on one fact: he was with Carlie, and she still cared. But as he leaned toward her, she protested.

"Ah, Tyler, I didn't mean…"

"Shh. Kiss me again, Carlie."

"You kissed me! I didn't…"

"Don't argue semantics. I can think of better things to do." His tone was deep and suggestive as his arms slowly tightened around her.

With slightly narrowed eyes and a dangerously soft voice, she inquired, "Are you suggesting we have sex?"

"I, ah, well, I suppose the thought had entered my mind." About a million times in the past hour, he silently added. But Carlie was suddenly looking so furious, he kept that little tidbit to himself.

"Because you donated money to needy children," she clarified, "you think I should sleep with you? That's despicable! How could you propose such a thing?"

Anger and frustration rushed through him, and he jumped to his feet. "All right, dammit! You don't like that proposition? Well, here's another one." He sucked in a deep breath. "Marry me."

Chapter 11

Carlie stared at Tyler blankly. "Don't you think humor is a little misplaced at this point?"

"I..." He shut his mouth. Truth be told, he'd surprised himself as much as he had Carlie with that sudden command. *Marry me.* Damn, but it did seem the right thing to say at the right time.

He grinned. "I'm not joking. I want to marry you."

She eyed him warily. "Why?"

He gave her a mock frown of disapproval over her rude questioning. "You don't seem to know any more about accepting proposals than you did about dates. Let me instruct you. This is the part where you fall into my arms, tearfully showing your gratitude and devotion, and shout a resounding, 'Yes!' You got all that?"

"Provided, of course, the answer would be yes?"

Tyler felt a moment's misgiving. "Don't toy with

me, Carlie. I've never proposed to anyone in my life. I could have a major attack of insecurity here, if you're not careful." He hoped his teasing tone belied the truth behind his words. He felt almost sick with dread.

Carlie chewed her bottom lip and her eyes were dark with shadows. "Tyler, I don't want to get married. It's not just you. I don't want to marry anyone. Ever. I followed that route once, and as you know, it didn't go all that well."

Tyler sat beside her and took her hands in his. He needed to touch her, to make her understand. "It wouldn't be that way with me, Carlie. I'm not like him."

She went on, all brisk and businesslike. "Of course you're not. I told you, you're amazing. Kind and compassionate, and too attractive to be turned loose on polite society. But I value my independence. I don't intend to give it up."

It took him a minute to recover from her compliments. He was still beaming when the rest of what she'd said sank in. "I'm not asking you to give up anything."

She gave him a sardonic look. "Be honest, Tyler. Don't you think you'd start hounding me right away over how I dress? Or how I wear my hair?"

"Well," he hedged. She had a point. But a poor one. "You can't go on hiding the rest of your life, Carlie. You're a beautiful woman. That's something to be proud of. It's a part of you. And once we're married, there won't be any reason to look so shabby. I wouldn't let other men ogle you."

She tossed up her hands in exasperation. "There, you see? Not only are you changing me, but you'll be playing barbarian protector as well. I don't need a protector, Tyler."

"Not dressed like that you won't."

Carlie sighed, ignoring his provocation. "Please try to understand."

"I understand. You said you cared for me, but it wasn't exactly the truth." He stood, towering over her. He felt dejected, rejected and unbearably weary. He tweaked her chin, giving her a crooked smile. "You know something, honey? You're just a bit selfish."

Carlie raised an eyebrow at the criticism, but he continued.

"I've bent over backward, made all the concessions I can make, humiliated myself several times now trying to win you over. But you have a hard heart. I don't hold that against you. Considering your past, I suppose it's even expected. But damned if I know what else to do.

"It hurts, Carlie. It hurts to care so much about someone, and then have them turn you away again and again. I've been closer to you than I have to any other soul on earth, Jason included. And I was determined not to give up on you."

Carlie was staring down at her lap, and Tyler couldn't see her face. He decided it was just as well. He was spilling his guts, laying his heart on the table, and if she looked at him with pity, he might very well lose it. His tone was indifferent now, his expression impassive. "I can't do it anymore. You must be stronger than I am, because I can't take the rejections again. If you want to go on living in a cocoon, there's no way I can stop you. But I won't hang around indefinitely waiting for you to emerge, either."

She remained silent, and Tyler sighed in disgust. She wasn't making it any easier for him. "I won't be at the practice on Monday. I'll get Jason to fill in until you can find someone more permanent. Explain to the kids for me, if you will. And if you need any more money, let me know. You can leave a message with my secretary." He walked to the door and waited, but she didn't move. He nearly choked on his rage and frustration. Damn her, she had pulled him in, made him love her and now she didn't care.

He walked out, closing the door softly behind him.

Carlie waited on Monday, her stomach roiling, her head aching, her eyes burning. And true to his word, Tyler didn't come. She felt awful, even though she hadn't wanted to marry him, *couldn't* marry him. The idea was absurd.

So why had her heart threatened to burst when he'd proposed? And when he'd left, after such a touching speech, she'd felt like she was coming apart.

Oh God, she hurt.

Jason entered, dressed in an old college sweatshirt and gym shorts that showed his hairy legs. He spared her a glance, then picked up a ball and began bouncing it. Carlie approached him.

"Hello, Jason."

He inclined his head. "Carlie."

"I appreciate your filling in like this. On such short notice, I mean."

He looked at her. "Tyler needed me. I love him. He's my brother."

"I... I know." She hesitated, swallowing hard. Jason's mood was apparently not conducive to small talk. But she needed to know. "How is Tyler?"

Very casually, still bouncing the ball, Jason said, "Miserable. Thanks for asking."

Carlie flinched at his tone. "Jason, I never meant to—"

"Of course, you didn't. In your book, all men are jerks, right? Tyler certainly can't be any different."

She shook her head, then started to turn away. Jason held the ball. "Carlie? I'm sorry. It's not my place to..."

She didn't look at him. "It's okay, Jason. I understand."

"No. I don't think you do. But it's my opinion you never will, so I'm glad you broke things off with Tyler now, before he got even more involved. I'm the only person he's ever had care for him. His life hasn't exactly encouraged him to trust women. So when he does marry, I damned well want it to be to a woman who's capable of loving him. He deserves that much."

She was crushed by the hard words, but acknowledged the truth in them. Tyler did deserve the best. If only...

Oh, God. She really had done it this time. No matter how deep she buried the past, it always seemed to come back and torment her.

Or was she only tormenting herself?

After two weeks had passed, Carlie knew it was time to face facts. She loved Tyler and always would. She missed him terribly, and with each day that went by, the feeling grew worse. When she was with him, she felt alive. Without him, she felt dull and drained.

She needed him, and even though she'd sworn never to need anyone again, she felt comforted by the admission. She no longer had to deny herself or her emotions. It wasn't a bad thing to need Tyler. He wouldn't take advantage of her feelings, wouldn't try to dominate her or weaken her to suit his own needs. She believed that. She trusted him.

But she had hurt him badly, and he might not forgive her.

Carlie knew she was too much the coward to call Tyler outright. She needed a reason for calling, and when more donations to the scholarship fund came in from various businesses, she decided that excuse would work well enough. She'd start out by thanking him, and work into telling him she loved him madly.

It was a bold plan, she thought, and would have worked, except that Tyler didn't answer the phone. She got a message saying he was out of the office for some time and all calls could be forwarded to Jason. When she tried him at home, his answering machine picked up. Concerned, she called Brenda.

What she discovered wasn't encouraging.

Tyler planned to take an extended vacation to Chicago, where he was considering joining a new firm. Jason, of course, was livid and blaming Carlie. Brenda was apologetic, but very upset by it all.

Carlie had a hard time breathing. She knew exactly what was happening. She'd done the same after her divorce. She'd tried to leave the pain behind.

She could have told Tyler it didn't work. Because right now, the pain was unbearable. Everything had gone wrong, and it was all her own fault. She was a miserable coward, and it was time she stopped hiding, just as Tyler had suggested.

She had to do something, and she had to do it now.

It was Jason who answered the door. Just the fact that Carlie was knocking at the front entrance, rather than entering through the kitchen, as usual, was indicative of her uneasiness. She had no idea if she'd be welcome, given the present situation. But Jason was polite. Painfully so.

"Hello, Carlie. Come in."

"Thanks. Ah, Tyler isn't here, is he?"

Jason eyed her. "No. He's been avoiding us as much as you have."

Carlie flushed, but she refused to back down. "I'm sorry about that." She came in and Jason shut the door behind her. With her hands in her pockets, she looked around the room. "Is Bren around?"

"I'll get her for you. Make yourself at home."

It felt exceedingly odd for Jason to say such a thing. It had never been necessary before.

Brenda flew into the room, her eyes alight with expectation. "Carlie! I'm so glad to see you!"

Carlie ducked out of reach. "No hugging, Bren. I'm dangerously close to coming unglued here, and any excess of kind consideration will definitely put me over the edge."

Brenda blinked. "What are you talking about?"

Carlie had been calm enough until that moment. The simple truth was, she still suffered a few qualms over her own appeal. She was unbelievably apprehensive about confronting Tyler, no matter how she tried to deny it. Her lips started to quiver. She felt like a fool, but she couldn't stop it. She clasped her hands, opened her mouth to calmly and intelligently explain, then broke into tears. "I love him!"

Brenda smiled. "Oh, Carlie."

Despite Carlie's objections, Brenda pulled her into a fierce hug. "I think that's wonderful."

"I don't know, Bren." She sniffed, then swiped the tears from her cheeks. "I hurt him. I've never hurt anyone in my life. I can't stand it."

"Have you told him?"

Carlie shook her head. "I can't just go up to him and say, 'Well, guess what? I do love you, after all.' I've been so terrible."

"No, you haven't. And Tyler will understand."

Carlie raised her chin. Enough was enough. She'd had her little show of vulnerability. "I sincerely hope you're right. Because I do love him. In fact, I'm crazy about him. But he's never actually said he loved me. He asked me to marry him, and he makes no bones about wanting me…that way. But he's never actually mentioned the word *love*."

Jason stepped into the room. "Gossiping about my brother again?"

Brenda turned and nearly snapped his head off. "We weren't gossiping! I was going to convince Carlie that Tyler loves her."

Jason rolled his eyes. "Of course he does. Why do you think he's been so impossible lately?"

"Don't tell me," Brenda demanded. "Tell Carlie."

Jason walked over to Carlie. "Tyler loves you. Now, what are you going to do about it?"

Carlie bit her bottom lip. Tyler had tried to tell her the depth of his feelings right before he left her house the last time. But she hadn't responded. At all. It made her ache to imagine how he must have felt. How could she tell him how scared she had been, that she'd been petrified at the idea of accepting too much happiness because it left her vulnerable?

Just as vulnerable as he must have felt when she'd failed to accept his proposal.

Suddenly, she realized what she had to do. "I have to make it up to him. I need to show him how much I care."

"Just tell him," Jason suggested.

But Carlie shook her head. "I have a plan. But I'll need your help."

"Oh, no." Jason put a hand to his head, looking ready to expire. "You're starting to sound just like my wife."

Brenda laughed. "Go ahead, Carlie, I'm listening. You know I dearly love a good plan."

Jason sat, and the women looked at him pointedly. "I'm not budging. You two are plotting something against my poor brother, and I need to be here to look after his interests."

"Well, all right." Carlie leaned forward, and Jason and Brenda followed suit. "Here's want I want to do."

Tyler stared at Jason, dressed in an elegant suit and obviously preparing to leave the house. "I thought you wanted me to help you with some work around here today."

Jason smacked his palm to his forehead theatrically. "Oh, boy. I forgot, Tyler. Bren made plans for us to go out tonight. Do you mind?"

"Well, no." Actually, Tyler had been looking forward to working with his brother. He needed some physical labor to drain him, to weary his mind enough to drive out thoughts of other things. He only hoped his disappointment didn't show.

Shoving his hands into his jeans pockets, Tyler

stepped around Jason. He didn't want to return to his apartment. The mere thought was enough to make him shudder. Lately, all he could do was think of Carlie. Oh, how the mighty did fall. Flat on their faces.

And it still hurt, dammit.

Moving away was a desperate decision. He couldn't be so close to Carlie, knowing she was only minutes away, and constantly be reminded of how he had failed, both her and himself. He needed to get on with his life, but no one had ever told him how to do that.

Jason interrupted his thoughts, slapping him on the shoulder. "I have a favor to ask. If you don't have anything else pressing to do, could you go ahead and get started on a few things for me? You know how I'm already rushed for time, especially now that I've started helping with the after-school basketball program."

Tyler winced. "How are they? The kids, I mean. Little Lucy is doing all right?"

"They're all the same." Jason's answer was deliberately vague. "A few of the parents asked me to extend their thanks for your help. It was great of you to figure out a way for them to earn extra money. I hadn't realized you were doing so much."

Tyler frowned, uncomfortable with the praise, but Jason didn't give him time to argue. "I made a list of a few jobs that had to be done."

Tyler forced a smile. "I wouldn't mind helping out. I don't have anything else to do today, anyway."

Jason almost grinned. "You're sure? I'd really appreciate it."

"No problem. What's first on the list?"

Jason produced a folded piece of paper and stuck

it into the front breast pocket of Tyler's flannel shirt. "I gotta run. Do me a favor first, though, will you? Carlie called the other day and said she left something in the pool house. I don't remember what. Go down and check it out, will you? Look around and see if you find anything."

Tyler didn't move a single muscle. "She's not stopping by here, is she?" He knew he sounded panicked, but to be alone with Carlie would nearly kill him. He couldn't trust himself not to act like an ass again.

Jason waved away his concern. "You don't have to worry about her dropping in." He turned away quickly. "I really do appreciate this, Tyler. Bren and I won't be home till late, so help yourself to anything you need, and…" Jason grinned suddenly. "Relax, will you? Things are never as bad as they seem."

Tyler had no answer for that. Things seemed pretty damned bad to him.

Despite himself, he was anxious to see what Carlie had left in the pool house. Her mask? Some small part of that alluring harem costume? Maybe he'd find it and keep it. As a memento. What could she say? Not a thing.

He waited till he heard Jason's car drive away, then went out the back, heading for the pool house. It seemed so achingly familiar, each step he took on the flagstone walk brought the memories closer. But instead of soft party lights to guide his way, the sun was shining brightly. The breeze chilled him, and he hunkered his shoulders forward, his head down.

The pool house door was slightly ajar, but Tyler paid no attention to that small detail. He was too overcome with memories. Odd, but knowing now that it had been Carlie, not another woman, only enhanced the memory, made it more erotic and more tantalizing.

Heat washed over him in waves as he closed the door behind him, but it wasn't from the warmth of the room. Just looking around caused his body to react, and when he spotted the couch, his thighs clenched and his stomach tightened.

"Tyler?"

He froze. He couldn't possibly be dreaming, not so vividly, not with such stark reality. He turned slowly, and felt his breath catch in his throat.

She was almost exactly as he remembered, hovering in the corner, her back to the wall. But there was no wig, and somehow he knew the mask was for effect, not concealment.

Tyler stared, his eyes so hot he could barely see. There were no shadows today. Each and every lamp had been turned on. Carlie's hair, appearing more blond than brown in the bright light, hung loose about her shoulders. It was in gentle waves, sexy and shimmering and tempting him to touch it. Her hazel eyes, brightly lit with anticipation and anxiety, stared at him, direct and unblinking.

Very slowly, not daring to breathe, he walked toward her. Reaching out, his fingers touched the mask. "May I remove it?"

Her smile quavered, dimpling her cheeks, but then vanished quickly. It was a nervous reaction, he knew, and his love for her doubled.

"If you like." Carlie held his eyes, her breathing suspended, her heart pounding erratically. She loved him so much. "Whatever you like, Tyler."

"I like you." He slipped the mask from her face, gently laying it aside. Cupping her cheeks, he smiled at her. "Do you realize how rare and special that is, Carlie? I like everything about you. I like being with you, I like looking at you, I like talking with you."

He kissed her lightly, fleetingly, on her trembling lips. "I'll never grow bored of you or try to change you."

Carlie rubbed her cheek against his palm. "Except my clothes?"

It was an attempt at humor, but Tyler didn't laugh. "You can wear any damned thing you like. I don't care."

Her eyes welled with tears, and she had to fight to keep from pressing herself against him. But they had to talk. She had to make him understand. Drawing a deep breath, she looked up at him. "I want to make you happy, Tyler. I… I love you."

He closed his eyes, then hugged her tight. "I love you, too, Carlie. So damned much."

Her smile was tremulous. "It's a little scary, isn't it?"

"No!" He held her away from him, his expression fierce. "Losing you is scary. Loving you is easy, and unbelievably exciting." Then he smiled, his hand dropping to finger the edge of her skimpy bodice. "Much like this costume of yours."

Very seriously, without any hesitation, Carlie whispered, "I want to be whatever you want me to be."

"I want you to be yourself." He pressed his face into her shoulder, inhaling her soft, feminine scent. "You're a beautiful woman, Carlie. And so special. Just be yourself for me, honey. Stop hiding."

She almost laughed out loud, she felt so relieved.

Teasing Tyler with a smile, she asked, "Did Jason tell you what I lost here?"

He looked struck, having all but forgotten about his brother. He grinned. "No. What did you lose?"

She ducked her head. "I lost my heart."

"No." He tipped her chin up. "It's not lost. I have it, and I'm not giving it back."

Carlie started to say something more, but Tyler touched his fingers to her lips. "Did you wear this costume only to torment me, or do you plan on making my fantasies come true?"

"A little of both." She almost made it out of reach before Tyler grabbed her and held her close.

A long kiss followed, and Carlie was finally able to hug herself to him. It felt so right, so perfect. Paper rattled when she leaned into his chest, and Tyler pulled away. With a suspicious look, he tugged out the note Jason had given him. Keeping Carlie close, he read the message aloud. "Women have fantasies, too, or so Bren insists. There's a large paper bag behind the couch. Have fun, kids."

Carlie laughed, then squirmed from his grasp to retrieve the bag. She looked inside, then grinning, she tossed the bag to Tyler. "Here you go."

He caught it automatically. "What is it?"

"Your pirate costume." She bobbed her eyebrows comically. "Remind me to thank your brother."

Tyler grinned wickedly as he began unbuttoning his shirt. "I'm not a man you can trifle with, sweetheart. If you want to play games, you're going to have to promise to marry me."

Carlie watched him remove his shirt, her gaze rapt. "I'll marry you, I'll choose a whole new wardrobe, I'll even get rid of my glasses. But you have to promise me something, too."

He unsnapped his jeans, then slowly shoved them down his hips. "What's that?"

"You can never stop being outrageous."

He laughed, sounding smug. "Told you you'd like it."

Carlie walked into his arms, feeling loved and in love. Happy. She didn't stop until Tyler was holding her close again. "Indeed I do, Tyler. Indeed I do."

* * * * *

Books by Brenda Jackson

Harlequin Desire

The Westmoreland Legacy

The Rancher Returns
His Secret Son
An Honorable Seduction
His to Claim
Duty or Desire

Forged of Steele

Seduced by a Steele
Claimed by a Steele

Visit her Author Profile page at Harlequin.com,
or brendajackson.net, for more titles.

"One Minute" Survey

You get up to **FOUR books** <u>and</u> Mystery Gifts...

ABSOLUTELY FREE!

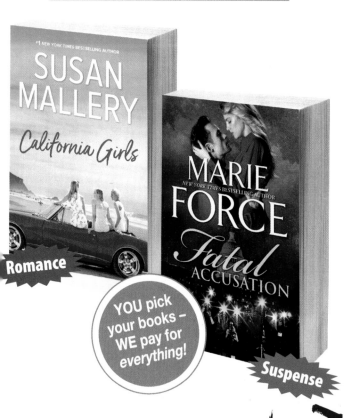

Romance

YOU pick your books – WE pay for everything!

Suspense

See inside for details.

Dear Reader,

Your opinions are important to us. So if you'll participate in our fast and free "One Minute" Survey, **YOU** can pick up to four wonderful books that **WE** pay for!

As a leading publisher of women's fiction, we'd love to hear from you. That's why we promise to reward you for completing our survey.

IMPORTANT: Please complete the survey and return it. We'll send your Free Books and Free Mystery Gifts right away. **And we pay for shipping and handling too!** *We pay for EVERYTHING!*

Try **Essential Suspense** featuring spine-tingling suspense and psychological thrillers with many written by today's best-selling authors.

Try **Essential Romance** featuring compelling romance stories with many written by today's best-selling authors.

Or TRY BOTH!

Thank you again for participating in our "One Minute" Survey. It really takes just a minute (or less) to complete the survey… and your free books and gifts will be well worth it!

Sincerely,

Pam Powers

Pam Powers
for Reader Service

"One Minute" Survey

GET YOUR FREE BOOKS AND FREE GIFTS!

✓ Complete this Survey ✓ Return this survey

1 Do you try to find time to read every day?
☐ YES ☐ NO

2 Do you prefer stories with happy endings?
☐ YES ☐ NO

3 Do you enjoy having books delivered to your home?
☐ YES ☐ NO

4 Do you share your favorite books with friends?
☐ YES ☐ NO

YES! I have completed the above "One Minute" Survey. Please send me my Free Books and Free Mystery Gifts (worth over $20 retail). I understand that I am under no obligation to buy anything, as explained on the back of this card.

☐ I prefer
Essential Suspense
191/391 MDL GNT4

☐ I prefer
Essential Romance
194/394 MDL GNT4

☐ I prefer BOTH
191/391 & 194/394
MDL GNUG

FIRST NAME

LAST NAME

ADDRESS

APT.#

CITY

STATE/PROV.

ZIP/POSTAL CODE

READER SERVICE—Here's how it works:

BUSINESS REPLY MAIL
FIRST-CLASS MAIL   PERMIT NO. 717   BUFFALO, NY

POSTAGE WILL BE PAID BY ADDRESSEE

READER SERVICE
PO BOX 1341
BUFFALO NY 14240-8571

NO POSTAGE
NECESSARY
IF MAILED
IN THE
UNITED STATES

THE PROPOSAL

Brenda Jackson

To Gerald Jackson, Sr. My one and only.
To all my readers who enjoy reading about the
Westmorelands, this book is especially for you!
To my Heavenly Father. How Great Thou Art.

He hath made every thing beautiful in his time.
—*Ecclesiastes* 3:11

Prologue

"Hello, ma'am, I'm Jason Westmoreland and I'd like to welcome you to Denver."

Even before she turned around, the deep, male voice had Bella Bostwick's stomach clenching as the throaty *sound* vibrated across her skin. And then when she gazed up into his eyes she had to practically force oxygen into her lungs. He had to be the most gorgeous man she'd ever seen.

For a moment she couldn't speak nor was she able to control her gaze from roaming over him and appreciating everything she saw. He was tall, way over six feet, with dark brown eyes, sculpted cheekbones and a chiseled jaw. And then there was his skin, a deep, rich chocolate-brown that had her remembering her craving for that particular treat and how delicious it was. But nothing could be more appealing than his lips and the way they were shaped. Sensuous. Sumptuous. A perfect pair for the sexy smile curving them.

He said he was a Westmoreland and because this charity ball was given on behalf of the Westmoreland Foundation, she could only assume he was one of *those* Westmorelands.

She took the hand he'd extended and wished she hadn't when a heated sizzle rode up her spine the moment she touched it. She tried forcing the sensation away. "And I'm Elizabeth Bostwick, but I prefer just Bella."

The smile curving his lips widened a fraction, enough to send warm blood rushing through her veins. "Hi, Bella."

The way he'd pronounce her name was ultrasexy. She thought his smile was intoxicating and definitely contagious, which was the reason she could so easily return it. "Hi, Jason."

"First, I'd like to offer my condolences on the loss of your grandfather."

"Thank you."

"And then I'm hoping the two of us could talk about the ranch you inherited. If you decide to sell it, I'd like to put in my bid for both the ranch and Hercules."

Bella drew in a deep breath. Her grandfather Herman Bostwick had died last month and left his land and prized stallion to her. She had seen the horse when she'd come to town for the reading of the will and would admit he was beautiful. She had returned to Denver from Savannah only yesterday to handle more legal matters regarding her grandfather's estate. "I haven't decided what I plan on doing regarding the ranch or the livestock, but if I do decide to sell I will keep your interest in mind. But I need to make you aware that according to my uncle Kenneth there are others who've expressed the same interest."

"Yes, I'm sure there are."

He had barely finished his sentence when her uncle suddenly appeared at her side and spoke up. "Westmoreland."

"Mr. Bostwick."

Bella immediately picked up strong negative undercurrents radiating between the two men and the extent of it became rather obvious when her uncle said in a curt tone, "It's time to leave, Bella."

She blinked. "Leave? But we just got here, Uncle Kenneth."

Her uncle smiled down at her as he tucked her arm underneath his. "Yes, dear, but you just arrived in town yesterday and have been quite busy since you've gotten here taking care of business matters."

She arched a brow as she stared at the grand-uncle she only discovered she had a few weeks ago. He hadn't been concerned with how exhausted she was when he'd insisted she accompany him here tonight, saying it was her place to attend this gala in her grandfather's stead.

"Good night, Westmoreland. I'm taking my niece home."

She barely had time to bid Jason farewell when her uncle escorted her to the door. As they proceeded toward the exit she couldn't help glancing over her shoulder to meet Jason's gaze. It was intense and she could tell he hadn't appreciated her uncle's abruptness. And then she saw a smile touch his lips again and she couldn't help reciprocate by smiling back. Was he flirting with her? Was she with him?

"Jason Westmoreland is someone you don't want to get to know, Bella," Kenneth Bostwick said in a gruff tone, apparently noticing the flirtatious exchange between them.

She turned to glance up at her uncle as they walked out into the night. People were still arriving. "Why?"

"He wants Herman's land. None of the Westmorelands are worth knowing. They think they can do whatever the hell they please around these parts." He interrupted her thoughts by saying, "There're a bunch of them and they own a lot of land on the outskirts of town."

She lifted an arched brow. "Near where my grandfather lived?"

"Yes. In fact Jason Westmoreland's land is adjacent to Herman's."

"Really?" She smiled warmly at the thought that Jason Westmoreland lived on property that connected to the land she'd inherited. Technically that made her his neighbor. *No wonder he wants to buy my land,* she thought to herself.

"It's a good thing you're selling Herman's land, but I wouldn't sell it to him under any circumstances."

She frowned when he opened the car for her to get in. "I haven't decided what I plan to do with the ranch, Uncle Kenneth," she reminded him.

He chuckled. "What is there to decide? You know nothing about ranching and a woman of your delicacy, breeding and refinement belongs back in Savannah and not here in Denver trying to run a hundred-acre ranch and enduring harsh winters. Like I told you earlier, I already know someone who wants to buy the ranch along with all the livestock—especially that stallion Hercules. They're offering a lot of money. Just think of all the shoes, dresses and hats you'll be able to buy, not to mention a real nice place near the Atlantic Ocean."

Bella didn't say anything. She figured this was probably not the time to tell him that as far as she was concerned there was a lot to decide because none of those things he'd mentioned meant anything to her. She refused to make a decision about her inheritance too hastily.

As her uncle's car pulled out of the parking lot, she settled back against the plush leather seats and remembered the exact moment her and Jason Westmoreland's eyes had met.

It was a connection she doubted she would ever forget.

Chapter 1

One month later

"Did you hear Herman Bostwick's granddaughter is back in Denver and rumor has it she's here to stay?"

Jason Westmoreland's ears perked up on the conversation between his sister-in-law Pam and his two cousins-in-laws Chloe and Lucia. He was at his brother Dillon's house, stretched out on the living room floor playing around with his six-month-old nephew, Denver.

Although the ladies had retired to the dining room to sit at the table and chat, it wasn't hard to hear what they were saying and he thought there was no reason for him not to listen. Especially when the woman they were discussing was a woman who'd captured his attention the moment he'd met her last month at a charity ball. She was a woman he hadn't been able to stop thinking about since.

"Her name is Elizabeth but she goes by Bella," Lucia, who'd recently married his cousin Derringer, was saying. "She came into Dad's paint store the other day and I swear she is simply beautiful. She looks so out of place here in Denver, a real Southern belle amidst a bunch of roughnecks."

"And I hear she intends to run the ranch alone. Her uncle Kenneth has made it known he won't be lifting one finger to help her," Pam said in disgust. "The nerve of the man to be so darn selfish. He was counting on her selling that land to Myers Smith who promised to pay him a bunch of money if the deal went through. It seems everyone would love to get their hands on that land and especially that stallion Hercules."

Including me, Jason thought, as he rolled the ball toward his nephew but kept his ears wide-open. He hadn't known Bella Bostwick had returned to Denver and wondered if she remembered he was interested in purchasing her land and Hercules. He definitely hoped so. His thoughts then shifted to Kenneth Bostwick. The man's attitude didn't surprise him. He'd always acted as if he was entitled, which is probably the reason Kenneth and Herman never got along. And since Herman's death, Kenneth had let it be known around town that he felt the land Bella had inherited should be his. Evidently Herman hadn't seen it that way and had left everything in his will to the granddaughter he'd never met.

"Well, I hope she's cautious as to who she hires to help out on that ranch. I can see a woman that beauti-

ful drawing men in droves, and some will be men who
she needs to be leery of," Chloe said.

Jason frowned at the thought of any man drawn to
her and didn't fully understand why he reacted that
way. Lucia was right in saying Bella was beautiful.
He had been totally captivated the moment he'd first
seen her. And it had been obvious Kenneth Bostwick
hadn't wanted him anywhere near his niece.

Kenneth never liked him and had envied Jason's relationship with old man Herman Bostwick. Most people around these parts had considered Herman mean,
ornery and craggy, but Jason was not one of them.
He would never forget the one time he had run away
from home at eleven and spent the night hidden in
Bostwick's barn. The old man had found him the next
morning and returned him to his parents. But not before feeding him a tasty breakfast and getting him to
help gather eggs from the chickens and milk the cows.
It was during that time he'd discovered Herman Bostwick wasn't as mean as everyone thought. In fact, Herman had only been a lonely old man.

Jason had gone back to visit Herman often over the
years and had been there the night Hercules had been
born. He'd known the moment he'd seen the colt that
he would be special. And Herman had even told him
that the horse would one day be his. Herman had died
in his sleep a few months ago and now his ranch and
every single thing on it, including Hercules, belonged
to his granddaughter. Everyone assumed she would
sell the ranch, but from what he was hearing she had
moved to Denver from Savannah.

He hoped to hell she had thought through her decision. Colorado's winters were rough, especially in

Denver. And running a spread as big as the one she'd inherited wasn't easy for an experienced rancher; he didn't want to think how it would be for someone who knew nothing about it. Granted if she kept Marvin Allen on as the foreman things might not be so bad, but still, there were a number of ranch hands and some men didn't take kindly to a woman who lacked experience being their boss.

"I think the neighborly thing for us to do is to pay her a visit and welcome her to the area. We can also let her know if there's anything she needs she can call on us," Pam said, interrupting his thoughts.

"I agree," both Lucia and Chloe chimed in.

He couldn't help but agree, as well. Paying his new neighbor a visit and welcoming her to the area was the right thing to do, and he intended to do just that. He might have lost out on a chance to get the ranch but he still wanted Hercules.

But even more than that, he wanted to get to know Bella Bostwick better.

Bella stepped out of the house and onto the porch and looked around at the vast mountains looming before her. The picturesque view almost took her breath away and reminded her of why she had defied her family and moved here from Savannah two weeks ago.

Her overprotective parents had tried talking her out of what they saw as a foolish move on her part mainly because they hadn't wanted her out of their sight. It had been bad enough while growing up when she'd been driven to private schools by a chauffeur each day and trailed everywhere she went by a bodyguard until she was twenty-one.

And the sad thing was that she hadn't known about her grandfather's existence until she was notified of the reading of his will. She hadn't been informed in time to attend the funeral services and a part of her was still upset with her parents for keeping that from her.

She didn't know what happened to put a permanent wedge between father and son, but whatever feud that existed between them should not have included her. She'd had every right to get to know Herman Bostwick and now he was gone. When she thought about the summers she could have spent here visiting him instead of being shipped away to some camp for the summer she couldn't help but feel angry. She used to hate those camps and the snooty kids that usually went to them.

Before leaving Savannah she had reminded her parents that she was twenty-five and old enough to make her own decisions about what she wanted to do with her life. And as far as she was concerned, the trust fund her maternal grandparents had established for her, as well as this ranch she'd now inherited from her paternal grandfather, made living that life a lot easier. It was the first time in her life that she had anything that was truly hers.

It would be too much to ask David and Melissa Bostwick to see things that way and they'd made it perfectly clear that they didn't. She wouldn't be surprised if they were meeting with their attorney at this very moment to come up with a way to force her to return home to Savannah. Well, she had news for them. This was now her home and she intended to stay.

If they'd had anything to say about it she would be in Savannah and getting engaged to marry Hugh Pierce. Although most women would consider Hugh, with his tall, dark and handsome looks and his old-money wealth, a prime catch. And if she really thought hard about it, then she would be one of those women who thought so. But that was the problem. She had to think real hard about it. They'd dated a number of times but there was never any connection, any spark and no real enthusiasm on her part about spending time with him. She had tried as delicately as she could to explain such a thing to her parents but that hadn't stopped them from trying to shove Hugh down her throat every chance they got. That only proved how controlling they could be.

And speaking of controlling…her uncle Kenneth had become another problem. He was her grandfather's fifty-year-old half brother, whom she'd met for the first time when she'd flown in for the reading of the will. He'd assumed the ranch would go to him and had been gravely disappointed that day to discover it hadn't. He had also expected her to sell everything and when she'd made the decision to keep the ranch, he had been furious and said his kindness to her had ended, and that he wouldn't lift a finger to help and wanted her to find out the hard way just what a mistake she had made.

She sank into the porch swing, thinking there was no way she could have made a mistake in deciding to build a life here. She had fallen in love with the land the first time she'd seen it when she'd come for the reading of the will. And it hadn't taken long to decide even though she'd been robbed of the opportunity to connect with her grandfather in life, she would connect with him in death by accepting the gift he'd given her. A part of her felt that although they'd never met, he had somehow known about the miserable childhood she had endured and was giving her the chance to have a way better adult life.

The extra men she had hired to work the ranch so far seemed eager to do so and appreciated the salary she was paying them which, from what she'd heard, was more than fair. She'd always heard if you wanted good people to work for you then you needed to pay them good money.

She was about to get up to go back into the house to pack up more of her grandfather's belongings when she noticed someone on horseback approaching in the distance. She squinted her eyes, remembering this was Denver and people living on the outskirts of town, in the rural sections, often traveled by horseback, and she was grateful for the riding lessons her parents had insisted that she take. She'd always wanted to own a horse and now she had several of them.

As the rider came closer she felt a tingling sensation in the pit if her stomach when she recognized him. Jason Westmoreland. She definitely remembered him from the night of the charity ball and one of the things she remembered the most was his warm smile. She had often wondered if he'd been as ruggedly handsome as she recalled. The closer the rider got she realized he was.

And she had to admit that in the three times she'd been to Denver, he was the closest thing to a modern-day cowboy she had seen. Even now he was riding his horse with an expertise and masculinity that had her heart pounding with every step the horse took. His gaze was steady on her and she couldn't help but stare back. Heat crawled up her spine and waves of sensuous sensations swept through her system. She could feel goose bumps form on her skin. He was definitely the first and only man she'd ever been this attracted to.

She couldn't help wondering why he was paying her a visit. He had expressed interest in her land and in Hercules when she'd met him that night at the charity ball. Was he here to convince her she'd made a mistake in moving here like her parents and uncle had done? Would he try to talk her into selling the land and horse to him? If that was the case then she had the same news for him she'd had for the others. She was staying put and Hercules would remain hers until she decided otherwise.

He brought his horse to a stop at the foot of the porch near a hitching post. "Hello, Bella."

"Jason." She gazed up into the dark brown eyes staring at her and could swear she felt heat radiating from them. The texture of his voice tingled against her skin just as it had that night. "Is there a reason for your visit?"

A smile curved his lips. "I understand you've decided to try your hand at ranching."

She lifted her chin, knowing what was coming next. "That's right. Do you have a problem with it?"

"No, I don't have a problem with it," he said smoothly. "The decision was yours to make. However, I'm sure you know things won't be easy for you."

"Yes, I'm very much aware they won't be. Is there anything else you'd like to say?"

"Yes. We're neighbors and if you ever need my help in any way just let me know."

She blinked. Had he actually offered his help? There had to be a catch and quickly figured what it was. "Is the reason you're being nice that you still want to buy Hercules? If so, you might as well know I haven't made a decision about him yet."

His smile faded and the look on his face suddenly became intense. "The reason I'm being *nice* is that I think of myself as a nice person. And as far as Hercules is concerned, yes, I still want to buy him but that has nothing to do with my offering my help to you as your neighbor."

She knew she had offended him and immediately regretted it. She normally wasn't this mistrusting of people but owning the ranch was a touchy subject with her because so many people were against it. He had wanted the land and Hercules but had accepted her decision and was even offering his help when her own uncle hadn't. Instead of taking it at face value, she'd questioned it. "Maybe I shouldn't have jumped to conclusions."

"Yes, maybe you shouldn't have."

Every cell in her body started to quiver under the intensity of his gaze. At that moment she knew his offer had been sincere. She wasn't sure how she knew; she just did. "I stand corrected. I apologize," she said.

"Apology accepted."

"Thank you." And because she wanted to get back on good footing with him she asked, "How have you been, Jason?"

His features relaxed when he said, "Can't complain." He tilted his Stetson back from his eyes before dismounting from the huge horse as if it was the easiest of things to do.

And neither can I complain, she thought, watching him come up the steps of the porch. There was nothing about seeing him in all his masculine form that any woman could or would complain about. She felt her throat tighten when moments later he was standing in front of her. Something she could recognize as hot, fluid desire closed in on her, making it hard to breathe. Especially when his gaze was holding hers with the same concentration he'd had the night of the ball.

Today in the bright sunlight she was seeing things about him that the lights in the ballroom that night hadn't revealed: the whiteness of his teeth against his dark skin, the thickness of his lashes, the smooth texture of his skin and the broadness of his shoulders beneath his shirt. Another thing she was seeing now as well as what she remembered seeing in full detail that night was the full shape of a pair of sensual lips.

"And what about you, Bella?"

She blinked, realizing he'd spoken. "What about me?" The smile curving his lips returned and in a way that lulled her into thoughts she shouldn't be thinking, like how she'd love kissing that smile on his face.

"How have you been…besides busy?" he asked.

Bella drew in a deep breath and said. "Yes, things have definitely been busy and at times even crazy."

"I bet. And I meant what I said earlier. If you ever need help with anything, let me know."

"Thanks for the offer, I appreciate it." She had seen the turnoff to his ranch. The marker referred to it as Jason's Place. And from what she'd seen through the trees it was a huge ranch and the two-story house was beautiful.

She quickly remembered her manners and said. "I was about to have a cup of tea. Would you like a cup, as well?"

He leaned against the post and his smile widened even more. "Tea?"

"Yes."

She figured he found such a thing amusing if the smile curving his lips was anything to go by. The last thing a cowboy would want after being in the saddle was a cup of tea. A cold beer was probably more to his liking but was the one thing she didn't have in her refrigerator. "I'd understand if you'd rather not," she said.

He chuckled. "A cup of tea is fine."

"You sure?"

He chuckled again. "Yes, I'm positive."

"All right then." She opened the door and he followed her inside.

Beside the fact Jason thought she looked downright beautiful, Bella Bostwick smelled good, as well. He wished there was some way he could ignore the sudden warmth that flowed through his body from her scent streaming through his nostrils.

And then there was the way she was dressed. He had to admit that although she looked downright delectable in her jeans and silk blouse she also looked out of place in them. But as she walked gracefully in front of him, Jason thought that a man could endure a lot of sleepless nights dreaming about a Southern-belle backside shaped like hers.

"If you'll have a seat, Jason, I'll bring the tea right out."

He stopped walking as he realized she must have a pot already made. "All right."

He watched her walk into the kitchen, but instead of taking the seat like she'd offered, he kept standing as he glanced around taking in the changes she'd already made to the place. There were a lot of framed art pieces on the wall, a number of vases filled with flowers, throw rugs on the wood floor and fancy curtains attached to the windows. It was evident that a woman lived here. And she was some woman.

She hadn't hesitated to get her back up when she'd assumed his visit here was less than what he'd told her. He figured Kenneth Bostwick, in addition to no telling how many others, probably hadn't liked her decision not to sell her land and was giving her pure grief about it. He wouldn't be one of those against her decision.

He continued to glance around the room, noting the changes. There were a lot of things that remained the same, like Herman's favorite recliner, but she'd added a spiffy new sofa to go with it. It was just as well. The old one had seen better days. The old man had claimed he would be getting a new one this coming Christmas, not knowing when he'd said it he wouldn't be around.

Jason drew in a deep breath remembering the last time he'd seen Herman Bostwick alive. It had been a month before he'd died. Jason had come to check on him and to ride Hercules. Jason was one of the few people who could do so mainly because he was the one Herman had let break in the horse.

He glanced down to study the patterns on the throw rug beneath his feet thinking how unique looking they were when he heard her reenter the room. He looked up and a part of him wished he hadn't. The short medium brown curls framing her face made her mahogany colored skin appear soft to the touch and perfect for her hazel eyes and high cheekbones.

There was a refinement about her, but he had a feeling she was a force to be reckoned with if she had to be. She'd proven that earlier when she'd assumed he was there to question her sanity about moving here. Maybe he should be questioning his own sanity for not convincing her to move on and return to where she came from. No matter her best intentions, she wasn't cut out to be a rancher, not with her soft hands and manicured nails.

He believed there had to be some inner conflict driving her to try to run the ranch. He decided then and there that he would do whatever he could to help her succeed. And as she set the tea tray down on the table he knew at that moment she was someone he wanted to get to know better in the process.

"It's herbal tea. Do you want me to add any type of sweetener?" she asked.

"No," he said flatly, although he wasn't sure if he did or not. He wasn't a hot tea drinker, but did enjoy a glass of cold sweet tea from time to time. However, for some reason he felt he would probably enjoy his hot tea like he did his coffee—without anything added to it.

"I prefer mine sweet," she said softly, turning and smiling over at him. His guts tightened and he tried like hell to ignore the ache deep within and the attraction for this woman. He'd never felt anything like this before.

He was still standing and when she crossed the room toward him carrying his cup of tea, he had to forcibly propel air through his lungs with every step she took. Her beauty was brutal to the eyes but soothing to the soul, and he was enjoying the view in deep male appreciation. How old was she and what was she doing out here in the middle of nowhere trying to run a ranch?

"Here you are, Jason."

He liked the sound of his name from her lips and when he took the glass from her hands they touched in the process. Immediately, he felt his stomach muscles begin to clench.

"Thanks," he said, thinking he needed to step away from her and not let Bella Bostwick crowd his space. But he also very much wanted to keep her right there. Topping the list was her scent. He wasn't sure what perfume she was wearing but it was definitely an attention grabber, although her beauty alone would do the trick.

"You're welcome. Now I suggest we sit down or I'm going to get a crook in my neck staring up at you."

He heard the smile in her voice and then saw it on her lips. It stirred to life something inside of him and for a moment he wondered if her smile was genuine or practiced and quickly came to the conclusion it was genuine. During his thirty-four years he had met women who'd been as phony as a four-dollar bill but he had a feeling Bella Bostwick wasn't one of them. In fact, she might be a little too real for her own good.

"I don't want that to happen," he said, easing down on her sofa and stretching his long legs out in front of him. He watched as she then eased down in the comfortable looking recliner he had bought Herman five years ago for his seventy-fifth birthday.

Jason figured this was probably one of the craziest things he'd ever done, sit with a woman in her living room in the middle of the day and converse with her while sipping tea. But he was doing it and at that moment, he couldn't imagine any other place he'd rather be.

* * *

Bella took a sip of her tea and studied Jason over the rim of her cup. Who was he? Why was she so attracted to him? And why was he attracted to her? And she knew the latter was true. She'd felt it that night at the ball and she could feel it now. He was able to bring out desires in her that she never felt before but for some reason she didn't feel threatened by those feelings. Instead, although she really didn't know him, she felt he was a powerhouse of strength, tenderness and protectiveness all rolled into one. She knew he would never hurt her.

"So, tell me about yourself Jason," she heard herself say, wanting so much to hear about the man who seemed to be taking up so much space in her living room as well as in her mind.

A smile touched his lips when he said, "I'm a Westmoreland."

His words raised her curiosity up a notch. Was being a Westmoreland supposed to mean something? She hadn't heard any type of arrogance or egotism in his words, just a sense of pride, self-respect and honor.

"And what does being a Westmoreland mean?" she asked as she tucked her legs beneath her to get more comfortable in the chair.

She watched him take a sip of his tea. "There's a bunch of us, fifteen in fact," Jason said.

She nodded, taking in his response. "Fifteen?"

"Yes. And that's not counting the three Westmoreland wives and a cousin-in-law from Australia. In our family tree we've now become known as the Denver Westmorelands."

"Denver Westmorelands? Does that mean there are more Westmorelands in other parts of the country?"

"Yes, there are some who sprung from the Atlanta area. We have fifteen cousins there, as well. Most of them were at the Westmoreland charity ball."

An amused smile touched her lips. She recalled seeing them and remembered thinking how much they'd resembled in looks or height. Jason had been the only one she'd gotten a real good close-up view of, and the only one she'd held a conversation with before her uncle had practically dragged her away from the party that night.

She then decided to bring up something she'd detected at the ball. "You and my uncle Kenneth don't get along."

If her statement surprised him the astonishment was not reflected in his face. "No, we've never gotten along," he said as if the thought didn't bother him, in fact he preferred it that way.

She paused and waited on him to elaborate but he didn't. He just took another sip of tea.

"And why is that?"

He shrugged massive shoulders and the gesture made her body even more responsive to his. "I can't rightly say why we've never seen eye-to-eye on a number of things."

"What about my grandfather? Did you get along with him?"

He chuckled. "Actually I did. Herman and I had a good relationship that started back when I was kid. He taught me a lot about ranching and I enjoyed our chats."

She took a sip of her tea. "Did he ever mention anything about having a granddaughter?"

"No, but then I didn't know he had a son, either. The only family I knew about was Kenneth and their relationship was rather strained."

She nodded. She'd heard the story of how her father had left for college at the age of seventeen, never to return. Her uncle Kenneth claimed he wasn't sure what the disagreement had been between the two men since he himself had been a young kid at the time. David Bostwick had made his riches on the east coast, first as a land developer and then as an investor in all sorts of moneymaking ventures. That was how he'd met her mother, a Savannah socialite, daughter of a shipping magnate and ten years her senior. The marriage had been based more on increasing their wealth instead of love. She was well aware of both of her parents' supposedly discreet affairs.

And as far as Kenneth Bostwick was concerned, she knew that Herman's widowed father at the age of seventy married a thirty-something-year-old woman and Kenneth had been their only child. Bella gathered from bits and pieces she'd overheard from Kenneth's daughter, Elyse, that Kenneth and Herman had never gotten along because Herman thought Kenneth's mother, Belinda, hadn't been anything but a gold digger who married a man old enough to be her grandfather.

"Finding out Herman had a granddaughter came as a surprise to everyone around these parts."

Bella chuckled softly. "Yes, and it came as quite a surprise to me to discover I had a grandfather."

She saw the surprise that touched his face. "You didn't know about Herman?"

"No. I thought both my father's parents were dead. My father was close to forty when he married my mother and when I was in my teens he was in his fifties already so I assumed his parents were deceased since he never mentioned them. I didn't know about Herman until I got a summons to be present at the reading of the will. My parents didn't even mention anything about the funeral. They attended the services but only said they were leaving town to take care of business. I assumed it was one of their usual business trips. It was only when they returned that they mentioned that Herman's attorney had advised them that I was needed for the reading of the will in a week."

She pulled in a deep breath. "Needless to say, I wasn't happy that my parents had kept such a thing from me all those years. I felt whatever feud was between my father and grandfather was between them and should not have included me. I feel such a sense of loss at not having known Herman Bostwick."

Jason nodded. "He could be quite a character at times, trust me."

For some reason she felt she could trust him…and in fact, that she already did. "Tell me about him. I want to get to know the grandfather I never knew."

He smiled. "There's no way I can tell you everything about him in one day."

She returned the smile. "Then come back again for tea so we can talk. That is, if you don't mind."

She held her breath thinking he probably had a lot more things to do with his time than to sip tea with her. A man like him probably had other things on his mind when he was with someone of the opposite sex.

"No, I don't mind. In fact I'd rather enjoy it."

She inwardly sighed, suddenly feeling giddy, pleased. Jason Westmoreland was the type of man who could make his way into any woman's hot and wild fantasies, and he'd just agreed to indulge her by sharing tea with her occasionally to talk about the grandfather she'd never known.

"Well, I guess I'd better get back to work."

"And what do you do for a living?" she asked, without thinking about it.

"Several of my cousins and I are partners in a horse breeding and horse training venture. The horse that came in second last year at the Preakness was one of ours."

"Congratulations!"

"Thanks."

She then watched as he eased his body off her sofa to stand. And when he handed the empty teacup back to her, she felt her body tingle with the exchange when their hands touched and knew he'd felt it, as well.

"Thanks for the tea, Bella."

"You're welcome and you have an open invitation to come back for more."

He met her gaze, held it for a moment. "And I will."

Chapter 2

On Tuesday of the following week, Bella was in her car headed to town to purchase new appliances for her kitchen. Buying a stove and refrigerator might not be a big deal to some, but for her it would be a first. She was looking forward to it. Besides, it would get her mind off the phone call she'd gotten from her attorney first thing this morning.

Not wanting to think about the phone call, she thought about her friends back home instead. They had teased her that although she would be living out in the boondocks on a ranch, downtown Denver was half an hour away and that's probably where she would spend most of her time—shopping and attending various plays and parties. But she had discovered she liked being away from city life and hadn't missed it at all. She'd grown up in Savannah right on the ocean. Her parents' estate had been minutes from downtown and was the place where lavish parties were always held.

She had talked to her parents earlier today and found the conversation totally draining. Her father insisted she put the ranch up for sale and come home immediately. When the conversation ended she had been more determined than ever to keep as much distance between her and Savannah as possible.

She had been on the ranch for only three weeks and already the taste of freedom, to do whatever she wanted whenever she wanted, was a luxurious right she refused to give up. Although she missed waking up every morning to the scent of the ocean, she was becoming used to the crisp mountain air drenched in the rich fragrance of dahlias.

Her thoughts then shifted to something else or more precisely, someone else. Jason Westmoreland. Good to his word he had stopped by a few days ago to join her for tea. They'd had a pleasant conversation, and he'd told her more about her grandfather. She could tell Jason and Herman's relationship had been close. Part of her was glad that Jason had probably helped relieve Herman's loneliness.

Although her father refused to tell her what had happened to drive him away from home, she hoped to find out on her own. Her grandfather had kept a number of journals and she intended to start reading them this week. The only thing she knew from what Kenneth Bostwick had told her was that Herman's father, William, had remarried when Herman was in his twenties and married with a son of his own. That woman had been Kenneth's mother, which was why he was a lot younger than her father. In fact her father and Kenneth had few memories of each other since David Bost-wick had left home for college at the age of seventeen.

Jason had also answered questions about ranching and assured her that the man she'd kept on as foreman had worked for her grandfather for a number of years and knew what he was doing. Jason hadn't stayed long but she'd enjoyed his visit.

She found Jason to be kind and soft-spoken and whenever he talked in that reassuring tone she would feel safe, protected and confident that no matter what decisions she made regarding her life and the ranch, it would be okay. He also gave her the impression that she could and would make mistakes and that would be okay, too, as long as she learned from those mistakes and didn't repeat them.

She had gotten to meet some of his family members, namely the women, when they'd all shown up a couple of days ago with housewarming goodies to welcome her to the community. Pamela, Chloe and Lucia had married into the family, and Megan and Bailey were Westmorelands by birth. They told her about Gemma, who was Megan and Bailey's sister and how she had gotten married earlier that year, moved with her husband to Australia and was expecting their first child.

Pamela and Chloe had brought their babies and being in their presence only reinforced a desire Bella always had of being a mother. She loved children and hoped to marry and have a houseful one day. And when she did, she intended for her relationship with them to be different than the one she had with her own parents.

The women had invited her to dinner at Pamela's home Friday evening so that she could meet the rest of the family. She thought the invitation to dinner was a nice gesture and downright neighborly on their part. They were surprised she had already met Jason because he hadn't mentioned anything to them about meeting her.

She wasn't sure why he hadn't when all the evidence led her to believe the Westmorelands were a close-knit group. But then she figured men tended to keep their activities private and not share them with anyone. He said he would be dropping by for tea again tomorrow and she looked forward to his visit.

It was obvious there was still an intense attraction between them, yet he always acted honorably in her presence. He would sit across from her with his long legs stretched out in front of him and sip tea while she talked. She tried not to dominate the conversation but found he was someone she could talk to and someone who listened to what she had to say. She could see him now sitting there absorbed in whatever she said while displaying a ruggedness she found totally sexy.

And he had shared some things about himself. She knew he was thirty-four and a graduate of the University of Denver. He also shared with her how his parents and uncle and aunt had been killed in a plane crash when he was eighteen, leaving him and his fourteen siblings and cousins without parents. With admiration laced in his voice he had talked about his older brother Dillon and his cousin Ramsey and how the two men had been determined to keep the family together and how they had.

She couldn't help but compare his large family to her smaller one. Although she loved her parents she couldn't recall a time she and her parents had ever been close. While growing up they had relinquished her care to sitters while they jet-setted all over the country. At times she thought they'd forgotten she existed. When she got older she understood her father's obsession with trying to keep up with his young wife. Eventually she saw that obsession diminish when he found other interests and her mother did, as well.

That was why at times the idea of having a baby without a husband appealed to her, although doing such a thing would send her parents into cardiac arrest. But she couldn't concern herself with how her parents would react if she chose to go that route. Moving here was her first stab at emancipation and whatever she decided to do would be her decision. But for a woman who'd never slept with a man to contemplate having a baby from one was a bit much for her to absorb right now.

She pulled into the parking lot of one of the major appliance stores. When she returned home she would meet with her foreman to see how things were going. Jason had said such meetings were necessary and she should be kept updated on what went on at her ranch.

Moments later as she got out of her car she decided another thing she needed to do was buy a truck. *A truck.* She chuckled, thinking her mother would probably gag at the thought of her driving a truck instead of being chauffeured around in a car. But her parents had to realize and accept her life was changing and the luxurious life she used to have was now gone.

As soon as she entered the store a salesperson was right on her heels and it didn't take long to make the purchases she needed because she knew just what she wanted. She'd always thought stainless steel had a way of enhancing the look of a kitchen and figured sometime next year she would give the kitchen a total make-

over with granite countertops and new tile flooring,
as well. But she would take things one step at a time.

"Bella?"

She didn't have to turn to know who'd said her
name. As far as she was concerned, no one could pronounce it in the same rugged yet sexy tone as Jason.
Although she had just seen him a few days ago when
he'd joined her for tea, there was something about seeing him now that sent sensations coursing through her.

She turned around and there he stood dressed in a
pair of jeans that hugged his sinewy thighs and long,
muscular legs, a blue chambray shirt and a lightweight
leather jacket that emphasized the broadness of his
shoulders.

She smiled up at him. "Jason, what a pleasant surprise."

It was a pleasant surprise for Jason, as well. He had
walked into the store and immediately, like radar, he
had picked up on her presence and all it took was following her scent to find her.

"Same here. I had to come into town to pick up a
new hot water heater for the bunkhouse," he said, smiling down at her. He shoved his hands into his pockets; otherwise, he would have been tempted to pull her
to him and kiss her. Kissing Bella was something he
wanted but hadn't gotten around to doing. He didn't
want to rush things and didn't want her to think his
interest in her had anything to do with wanting to buy
Hercules, because that wasn't the case. His interest in
her was definitely one of want and need.

"I met the ladies in your family the other day. They
came to pay me a visit," she said.

"Did they?"

"Yes."

He'd known they would eventually get around to doing so. The ladies had discussed a visit to welcome her to the community.

"They're all so nice," she said

"I think they are nice, too. Did you get whatever you needed?" He wondered if she would join him for lunch if he were to ask.

"Yes, my refrigerator and stove will be delivered by the end of the week. I'm so excited."

He couldn't help but laugh. She was genuinely excited. If she got that excited over appliances he could imagine how she would react over jewelry. "Will you be in town for a while, Bella?"

"Yes. I have a meeting with Marvin later this evening."

He raised a brow. "Is everything all right?"

She nodded, smiling. "Yes. I'm just having a weekly meeting like you suggested."

He was glad she had taken his advice. "How about joining me for lunch? There's a place not far from here that serves several nice dishes."

She smiled up at him. "I'd love that."

Jason knew he would love it just as much. He had been thinking about her a lot, especially at night when he'd found it hard to sleep. She was getting to him. No, she had gotten to him. He didn't know of any other woman that he'd been this attracted to. There was something about her. Something that was drawing him to her on a personal level that he could not control. But then a part of him didn't want to control it. Nor did he want to fight it. He wanted to see how far it would go and where it would stop.

"Do you want me to follow you there, Jason?"

No, he wanted her in the same vehicle with him. "We can ride in my truck. Your car will be fine parked here until we return."

"Okay."

As he escorted her toward the exit, she glanced up at him. "What about your hot water heater?"

"I haven't picked it out yet but that's fine since I know the brand I want."

"All right."

Together they walked out of the store toward his truck. It was a beautiful day in May but when he felt her shiver beside him, he figured a beautiful day in Savannah would be a day in the eighties. Here in Denver if they got sixty-something degree weather in June they would be ecstatic.

He took his jacket off and placed it around her shoulders. She glanced up at him. "You didn't have to do that."

He smiled. "Yes, I did. I don't want you to get cold on me." She was wearing a pair of black slacks and a light blue cardigan sweater. As always she looked ultrafeminine.

And now she was wearing his jacket. They continued walking and when they reached his truck she glanced up and her gaze connected with his and he could feel electricity sparking to life between them. She looked away quickly, as if she'd been embarrassed that their attraction to each other was so obvious.

"Do you want your jacket back now?" she asked softly.

"No, keep it on. I like seeing you in it."

She blushed again and at that moment he got the most ridiculous notion that perhaps this sort of intense attraction between two people was sort of new to Bella. He wouldn't be surprised to discover that she had several innocent bones in her body; enough to shove him in another direction rather quickly. But for some reason he was staying put.

She nibbled on her bottom lip. "Why do you like seeing me in it?"

"Because I do. And because it's mine and you're in it."

He wasn't sure if what he'd said made much sense or if she was confused even more. But what he *was* sure about was that he was determined to find out just how much Bella Bostwick knew about men. And what she didn't know he was going to make it his business to teach her.

Bella was convinced there was nothing more compelling than the feel of wearing the jacket belonging to a man whose very existence represented true masculinity. It permeated her with his warmth, his scent and his aura in every way. She was filled with an urge to get more, to know more and to feel more of Jason Westmoreland. And as she stared at him through the car's window as he pulled out his cell phone to make arrangements for their lunch, she couldn't help but feel the hot rush of blood in her veins while heat churned deep down inside of her.

And there lay the crux of her problem. As beguiling as the feelings taking over her senses, making ingrained curiosity get the best of her, she knew better than to step beyond the range of her experience. That range didn't extend beyond what the nuns at the private Catholic schools she'd attended most of her life had warned her about. It was a range good girls just didn't go beyond.

Jason was the type of man women dreamed about. He was what fantasies were made of. She watched him ease his phone back into the pocket of his jeans, walk around the front of his truck to get in. He was the type of man a woman would love to snuggle up with on a cold Colorado winter night…especially the kind her parents and uncle had said she would have to endure. Just the thought of being with him in front of a roaring fire that blazed in a fireplace would be an unadulterated fantasy come true for any woman…. And her greatest fear.

"You're comfortable?" he asked, placing a wide-brimmed Stetson on his head.

She glanced over at him and she held his gaze for a moment and then nodded. "Yes, I'm fine. Thanks."

"You're welcome."

He backed up the truck and then they headed out of the parking lot in silence but she was fully aware of his hands that gripped the steering wheel. They were large and strong hands and she could imagine those same hands gripping her. That thought made heat seep into every cell and pore of her body, percolating her bones and making her surrender to something she'd never had before.

Her virginal state had never bothered her before and it didn't really bother her now except the unknown was making the naughtiness in her come out. It was making her anticipate things she was better off not getting.

"You've gotten quiet on me, Bella," Jason said.

She glanced over at him and again met his gaze thinking, yes she had. But she figured he didn't want to hear her thoughts out loud and certain things she needed to keep to herself.

"Sorry," she said. "I was thinking about Friday," she decided to say.

"Friday?"

"Yes. Pamela invited me to dinner."

"She did?"

Bella heard the surprise in his voice. "Yes. She said it would be the perfect opportunity to meet everyone. It seems all of my neighbors are Westmorelands. You're just the one living the closest to me."

"And what makes you so preoccupied about Friday?"

"Meeting so many of your family members."

He chuckled. "You'll survive."

"Thanks for the vote of confidence." Then she said, "Tell me about them." He had already told her some but she wanted to hear more. And the ladies who came to visit had also shared some of their family history with her. But she wanted to hear his version just to hear the husky sound of his voice, to feel how it would stir across her skin and tantalize several parts of her body.

"You already met the ones who think they run things, namely the women."

She laughed. "They don't?"

"We let them think that way because we're slowly getting outnumbered. Although Gemma is in Australia she still has a lot to say and whenever we take a vote about anything, of course she sides with the women."

She grinned. "You all actually take votes on stuff?"

"Yes, we believe in democracy. The last time we voted we had to decide where Christmas dinner would be held. Usually we hold everything at Dillon's because he has the main family house, but his kitchen was being renovated so we voted to go to Ramsey's."

"All of you have homes?"

"Yes. When we each turned twenty-five we inherited one hundred acres. It was fun naming my own spread."

"Yours is Jason's Place, right?"

He smiled over at her. "That's right."

While he'd been talking her body had responded to the sound of his voice as if it was on a mission to capture each and every nuance. She inhaled deeply and they began chatting again but this time about her family. He'd been honest about his family so she decided to be honest about hers.

"My parents and I aren't all that close and I can't remember a time that we were. They didn't support my move out here," she said and wondered why she'd wanted to share that little detail.

"Is it true that Kenneth is upset you didn't sell the land to Myers Smith?" he asked.

She nodded slowly. "Yes, he told me himself that he thinks I made a mistake in deciding to move here and is looking forward to the day I fail so he can say, 'I told you so.'"

Jason shook his head, finding it hard to believe this was a family member who was hoping for her failure. "Are he and your father close?"

Bella chuckled softly. "They barely know each other. According to Dad he was already in high school when Kenneth was born, although technically Kenneth is my father's half uncle. My father's grandfather married Kenneth's mother who was twenty-five years his junior."

"Do you have any other family, like cousins?"

She shook her head. "Both my parents were the only children. Of course Uncle Kenneth has a son and daughter but they hadn't spoken to me since the reading of the will. Uncle Kenneth only spoke to me when he thought I'd be selling the ranch and livestock to his friend."

By the time he had brought the truck to a stop in front of a huge building, she had to wipe tears of laughter from her eyes when he'd told her about all the trouble the younger Westmorelands had gotten into.

"I just can't imagine your cousin Bailey—who has such an innocent look about her—being such a hell-raiser while growing up."

Jason laughed. "Hey, don't let the innocent act fool you. The cousins Aiden and Adrian are at Harvard and Bane joined the navy. We talked Bailey into hanging around here to attend college so we could keep an eye on her."

He chuckled and then added, "It turned out to be a mistake when she began keeping an eye on us instead."

When he turned off the truck's engine she glanced through the windshield at the building looming in front of them and raised a brow. "This isn't a restaurant?"

He glanced over at her. "No, it's not. It's the Blue Ridge Management, a company my father and uncle founded over forty years ago. After they were killed Dillon and Ramsey took over. Ramsey eventually left Dillon in charge to become a sheep rancher and Dillon is currently CEO."

He glanced out the windshield to look up at the forty-story building with a pensive look on his face and moments later added, "My brother Riley holds an upper management position here. My cousins Zane and Derringer, as well as myself, worked for the company after college until last year when we decided to join the Montana Westmorelands in the horse training and breeding business."

He smiled. "I guess you can say that nine-to-five gig was never our forte. Like Ramsey we prefer being outdoors."

She nodded and followed his gaze to the building. "And we're eating lunch here?"

He glanced over at her. "Yes, I have my office that I still use from time to time to conduct business. I called ahead and Dillon's secretary took care of everything for me."

A few moments later they were walking into the massive lobby of Blue Ridge Land Management and the first thing Bella noticed was the huge, beautifully decorated atrium with a waterfall amidst a replica of mountains complete with blooming flowers and other types of foliage. After stopping at the security guard station they caught an elevator up to the executive floor.

"I remember coming up here a lot with my dad," Jason said softly, reflecting on that time. "Whenever he would work on the weekends, he would gather us all together to get us out of Mom's hair for a while. Once we got up to the fortieth floor we knew he would probably find something for us to do."

He chuckled and then added, "But just in case he didn't. I would always travel with a pack of crayons in my back pocket."

Bella smiled. She could just imagine Jason and his six brothers crowded on the elevator with their father. Although he would be working they would have gotten to spend the day with him nonetheless. She couldn't ever recall a time her father had taken her to work with him. In fact she hadn't known where the Bostwick Firm had been located until she was well into her teens. Her mother never worked outside the home but was mainly the hostess for the numerous parties her parents would give.

It seemed the ride to the top floor took forever. A few times the elevator stopped to let people either on or off. Some of them recognized Jason and he took the time to inquire about the family members he knew, especially their children or grandchildren.

The moment they stepped off the elevator onto the fortieth floor Bella could tell immediately that this was where all the executive offices were located. The furniture was plush and the carpeting thick and luxurious looking. She was quickly drawn to huge paintings of couples adorning the walls in the center of the lobby. Intrigued she moved toward them.

"These are my parents," Jason said, coming to stand by her side. "And the couple in the picture over there is my aunt and uncle. My father and Uncle Thomas were close, barely fourteen months apart in age. And my mother and Aunt Susan got along beautifully and were just as close as sisters."

"And they died together," she whispered softly. It was a statement not a question since he had already told her what had happened when they'd all died in a plane crash. Bella studied the portrait of his parents in detail. Jason favored his father a lot but he definitely had his mother's mouth.

"She was beautiful," she said. "So was your aunt Susan. I take it Ramsey and Chloe's daughter was named after her?"

Jason nodded. "Yes, and she's going to grow up to be a beauty just like her grandmother."

She glanced over at him. "And what was your mother's name?"

"Clarisse. And my father was Adam." Jason then looked down at his watch. "Come on. Our lunch should have arrived by now."

He surprised her when he took her arm and led her toward a bank of offices and stopped at one in particular with his name on it. She felt her heart racing. Although he hadn't called it as such, she considered this lunch a date.

That thought was reinforced when he opened the door to his office and she saw the table set for lunch. The room was spacious and had a downtown view of Denver. The table, completely set with everything, including a bottle of wine, had been placed by the window so they could enjoy the view while they ate.

"Jason, the table and the view are beautiful. Thanks for inviting me to lunch."

"You're welcome," he said, pulling a chair out for her. "There's a huge restaurant downstairs for the employees but I thought we'd eat in here for privacy."

"That's considerate of you."

And done for purely selfish reasons, Jason thought as he took the chair across from her. He liked having her all to himself. Although he wasn't a tea drinker, he had become one and looked forward to visiting her each week to sit down and converse while drinking tea. He enjoyed her company. He glanced over at her and their gazes connected. Their response to each other always amazed him because it seemed so natural and out of control. He couldn't stop the heat flowing all through his body at that precise moment even if he wanted to.

He doubted she knew she had a dazed look in the depths of her dark eyes or that today everything about her looked soft, feminine but not overly so. Just to the right degree to make a man appreciate being a man.

She slowly broke eye contact with him to lift the lid off the platter and when she glanced back up she was smiling brightly. "Spaghetti."

He couldn't help but return her smile. "Yes. I recall you saying the other day how much you enjoyed Italian food." In fact they had talked about a number of things in the hour he had been there.

"I do love Italian food," she said excitedly, taking a hold of her fork.

He poured wine into their glasses and glanced over and caught her slurping up a single strand of spaghetti through a pair of luscious lips. His gut clenched and when she licked her lips he couldn't help but envy the noodle.

When she caught him staring she blushed, embarrassed at being caught doing something so inelegant. "Sorry. I know that showed bad manners but I couldn't resist." She smiled. "It was the one thing I always wanted to do around my parents whenever we ate spaghetti that I couldn't do."

He chuckled. "No harm done. In fact you can slurp the rest of it if you'd like. It's just you and me."

She grinned. "Thanks, but I better not." He then

watched as she took her fork in her hand, preparing to eat the rest of her spaghetti in the classical and cultured way.

"I take it your parents were strong disciplinarians," he said, taking a sip of his wine.

Her smile slowly faded. "They still are or at least they try to be. Even now they will stop at nothing to get me back to Savannah so they can keep an eye on me. I got a call from my attorney this morning warning me they've possibly found a loophole in the trust fund my grandparents established for me before they died."

He lifted a brow. "What kind of a loophole?"

"One that says I'm supposed to be married after the first year. If that's true I have less than three months," she said in disgust. "I'm sure they're counting on me returning to Savannah to marry Hugh."

He sipped his wine. "Hugh?"

She met his gaze and he could see the troubled look in hers. "Yes, Hugh Pierce. His family comes from Savannah's old money and my parents have made up their minds that Hugh and I are a perfect match."

He watched her shoulders rise and fall after releasing several sighs. Evidently the thought of becoming Mrs. Hugh Pierce bothered her. Hell, the thought bothered him, as well.

In a way he should be overjoyed, elated, that there was a possibility she was moving back to Savannah. That meant her ranch and Hercules would probably be up for sale. And when they were, he would be ready to make her an offer he hoped she wouldn't refuse. He knew he wasn't the only one wanting the land and no telling how many others wanted Hercules, but he was determined that the prized stallion wouldn't fall into anyone's hands but his.

And yet, he wasn't overjoyed or elated at the thought that she would return to Savannah.

He got the impression her parents were controlling people or at least they tried to be. He began eating, wondering why her parents wanted to shove this Hugh Pierce down her throat when she evidently wasn't feeling the guy. Would they coerce her to marry someone just because the man came from "old money"?

He forced the thought to the back of his mind, thinking who she ended up marrying was no concern of his. But making sure his name headed the list as a potential buyer for her ranch and livestock was. He glanced over at her. "When will you know what you'll have to do?"

She looked up after taking a sip of her wine. "I'm not sure. I have a good attorney but I have to admit my parents' attorney is more experienced in such matters. In other words, he's crafty as sin. I'm sure when my grandparents drew up my trust they thought they were looking out for my future because in their social circles, ideally, a young woman married by her twenty-sixth birthday. For her to attend college was just a formality since she was expected to marry a man who had the means to take care of her."

"And your parents have no qualms in forcing you to marry?"

"No, not one iota," she said without pause. "They don't truly care about my happiness. All they care about is that they would be proving once again they control my life and always will."

He heard the trembling in her voice and when she looked down as to study her silverware, he knew her composure was being threatened. At that moment, something inside of him wanted to get up, pull her into his arms and tell her things would be all right. But he couldn't rightly say that. He had no way of knowing they would be for her, given the situation she was in. Actually it was her problem not his. Still another part of him couldn't help regretting that her misfortune could end up being his golden opportunity.

"I thought I'd finally gotten free of my parents' watchful eyes at college, only to discover they had certain people in place, school officials and professors, keeping tabs on me and reporting to them on my behavior," she said, interrupting his thoughts.

"And I thought, I truly believed, the money I'm getting from my trust fund and inheriting the ranch were my way of living my life the way I want and an end to being under my parents' control. I was going to exert my freedom for the first time in my life."

She paused briefly. "Jason. I really love it here. I've been able to live the way I want, do the things I want. It's a freedom I've never had and I don't want to give it up."

They sat staring at each other for what seemed like several mind-numbing moments and then Jason spoke. "Then don't give it up. Fight them for what you want."

Her shoulders slumped again. "Although I plan to try, it's easier said than done. My father is a well-known and powerful man in Savannah and a lot of the judges are his personal friends. For anyone to even try something as archaic as forcing someone to marry is ludicrous. But my parents will do it with their friends' help if it brings me to heel."

Once again Bella fell silent for a moment. "When

I received word about Herman and confronted my father as to why he never told me about his life here in
Denver, he wouldn't tell me, but I've been reading my
grandfather's journals. He claims my father hated living here while growing up. His mother had visited this
area from Savannah, met Herman and fell in love and
never went back east. Her family disowned her for it.
But after college my father moved to Savannah and
sought out his maternal grandparents and they were
willing to accept him in their good graces but only
if he never reminded them of what they saw as their
daughter's betrayal, so he didn't."

She then straightened her shoulders and forced a
smile to her lips. "Let's change the subject," she suggested. "Thinking about my woes is rather depressing
and you've made lunch too nice for me to be depressed
about anything."

They enjoyed the rest of their meal conversing about
other things. He told her about his horse breeding business and about how he and the Atlanta Westmorelands
had discovered they were related through his great-
grandfather Raphel Westmoreland.

"Was your grandfather really married to all those
women?" she asked after he told her the tale of how
Raphel had become a black sheep in the family after
running off in the early nineteen hundreds with the
preacher's wife and all the other wives he supposedly
collected along the way.

He took another sip of wine. "That's what everyone is trying to find out. We need to know if there are
any more Westmorelands out there. Megan is hiring
a private detective to help solve the puzzle about Ra-

phel's wives. We've eliminated two and now we have two more to check out."

When they finished the main course Jason used his cell phone to call downstairs to say they were ready for dessert. Moments later banana pudding was delivered to them. Bella thought the dessert was simply delicious. She usually didn't eat a lot of sweets but once she'd taken a bite she couldn't help but finish the whole thing.

A short while later, after they'd devoured the dessert with coffee, Jason checked his watch. "We're right on schedule. I'll take you back in time to get your car so you can make your meeting with Marvin."

Jason stood, rounded the table and reached for her hand. The instant they touched it seemed a rush of heated sensations tore through the both of them at the same time. It was absorbed in their bones, tangled their flesh and he all but shuddered under the impact. The alluring scent of her filled his nostrils and his breath was freed on a ragged sigh.

Some part of his brain told him to take a step back and put distance between them. But then another part told him he was facing the inevitable. There had been this blazing attraction, this tantalizing degree of lust between them from the beginning. For him it had been since the moment he had seen her when she'd entered the ballroom with Kenneth Bostwick. He had known then he wanted her.

They stared at each other and for a second he thought she would avert her gaze from his but she didn't. She couldn't resist him any more than he could resist her and they both knew it, which was probably why, when he took a step closer and began lowering his head, she went on tiptoes and lifted her mouth to meet his.

The moment their lips connected, a low, guttural sound rumbled from deep in his throat and he deepened the kiss the moment she wrapped her arms around his neck. His tongue slid easily into her mouth, exploring one side and then another, as well as all the areas in between before tangling with her own, mating deeply, and when she reciprocated the move sent a jolt of desire all through his bones.

And then it was on.

Holy crap. Hunger the likes he'd never felt before infiltrated his mind. He felt a sexual connection with her that he'd never felt with any woman before. As his tongue continued to slide against hers, parts of him felt primed and ready to explode at any moment. Never had he encountered such overwhelming passion, such blatant desire and raw primal need.

His mouth was doing a good job tasting her, but the rest of him wanted to feel her, draw her closer into his arms. On instinct he felt her lean into him, plastering their bodies from breast to knee and as Jason deepened the kiss even more, he groaned, wondering if he would never get enough of her.

Bella was feeling the same way about Jason. No man had ever held her this close, taken her mouth this passionately and made sensations she'd never felt before rush through her quicker than the speed of light.

And she felt him, his erection, rigid and throbbing, against her middle, pressing hard at the juncture of her thighs, making her feel sensations there—right there—she hadn't felt before. It was doing more than just tingling. She was left aching in that very spot. She felt like a mass of kerosene and he was a torch set to ignite her, making her explode into flames. He was all solid muscle pressing against her and she wanted it all. She wanted him. She wasn't sure what wanting him entailed but she knew he was the only man who made her feel this way. He was the only man she wanted to make her feel this way.

When at last he drew his mouth away from her, his face remained close. Acting by instinct, she took her tongue and licked around his lips from corner to corner, not ready to relinquish the taste of him. When a guttural sound emitted from his throat, need rammed through her and when she tilted her lips toward his, he took her mouth once again. He eased his tongue into her mouth like it had every right to be there and at the moment she was of the conclusion that it did.

He slowly broke off the kiss and stared into her face for a long moment before caressing his thumb across her lips then running his fingers through the curls on her head.

"I guess we better leave now so you won't miss your meeting," he said in a deep, husky tone.

Unable to utter a single word she merely nodded.

And when he took her hand and entwined her fingers in his, the sensations she'd felt earlier were still strong, nearly overpowering, but she was determined to fight it this time. And every time after that. She could not become involved with anyone, especially someone like Jason. And especially not now.

She had enough on her plate in dealing with the ranch and her parents. She had to keep her head on straight and not get caught up in the desires of the flesh. She didn't need a lover; she needed a game plan.

And as Jason led her out of his office, she tried sorting out all the emotions she was feeling. She'd just been kissed senseless and now she was trying to convince herself that no matter what, it couldn't happen again.

Only problem with that was her mind was declaring one thing and her body was claiming another.

Chapter 3

He was in serious trouble.

Jason rubbed his hand across his face as he watched Bella rush off toward her car. He made sure she had gotten inside and driven off before pulling out of the parking lot behind her. The Westmoreland men were known to have high testosterone levels but his had never given him pause until today and only with Bella Bostwick.

He wouldn't waste his time wondering why he had kissed her since he knew the reason. She was walking femininity at its finest, temptation not too many men could resist and a lustful shot in any man's arms. He had gotten a sampling of all three. And it hadn't been a little taste but a whole whopping one. Now that he knew her flavor he wanted to savor it again and again and again.

When he brought his truck to a stop at a traffic light he checked his watch. Bella wasn't the only one who had a meeting this afternoon. He, Zane and Derringer had a conference call with their partners in Montana in less than an hour. He hadn't forgotten about the meeting but spending time with Bella had been something he hadn't been willing to shorten. Now with the taste of her still lingering in his mouth, he was glad he hadn't.

He shook his head, still finding it hard to believe just how well they had connected with that kiss, which made him wonder how they would connect in other ways and places…like in the bedroom.

The thought of her naked, thighs opened while he entered her was something he couldn't get out of his mind. He was burning for her and although he'd like to think it was only a physical attraction he wasn't sure that was the case. But then if it wasn't the case, what was it?

He didn't get a chance to think any further because at that moment his cell phone rang. He pulled it off his belt and saw it was his cousin Derringer. The newlywed of just a little over a month had been the last person he'd thought would fall in love with any woman. But he had and Jason could see why. Lucia was as precious as they came and everyone thought she was a great addition to the Westmoreland family.

"Yes, Derringer?"

"Hey, man, where are you? Did you forget about today's meeting?"

Jason couldn't help but smile as he remembered how he'd called to ask Derringer the same question since he'd gotten married. It seemed these days it was hard for his cousin to tear himself away from his wife at times.

"No, I didn't forget and I'm less than thirty minutes away."

"Okay. And I hear your lady is joining the family for dinner on Friday night."

He considered that for a moment. Had anyone else made that comment he probably would have gotten irritated by it, but Derringer was Derringer and the two people who knew more than anyone that he didn't have a "lady" were his cousins Derringer and Zane. Knowing that was the case he figured Derringer was fishing for information.

"I don't have a *lady* and you very well know it, Derringer."

"Do I? If that's the case when did you become a tea sipper?"

He laughed as his gaze held steady to the road. "Ah, I see our precious Bailey has been talking."

"Who else? Bella might have mentioned it to the ladies when they went visiting, but of course it's Bailey who's decided you have the hots for the Southern belle. And those were Bailey's words not mine."

"Thanks for clarifying that for me." The hots weren't all he had for Bella Bostwick. Blood was pumping fast and furious in his veins at the thought of the kiss they had shared.

"No problem. So level with me, Jason. What's going on with you and the Southern Bella?"

Jason smiled. The Southern Bella fit her. But then so did the Sensuous Bella. The Sexy Bella. The Sumptuous Bella. "And what makes you think something is going on?"

"I know you."

True. Derringer and Zane knew him better than any of the other Westmorelands because they'd always been close, thick as thieves while growing up. "I admit I'm attracted to her but what man wouldn't be? Otherwise, it's not that serious."

"You sure?"

Jason's hand tightened on his steering wheel—that was the crux of his problem. When it came to Bella the only thing he was sure about was that he wanted her in a way he'd never wanted any other woman. When they'd kissed she kissed him back in a way that had his body heating up just thinking how her tongue had mated with his. He had loved the way her silken curls had felt flowing through his fingers and how perfect their bodies fit together.

He was probably treading on dangerous ground but for reasons he didn't quite understand, he couldn't admit to being sure right now. So instead of outright lying he decided to plead the fifth by saying, "I'll get back to you on that."

Irritation spread all through his gut at the thought that he hadn't given Derringer an answer mainly because he couldn't. And for a man who'd always been decisive when it came to a woman's place in his heart, he could just imagine what Derringer was thinking.

He was trying not to think the same thing himself. Hell, he'd only set out to be a good neighbor and then realized how much he enjoyed her company. And then there had been the attraction he hadn't been able to overlook.

"I'll see you when you get here, Jason. Have a safe

drive in," Derringer said without further comment about Bella.

"Will do."

Bella stood staring out her bedroom window at the mountains. Her meeting with Marvin had been informative as well as a little overwhelming. But she had been able to follow everything the man had said. Heading the list was Hercules. The horse was restless, agitated and it seemed when Hercules wasn't in a good mood everybody knew it.

According to Marvin, Hercules hadn't been ridden in a while mainly because very few men would go near him. The only man capable to handling Hercules was Jason. The same Jason she had decided to avoid from now on. She recognized danger when she saw it and in this case it was danger she could feel. Physically.

Even now she could remember Jason mesmerizing her with his smile, seducing her with his kiss and making her groan over and over again. And there was the way his gaze had scanned over her body while in the elevator as they left his office after lunch, or the hot, lusty look he gave her when she got out of the truck at the appliance store. That look had her rushing off as if a pack of pit bulls were nipping at her heels.

And last but not least were Jason's hands on her. Those big, strong hands had touched her in places that had made her pause for breath, had made sensations overtake her and had made her put her guard up in a way she didn't feel safe in letting down.

Of course she'd known they were attracted to each other from the first, but she hadn't expected that attraction to become so volatile and explosive. And she'd experienced all that from just one kiss. Heaven help them if they went beyond kissing.

If he continued to come around, if he continued to spend time with her in any way, they would be tempted to go beyond that. Today proved she was virtually putty in his hands and she didn't want to think about what that could mean if it continued. She liked it but then she was threatened by it. She was just getting to feel free and the last thing she wanted to be was held in bondage by anything, especially by emotions she couldn't quite understand. She wasn't ready to become the other part of anyone. Jeez, she was just finding herself, enjoying her newfound independence. She didn't want to give it up before experiencing it fully.

At that moment her cell phone went off and she rolled her eyes when she saw the caller was her mother. She pulled in a deep breath before saying, "Yes, Mother?"

"I'm sure you've heard from your attorney about that little stipulation we found out about in your trust fund. My mother was definitely smart to think of it."

Bella frowned. "Yes, I heard all about it." Of course Melissa Bostwick would take the time to call and gloat. And of course she wanted to make it seem that they had discovered the stipulation by accident when the truth was that they'd probably hired a team of attorneys to look for anything in the trust fund they could use against her to keep her in line. If they had their way she would be dependent on them for life.

"Good. Your father and I expect you to stop this nonsense immediately and come home."

"Sorry, Mom, but I am home."

"No, you're not and if you continue with this foolishness you will be sorry. With no money coming in, what on earth will you do?"

"Get a job I guess."

"Don't be ridiculous."

"I'm being serious. Sorry you can't tell the difference."

There was a pause and then her mother asked, "Why do you always want to have your way?"

"Because it's my way to have. I'm twenty-five for heaven's sake. You and Dad need to let me live my own life."

"We will but not there, and Hugh's been asking about you."

"That's nice. Is there anything else you wanted, Mom?"

"For you to stop being difficult."

"If wanting to live my life the way I want is being difficult then get prepared for more difficult days ahead. Goodbye, Mom."

Out of respect Bella didn't hang up the phone until she heard her mother's click. And when she did she clicked off and shook her head. Her parents were so sure they had her where they wanted her.

And that possibility bothered her more than anything.

Jason glanced around the room. All of his male cousins had Bella to the side conversing away with her. No doubt they were as fascinated by her intellect as well as her beauty. And things had been that way since she'd arrived. More than once he'd sent Zane dirty looks that basically told his cousin to back off.

Why he'd done such a thing he wasn't sure. He and Bella weren't an item or anything of the sort.

In fact, to his way of thinking, she was acting rather coolly toward him. Although she was polite enough, no one would have thought he had devoured her mouth the way he had three days ago in his office. And maybe that was the reason she was acting this way. No one was supposed to know. It was their secret. Right?

Wrong.

He knew his family well, a lot better than she did. Their acting like cordial acquaintances only made them suspect. His brother Riley had already voiced his suspicions. "Trouble in paradise with the Southern Bella?"

He'd frown and had been tempted to tell Riley there was no trouble in paradise because he and Bella didn't have that kind of relationship. They had kissed only once for heaven's sake. Twice, if you were to take into consideration that he'd kissed her a second time that day before leaving his office.

So, okay, they had kissed twice. No big deal. He drew in a deep breath wondering if it wasn't a big deal, why was he making it one? Why had he come early and anticipated her arrival like a kid waiting for Christmas to get here?

Everyone who knew him, especially his family, was well aware that he dated when it suited him and his reputation with women was nothing like Derringer's had been or Zane's was. It didn't come close. The thought of meeting someone and getting married and having a family was something at the bottom of his list, but at least he didn't mind claiming it was on his list. That was something some of his other single brothers and cousins refused to do.

"You're rather quiet tonight, Jason."

He glanced over and saw his cousin Bailey had come to stand beside him and knew why she was there. She wanted to not just pick his brain but to dissect his mind. "I'm no quieter than usual, Bail."

She tilted her head and looked up at him. "Hmm, I think you are. Does Bella have anything to do with it?"

He took a sip of his wine. "And what makes you think that?"

She shrugged. "Because you keep glancing over there at her when you think no one is looking."

"That's not true."

She smiled. "Yes, it is. You probably don't realize you're doing it."

He frowned. Was that true? Had he been that obvious whenever he'd glanced over at Bella? Of course someone like Bailey—who made it her business to keep up with everything and everyone or tried to—would notice such a thing.

"I thought we were just having dinner," he decided to say. "I didn't know it was an all-out dinner party."

Bailey grinned. "I remember the first time Ramsey brought Chloe to introduce her to the family. He'd thought the same thing."

Nodding, he remembered that time. "Only difference in that is that Ramsey *brought* Chloe. I didn't bring Bella nor did I invite her."

"Are you saying you wished she wasn't here?"

He hated when Bailey tried putting words into his mouth. And speaking of mouth...he glanced across the room to Bella and watched hers move and couldn't help remembering all he'd done to that mouth when he'd kissed her.

"Jason?"

He then recalled what Bailey had asked him and figured until he gave her an answer she wasn't going anywhere. "No, that's not what I'm saying and you darn well know it. I don't have a problem with Bella being here. I think it's important for her to get to know her neighbors."

But did his brothers and cousins have to stay in her face, hang on to her every word and check her out so thoroughly? He knew everyone who hadn't officially met her had been taken with her the moment Dillon had opened the door for her. She had walked in with a gracefulness and pristine elegance that made every male in the house appreciate not only her beauty but her poise, refinement and charming personality.

Her outfit, an electric-blue wrap dress with a flattering scoop neckline and a hem line that hit just above her knees greatly emphasized her small waist, firm breasts and shapely legs, and looked stylishly perfect on her. He would admit that his heart had slammed hard in his chest the moment she'd entered the room.

"Well, dinner is about to be served. You better hope you get a seat close to her. It won't take much for the others to boot you out the way." She then walked off.

He glanced back over to where Bella was standing and thought that no one would boot him out the way when it came to Bella. They better not even try.

Bella smiled at something Zane had said while trying not to glance across the room at Jason. He had spoken to her when she'd first arrived but since then had pretty much kept his distance, preferring to let his brothers and cousins keep her company.

You would never know they had been two people who'd almost demolished the mouths right off their faces a few days ago. But then maybe that was the point. Maybe he didn't want anyone to know. Come to think of it, she'd never asked if he even had a girlfriend. For all she knew he might have one. Just because he'd dropped by for tea didn't mean anything other than he was neighborly. And she had to remember that he had never gotten out of the way with her.

Until that day in his office.

What had made him want to kiss her? There had been this intense chemistry between them from the first, but neither of them had acted on it until that day. Had stepping over those boundaries taken their relationship to a place where it couldn't recover? She truly hoped not. He was a nice person, a charmer if ever there was one. And although she'd decided that distance between them was probably for the best right now, she did want him to remain her friend.

"Pam's getting everyone's attention for dinner," Dillon said as he approached the group. "Let me escort you to the dining room," he offered and tucked Bella's arm beneath his.

She smiled at him. The one thing she noticed was that all the Westmoreland men resembled in some way. "Thank you."

She glanced over at Jason. Their gazes met and she felt it, the same sensations she felt whenever he was near her. That deep stirring in the pit of her stomach had her trying to catch her breath.

"You okay?" Dillon asked her.

She glanced up and saw concern in his deep dark

eyes. He'd followed her gaze and noted it had lit on his brother. "Yes, I'm fine."

She just hoped what she'd said was true.

Jason wasn't surprised to discover he had been placed beside Bella at the dinner table. The women in the family tended to be matchmakers when they set their minds to it, which he could overlook considering three of them were all happily married themselves. The other two, Megan and Bailey, were in it for the ride.

He dipped his head, lower than he'd planned, to ask Bella if she was enjoying herself, and when she turned her head to look at him their lips nearly touched. He came close to ignoring everyone sitting at the table and giving in to the temptation to kiss her.

She must have read his mind and a light blush spread into her cheeks. He swallowed, pulled his lips back. "Are you having a good time?"

"Yes. And I appreciate your family for inviting me."

"And I'm sure they enjoy having you here," he said. Had she expected him to invite her? He shrugged off the thought as wrong. There had been no reason for him to invite her to meet his family. Come to think of it, he had never invited a woman home for dinner. Not even Emma Phillips and they'd dated close to a year before she tried giving him an ultimatum.

The meal went off without a hitch with various conversations swirling around the table. Megan informed everyone that the private investigator she had hired to dig deeper into their great-grandfather Raphel's past was Rico Claiborne, who just happened to be the brother of Jessica and Savannah who were married to their cousins Chase and Durango. Rico, whom Megan hadn't yet met, was flying into Denver at some point in time to go over the information he'd collected on what was supposed to be Raphel's third wife.

By the time dinner was over and conversations wound down it was close to ten o'clock. Someone suggested given the lateness of the hour that Bella be escorted back home. Several of his cousins spoke up to do the honor and Jason figured he needed to end the nonsense once and for all and said in a voice that brooked no argument, "I'll make sure Bella gets home."

He noticed that all conversation automatically ceased and no one questioned his announcement. "Ready to go?" he asked Bella softly.

"Yes."

She thanked everyone and openly gave his cousins and brothers hugs. It wasn't hard to tell that they all liked her and had enjoyed her visit. After telling everyone good-night he followed her out the door.

Bella glanced out her rearview mirror and saw Jason was following her at a safe distance. She laughed, thinking when it came to Jason there wasn't a safe zone. Just knowing he was anywhere within her area was enough to rattle her. Even sitting beside him at dinner had been a challenge for her, but thanks to the rest of his family who kept lively conversation going on, she was able to endure his presence and the sexual tension she'd felt. Each time he talked to her and she looked into his face and focused on his mouth, she would remember that same mouth mating with hers.

A sigh of relief escaped her lips when they pulled into her yard. Figuring it would be dark when she returned she had left lights burning outside and her yard was practically glowing. She parked her car and was opening the door to get out when she saw Jason already standing there beside it. Her breathing quickened and panic set in. "You don't need to walk me to the door, Jason," she said quickly.

"I want to," he said simply.

Annoyance flashed in her eyes when she recalled how he'd gone out of his way most of the evening to avoid her. "Why would you?"

He gave her a look. "Why wouldn't I?" Instead of waiting for her to respond he took her hand in his and headed toward her front door.

Fine! she thought, fuming inside and dismissing the temptation to pull her hand away from his. Because her foreman lived on the ranch, she knew the last thing she needed to do was make a scene with Jason outside under the bright lights. He stood back while she unlocked the door and she had a feeling he intended to make sure she was safely inside before leaving. She was right when he followed her inside.

When he closed the door behind them she placed her hands on her hips and opened her mouth to say what was on her mind, but he beat her to the punch. "Was I out of line when I kissed you that day, Bella?"

The softly spoken question gave her pause and she dropped her hands to her side. No, he hadn't been out of line mainly because she'd wanted the kiss. She had wanted to feel his mouth on hers, his tongue tangling with her own. And if she was downright truthful about it, she would admit to wanting his hands on her, all over her, touching her in ways no man had touched her before.

He was waiting for her response.

"No, you weren't out of line."

"Then why the coldness today?"

She tilted her chin. "I can be asking you the same thing, Jason. You weren't Mr. Congeniality yourself tonight."

He didn't say anything for a moment but she could tell her comment had hit a mark with him. "No, I wasn't," he admitted.

Although she had made the accusation she was stunned by the admission. It had caught her off guard. "Why?" She knew the reason for her distance but was curious to know the reason for his.

"Ladies first."

"Fine," she said, placing her purse on the table. "We might as well get this little talk over with. Would you like something to drink?"

"Yes," he said, rubbing his hand down his face in frustration. "A cup of tea would be nice."

She glanced up at him, surprised by his choice. There was no need to mention since that first day when he'd shown up she had picked up a couple bottles of beer and wine at the store to give him more of a choice. Since tea was also her choice she said, "All right, I'll be back in a moment." She then swept from the room.

Jason watched her leave and felt more frustrated than ever. She was right, they needed to talk. He shook his head. When had things between them gotten so complicated? Had it all started with that kiss? A kiss that was destined to happen sooner or later given the intense attraction between them?

He sighed deeply, wondering how he would explain his coldness to her tonight. How could he tell her his behavior had been put in place as a safety mechanism stemming from the fact that he wanted her more than he'd ever wanted any other woman? And how could he explain that the thought of any woman getting under his skin to the extent she had scared the hell out of him?

Chances were if he hadn't run into her at the appliance store he would have sought out her company anyway. More than likely he would have dropped by later for tea, although he had tried limiting his visits for fear of wearing out his welcome.

Her phone rang and he wondered who would be calling her at this late hour but knew it was none of his business when she picked it up on the second rang. He'd never gotten around to asking if she had a boyfriend or not and assumed she didn't.

Moments later Jason glanced toward the kitchen door when he heard a loud noise, the sound of something crashing on her floor. He quickly moved toward the kitchen to see what had happened and to make sure she was all right.

He frowned when he entered the kitchen and saw Bella stooping to pick up the tray she'd dropped along with two broken cups.

He quickly moved forward. "Are you okay, Bella?" he asked.

She didn't look at him as she continued to pick up broken pieces of the teacups. "I'm fine. I accidentally dropped it."

He bent down toward her. "That's fine. At least you didn't have tea in the cups. You could have burned yourself. I can help you get that up."

She turned to look up at him. "I can do this, Jason. I don't need your help."

He met her gaze and would have taken her stinging words to heart if he hadn't seen the redness of her eyes. "What's wrong?"

Instead of answering she shook her head and averted her gaze, refusing to look at him any longer. Quickly recovering his composure at seeing her so upset, he was pushed into action and wrapped his arms around her waist and assisted her up off the floor.

He stood facing her and drew in a deep, calming breath before saying, "I want to know what's wrong, Bella."

She drew in her own deep breath. "That was my father. He called to gloat."

Jason frowned. "About what?"

He watched her when she swallowed deeply. "He and his attorney were able to get an injunction against my trust fund and wanted me to know my monthly funds are on hold."

He heard the tremor in her voice. "But I thought you had three months before your twenty-sixth birthday."

"I do, but some judge—probably a close friend of Dad's—felt my parents had grounds to place a hold on my money. They don't believe I'll marry before the trust fund's deadline date."

She frowned. "I need my money, Jason. I was counting on the income to pay my men as well as to pay for all the work I've ordered to be done around here. There were a number of things my grandfather hadn't taken care of around here that need to be done, like repairing the roof on the barn. My parents are deliberately placing me in a bind and they know it."

Jason nodded. He had started noticing a number of things Herman had begun overlooking that had needed to be done. He then shook his head. He'd heard of controlling parents but felt hers were ridiculous.

"Certainly there is something your attorney can do."

She drew in a deep breath. "He sent me a text moments ago and said there's nothing he can do now that a judge has gotten involved. And even if there were, it would take time and my parents know it. It is time they figure I don't have, which will work in their favor. True, I got this ranch free and clear but it takes money to keep it operational."

He shook his head. "And all because you won't get married?"

"Yes. They believe I was raised and groomed to be the wife of someone like Hugh who already has standing in Savannah's upper-class society."

Jason didn't say anything for a few moments. "Does your trust fund specifically state who you're to marry?"

"No, it just says I have to be a married woman. I guess my grandparents figured in their way of thinking that I would automatically marry someone they would consider my equal and not just anyone."

An idea suddenly slammed into Jason's head. It was a crazy one…but it would serve a purpose in the long run. In the end, she would get what she wanted and he would get what he wanted.

He reached out and took her hand in his, entwined their fingers and tried ignoring the sensations touching her caused. "Let's sit down for a moment. I might have an idea."

Bella allowed him to lead her over to the kitchen table and she sat down with her hands on top of the table and glanced up at him expectantly.

"Promise you'll keep an open mind when you hear my proposal."

"All right, I promise."

He paused a moment and then said, "I think you should do what your parents want and get married."

"What!"

"Think about it, Bella. You can marry anyone to keep your trust fund intact."

He could tell she was even more confused. "I don't understand, Jason. I'm not seriously involved with anyone, so who am I supposed to marry?"

"Me."

Chapter 4

Bella's jaw dropped open. "You?"

"Yes."

She stared at Jason for a long moment and then she adamantly shook her head.

"Why would you agree to marry me?" she asked, confused.

"Think about it, Bella. It will be a win-win situation for the both of us. Marriage to me will guarantee you'll keep your trust fund rolling in without your parents' interfering. And it will give me what I want, as well, which is your land and Hercules."

Her eyes widened. "A marriage of convenience between us?"

"Yes." He could see the light shining bright in her wide-eyed innocent gaze. But then caution eased into the hazel depths.

"And you want me to give you my land as well as Hercules?"

"Co-ownership of the land and total ownership of Hercules."

Bella nibbled on her bottom lip, giving his proposal consideration while trying not to feel the disappointment trying to crowd her in. She had come here to Denver to be independent and not dependent. But what he was proposing was not how she had planned things to go. She was just learning to live on her own without her parents looking over her shoulder. She wanted her own life and now Jason was proposing that he share it. Even if it was on a temporary basis, she was going to feel her independence snatched away. "And how long do we have to remain married?"

"For as long as we want but at least a year. Anytime after that either of us are free to file for a divorce to end things. But think about it, once we send your father's attorney proof we're officially married he'll have no choice but to release the hold on your trust fund."

Bella knew that her parents would always be her parents and although she loved them, she could not put up with their controlling ways any longer. She thought Jason's proposal might work but she still had a few reservations and concerns.

"Will we live in separate households?" she decided to ask.

"No, we will either live here or at my place. I have no problem moving in here but we can't live apart. We don't want to give your parents or anyone a reason to think our marriage isn't the real thing."

She nodded thinking what he said made sense but she needed to ask another question. This one was of a delicate nature but was one she definitely needed to know the answer to. She cleared her throat. "If we lived in the same house would you expect for us to sleep in the same bed?"

He held her gaze intently. "I think by now it's apparent we're attracted to each other, which is the reason I wasn't Mr. Congeniality tonight as you've indicated. That kiss we shared only made me want more and I think you know where wanting more would have led."

Yes, she knew. And because he was being honest with her she might as well be honest with him. "And the reason I acted 'cold' as you put it was that I felt sensations kissing you that I'd never felt before and with everything going on in my life, the last thing I needed to take on was a lover. And now you want me to take on a husband, Jason?"

"Yes, and only because you won't have all those issues you had before. And I would want us to share a bed, but I'll leave the decision of what we do up to you. I won't rush you into doing anything you're not comfortable with doing. But I think you can rightly say with us living under the same roof such a thing is bound to happen eventually."

She swallowed. Yes, she could rightly say that. Marrying him would definitely be a solution to her problem and like he'd said, he would be getting what he wanted out of the deal as well—co-ownership of her land and Hercules. It would be a win-win situation.

But still.

"I need to think about it, Jason. Your proposal sounds good but I need to make sure it's the right answer."

He nodded. "I have an attorney who can draw up the

papers so you won't have to worry about everything I'm proposing being legit and binding. Your attorney can look at them as well if you'd like. He will be bound by attorney-client privilege not to disclose the details of our marriage to anyone."

"I still need time to think things through, Jason."

"And I'll give you that time but my proposal won't be out there forever."

"I understand."

And whether or not he believed her, she *did* understand, which was why she needed time to think about it. From his standpoint things probably looked simple and easy. But to her there were several "what ifs" she had to consider.

What if during that year she fell in love with him but he wanted out of the marriage? What if he was satisfied with a loveless marriage and like her parents wanted to be discreet in taking lovers? What if—

"How much time do you think you'll need to think about it?"

"No more than a week at the most. I should have my answer to you by then." And she hoped more than anything it would be the right one.

"All right, that will work for me."

"And you're not involved with anyone?" she asked, needing to know for certain.

He smiled. "No, I'm not. Trust me. I couldn't be involved with anyone and kiss you the way I did the other day."

Bringing up their kiss made her remember how it had been that day, and how easily her lips had molded to his. It had been so easy to feel his passion, and some of the things his tongue had done inside her mouth nearly short-circuited her brain. Even now her body was inwardly shuddering with the force of those memories. And she expected them to live under the same roof and not share a bed? That was definitely an unrealistic expectation on her part. It seemed since their kiss, being under the same roof for any period of time was a passionate time bomb waiting to happen for them and they both knew it.

She glanced across the table at him and her stomach clenched. He was looking at her the same way he'd done that day right before he'd kissed her. And she'd kissed him back. Mated with his mouth and loved every minute doing so.

Even now she recognized the look in his eyes. It was a dark, hungry look that did more than suggest he wanted her and if given the chance he would take her right here, on her kitchen table. And it would entail more than just kissing. He would probably want to sample her the same way she'd done the seafood bisque Pam had served at dinner. And heaven help her but she would just love to be sampled.

She knew what he wanted but was curious to know what he was thinking at this moment. He was staring at her with such intensity, such longing and such greed. Then she thought, maybe it was best that she didn't know. It would be safer to just imagine.

Swallowing hard, she broke eye contact with him and thought changing the subject was a good idea. The discussion of a possible marriage between them was not the way to go right now.

"At least I've paid for the appliances they are delivering next week," she said, glancing over at her stove that had seen better days. "I think that stove and refrigerator were here when my Dad lived here," she added.

"Probably."

"So it was time for new ones, don't you think?"

"Yes. And I think we need to get those broken pieces of the teacups off the floor," he said.

"I'll do it later. It will give me something to do after you leave. I'm going to need to stay busy for a while. I'm not sleepy."

"You sure you won't need my help cleaning it up?"

"Yes, I'm sure" was her response.

"All right."

"I have beer in the refrigerator if you'd like one," she offered.

"No, I'm straight."

For the next ten minutes they continued to engage in idle chatter. Anything else was liable to set off sparks that could ignite into who knows what.

"Bella?"

"Yes."

"It's not working."

She knew just what he meant. They had moved the conversation from her appliances, to the broken teacups, to him not wanting a beer, to the furniture in her living room, to the movie that had made number one at the box office last weekend like either of them really gave a royal flip. "It's not?"

"No. It's okay to feel what we're feeling right now, no matter what decision you make a week from now. And on that note," he said, standing, "if you're sure you don't want me to help clean up the broken teacups, I think I'd better go before…"

"Before what?" she asked when he hesitated in completing the statement.

"Before I try eating you alive."

She sucked in a quick breath while a vision of him doing that very thing filtered through her mind. And then instead of leaving well enough alone, she asked something really stupid. "Why would you want to do something like that?"

He smiled. And the way he smiled had her pulse beating rapidly in several areas of her body. It wasn't a predatory smile but one of those "if you really want to know" smiles. Never before had she been aware of the many smiles a person's lips could convey.

In truth, with the little experience she had when it came to men, she was surprised she could read him at all. But for some strange reason she could read Jason and she could do so on a level that could set off passion fizzing to life inside of her.

Like it was doing now.

"The reason I'd try eating you alive is that the other day I only got a sample of your taste. But it was enough to give me plenty of sleepless nights since then. Now I find that I crave knowing how you taste all over. So if you're not ready for that to happen, come on and walk me to the door."

Honestly, at that moment she wasn't quite sure what she was ready for and figured that degree of uncertainty was reason to walk him to the door. She had a lot to think about and work out in her mind and only a week to do it.

She stood and moved around the table. When he extended his hand to her, she knew if they were to touch it would set off a chain of emotions and events she wasn't sure she was ready for. Her gaze moved away from his hand up to his face and she had a feeling that he knew it, as well. Was this supposed to be a challenge? Or was it merely a way to get her to face the facts of how living under the same roof with him would be?

She could ignore his outstretched hand but doing so would be rude and she wasn't a rude person. He was watching her. Waiting for her next move. So she made it and placed her hand in his. And the instant their hands touched she felt it. The heat of his warmth spread through her and instead of withstanding it she was drawn deeper and deeper into it.

Before she realized his intentions he let go of her hand to slide his fingertips up and down her arm in a caress so light and so mind-bogglingly sensual that she had to clamp down her mouth to keep from moaning.

The look in the dark eyes staring at her was intense and she knew at that moment his touch wasn't the only thing making her come apart. His manly scent was flowing through her nostrils and drawing him to her in a way that was actually making her panties wet.

My goodness.

"Maybe my thinking is wrong, Bella," he said in a deep, husky voice as his fingers continued to caress her arms, making her stomach clench with every heated stroke against her skin.

"Maybe you are ready for me to taste you all over, let my tongue glide across your skin, sample you in my mouth and feast on you with the deep hunger I need assuaged. And while your delicious taste sinks into my mouth, I will use my tongue to push you over the edge time and time again and drown you in a need that I intend to fulfill."

His words were pushing her over the edge just as much as his touch was doing. They were making her feel things. Want things. And increasing her desire to explore. To experience. To exert her freedom this way.

"Tell me you're ready," he urged softly in a heated voice. "Just looking at you makes me hot and hard," he said in a tone that heated her skin. "So please tell me you're ready for me."

Bella thought Jason's words had been spoken in the huskiest whisper she'd ever heard, and they did something to her both physically and mentally. They prodded her to want whatever it was he was offering. Whatever she was supposed to be ready for.

Like other women, sex was no great mystery to her. At least not since she had seen her parents' house-keeper Carlie have sex with the gardener when she was twelve. She hadn't understood at the time what all the moans and groans were about and why they had to be naked while making them. As she got older she'd been shielded from any encounters with the opposite sex and never had time to dwell on such matters.

But there had been a time when she'd become curious so she had begun reading a lot. Her parents would probably die of shame if they knew about all the romance novels Carlie would sneak in to her. It was there between the pages of those novels that she began to dream, fantasize and hope that one day she would fall in love and live happily ever after like the women she read about. Her most ardent desire was to one day find the one man who would make her sexually liberated. She wouldn't press her luck and hold out for love.

She swallowed deeply as she gazed up at Jason,

knowing he was waiting for her response, and she knew at that moment what it would be. "Yes, Jason, I'm ready."

He didn't say anything for the longest time; he just stood there and stared at her. For a moment she wondered if he'd heard her. But his darkened eyes, the sound of his breathing alerted her that he had. And his eyes then traveled down the length of her throat and she knew he saw how erratically her pulse was throbbing there at the center.

And then before she could blink, he lowered his head to kiss her. His tongue drove between her lips at the same time his hand reached under her wrap dress. While his tongue relentlessly probed her mouth, his fingers began sliding up her thighs and the feel of his hands on that part of her, a part no other man had touched, made something inside of her uncoil and she released a breathless sigh. She knew at that moment the heat was on. Before she realized he'd done so, he had inched her backward and the cheeks of her behind aligned with the table.

He withdrew his mouth from hers long enough to whisper, "I can't wait to get my tongue inside of you."

His words sent all kinds of sensations swirling around in her stomach and a deep ache began throbbing between her legs. The heat was not just on, it was almost edging out of control. She felt it emitting even more when his fingers moved from her thighs to her panties.

And when he reclaimed her mouth again she moaned at how thoroughly he was kissing her and thinking her brain would overload from all the sensations ramming through her. She tried keeping up as his tongue did a methodical sweep of her mouth. And when she finally thought her senses were partially back under control, he proved her wrong when his fingers wiggled their way beneath the waistband of her panties to begin stroking her in a way that all but obliterated her senses.

"Jason…"

She felt her body being eased back onto the table at the same time her dress was pushed up to her waist. She was too full of emotions, wrapped up in way too many sensations, to take stock in what he was doing, but she got a pretty good idea when he eased her panties down her legs, leaving her open and bare to his sight. And when he eased her back farther on the table and placed her legs over his shoulders to nearly wrap around his neck she knew.

Her breath quickened at the smile that then touched his lips, a smile like before that was not predatory and this time wasn't even one of those "if you really want to know" smiles. This one was a "you're going to enjoy this" smile that curved the corners of his mouth and made a hidden dimple appear in his right cheek.

And before she could release her next breath he lifted her hips to bury his face between her legs. She bit her tongue to keep from screaming when his hot tongue slid between her womanly folds.

She squirmed frantically beneath his mouth as he drove her crazy with passion, using his tongue to coax her into the kind of climax she'd only read about. It was the kind that had preclimactic sensations rushing through her. He shoved his tongue deeper inside her, doing more than tasting her dewy wetness; he was using the hot tip of his tongue to greedily lick her from core to core.

She threw her head back and closed her eyes, as his tongue began making all kinds of circles inside her, teasing her flesh, branding it. But he wouldn't let up and she saw he had no intentions of doing so. She felt the buildup right there at the center of her thighs where his mouth was. Pleasure and heat were taking their toll.

Then suddenly her body convulsed around his mouth and she released a moan from deep within her throat as sharp jolts of sexual pleasure set ripples off in her body. And she moaned while the aftershocks made her body shudder uncontrollably. What she was enduring was unbearably erotic, pleasure so great she thought she would pass out from it.

But she couldn't pass out, not when his tongue continued to thrust inside her, forcing her to give even more. And then she was shoved over the edge. Unable to take anymore, she tightened her legs around his neck and cried out in ecstasy as waves after turbulent waves overtook her.

It was only when the last spasm had eased from her body did he tear his mouth away from her, lower her legs, lean down and kiss her, letting her taste the essence of herself from his lips.

She sucked hard on his tongue, needing it like a lifeline and knowing at that moment he had to be the most sensual and passionate man to walk on the planet. He had made her feel things she'd never felt before, far greater than what she had imagined in any of those romance novels. And she knew this was just the beginning, an introduction to what was out there…and she had a feeling of what was to come.

She knew at that moment, while their tongues continued to mate furiously, that after tonight there was no way they could live under the same roof and not want to discover what was beyond this. How far into pleasure could he take her?

She was definitely going to have to give the proposal he'd placed out there some serious thought.

Jason eased Bella's dress back down her thighs before lifting her from the table to stand on her feet. He studied her features and was pleased with what he saw. Her eyes glowed, her lips were swollen and she looked well rested when she hadn't slept.

But more than anything he thought she was the most beautiful woman he'd ever seen. He hoped he'd given her something to think about, something to anticipate, because more than anything he wanted to marry her.

He intended to marry her.

"Come on, walk me to the door," he whispered thickly. "And this time I promise to leave."

He took her hand in his and ignored the sensations he felt whenever he touched her. "Have breakfast with me tomorrow."

She glanced up at him. "You don't intend to make my decision easy, do you?"

A soft chuckle escaped his lips. "Nothing's wrong with me giving you something to think about. To remember. And to anticipate. It will only help you to make the right decision about my proposal."

When they reached her door he leaned down and kissed her again. She parted her lips easily for him and he deepened the kiss, finding her tongue and then enjoying a game of hide-and-seek with it before finally releasing her mouth on a deep, guttural moan. "What about breakfast in the morning at my place?" he asked huskily.

"That's all it's going to be, right? Breakfast and nothing more?" she asked, her voice lower than a whisper.

He smiled at her with a mischievous grin on his face. "We'll see."

"In that case I'll pass. I can't take too much of you, Jason Westmoreland."

He laughed as he pulled her closer into his arms. "Sweetheart, if I have my way, one of these days you're going to take *all* of me." He figured she knew just what he meant with his throbbing erection all but poking at her center. Maybe she was right and for them to share breakfast tomorrow wasn't a good idea. He would be pouncing on her before she got inside his house.

"A rain check, then?" he prompted.

"Um, maybe."

He lifted a brow. "You're not trying to play hard to get, are you?"

She smiled. "You can ask me that after what happened a short while ago in my kitchen? But I will warn you that I intend to build up some type of immunity to your charms by the time I see you again. You can be overwhelming, Jason."

He chuckled again, thinking she hadn't seen anything yet. Leaning over he brushed a kiss across her lips. "Think about me tonight, Bella."

He opened the door and walked out, thinking the next seven days were bound to be the longest he'd ever endured.

Later that night Bella couldn't get to sleep. Her body was tingling all over from the touch of a man. But it hadn't been any man, it had been Jason. When she tried closing her eyes all she could see was how it had been in her kitchen, the way Jason had draped her across the table and proceeded to enjoy her in such a scandalous way. The nuns at her school would have heart failure to know what had happened to her…and to know how much she had enjoyed it.

All her life she'd been taught—it had virtually been drilled into her head—all about the sins of the flesh. It was wrong for a woman to engage in any type of sexual encounter with a man before marriage. But how could something be so wrong if it felt so right?

Color tinted her cheeks. She needed to get to Confessions the first chance she got. She'd given in to temptation tonight and as much as she had enjoyed it, it would be something she couldn't repeat. Those kinds of activities belonged to people who were married and doing otherwise was improper.

She was just going to have to make sure she and Jason weren't under the same roof alone for a long period of time. Things could get out of hand. She was a weakling when it came to him. He would tempt her to do things she knew she shouldn't.

And now she was paying the price for her little indulgence by not being able to get to sleep. There was no doubt in her mind that Jason's mouth should be outlawed. She inwardly sighed. It was going to take a rather long time to clear those thoughts from her mind.

Chapter 5

"I like Bella, Jason."

He glanced over at his cousin Zane. It was early Monday morning and they were standing in the round pen with one of the mares while waiting for Derringer to bring the designated stallion from his stall for the scheduled breeding session. "I like her, too."

Zane chuckled. "Could have fooled me. Because you weren't giving her your attention at dinner Friday night. We all felt that it was up to us to make her feel welcome, because you were ignoring the poor girl."

Jason rolled his eyes. "And I bet it pained all of you to do so."

"Not really. Your Southern Bella is a real classy lady. If you weren't interested in her I'd make a play for her."

"But I *am* interested in her."

"I know," Zane said, smiling. "It was pretty obvious. I intercepted your dirty looks loud and clear. In any case, I hope things get straightened out between you two."

"I hope so, too. I'll find out in five more days."

Zane lifted a curious brow. "Five days? What's supposed to happen in five days?"

"Long story and one which I prefer not to share right now." He had intentionally not contacted Bella over the past two days to give her breathing space from him to think his proposal through. He'd thought it through and it made perfect sense to him. He was beginning to anticipate her answer. It would be yes; it just had to be.

But what if yes wasn't her answer? What if even after the other night and the sample lovemaking they'd shared that she thought his proposal wasn't worth taking the chance? He would be the first to admit that his proposal was a bit daring. But he felt the terms were fair. Hell, he was giving her a chance to be the first to file for a divorce after the first year. And he—

Zane snapped a finger in front of his face. "Hellooo. Are you with us? Derringer is here with Fireball. Are you up to this or are you thinking about mating of another kind?" Zane was grinning.

Jason frowned when he glanced over at Derringer and saw a smirk on his face, as well. "Yes, I'm up to this and it's none of your business what I'm thinking about."

"Fine, just keep Prancer straight while Fireball mounts her. It's been a while since he's had a mare and he might be overly eager," Zane said with a meaningful smile.

Just like me, Jason thought, remembering every

vivid detail of Bella spread out on her kitchen table for him to enjoy. "All right, let's get this going. I have something to do later."

Both Zane and Derringer gave him speculative looks but said nothing.

Bella stepped out of the shower and began toweling herself dry. It was the middle of the day but after going for a walk around the ranch she had gotten hot and sticky. Now she intended to slip into something comfortable and have a cup of tea and relax…and think about Jason's proposal.

The walk had done her good and walking her land had made her even more determined to hold on to what was hers. But was Jason's proposal the answer? Or would she be jumping out of the pot and into the fire?

After Friday night and what had gone down in her kitchen, there was no doubt in her mind that Jason was the kind of lover women dreamed of having. And he had to be the most unselfish person she knew. He had given her pleasure without seeking his own. She had read enough articles on the subject to know most men weren't usually that generous. But he had been and her body hadn't been the same since. Every time she thought about him and that night in the kitchen, she had to pause and catch her breath.

She hadn't heard from him since that night but figured he was giving her time to think things through before she gave him her answer. She had talked to her attorney again and he hadn't said anything to make her think she had a chance of getting the hold on her trust fund lifted.

She had run into her uncle yesterday when she'd

gone into town and he hadn't been at all pleasant. And neither had his son, daughter and two teenage grandsons. All of them practically cut her with their sharp looks. She just didn't get it. Jason had wanted her land as well but he hadn't been anything but supportive of her decision to keep it and had offered his help from the first.

She understood that she and her Denver relatives didn't have the same bond as the Westmorelands but she would think they wouldn't be dismissing her the way they were doing over some land.

She had dressed and was heading downstairs when something like a missile sailed through her living room window, breaking the glass in the process. "What on earth!" She nearly missed her step when she raced back up the stairs to her bedroom, closing the door and locking it behind her.

Catching her breath she grabbed her cell phone off the nightstand and called the police.

"Where is she, Marvin?" Jason asked, walking into Bella's house with Zane and Derringer on his heels.

"She's in the kitchen," the man answered, moving quickly out of Jason's way.

Jason had gotten a call from Pam to tell him what had happened. He had jumped in his truck and left Zane's ranch immediately with Derringer and Zane following close behind in their vehicles.

From what Pam had said, someone had thrown a large rock through Bella's window with a note tied to it saying, "Go back to where you came from." The thought of anyone doing that angered him. Who on earth would do such a thing?

He walked into the kitchen and glanced around, dismissing memories of the last time he'd been there and his focus immediately went to Bella. She was sitting at the kitchen table talking to Pete Higgins, one of the sheriff's deputies and a good friend of Derringer's.

Everyone glanced up when he entered and the look on Bella's face was like a kick in his gut. He could tell she was shaken and there was a hurt expression in her eyes he'd never seen before. His anger flared at the thought that someone could hurt her in any way. The rock may not have hit her but she'd taken a hit just the same. Whoever had thrown that rock through the window had hit her spirit and left her shaken.

"Jason, Zane and Derringer," Pete said, acknowledging their arrival. "Why am I not surprised to see the three of you here?"

Jason didn't respond as he moved straight toward Bella and, disregarding the onlookers, he reached out to caress the soft skin beneath her ear. "Are you all right?" he whispered in a husky tone.

She held his gaze and nodded slowly. "Yes, I'm fine. I was on my way downstairs when that rock came flying through the window. It scared me more than anything."

He glanced at the rock that someone had placed on the table. It was a huge rock, big enough to hurt her had she been in her living room anywhere near the window. The thought of anyone harming one single hair on her head infuriated him.

He glanced over at Pete. "Do you have any idea who did it?"

Peter shook his head. "No, but both the rock and

note have been dusted for fingerprints. Hopefully we'll know something soon."

Soon? He wanted to know something now. He glanced down at the note and read it.

"I was just asking Ms. Bostwick if she knew of anyone who wanted her off this property. The only people she could think of are her parents and possibly Kenneth Bostwick."

"I can't see my parents behind anything like this," Bella said in a soft voice. "And I don't want to think Uncle Kenneth is capable of doing anything like this, either. However, he does want me off the land because he knows of someone who wants to buy it."

Pete nodded. "What about Jason here? I think we all know he wants your land and Hercules, as well," the deputy said as if Jason wasn't standing right there listening to his every word. "Do you think he'd want you gone, too?"

Bella seemed surprised by the question and moved her gaze from Pete to Jason. Jason figured she saw remnants of passion behind the anger in his eyes.

"No, he'd want me to stay," she said with a soft sigh.

Pete closed his notepad, evidently deciding not to ask why she was so certain of that. "Well, hopefully we'll have something within a week if those fingerprints are identified," he said.

"And what is she supposed to do in the meantime, Pete?" Jason asked in a frustrated tone.

"Report anything suspicious," Pete responded dryly. He turned to face Bella. "I'll request that the sheriff beef up security around here starting today."

"Thank you, Deputy Higgins," Bella said softly. "I'd appreciate that tremendously. Marvin is getting the window replaced and I'll be keeping the lights on in the yard all night now."

"Doesn't matter," Jason said. "You're staying at my place tonight."

Bella tilted her head to the side and met Jason's intense gaze. "I can't do that. You and I can't stay under the same roof."

Jason crossed his arms over his chest. "And why not?"

A flush stole into her cheeks when she noted Jason wasn't the only one waiting on her response. "You know why," she finally said.

Jason's forehead bunched up. Then when he remembered what could possibly happen if they stayed overnight under the same roof, he smiled. "Oh, yeah."

"Oh, yeah, what?" Zane wanted to know.

Jason frowned at his cousin. "None of your business."

Pete cleared his throat. "I'm out of here but like I said, Miss Bostwick, the department will have more police checking around the area." He slipped both the rock and note into a plastic evidence bag.

Zane and Derringer followed Pete out the door, which Jason appreciated since it gave him time alone with Bella. The first thing he did was lean down and kiss her. He needed the taste of her to know she was really okay.

She responded to his kiss and automatically he deepened it, drawing her up out of the chair to stand on her feet in the process. He needed the feel of all of her to know she was safe. He would protect her with his life if he had to. He'd aged a good twenty years when he'd gotten that call from Pam telling him what had happened. And speaking of Pam's phone call...

He broke off the kiss and with an irritated frown on his features he looked down at Bella. "Why didn't you call me? Why did I have to hear what happened from someone else?"

She gazed right back at him with an irritated frown of her own. "You've never given me your phone number."

Jason blinked in surprise and realized what she'd said was true. He hadn't given her his phone number.

"I apologize for that oversight," he said. "You will definitely have it from here on out. And we need to talk about you moving in with me for a while."

She shook her head. "I can't move in with you, Jason, and as I said earlier, we both know why."

"Do you honestly think if you gave me an order not to touch you that I wouldn't keep my hands off you?" he asked.

She shrugged delicate shoulders. "Yes, I believe you'd do as I ask, but I'm not sure given that same scenario, in light of what happened in this very kitchen Friday night, that I'd be able to keep my hands off you."

He blinked. Stared down at her and blinked again. This time with a smile on his lips. "You don't say?"

"I do say and I know it's an awful thing to admit, but right now I can't make you any promises," she said, rubbing her hands together as if distressed by the very notion.

He wasn't distressed, not even a little bit. In fact, he was elated. For a minute he couldn't say a word and then said, "And you think I have a problem with you not being able to keep your hands off me?"

She nodded. "If you don't have a problem with it then you should. We aren't married. We aren't even engaged."

"I asked you to marry me Friday night."

She used her hand to wave off his reminder. "Yes, but it would be a marriage of convenience, which I haven't agreed to yet since the issue of the sleeping arrangements is still up in the air. Until I do decide I think it's best if you stay under your roof and I stay under mine. Yes, that's the proper thing to do."

He lifted a brow. "The proper thing to do?"

"Yes, proper, appropriate, suitable, fitting, which of those words do you prefer using?"

"What about none of them?"

"It doesn't matter, Jason. It's bad enough that we got carried away the other night in this kitchen. But we can't repeat something like that."

He didn't see why they couldn't and was about to say as much when he heard footsteps approaching and glanced over as Derringer and Zane entered the kitchen.

"Pete thinks he's found a footprint outside near the bushes and is checking it out now," Derringer informed them.

Jason nodded. He then turned back to Bella and his expression was one that would accept no argument on the matter. "Pack an overnight bag, Bella. You're staying at my place tonight even if I have to sleep in the barn."

Chapter 6

Bella glared at Jason. It was a ladylike glare but a glare nonetheless. She opened her mouth to say something then remembered they had an audience and immediately closed it. She cast a warm smile over at Zane and Derringer. "I'd like a few minutes alone with Jason to discuss a private matter, please."

They returned her smile, nodded and gave Jason "you've done it now" smiles before walking out of the kitchen.

It was then that she turned her attention back to Jason. "Now then, Jason, let's not be ridiculous. You are not sleeping in your barn just so I can sleep under your roof. I'm staying right here."

She could tell he did not appreciate his order not being obeyed when she saw his irritation with her increase. "Have you forgotten someone threw a rock through your window with a note demanding you leave town?"

She nibbled a minute on her bottom lip. "No, I didn't forget the rock or the note attached to it, but I can't let them think they've won by running away. I admit to being a little frightened at first but I'm fine now. Marvin is having the window replaced and I'll keep lights shining around here all night. And don't forget Marvin sleeps in the bunkhouse each night so technically, I won't be here by myself. I'll be fine but I appreciate your concern."

Jason stared at her for a moment and didn't say anything. He hadn't lied about aging twenty years when he'd gotten that call from Pam. He had walked into her house not knowing what to expect. The thought that someone wanted her gone bothered him, because he knew she wasn't going anywhere and that meant he needed to protect her.

"Fine, you stay inside here and I'll sleep in your barn," he finally said.

She shook her head after crossing her arms over her chest. "You won't be sleeping in anyone's barn. You're going to sleep in your own bed tonight and I intend to sleep in mine."

"Fine," he snapped like he was giving in to her suggestion when he wouldn't do anything of the sort. But if she wanted to think it he would let her. "I need to take you to Pam's to show her and the others you're okay and in one piece."

A smile touched her lips. "They were worried about me?"

She seemed surprised by that. "Yes, everyone was worried."

"In that case let me grab my purse."

"I'll be waiting outside," he said to her fleeing back.

He shook his head and slowly left the kitchen and walked through the dining room to the living room where Marvin and a couple of the men were replacing the window. They had cleaned up all the broken glass but a scratch mark on the wooden floor clearly showed where the rock had landed once it entered the house.

He drew in a sharp breath at the thought of Bella getting hit by that rock. If anything would have happened to her he would have…

At that moment he wasn't sure just what he would do. The thought of anything happening to her sent sharp fear through him in a way he'd never known before. Why? Why were his feelings for her so intense? Why was he so possessive when it came to her?

He shrugged off the responses that flowed through his mind, not ready to deal with any of them. He walked out the front door to where Zane and Derringer were waiting.

"You aren't really going to let her stay here unprotected?" Derringer asked, studying his features.

Jason shook his head. "No."

"And why can't the two of you stay under the same roof?" Zane asked curiously.

"None of your business."

Zane chuckled. "If you don't give me an answer I'm going to think things."

That didn't move Jason. "Think whatever you want." He then checked his watch. "I hate to do this but I'm checking out for the rest of the day. I intend to keep an eye on Bella until Pete finds out who threw that rock through her window."

"You think Kenneth Bostwick had something to do with it?" Derringer asked.

"Not sure, but I hope for his sake he didn't," Jason said in a voice laced with tightly controlled anger.

He stopped talking when Bella walked onto the porch. Not only had she grabbed her purse but she'd also changed her dress. At his curious look, she said, "The dress I was wearing wasn't suitable for visiting."

He nodded and decided not to tell her she looked good now and had looked good then. Whatever she put on her body she wore with both grace and style. He met her in the middle of the porch and slipped her hand in his. "You look nice. And I thought we could grab dinner someplace before I bring you back here."

Her eyes glowed in a way that tightened his stomach and sent sensations rushing through his gut. "I'd like that, Jason."

It was close to ten at night when Bella returned home. Jason entered her house and checked around, turning on lights as he went from room to room. It made her feel extra safe when she saw a police patrol car parked near the turnoff to her property.

"Everything looks okay," Jason said, breaking into her thoughts.

"Thanks. I'll walk you to the door," she said quickly, heading back downstairs.

"Trying to rush me out of here, Bella?"

At the moment she didn't care what he thought. She just needed him gone so she could get her mind straightened out. Being with him for the past eight hours had taken its toll on her mind and body.

She hadn't known he was so touchy and each time

he'd touched her, even by doing something simple as placing a hand in the center of her back when they'd been walking into the movies, it had done something to her in a way that had her hot and bothered for the rest of the evening.

But she had enjoyed the movies they'd gone to after dinner. She had enjoyed sitting beside him while he held her hand when he wasn't feeding her popcorn.

"No, I'm not trying to rush you, Jason, but it is late," she said. "If your goal this evening was to tire me out then you've done a good job of it. I plan to take a shower and then go to bed."

They were standing facing each other and he wrapped his arms around her and took a step closer, almost plastering his body to hers. She could feel all of him from chest to knee; but especially the erect body part in between.

"I'd love to take a shower with you, sweetheart," he whispered.

She didn't know what he was trying to do, but he'd been whispering such naughty come-ons to her all evening. And each and every one of them had only added to her torment. "Taking a shower together wouldn't be right, Jason, and you know it."

He chuckled. "Trying to send me home to an empty bed isn't right, either. Why don't you just accept my proposal? We can get married the same day. No waiting. And then," he said, leaning closer to begin nibbling around her mouth, "we can sleep under the same roof that night. Just think about that."

Bella moaned against the onslaught of his mouth on hers. She was thinking about it and could just imagine it. Oh, what a night that would be. But then she also had to think about what would happen if he got tired of her like her father had eventually gotten tired of her mother. The way her mother had gotten tired of her father. What if he approached her about wanting an open marriage? What if he told her after the first year that he wanted a divorce and she'd gotten attached to him? She could just imagine the heartbreak she would feel.

"Bella?"

She glanced up at him. "Yes?"

Jason Westmoreland was such a handsome man that it made her heart ache. And at the same time he made parts of her sizzle in desire so thick you could cut it with a knife. She thought his features were flawless and he had to have the most irresistible pair of lips born to any man. Staring at his mouth pushed her to recall the way their tongues would entangle in his mouth while they mated them like crazy. It didn't take much to wonder how things would be between them in the bedroom. But she knew as tempting as it was, there was more to a marriage than just great sex. But could she really ask for more from a marriage of convenience?

"Are you sure you don't want me to stay tonight? I could sleep on the sofa."

She shook her head. Even that would be too close for comfort for her. "No, Jason, I'll be fine. Go home."

"Not before I do this," he said, leaning down and capturing her mouth with his. She didn't have a problem offering him what he wanted and he proved he didn't have a problem taking it. He kissed her deeply, thoroughly and with no reservations about making her feel wanted, needed and desired. She could definitely feel heat radiating from his body to hers and wasn't put off by it. Instead it ignited passion within her so acute she had to fight to keep a level head or risk the kiss taking them places she wasn't ready to go.

Moments later she was the one who broke off the kiss. Desperately needing to breathe, she inhaled a deep breath. Jason just simply stood there staring and waiting, as if he was ready to go another round.

Bella knew she disappointed him when she took a step back. "Good night, Jason."

His lips curved into a too-sexy smile. "Tell me one thing that will be good about it once I walk out that door."

She really wasn't sure what she could say to that and in those cases she'd always been told it was better not to say anything at all. Instead she repeated herself while turning the knob on the door to open it. "Good night, Jason.

He leaned in, brushed a kiss across her lips and whispered, "Good night, Bella."

Bella wasn't sure what brought her awake during the middle of the night. Glancing over at the clock on her nightstand she saw it was two in the morning. She was restless. She was hot. And she was definitely still bothered. She hadn't known just spending time with a man could put a woman in such an erotic state.

Sliding out of bed she slipped into her robe and house shoes. A full moon was in the sky and its light spread into the room. She was surprised by how easily sleep had come to her at first. But that had been a few hours ago and now she was wide-awake.

She moved over to the windows to look out. Under the moon-crested sky she could see the shape of the mountains in their majestic splendor. At night they were just as overpowering as they were in the daylight.

She was about to move away from the window when she happened to glance down below and saw a truck parked in her yard. She frowned and pressed her face closer to the window to make out just whose vehicle was parked in her yard and frowned when she recognized the vehicle was Jason's.

What was his truck doing in her yard at two in the morning? Was he in it?

She rushed downstairs. He couldn't be in a truck in front of her house at two in the morning. What would Marvin think? What would the police officers cruising the area think? His family?

When she made it to the living room she slowly opened the door and slipped out. She then released a disgusted sigh when she saw he was sitting in the truck. He had put his seat in a reclining position, but that had to be uncomfortable for him.

As if he'd been sleeping with one eye open and another one closed, he came awake when she rounded the truck and tapped on his window. He slowly tilted his Stetson back from covering his eyes. "Yes, Bella?"

She opened her mouth to speak and then closed it. If she thought he was a handsome man before then he was even more now with the shadow covering his jaw. There was just something ultrasexy about a man who hadn't shaved.

She fought her attention away from his jaw back to his gaze. "What are you doing here? Why did you come back?"

"I never left."

She blinked. "You never left? You mean to tell me

you've been out here in the car since I walked you to the door?"

He smiled that sexy smile. "Yes, I've been here since you walked me to the door."

"But why?"

"To protect you."

That simple statement suddenly took the wind out of her sail for just a moment. Merely a moment. That was all the time she needed to be reminded that no one had tried truly protecting her before. She'd always considered her parents' antics more in the line of controlling than protecting.

She then recovered and remembered why he couldn't sit out here protecting her. "But you can't sit out here, Jason. It's not proper. What will your family think if any of them see your car parked in front of my house at this hour? What would those policemen think? What would—"

"Honestly, Bella, I really don't give a royal damn what anyone thinks. I refuse to let you stay here without being close by to make sure you're okay. You didn't want me to sleep in the barn so this is where I am and where I will stay."

She frowned. "You're being difficult."

"No, I'm being a man looking out for the woman I want. Now go back inside and lock the door behind you. You interrupted my sleep."

She stared at him for a long moment and then said, "Fine, you win. Come on inside."

He stared back at her. "That wasn't what this was about, Bella. I recognize the fact just as much as you do that we don't need to be under the same roof alone. I'm fine with being out here tonight."

"Well, I'm not fine with it."

"Sorry about that but there's nothing I can do about it."

She glared at him and seeing he was determined to be stubborn, she threw up her hands before going back into the house, closing the door behind her.

Jason heard the lock click in place and swore he could also hear her fuming all the way up the stairs. She could fume all she wanted but he wasn't leaving. He had been sitting out there for the past four hours thinking, and the more he thought the more he realized something vital to him. And it was something he could not deny or ignore. He had fallen in love with Bella. And accepting how he felt gave his proposal much more meaning than what he'd presented to her. Now he fully understood why Derringer had acted so strangely while courting Lucia.

He had dated women in the past but had never loved any of them. He'd known better than to do so after that fiasco with Mona Cardington in high school. He'd admitted he loved her and when a new guy moved to town weeks later she had dumped him like a hot potato. That had been years ago but the pain he'd felt that day had been real and at seventeen it had been what had kept him from loving another woman.

And now he had fallen head over heels in love with a Southern belle and for the time being would keep how he felt to himself.

An hour later Bella lay in bed staring up at the ceiling, still inwardly fuming. How dare Jason put her in such a compromising position? No one would think he was sleeping in the truck. People were going to assume they were lovers and he was sleeping in her bed, lying with her between silken sheets with their limbs entwined and mouths fused while making hot, passionate and steamy love.

Her thighs began to quiver and the juncture between her legs began to ache just thinking of how it would probably be if they were to share a bed. He would stroke her senseless with his fingers in her most intimate spot first, taking his time to get her primed and ready for the next stage of what he would do to her.

She shifted to her side and held her legs tightly together, hoping the ache would go away. She'd never craved a man before and now she was craving Jason something fierce, more so than ever since he'd tasted her there. All she had to do was close her eyes and remember being stretched out on her kitchen table with his head between her legs and how he had lapped her into sweet oblivion. The memories sent jolts of electricity throughout her body, making the tips of her breasts feel sensitive against her nightgown.

And the man causing her so much torment and pleasure was downstairs sleeping in his truck just to keep her safe. She couldn't help but be touched that he would do such a thing. He had given up a nice comfortable bed and was sleeping in a position that couldn't be relaxing with his hat over his eyes to shield the brightness of the lights around her yard. Why? Was protecting her that important to him?

If it was, then why?

Deep down she knew the reason and it stemmed from him wanting her land and Hercules. He had been up-front about it from the beginning. She had respected him for it and for accepting the decision was hers to make. So, in other words, he wasn't really protecting her per se but merely protecting his interest, or what he hoped to be his interest. She figured such a thing made sense but...

Would accepting the proposal Jason placed on the table be in her best interest? Did she have a choice if she wanted the hold lifted on her trust fund? Was being legally bound to Jason as his wife for a minimum of a year something she wanted? What about sleeping under the same roof with him and sharing his bed— she'd accepted they would be synonymous—be in her best interest? Was it what she wanted to do, knowing in a year's time he could walk away without looking back? Knowing after that time he would be free to marry someone else? Free to make love to someone else the same way he'd make love to her?

And then there was the question of who was re- sponsible for throwing the rock inside her house. Why was someone trying to scare her off? Although she doubted it, could it be her parents' doing to get her to run back home?

She yawned when she felt sleep coming down on her. Although she regretted Jason was sleeping in his truck, she knew she could sleep a lot more peacefully knowing he was the one protecting her.

Bella woke to the sound of someone knocking on her door and discovered it was morning. She quickly eased out of bed and slid into her bathrobe and bed- room shoes to head downstairs.

"I'm coming!" she called out, rushing to the door. She glanced out the peephole and saw it was Jason. Her heart began beating fast and furiously in her chest at the sight of him, handsome and unshaven with his Stetson low on his brow. Mercy!

Taking a deep breath she opened the door. "Good morning, Jason."

"Good morning, Bella. I wanted to let you know I'm leaving to go home and freshen up, but Riley is here."

"Your brother Riley?" she asked, looking over his shoulder to see the truck parked next to his and the man sitting inside. Riley threw up his hand in a wave which she returned. She recalled meeting him that night at dinner. Jason was older than Riley by two and a half years.

"Yes, my brother Riley."

She was confused. "Why is he here?"

"Because I'm going home to freshen up." He tilted his head and smiled at her. "Are you awake yet?"

"Yes, I'm awake and I know you said you're going home to change but why does Riley have to be here? It's not like I need a bodyguard or something. A rock got thrown through my window, Jason. Not a scud missile."

He merely kept smiling at her while leaning in her doorway. And then he said, "Has anyone ever told you how beautiful you look in the morning?"

She stood there and stared at him. Not ready for him to change the subject and definitely not prepared for him to say something so nice about how she looked. She could definitely return the favor and ask, had anyone ever told him how handsome he looked in the morning. However, she was certain a number of women already had.

So she answered him honestly. "No one has ever told me that."

"Then let me go on record as being your first."

She drew in a deep breath. He didn't say "the" first but had said "your" first. He had made it personal and exclusive. She wondered what he would think to know she had drifted off to sleep last night with images of him flittering through her mind. Memories of his mouth on her probably elicited pleasurable sighs from her even while she slept.

"Doesn't Riley have to go to work today?" she asked, remembering when he'd mentioned that Riley worked for Blue Ridge Management. She'd even seen his name on one of the doors when they'd exited from the elevator on the fortieth floor.

"Yes, but he'll leave whenever I get back."

She crossed her arms over her chest. "And what about you? Don't you have horses to breed or train?"

"Your safety is more important to me."

"Yeah, right."

He lifted a brow. "You don't believe me? Even after I spent the entire night in my truck?"

"You were protecting your interest."

"And that's definitely you, sweetheart."

Don't even go there. Bella figured it was definitely time to end this conversation. If she engaged in chatter with him too much longer he would be convincing her that everything he was saying was true.

"You will have an answer for me in four days, right, Bella?"

"That's my plan."

"Good. I'll be back by the time you're dressed and we can do breakfast with Dillon and Pam, and then I want to show you what I do for a living."

Before she could respond he leaned in and kissed

her on the lips. "See you in an hour. And wear your riding attire."

She sucked in a deep breath and watched as he walked off the porch to his truck to drive away. The man was definitely something else. She cast a quick glance to where Riley sat in his own truck sipping a cup of coffee. There was no doubt in her mind Riley had seen his brother kiss her, and she could only imagine what he was thinking.

Deciding the least she could do was invite him in, she called out to him. "You're welcome to come inside, Riley," she said, smiling broadly at him.

The smile he returned was just as expansive as he leaned his head slightly out the truck's window and said, "Thanks, but Jason warned me not to. I'm fine."

Jason warned him not to? Of course he was just joking, although he looked dead serious.

Instead of questioning him about it, she nodded, closed the door and headed back upstairs. As she entered her bedroom she couldn't ignore the excitement she felt about riding with Jason and checking out his horse training business.

Jason had grabbed his Stetson off the rack and was about to head out the door when his cell phone rang. He pulled it off his belt and saw it was Dillon.

"Yes, Dil?"

"Pam wanted me to call and verify that you and Bella are coming for breakfast."

Jason smiled. "Yes, we'll be there. In fact I'm about to saddle up one of the mares. I thought we'd ride over on horseback. We can enjoy the sights along the way."

"That's a good idea. Everything's okay at her place?"

"Yes, so far so good. The sheriff has increased the patrols around Bella's house and I appreciate it. Thank him the next time the two of you shoot pool together."

Dillon chuckled. "I will. And just so you know, I like Bella. She has a lot of class."

Jason smiled. That meant a lot coming from his older brother. While growing up he'd always thought Dillon was smart with a good head on his shoulders. Jason's admiration increased when Dillon had worked hard to keep the family together.

"And thanks, Dillon."

"For what?"

"For being you. For being there when all of us needed you to be. For doing what you knew Mom and Dad, as well as Uncle Thomas and Aunt Susan would have wanted you to do."

"You don't have to thank me, Jason."

"Yes, I do."

Dillon didn't say anything for a moment. "Then you're welcome. Now don't keep us waiting with Bella. We won't start breakfast until the two of you get here. At least all of us except Denver. He wakes up hungry. Pam has fed him already," Dillon said.

Jason couldn't help but smile, and not for the first time, as he thought of one day having a son of his own. Being around Denver had the tendency to put such thoughts into his head. He enjoyed his nephew immensely.

"We'll get there in good time, I promise," he said before clicking off the phone.

Bella glanced down at her riding attire and smiled. She wanted to be ready when Jason returned.

Grabbing her hat off the rack she placed it on her head and opened the door to step outside on the porch. Riley had gotten out of the truck and was leaning against it. He glanced over at her and smiled.

"Ready to go riding I see," he said.

"Yes, Jason told me to be ready. We're having breakfast with Dillon and Pam."

"Yes, I had planned to have breakfast with them as well but I have a meeting at the office."

Bella nodded. "You enjoy working inside?"

Riley chuckled. "Yes, I'll leave the horses, dirt and grime to Jason. He's always liked being outdoors. When he worked at Blue Ridge I knew it was just a matter of time before wanderlust got ahold of him. He's good with horses, so are Zane and Derringer. Joining in with the Montana Westmorelands in that horse business was great for them."

Bella nodded again. "So exactly what do you do at Blue Ridge?"

"Mmm, a little bit of everything. I like to think of myself as Dillon's right-hand man. But my main job is PR. I have to make sure Blue Ridge keeps a stellar image."

Bella continued to engage in conversation with Riley while thinking he was another kind Westmoreland man. It seemed that all of them were. But she'd heard Bailey remark more than once that Riley was also a ladies' man, and she could definitely believe that. Like Jason, he was handsome to a fault.

"So, Riley, when will you settle down and get married?" she asked him, just to see what his response would be.

"Married? Me? Never. I like things just the way they are. I am definitely not the marrying kind."

Bella smiled, wondering if Jason wasn't the marrying kind, as well, although he'd given a marriage proposal to her. Did he want joint ownership of her land and Hercules that much? Evidently so.

Jason smiled as he headed back to Bella's ranch with a horse he knew she would love riding. Fancy Free was an even tempered mare. In the distance, he could see Bella was standing on the porch waiting for him. He would discount the fact that she seemed to be having an enjoyable conversation with Riley, who seemed to be flirting with her.

He ignored the signs of jealousy seeping into his bones. Riley was his brother and if you couldn't trust your own brother who could you trust? A lightbulb suddenly went off in his head. Hell. Had Abel assumed the same thing about Cain?

He tightened his hands on his horse and increased his pace to a gallop. What was Riley saying to Bella to make her laugh so much anyway? Riley was becoming a regular ladies' man around town. It seemed he was trying to keep up with Zane in that aspect. Jason had always thought Riley's playboy ways were amusing. Until now.

Moments later he brought his horse to a stop by the edge of Bella's porch. He tilted his Stetson back on his head so it wouldn't shield his eyes. "Excuse me if I'm interrupting anything."

Riley had the nerve to grin up at him. "No problem but you're twenty minutes late. You better be glad I enjoy Bella's company."

Jason frowned at his brother. "I can tell."

His gaze then shifted to Bella. She looked beautiful standing there in a pair of riding breeches that fitted her body to perfection, a white shirt and a pair of riding boots. She didn't just look beautiful, she looked hot as sin and a side glance at Riley told him that his brother was enjoying the view as much as he was.

"Don't you need to be on your way to work, Riley?"

His brother gave him another grin. "I guess so. Call if you need me as Bella's bodyguard again." He then got into his truck and pulled off.

Jason watched him leave before turning his full attention back to Bella. "Ready to go riding, sweetheart?"

As Bella rode with Jason she tried concentrating on the sheer beauty of the rustic countryside instead of the sexiness of the man in the saddle beside her. He was riding Hercules and she could tell he was an expert horseman. And she could tell why he wanted to own the stallion. It was as if he and the horse had a personal relationship. It was evident Hercules had been glad to see him. Whereas the stallion had been like putty in Jason's hands the horse had given the others grief in trying to handle him. Even now the two seemed in sync.

This was beautiful countryside and the first time she'd seen it. She was stunned by its beauty. The mare he'd chosen for her had come from his stable and was the one he'd rode over to her place. She liked how easily she and the horse were able to take the slopes that stretched out into valleys. The landscape looked majestic with the mountains in the distance.

First they rode over to Dillon and Pam's for break-

fast. She had fallen in love with the Westmoreland Estate the first time she had seen it. The huge Victorian
style home with a wide circular driveway sat on three
hundred acres of land. Jason had told her on the ride
over that as the oldest cousin, Dillon had inherited the
family home. It was where most of the family seemed
to congregate the majority of the time.

She had met Pam's three younger sisters the other
night at dinner and enjoyed their company again
around the breakfast table. Everyone asked questions
about the rock throwing incident and Dillon, who knew
the sheriff personally, felt the person or persons responsible would eventually get caught.

After breakfast they were in the saddle again. Jason
and Bella rode to Zane's place. She was given a front
row seat and watched as Zane, Derringer and Jason ex-
ercised several of the horses. Jason had explained some
of the horses needed both aerobic and anaerobic training, and that so many hours each day were spent on that
task. She could tell that it took a lot of skill as well as
experience for any trainer to be successful and achieve
the goals they wanted for the horses they trained.

At noon Lucia arrived with box lunches for everyone
and Bella couldn't help noticing how much the newly-
weds were still into each other. She knew if she decided
to marry Jason they would not share the type of marriage Derringer and Lucia did since their union would
be more of a business arrangement than anything else.
But it was so obvious to anyone around Derringer and
Lucia they were madly in love with each other.

Later that day they had dinner with Ramsey and
Chloe and enjoyed the time they spent with the couple immensely. Over dinner Ramsey provided tidbits

about sheep ranching and how he'd made the decision to move from being a businessman to operating a sheep ranch.

The sun was going down when she and Jason mounted their horses to return to her ranch. It had been a full day of activities and she had learned a lot about both the horse training business and sheep ranching.

She glanced over at Jason. He hadn't said a whole lot since they'd left his brother's ranch and she couldn't help wondering what he was thinking. She also couldn't help wondering if he intended to sleep in his truck again tonight.

"I feel like a freeloader today," she said to break the silence between them.

He glanced over at her. "Why?"

"Your family fed me breakfast, lunch and dinner today."

He smiled. "They like you."

"And I like them."

She truly did. One of the benefits of accepting Jason's proposal would be his family. But what would happen after the year was up and she'd gotten attached to them? Considered herself part of the family?

They had cleared his land and were riding on her property when up ahead in the distance they saw what appeared to be a huge fiery red ball filled with smoke. They both realized at the same time what it was.

Fire.

And it was coming from the direction of her ranch.

Chapter 7

Bella stood in what used to be the middle of her living room, glanced around and fought the tears stinging her eyes. More than half of her home was gone, destroyed by the fire. And according to the fire marshal it had been deliberately set. If it hadn't been for the quick thinking of her men who begun using water hoses to douse the flames, the entire ranch house would have gone up in smoke.

Her heart felt heavy. Oppressed. Broken. All she'd wanted when she had left Savannah was to start a new life here. But it seemed that was not going to happen. Someone wanted her gone. Who wanted her land that much?

She felt a touch to her arm and without looking up she knew it was Jason. Her body would recognize his touch anywhere. He had been by her side the entire time and watched as portions of her house went up in flames. And he had held her when she couldn't watch any longer and buried her face in his chest and clung to him. At that moment he had become the one thing that was unshakable in a world that was falling down all around her; intentionally being destroyed by someone who was determined to steal her happiness and joy. And he had held her and whispered over and over that everything was going to be all right. And she had tried to believe him and had managed to draw strength from him.

His family had arrived and had given their support as well and had let the authorities know they wanted answers and wanted the person or persons responsible brought to justice. Already they were talking about helping her rebuild and like Jason had done, assured her that everything would be all right.

Sheriff Harper had questioned her, making inquiries similar to the ones Pete had yesterday when the rock had been thrown through her living room window. Did she know of anyone who wanted her out of Denver? Whoever was responsible was determined to get their message through to her loud and clear.

"Bella?"

She glanced up and met Jason's gaze. "Yes?"

"Come on, let's go. There's nothing more we can do here tonight."

She shuddered miserably and the lungs holding back her sob constricted. "Go? Go where, Jason? Look around you. I no longer have a home."

She couldn't stop the single tear that fell from her eyes. Instead of responding to what she'd said Jason brushed the tear away with the pad of his thumb before entwining his fingers in hers. He then led her away toward the barn for a moment of privacy. It was then that he turned her to face him, sweeping the curls back from her face. He fixed her with a gaze that stirred everything inside of her.

"As long as I have a home, Bella, you do, too."

He then drew in a deep breath. "Don't let whoever did this win. This is land that your grandfather gave you and you have every right to be here if that's what you want. Don't let anyone run you off your land," Jason said in a husky whisper.

She heard his words, she felt his plea, but like she'd told him, she no longer had a home now. She didn't want to depend on others, become their charity case. "But what can I do, Jason? It takes money to rebuild and thanks to my parents, my trust fund is on hold." She paused and then with sagging shoulders added, "I don't have anything now. The ranch was insured, but it will take time to rebuild."

"You have me, Bella. My proposal still stands and now more than ever you should consider taking it. A marriage between us means that we'll both get what we want and will show the person who did this that you aren't going anywhere. It will show them they didn't win after all and sooner or later they will get caught. And even if it happens to be a member of your family, I'm going to make sure they pay for doing this."

Jason lowered his gaze to the ground for a moment and then returned it to her. "I am worse than mad right now, Bella, I'm so full of rage I could actually hurt someone for doing this to you. Whoever is behind this probably thought you were inside the house. What if you had been? What if you hadn't spent the day with me?"

Bella took a deep breath. Those were more "what ifs" she didn't want to think about or consider. The only thing she wanted to think about right now was the proposal; the one Jason had offered and still wanted her to take. And she decided at that very moment that she would.

She would take her chances on what might or might not happen within that year. She would be the best wife possible and hopefully in a year's time even if he wanted a divorce they could still be friends.

"So what about it, Bella? Will you show whoever did this today that you are a fighter and not a quitter and that you will keep what's yours? Will you marry me so we can do that together?"

She held his gaze, exhaled deeply. "Yes, I'll marry you, Jason."

She thought the smile that touched his lips was priceless and she had to inwardly remind herself he wasn't happy because he was marrying her but because marrying her meant he would co-own her land and get full possession of Hercules. And in marrying him she would get her trust fund back and send a message to whomever was behind the threats to her that they were wasting their time and she wasn't going anywhere.

He leaned down, brushed a kiss across her lips and tightened his hold on her hand. "Come on. Let's go tell the family our good news."

If Jason's brothers and cousins were surprised by their announcement they didn't let on. Probably because they were too busy congratulating them and then making wedding plans.

She and Jason had decided the true nature of their marriage was between them. They planned to keep it that way. The Westmorelands didn't so much as bat an eye when Jason further announced they would be getting married as soon as possible. Tomorrow in fact. He assured everyone they could plan a huge reception for later.

Bella decided to contact her parents *after* the wedding tomorrow. A judge who was a friend of the Westmorelands was given a call and he immediately agreed to perform the civil ceremony in his chambers around three in the afternoon. Dillon and Ramsey suggested the family celebrate the nuptials by joining them for dinner after the ceremony at a restaurant downtown.

The honeymoon would come later. For now they would spend the night at a hotel downtown. With so many things to do to prepare for tomorrow, Bella was able to put the fire behind her and she actually looked forward to her wedding day. She was also able to put out of her mind the reason they were marrying in the first place. Dillon and Pam invited her to spend the night in their home, and she accepted their invitation.

"Come walk me out to my truck," Jason whispered, taking her hand in his.

"All right."

When they got to where his truck was parked, he placed her against it and leaned over and kissed her in a deep, drugging kiss. When he released her lips he whispered, "You can come home with me tonight, you know."

Yes, she knew but then she also knew if she did so,

they would consummate a wedding that was yet to take place. She wanted to do things in the right order. The way she'd always dreamed of doing them when she read all those romance novels.

"Yes, I know but I'll be fine staying with Dillon and Pam tonight. Tomorrow will be here before you know it." She then paused and looked up at him, searched his gaze. "And you think we're doing the right thing, Jason?"

He smiled, nodding. "Yes, I'm positive. After the ceremony we'll contact your parents and provide their attorney with whatever documentation needed to kick your trust fund back in gear. And I'm sure word will get around soon enough for whoever has been making those threats to hear Bella Bostwick Westmoreland is here to stay."

Bella Bostwick Westmoreland. She liked the sound of it already but deep down she knew she couldn't get attached to it. She stared into his eyes and hoped he wouldn't wake up one morning and think he'd made a mistake and the proposal hadn't been worth it.

"Everything will work out for the best, Bella. You'll see." He then pulled her into his arms and kissed her again.

"I now pronounce you man and wife. Jason, you may kiss your bride."

Jason didn't waste any time pulling Bella into his arms and devouring her mouth the way he'd gotten accustomed to doing.

He had expected a small audience but every Westmoreland living in Denver was there, except Micah, his brother who was a year older and an epidemiologist with the federal government, as well as his brothers Canyon and Stern who were away attending law school. And of course he missed his cousin Gemma who was living with her husband in Australia, and his younger brother Bane who was in the navy. Jason also missed the twins, Aiden and Adrian. They were away at college.

When he finally released Bella's mouth, cheers went up and he glanced at Bella and knew at that moment just how much he loved her. He would prove the depth of his love over the rest of their lives. He knew she assumed after the first year either of them could file for divorce, but he didn't intend for that to happen. Ever. There would be no divorce.

He glanced down at the ring he'd placed on her finger. He had picked her up at eight that morning, taken her into town for breakfast and from there a whirlwind of activities had begun with a visit to the jeweler. Then to the courthouse to file the necessary papers so they could marry on time. Luckily there was no waiting period in Colorado and he was grateful for that.

"Hey, Jason and Bella. Are the two of you ready for dinner?" Dillon asked, smiling.

Jason smiled back. "Yes, we are." He took Bella's hand in his, felt the sensations touching her elicited and knew that, personally, he was ready for something else, as well.

Bella cast a quick glance over at Jason as they stepped on the elevator that would take them up to their hotel room in the tower—the honeymoon suite—compliments of the entire Westmoreland family. She realized she hadn't just married the man but had also inherited his entire family. For someone who'd never had an extended family before, she could only be elated.

Dinner with everyone had been wonderful and Jason's brothers and cousins had stood to offer toasts to what everyone saw as a long marriage. There hadn't been anything in Jason's expression indicating they were way off base in that assumption or that it was wishful thinking on their parts.

All of the Westmoreland ladies had given her hugs and welcomed her to the family. The men had hugged her, as well, and she could tell they were genuinely happy for her and Jason.

And now they were on the elevator that would carry them to the floor where their room was located. They would be spending the night, sleeping under the same roof and sharing the same bed. They hadn't discussed such a thing happening, but she knew it was an unspoken understanding between them.

Jason had become quiet and she wondered if he'd already regretted making the proposal. The thought that he had sent her into a panic mode, made her heart begin to break a piece at a time. Then without warning, she felt his hand touch her arm and when she glanced over at him he smiled and reached for her and pulled her closer to his side, as if refusing to let her stand anywhere by herself…without him. It was as if he was letting her know she would never ever be alone again.

She knew a part of her was probably rationalizing things the way she wished they were, the way she wanted them to be but not necessarily how they really were. But if she had to fantasize then she would do that. If she had to pretend they had a real marriage for the next year then she would do that, too. However, a part of her would never lose sight of the real reason she was here. A part of her would always be prepared for the inevitable.

"You were a beautiful bride, Bella."

"Thank you." Warmth spread through her in knowing that he'd thought so because she had tried so hard to be. She had been determined to make some part of today resemble a real wedding—even if it was a civil one in the judge's chambers. The ladies in the family had insisted that she be turned over to them after securing a license at the Denver County Court House and had promised Jason she would be on time for her wedding.

It had taken less than an hour to obtain the marriage license and Lucia had been there to pick her up afterward. Bella had been whisked away for a day of beauty and to visit a very exclusive bridal shop to pick up the perfect dress for her wedding. Since time was of the essence, everything had been arranged beforehand. When they had delivered her back to Jason five hours later, the moment she'd joined him in the judge's chambers his smile had let her know he thought her time away from him had been well worth it. She would forever be grateful to her new in-laws and a part of her knew that Pam, Chloe, Megan, Lucia and Bailey would also be friends she could count on for life.

"You look good yourself," she said softly.

She thought that was an understatement. She had seen him in a suit the night at the charity ball. He had taken her breath away then and was taking it away now. Tall, dark and handsome, he was the epitome of every woman's fantasy and dream. And for at least one full year, he would be hers.

The elevator stopped on their floor and tightening his hand on hers, they stepped out. Her breath caught when the elevator doors whooshed closed behind them and they began walking toward room 4501. She knew once they reached those doors and she stepped inside there would be no turning back.

They silently strolled side by side holding hands. Everything about the Four Seasons Hotel spoke of its elegance and the decorative colors all around were vibrant and vivid.

Jason released her hand when they reached their room to pull the passkey from the pocket of his suit jacket. Once he opened the door he extended his hand to her and she took it, felt the sensations flowing between them. She gasped when she was suddenly swept off her feet and into his arms and carried over the threshold into the honeymoon suite.

Jason kicked the door closed with his foot before placing Bella on her feet. And then he just stood there and looked at her, allowing his gaze to roam all over her. What he'd told her earlier was true. She was a beautiful bride.

And she was his.

Absolutely and positively his.

Her tea-length dress was ivory in color and made of silk chiffon and fitted at her small waist with a rose in the center. It was a perfect match for the ivory satin rose-heeled shoes on her feet. White roses were her favorite flower and she'd used them as the theme in their wedding. Even her wedding bouquet had consisted of white roses.

His chest expanded with so much love for her, love she didn't know about yet. He had a year to win her over and intended to spend the next twelve months doing just that. But now, he needed for her to know just how much she was desired.

He lowered his head and kissed her, letting his tongue tangle with hers, reacquainting himself with the taste of her, a taste he had not forgotten and had so desperately craved since the last time. He kissed her deeply, not allowing any part of her mouth to go untouched. And she returned the kiss with a hunger that matched his own and he was mesmerized by how she was making him feel.

He tightened his hold on her, molding his body to hers, and was certain she could feel the hot ridge of his erection pressing against her. It was throbbing something awful with a need for her that was monumental. He had wanted her for a long time…ever since he'd seen her that night at the ball, and his desire for her hadn't diminished any since. If anything, it had only increased to a level that even now he could feel his gut tighten in desire. Taking her hands he deliberately began slowly lifting her dress up toward her waist.

"Wrap your legs around me, Bella," he whispered and assisted by lifting her hips when she wrapped her legs around him to walk her toward the bedroom. It was a huge suite and he was determined that later, after they took care of business in the bedroom, they would check out all the amenities the suite had to offer; especially the large Jacuzzi bathtub. Already he saw the beauty of downtown Denver from their hotel room window.

But downtown Denver was the last thing on his mind right now. Making love to his wife was.

His wife.

He began kissing her again, deeper and longer, loving the way her tongue mated with his over and over again. He placed her on the bed while reaching behind her to unfasten her dress and slide it from her body. It was then that he took a step back and thought he was dreaming. No fantasy could top what he was seeing now.

She was wearing a white lace bra and matching panties. On any other woman such a color would come across as ultrainnocence, but on Bella it became the epitome of sexual desire.

He needed to completely undress her and did so while thinking of everything he wanted to do to her. When she was on her knees in the middle of the bed naked, he could tell from her expression that this was the first time a man had seen her body and the thought sent shivers through him as his gaze roamed over her in male appreciation. A shudder of primal pride flowed through him and he could only stand there and take her all in.

An erection that was already hard got even harder when he looked at her chest, an area he had yet to taste. Her twin globes were firm. His tongue tingled at the thought of being wrapped around those nipples.

No longer able to resist temptation, he moved toward the bed and placed a knee on it and immediately leaned in to capture a nipple in his mouth. His tongue latched on the hard nub and began playing all kinds of games with it. Games she seemed to enjoy if the way she was pushing her breasts deeper into his mouth was anything to go by.

He heard her moan as he continued to torture her nipples, with quick nips followed by sucking motions and when he reached down to let his hands test her to see how ready she was, he found she was definitely ready for him. Pulling back he eased from the bed to remove his clothes as she watched.

"I'm not on the Pill, Jason."

He glanced over at her. "You're not?"

"No."

And evidently thinking she needed to explain further she said, "I haven't been sexually active with anyone."

"Since?"

"Never."

A part of him wasn't surprised. In fact he had suspected as much. He'd known no other man had performed oral sex on her but hadn't been sure of the depth of any other sexual experience. "Any reason you hadn't?"

She met his gaze and held it. "I've been waiting for you."

He drew in a sharp breath and wondered if she knew what she'd just insinuated and figured she hadn't. Maybe she hadn't insinuated anything and it was just wishful thinking on his part. He loved her and would give just about anything for her to love him in return. And until she said the words, he wouldn't assume anything.

"Then your wait is over, sweetheart," he said, sliding on a condom over the thickness of his erection while she looked on. And from the fascinated expression on her face he could tell what she was seeing was another first for her.

When he completed that task he moved to the bed and toward her. "You are so beautifully built, Jason," she said softly, and as if she needed to test her ability to arouse him, she leaned up and flicked out her tongue, licking one of the hardened nubs on his breast like he'd done earlier to her.

He drew in a sharp intake of breath. "You're a quick learner," he said huskily.

"Is that good or bad?"

He smiled at her. "For us it will always be good."

Since this would be her first time he wanted her more than ready and knew of one way to do it. He eased her down on the bed and decided to lick her into an orgasm. Starting at her mouth, he slowly moved downward to her chin, trekked down her neck to her breasts. By the time he'd made it past her midriff to her flat tummy she was writhing under his mouth but he didn't mind. That was a telltale sign of how she was feeling.

"Open your legs, baby," he whispered. The moment she did so he dipped his head to ease his tongue between the folds of her femininity. He recalled doing this to her the last time and knew just what spots would make her moan deep in her throat. Tonight he wanted to do better than that. He wanted to make her scream.

Over and over again he licked her to the edge of an orgasm then withdrew his tongue and began torturing her all over again. She sobbed his name, moaned and groaned. And then, when she was on the verge of an explosion he shifted upward and placed his body over hers.

When he guided his erection in place, he held her

gaze and lowered his body to join with hers, uniting them as one. She was tight and he kept a level of control as he eased inside her, feeling how firm a hold her clenched muscles had on him. He didn't want to hurt her and moved inch by slow inch inside her. When he had finally reached the hilt, he closed his eyes but didn't move. He needed to be still for a moment and grasp the significance of what was taking place. He was making love to his wife and she was a wife he loved more than life.

He slowly opened his eyes and met hers and saw she had been watching...waiting and needing him to finish what he'd started. So he did. He began moving slowly, with an extremely low amount of pressure as he began moving in and out of her. When she arched her back, he increased the pressure and the rhythm.

The sounds she began making sent him spiraling and let him know she was loving it. The more she moaned, the more she got. Several times he'd gone so deep inside her he knew he had touched her womb and the thought that he had done so made him crave her that much more.

She released a number of shuddering breaths as he continued to thrust, claiming her as his while she claimed him as hers. And then she threw her head back and screamed out his name.

That's when he came, filling her while groaning thickly as an orgasm overtook them both. The spasms that rammed through his body were so powerful he had to force himself to breathe. He bucked against her several times as he continued to ride her through the force of his release.

He inhaled the scent of their lovemaking before

leaning down to capture her mouth, and knew at that moment the night for them was just beginning.

Sometime during the night Jason woke up from the feel of Bella's mouth on him. Immediately his erection began to swell.

"Oh." She pulled her mouth away and looked up at him with a blush on her face. "I thought you were asleep."

His lips curved into a smile. "I was but there are some things a man can't sleep through. What are you doing down there?"

She raised her head to meet his gaze. "Tasting you the way you tasted me," she said softly.

"You didn't have to wait until I was asleep, you know," he said, feeling himself get even harder. Although he was no longer inside her mouth, it was still close. Right there. And the heat of her breath was way too close.

"I know, but you were asleep and I thought I would practice first. I didn't want to embarrass myself while you were awake and get it wrong," she said, blushing even more.

He chuckled, thinking her blush was priceless. "Baby, this is one of those things a woman can never get wrong."

"Do you want me to stop?"

"What do you think?"

She smiled up at him shyly. Wickedly. Wantonly. "I think you don't. Just remember this is a practice session."

She then leaned closer and slid him back into her mouth. He groaned deep in his throat when she began making love to him this way. Earlier that night he had licked her into an orgasm and now she was licking him to insanity. He made a low sound in the back of his throat when she began pulling everything out of him with her mouth. If this was a practice session she would kill him when it came to the real thing.

"Bella!"

He quickly reached down and pulled her up to him and flipped her onto her back. He moved on top of her and pushed inside of her, realizing too late when he felt himself explode that he wasn't wearing a condom. The thought that he could be making her pregnant jutted an even bigger release from his body into hers.

His entire body quivered from the magnitude of the powerful thrusts that kept coming, thrusts he wasn't able to stop. The more she gave, the more he wanted and when her hips arched off the bed, he drove in deeper and came again.

"Jason!"

She was following him to sweet oblivion and his heart began hammering at the realization that this was lovemaking as naked as it could get, and he clung to it, clung to her. A low, shivering moan escaped his lips and when her thighs began to tremor, he felt the vibration to the core.

Moments later he collapsed on top of her, moaned her name as his manhood buried inside of her continued to throb, cling to her flesh as her inner muscles wouldn't release their hold.

What they'd just shared as well as all the other times they'd made love tonight was so unbearably pleasurable he couldn't think straight. The thought of what she'd been doing when he had awakened sent sensuous chills down his body.

He opened his mouth to speak but immediately closed it when he saw she had drifted off to sleep. She made such an erotic picture lying there with her eyes closed, soft dark curls framing her face and the sexiest lips he'd ever had the pleasure of kissing slightly parted.

He continued to look at her, thinking he would let her get some rest now. Later he intended to wake her up the same way she'd woken him.

Chapter 8

The following morning after they'd enjoyed breakfast in bed, Bella figured now was just as good a time as any to let her parents know she was a married woman.

She picked up her cell phone and then glanced over at Jason and smiled. That smile gave her the inner strength for the confrontation she knew was coming. The thought of her outwitting them by marrying—and someone from Denver—would definitely throw her parents into a tizzy. She could just imagine what they would try to do. But just as Jason had said, they could try but wouldn't succeed. She and Jason were as married as married could get and there was nothing her parents could do about it.

Taking a deep breath she punched in their number and when the housekeeper answered she was put on hold, waiting for her father to pick up the line.

"Elizabeth. I hope you're calling to say you've come to your senses and have purchased a one-way plane ticket back home."

She frowned. He didn't even take the time to ask how she was doing. Although she figured her parents had nothing to do with those two incidents this week, she decided to ask anyway. "Tell me something, Dad. Did you and Mom think using scare tactics to get me to return to Savannah would work?"

"What are you talking about?"

"Three days ago someone threw a rock through my living room window with a threatening note for me to leave town, and two days ago someone torched my house. Luckily I wasn't there at the time."

"Someone set Dad's house on fire?"

She'd heard the shock in his voice and she heard something else, too. Empathy. This was the first time she'd heard him refer to Herman as "Dad."

"Yes."

"I didn't have anything to do with that, Elizabeth. Your mother and I would never put you in danger like that. What kind of parents do you think we are?"

"Controlling. But I didn't call to exchange words, Dad. I'm just calling for you and Mother to share my good news. I got married yesterday."

"What!"

"That's right. I got married to a wonderful man by the name of Jason Westmoreland."

"Westmoreland?"

"Yes."

"I went to schools with some Westmorelands. Their land was connected to ours."

"Probably his parents. They're deceased now."

"Sorry to hear that, but I hope you know why he married you. He wants that land. But don't worry about it, dear. It can easily be remedied once you file for an annulment."

She shook her head. Her parents just didn't get it. "Jason didn't force me to marry him, Dad. I married him of my own free will."

"Listen, Elizabeth, you haven't been living out there even a full month. You don't know this guy. I will not allow you to marry him."

"Dad, I am already married to him and I plan to send your attorney a copy of our marriage license so the hold on my trust fund will be lifted."

"You think you're smart, Elizabeth. I know what you're doing and I won't allow it. You don't love him and he can't love you."

"Sounds pretty much like the same setup you and Mom have got going. The same kind of marriage you wanted me to enter with Hugh. So what's the problem? I don't see where there is one and I refuse to discuss the matter with you any longer. Goodbye, Dad. Give Mom my best." She then clicked off the phone.

"I take it the news of our marriage didn't go over well with your father."

She glanced over at Jason who was lying beside her and smiled faintly. "Did you really expect that it would?"

"No and it really doesn't matter. They'll just have to get over it."

She snuggled closer to him. That was one of the things she liked about Jason. He was his own man. "What time do we have to check out of here?"

"By noon. And then we'll be on our way to Jason's Place."

She had to restrain the happiness she felt upon knowing they would be going to his home where she would live for at least the next twelve months. "Are there any do's and don'ts that I need to know about?"

.He lifted a brow. "Do's and don'ts?"

"Yes. My time at your home is limited. I don't want to jeopardize my welcome." She could have sworn she'd seen something flash in his eyes but couldn't be certain.

"You'd never jeopardize your welcome and no, there are no do's and don'ts that will apply to you, unless…"

Now it was her turn to raise a brow. "Unless what?"

"You take a notion to paint my bedroom pink or something."

She couldn't help bursting out in laughter. She calmed down enough to ask, "What about yellow? Will that do?"

"Not one of my favorite colors but I guess it will work."

She smiled as she snuggled even closer to him. She was looking forward to living under the same roof with Jason.

"Bella?"

She glanced up. "Yes?"

"The last time we made love, I didn't use a condom."

She'd been aware of it but hadn't expected him to talk about it. "Yes, I know."

"It wasn't intentional."

"I know that, too," she said softly. There was no reason he would want to get her pregnant. That would only throw a monkey wrench in their agreement.

They didn't say anything for a long moment and then he asked, "Do you like children?"

She wondered why he was asking such a thing. Surely he had seen her interactions with Susan and Denver enough to know that she did. "Yes, I like children."

"Do you think you'd want any of your own one day?"

Was he asking because he was worried that she would use that as a trap to stay with him beyond the one year? But he'd asked and she needed to be honest. "Yes, I'd love children, although I haven't had the best of childhoods. Don't get me wrong, my parents weren't monsters or anything like that but they just weren't affectionate…at least not like your family."

She paused for a moment. "I love my parents, Jason, although I doubt my relationship with them will ever be what I've always wished for. They aren't that kind of people. Displaying affection isn't one of their strong points. If I become a mother I want to do just the opposite. There will never be a day my child will not know he or she is loved." She hadn't meant to say all of that and now she couldn't help wondering if doing so would ruin things between them.

"I think you would make a wonderful mother."

His words touched her. "Thank you for saying that."

"You're welcome, and I meant it."

She drew in a deep breath, wondering how he could be certain of such a thing. She continued to stare at him for a long moment. He would be a gift to any woman and he had sacrificed himself to marry her—just because he'd wanted her land and Hercules. When she thought about it she found it pitiful that it had taken that to make him want to join his life to hers.

He lifted her hand and looked at the ring he'd placed there. She looked at it, too. It was beautiful. More than she'd expected and everyone had oohed and aahed over it.

"You're wearing my ring," he said softly.

The sound of his deep, husky voice made her tummy tingle and a heated sensation spread all through her. "Yes, I'm wearing your ring. It's beautiful. Thank you."

Then she lifted his hand. Saw the gold band brilliantly shining in the sunlight. "And you're wearing mine."

And then she found herself being kissed by him and she knew that no matter how their marriage might end up, right now it was off to a great beginning.

For the second time in two days Jason carried the woman he loved over the threshold. This time he walked into his house. "Welcome to Jason's Place, sweetheart," he said, placing her on her feet.

Bella glanced around. This was the first time she'd been inside Jason's home. She'd seen it a few times from a distance and thought the two-story dwelling flanked by a number of flowering trees was simply beautiful. On the drive from town he'd given her a little history of his home. It had taken an entire year to build and he had built it himself, with help from all the other Westmorelands. And with all the pride she'd heard when he spoke of it, she knew he loved his home. She could see why. The design was magnificent. The decorating—which had been done by his cousin

Gemma—was breathtaking and perfect for the single
man he'd been.

Jason's eyes never left Bella's as he studied her reaction to being in his home. As far as he was concerned,
she would be a permanent fixture. His heart would
beat when hers did. His breath was released the same
time hers was. He had shared something with her he
had never done with any woman—the essence of himself. For the first time in his life he had made love to
a woman without wearing a condom. It had felt wonderful being skin to skin, flesh to flesh with her—but
only with her. The wife he adored and intended to
keep forever.

He knew he had a job to do where she was concerned and it would be one that would give him the
greatest of pleasure and satisfaction. Her pain was his
pain, her happiness was his. Their lives were now entwined and all because of the proposal he'd offered
and she'd taken.

Without thought he turned her in his arms and lowered his head to kiss her, needing the feel of his mouth
on hers, her body pressed against his. The kiss was
long, deep and the most satisfying experience he could
imagine. But then, he'd had nothing but satisfying ex-
periences with her. And he planned on having plenty
more.

"Aren't you going to work today?" Bella asked Jason
the following day over breakfast. She was learning her
way around his spacious kitchen and loved doing it.
They had stayed inside yesterday after he'd brought
her here. He had kept her mostly in the bedroom, saying their honeymoon was still ongoing. And she had

been not one to argue considering the glow she figured had to be on her face. Jason was the most ardent and generous of lovers.

Her mother had called last night trying to convince her she'd made a mistake and that she and her father would be flying into Denver in a few days to talk some sense into her. Bella had told her mother she didn't think coming to Denver was a good idea, but of course Melissa Bostwick wouldn't listen.

When Bella had told Jason about the latest developments—namely her parents' planned trip to Denver—he'd merely shrugged and told her not to worry about it. That was easy for him to say. He'd never met her parents.

"No, I'm not going to work today. I'm still on my honeymoon," Jason said, breaking into her thoughts. "You tell me what you want to do today and we'll do it."

She turned away from the stove where she'd prepared something simple like French toast. "You want to spend more time with me?"

He chuckled. "Of course I do. You sound surprised."

She was. She figured as much time as they'd spent in the bedroom he would have tired of her by now. She was about to open her mouth when his house phone rang. He smiled over at her. "Excuse me for a minute while I get that."

Bella figured the caller was one of his relatives. She turned back to the stove to turn it off. She couldn't help but smile at the thought that he wanted to spend more time with her.

A few moments later Jason hung up the phone. "That was Sheriff Harper."

She turned back around to him. "Has he found out anything?"

"Yes, they've made some arrests."

A lump formed in her throat. She crossed the floor to sit down at the table, thinking she didn't want to be standing for this. "Who did it?"

He came to sit across from her. "Your uncle Kenneth's twin grandsons."

Bella's hand flew to her chest. "But they're only fourteen years old."

"Yes, but the footprints outside your window and the fingerprints on the rock matched theirs. Not to mention that the kerosene can they used to start the fire at your ranch belonged to their parents."

Bella didn't say anything. She just continued to stare at him.

"Evidently they heard their grandfather's grumblings about you and figured they were doing him a favor by scaring you away," Jason said.

"What will happen to them?" she asked quietly.

"Right now they're in police custody. A judge will decide tomorrow if they will be released into the custody of their parents until a court date is set. If they are found guilty, and chances are they will be since the evidence against them is so strong, they will serve time in a detention center for youth for about one or two years, maybe longer depending on any prior arrests."

Jason's face hardened. "Personally, it wouldn't bother me in the least if they locked them up and threw away the key. I'm sure Kenneth is fit to be tied, though. He thinks the world of those two."

Bella shook her head sadly. "I feel so badly about this."

A deep scowl covered Jason's face. "Why do you feel badly? You're the victim and they broke the law."

, She could tell by the sound of his voice that he was still upset. "But they're just kids. I need to call Uncle Kenneth."

"Why? As far as I'm concerned this is all his fault for spouting off at the mouth around them about you."

A part of Bella knew what Jason said was true and could even accept he had a right to be angry, but still, the thought that she was responsible for the disruption of so many lives was getting to her. Had she made a mistake in moving to Denver after all?

"Don't even think it, Bella."

She glanced across the table at Jason. "What?"

"I know what's going through your mind, sweetheart. I can see it all over your face and you want to blame yourself for what happened but it's not your fault."

"Isn't it?"

"No. You can't hold yourself responsible for the actions of others. What if you had been standing near the window the day that rock came flying through, or worse yet, what if you'd been home the day they set fire to the house? If I sound mad it's because I still am. And I'm going to stay mad until justice is served."

He paused a moment and then said, "I don't want to talk about Kenneth or his grandsons any longer. Come on, let's get dressed and go riding."

When they returned from riding and Bella checked her cell phone, she had received a call from her parents saying that they had changed their minds and would not be coming to Denver after all. She couldn't help wondering why, but she figured the best thing to do was count her blessings and be happy about their change in plans.

Jason was outside putting the horses away and she decided to take a shower and change into something relaxing. So far, other than the sheriff, no one else had called. She figured Jason's family was treating them as honeymooners and giving them their privacy.

When her cell phone rang, she didn't recognize the caller but figured it might be one of her parents calling from another number. "Yes?"

"This is all your fault, Bella."

She froze upon hearing her uncle's voice. He was angry. "My grandsons might be going to some youth detention center for a couple of years because of you."

Bella drew in a deep breath and remembered the conversation she and Jason had had earlier that day. "You should not have talked badly about me in front of them."

"Are you saying it's my fault?"

"Yes, Uncle Kenneth, that's exactly what I'm saying. You have no one else to blame but yourself."

"Why you… How dare you speak to me that way. You think you're something now that you're married to a Westmoreland. Well, you'll see what a mistake you made. All Jason Westmoreland wanted was your land and that horse. He doesn't care anything about you. I told you I knew someone who wanted to buy your land."

"And I've always told you my land isn't for sale."

"If you don't think Westmoreland plans to weasel it from you then you're crazy. Just mark my word. You mean nothing to him. All he wants is that land. He is nothing but a controller and a manipulator."

Her uncle then hung up the phone on her.

Bella tried not to let her uncle's words get to her. No one knew the details of their marriage so her uncle had no idea that she was well aware that Jason wanted her land and horse. For what other reason would he have presented her with that proposal? She wasn't the crazy person her uncle evidently assumed she was. She was operating with more than a full deck and was also well aware Jason didn't love her.

She glanced up when Jason walked through the back door. He smiled when he saw her. "I thought you were going to take a shower."

"I was, but I got a phone call."

"Oh, from who?"

She knew now was not the time to tell him about her uncle's call—especially after all he'd said earlier. So she decided to take that time to tell him about her parents' decision.

"Dad and Mom called. They aren't coming after all."

"What changed their minds?" he asked, taking a seat on the sofa.

"Not sure. They didn't say."

He caught her wrist and pulled her down on the sofa beside him. "Well, I have a lot to say, none of it nice. But the main thing is they've decided not to come and I think it's a good move on their part because I don't want anyone to upset you."

"No one will," she said softly. "I'm fine."

"And I want to make sure you stay that way," he said and pulled her closer into his arms.

She was quiet as her head lay rested against his chest and could actually hear his heart pounding. She wondered if he could hear the pounding of her heart.

She still found it strange how attracted they were to each other. Getting married hadn't lessened that any.

She lifted her head to look up at him and saw the intense look that was there in his eyes. It was a look that was so intimate it sent a rush of heat sprinting all through her.

And when he began easing his mouth toward hers, all thoughts left her mind except for one, and that was how much he could make her feel loved even when he was pretending. The moment their lips touched she refused to believe her uncle Kenneth's claim that he was controlling.

Instead she concentrated on how he was making her feel with the way his mouth was mating with hers. And she knew this kiss was just the beginning.

Chapter 9

During the next few weeks Bella settled into what she considered a comfortable routine. She'd never thought being married would be such a wonderful experience and could only thank Jason for making the transition easy for her.

They shared a bed and made passionate love each night. Then in the morning they would get up early and while he sat at the table drinking coffee she would enjoy a cup of tea while he told her about what horses he would be training that day.

While he was away she usually kept busy by reading her grandfather's journals, which had been upstairs in her bedroom and so were spared by the fire. Because she'd been heavily involved with a lot of charity work while living in Savannah, she'd already volunteered a lot of her time at the children's hospital and the West-moreland Foundation.

Hercules was now in Jason's stalls and Jason was working with the insurance company on the repairs of her ranch. He had arranged for all the men who'd worked with her before the fire to be hired on with his horse training business.

Although she appreciated him stepping in and taking charge of her affairs the way he'd done, she hadn't been able to put her uncle Kenneth's warning out of her mind. She knew it was ludicrous to worry about Jason's motivation because he had been honest with her from the beginning and she knew why he'd made the proposal for their marriage. She was well aware that he didn't love her and that he was only married to her for the land and Hercules. But now that he had both was it just a matter of time for him before he tried to get rid of her?

She would be the first to admit he never acted as if he was getting tired of her and still treated her as if he enjoyed having her around. In the afternoons when he returned home for work, the first thing he did after placing his Stetson on the hat rack was to seek her out. Usually he didn't have far to look because she would be right there, close by. Anticipating his return home always put her near the door when he entered the house.

Bella couldn't help noticing that over the last couple of days she had begun getting a little antsy where Jason was concerned because she was uncertain as to her future with him. And to make matters even worse she was late, which was a good sign she might be pregnant. She hadn't told him of her suspicions because she wasn't sure how he would take the news.

If she were pregnant, the baby would be born within the first year of their marriage. Would he still want a divorce even if she was the mother of his child or would he want to keep her around for that same reason; because he felt obligated to do so? But an even more important question was, did he even want to become a father? He had questioned her feelings on motherhood but she'd never questioned his. She could tell from his interactions with Susan and Denver that he liked kids, but that didn't necessarily mean he wanted any of his own.

Bella knew she should tell him about the possibility she could be pregnant and discuss her concerns with him now, but each time she was presented with the opportunity to do so, she would get cold feet.

She walked into an empty room he'd converted into an office and sat down at the desk to glance out the window. She would finally admit that another reason she was antsy was that she knew without a shadow of doubt that she had fallen in love with Jason and could certainly understand how such a thing had happened. She could understand it, but would he? He'd never asked for her love, just her land and horse.

She heard the sound of a vehicle door closing and stood from the desk, went to the window and looked down. It was Jason. He glanced up and saw her and a smile touched the corners of his mouth. Instantly she felt the buds of her nipples harden against her blouse. A flush of desire rushed through her and she knew at that moment her panties had gotten wet. The man could turn her on with a single look. He was home earlier than usual. Three hours earlier.

Now that he was here a lot of ideas flowed in her

mind on how they could use those extra hours. What she wanted to do first was to take him into her mouth, something she discovered she enjoyed doing. And then he could return the favor by putting that tongue of his to work between her legs. She shuddered at the thought and figured her hormones were on the attack; otherwise, she wouldn't be thinking such scandalous things. They were definitely not things a Miss Prim and Proper lady would think.

He broke eye contact with her to walk up the steps to come into the house and she rushed out of the office to stand at the top of the stairs. She glanced down the moment he opened the door. Jason's dark gaze latched on her and immediately her breath was snatched from her lungs. As she watched, he locked the door behind him and slowly began removing the clothes from his body, first tossing his hat on the rack and then unbuttoning his shirt.

She felt hot as she watched him and he didn't stop. He had completely removed his shirt and she couldn't help admiring the broad shoulders and sinewy muscular thighs in jeans. The masculine sight had blood rushing fast and furious through her veins.

"I'm coming up," he said in a deep, husky voice.

She slowly began backing up when he started moving up the stairs with a look in his eyes that was as predatory as anything she'd ever seen. And there was a deep, intense hunger in his gaze that had her heart hammering like crazy in her chest.

When he cleared the top stair and stepped onto the landing, she breathed in deeply, taking in his scent, while thinking that no man had a right to smell so good, look so utterly male and be so damn hot in a way that would overwhelm any woman's senses.

At least no man but Jason Westmoreland.

"Take off your clothes, Bella," he said in a deep, throaty voice.

She then asked what some would probably think was a dumb question. "Why?"

He moved slowly toward her and it was as if her feet were glued to the spot and she couldn't move. And when he came to a stop in front of her, she tilted back her head to look up at him, saw the hunger in his dark brown gaze. The intensity of that look sent a shudder through her.

He reached out and cupped her face in the palms of his hands and lowered his head slightly to whisper, "I came home early because I need to make love to you. And I need to do it now."

And then he captured her mouth with his, kissing her with the same intensity and hunger she'd seen in his eyes. She returned his kiss, not understanding why he needed to make love to her and why now. But she knew she would give him whatever he wanted and whatever way he wanted it.

He was ravishing her mouth, making her moan deep in her throat. His kiss seemed to be making a statement and staking a claim all at the same time. She couldn't do anything but take whatever he was giving, and she did so gladly and without shame. He had no idea she loved him. How much sharing these past few weeks had meant to her.

And then he jerked his mouth away and quickly removed his boots. Afterward, he carried her into the office and stood her by the desk as he began taking off her clothes with a frenzy that had her head spinning. One part of her wanted to tell him to slow down and to assure him she wasn't going anywhere. But another part was just as eager and excited as he was to get naked, and kept insisting that he hurry up.

Within minutes, more like seconds, spooned between his body and the desk, she was totally naked. The cool air from the air conditioner that swept across her heated skin made her want to cover herself with her hands, but he wouldn't let her. He gently grabbed her wrists in his and held them up over her head, which made her breasts tilt up in perfect alignment to his lips when he leaned down.

On a breathless sigh he eased a nipple into his mouth, sucking it in between his lips and then licking the throbbing tip. She arched her back, felt him gently ease her onto the desk and realized he was practically on the desk with her. The metal surface felt cool to her back, but the warmth of his body felt hot to her front.

He lowered his hand to her sex and the stroke of his fingers on the folds of her labia made her groan out sounds she'd never made before. She'd thought from the first that he had skillful fingers and they were thrumming through her, stirring all kinds of sensations within her. Their lovemaking would often range from gentle to hard and she knew today would be one of those hard times. For whatever reason, he was driven to take her now, without any gentleness of any kind. He was stroking a need within her that wanted it just as fast and hard as he could deliver.

He took a step back and quickly removed his jeans and boxers. When she saw him—in his engorged splendor—a sound of dire need erupted from deep within her throat. He was bringing her to this, this intense state of want and need that was fueled by passion and desire.

"I want to know your taste, baby."

It was on the tip of her tongue to say that as many times as he'd made a meal out of her that he should know it pretty well by now. Instead when he crouched down in front of her body, which was all but spread out on the desk, and proceeded to wrap her legs over his shoulders, she automatically arched her back.

And when she felt his hot mouth close in on her sex, slide his tongue through her womanly folds, she lifted her hips off the table with the intimate contact. And when he began suckling hard, using his tongue to both torture and pleasure, she let out an intense moan as an orgasm tore through her body; sensations started at the soles of her feet and traveled like wildfire all the way to the crown of her head. And then she screamed at the top of her lungs.

Shudders continued to rip through her, made her muscles both ache and rejuvenate. And she couldn't help but lie there while Jason continued to get the taste he wanted.

When her shudders finally subsided, he gave her body one complete and thorough lick before lifting his head and looking up at her with a satisfied smile on his face, and the way he began licking his lips made her feel hot all over again.

He reached out and spread her legs wide and began stroking her again and she began moaning at the contact. "My fingers are all wet, which means you're ready," he said. "Now for me to get ready."

And she knew without looking that he was tearing

into a condom packet and soon would be sliding the latex over his erection. After that first time in the hotel he'd never made love to her unprotected again, which gave her even more reason to think he wasn't ready for children. At least not with her, anyway.

From the feel of his erection pressing against her thigh she would definitely agree that at least he was ready for this, probably more ready than any man had a right to be, but she had no complaints.

She came to full attention when she felt his swollen, engorged member easing between her legs, and when he centered it to begin sliding between the folds of her labia and then suddenly thrust forward without any preamble, she began shuddering all over again.

"Look at me, baby. I want to be looking in your eyes when you come. I need to see it happen, Bella."

She looked up and met his gaze. He was buried deep inside of her and then holding tight to her gaze, he began moving, holding tight to the hips whose legs were wrapped firmly around him. They began moving together seemingly in perfect rhythm, faultless harmony and seamless precision. With each deep and thorough stroke, she felt all of him…every glorious inch.

"You tasted good and now you feel good," he said in a guttural voice while holding steadfast to her gaze. "Do you have any idea how wonderful you are making me feel?"

She had an idea. If it was anything close to how he was making her feel then the feelings were definitely mutual. And to show him just how mutual, her inner muscles began clamping down on him, milking him. She could tell from the look in his eyes the exact moment he realized what she was doing and the effect it was having on him. The more she milked him the bigger he seemed to get inside of her, as if he intended for her to have it all.

Today she felt greedy and was glad he intended to supply her needs. She dug her nails into his shoulders, at the moment not caring if she was branding him for life. And then he picked up the tempo and pleasure, the likes of nothing she'd experienced before dimming her vision. But through it all, she kept her gaze locked on his and saw how every sound, every move she made, got to him and triggered him to keep it coming.

And then when she felt her body break into fragments, she screamed out his name and he began pumping into her as if his very life depended on it. The orgasm that ripped through her snatched the breath from her lungs as his intense, relentless strokes almost drove her over the edge. And when she heard the hoarse cry from his own lips, saw the flash of something dark and turbulent in the depths of his eyes, she lost it and screamed again at the top of her lungs as another orgasm shook the core of everything inside her body.

And he followed her, pushed over the edge, while he continued to thrust even deeper. He buried his fingers into her hair and leaned down and captured her mouth to kiss the trembles right off her lips. At that moment she wished she could say all the words that had formed in her heart, words of love she wanted him to know. But she couldn't. This was all there was between them. She had accepted that long ago. And for the moment she was satisfied and content.

And when the day came that he wanted her gone,

memories like these would sustain her, get her through each day without him.

And she prayed to God the memories would be enough.

"So when can we plan your wedding reception?" Megan asked when the Westmorelands had assembled around the dinner table at Dillon's place a few weeks later.

When Bella didn't say anything but looked over at Jason, he shrugged and said, "Throw some dates out to see if they will work for us."

Megan began rambling off dates, saying the first weekend in August would be perfect since all the Westmorelands away at college would be home and Micah, who was presently in Beijing, had sent word he would be back in the States during that time, as well. Gemma, who was expecting, had gotten the doctor's okay to travel from Australia then.

"And," Megan continued, "I spoke with Casey yesterday and she's checked with the other Westmorelands and that will give them plenty of time to make plans to be here, as well. I'm so excited."

Jason glanced over at Bella again thinking he was glad someone was. There was something going on with his wife that he just couldn't put a finger on and whatever it was had put him at a disadvantage. He knew she was upset with the outcome of the Bostwick twins. With all the evidence mounted against the twins, their attorney had convinced their parents to enter a guilty plea in hopes they would get a lesser sentence.

However, given prior mischievous pranks that had gotten the pair into trouble with the law before, the judge was not all that lenient and gave them two years. Bella had insisted on going to the sentencing hearing and he'd warned her against it but she'd been adamant. Things hadn't gone well when Kenneth, who still refused to accept blame for his part in any of it, made a scene, accusing Bella as the one responsible for what had happened to his grandsons. Since that day Jason had noted a change in her and she'd begun withdrawing from him. He'd tried getting her to talk, but she refused to do so.

"So what do the two of you think?" Megan asked, drawing his attention again.

He glanced at Bella. "What do you think, sweetheart?"

She placed a smile on her lips that he knew was forced. "That time is fine with me, but I doubt Mom and Dad will come either way."

"Then they will miss a good party," Jason replied. He then turned to Megan. "The first weekend in August is fine."

Later, on the ride back to their place, Jason finally found out what was troubling Bella. "I rode over to my ranch today, Jason. Why didn't you tell me work hadn't begun on the house yet?"

"There was no reason to tell you. You knew I was taking care of things, didn't you?"

"Yes. But I assumed work had gotten started already."

"I saw no reason to begin work on the place yet, given we're having a lot of rainy days around here now. It's not a good time to start any type of construction. Besides, it's not like you're going to move into the house or anything."

"You don't know that."

He had pulled into the yard and brought the truck to a stop and turned the ignition off. He glanced over at her. "I don't? I thought I did."

He tilted his hat back from his eyes and stared over at her. "Why would you need to move back into the house?"

Instead of holding his gaze she glanced out the window and looked ahead at his house, which he now considered as their house. "Our marriage is only supposed to last a year and I'm going to need somewhere to live when it ends."

Her words were like a kick in the gut. She was already planning for the time when she would be leaving him? Why? He thought things were going great between them. "What's going on, Bella?"

"Nothing is going on. I just need to be realistic and remember that although we enjoy being bed partners, the reason we married stemmed from your proposal, which I accepted knowing full well the terms. And they are terms we must not forget."

Jason simply looked at her as he swore under his breath. She thought the only thing between them was the fact they were bed partners? "Thanks for reminding me, Bella." He then got out of the truck.

That was the first night they slept in the same bed but didn't make love and Bella lay there hurting inside and wasn't sure what she could do about it. She was trying to protect her heart, especially after the results of the pregnancy test she'd taken a few days ago.

Jason was an honorable man. Just the kind of man who'd keep her around just because she was the mother of his child. She wasn't particularly thinking of herself per se but of her child. She had grown up in a loveless household and simply refused to subject her child to one. Jason would never understand how that could be because he'd grown up with parents who'd loved each other and had set a good example for their children to follow. That was evident in the way his cousins and brother treated the wives they loved. It was easy to see their relationships were loving ones, the kinds that last until death. She didn't expect that kind of long-term commitment from Jason. That was not in the plan and had not been in his proposal.

She knew he was awake by the sound of his breathing but his back was to her as hers was to him. When he had come up to bed he hadn't said anything. In fact he had barely cast a glance her way before sliding under the covers.

His family was excited about hosting a wedding reception for them but she had been tempted to tell them not to bother. Their year would be up before she knew it anyway. However, she had sat there and listened while plans were being made and fighting the urge to get pulled into the excitement.

The bed shifted and she held her breath hoping that, although she'd given him that reminder, he would still want her. He dashed that hope when instead of sliding toward her he got out of the bed and left the room. Was he coming back to bed or did he plan on sleeping somewhere else tonight? On the sofa? In his truck?

She couldn't help the tears that begin falling from her eyes. She only had herself to blame. No one told her to fall in love. She should have known better. She should not have put her heart out there. But she had and now she was paying the price for doing so.

"Okay, what the hell is wrong with you, Jason? It's not like you to make such a stupid mistake and the one you just made was a doozy," Zane stormed. "That's the sheikh's prized horse and what you did could have cost him a leg."

Anger flared up inside of Jason. "Dammit, Zane, I know what I did. You don't have to remind me."

He then glanced over at Derringer and waited to see what he had to say and when he didn't say anything, Jason was grateful.

"Look, guys, I'm sorry about the mistake. I've got a lot on my mind. I think I'll call it a day before I cause another major screwup." He then walked off toward Zane's barn.

He was in the middle of saddling his horse to leave when Derringer walked up. "Hey, man, you want to talk about it?"

Jason drew in a deep breath. "No."

"Come on, Jas, there's evidently trouble in paradise at Jason's Place. I don't profess to be an expert when it comes to such matters, but even you will admit that me and Lucia had a number of clashes before we married."

Jason glanced over at him. "What about *after* you married?"

Derringer threw his head back and laughed. "Want a list? The main thing to remember is the two of you are people with different personalities and that in itself is bound to cause problems. The most effective solution is good, open communication. We talk it out and then we make love. Works every time. Oh, and you need to remind her every so often how much you love her."

Jason chuckled dryly. "The first two things you said I should do are things I can handle but not the latter."

Derringer raised a brow. "What? You can't tell your wife you love her?"

Jason sighed. "No, I can't tell her."

Derringer looked confused. "Why? You do love her, don't you?"

"Yes, more than life."

"Then what's the problem?"

Jason stopped what he was doing and met Derringer's gaze. "She doesn't love me back."

Derringer blinked and then drew back slightly and said, "Of course she loves you."

Jason shook his head. "No, she doesn't." He paused for a moment and then said, "Our marriage was based on a business proposition, Derringer. She needed a husband to retain her trust fund and I wanted her land—at least co-ownership of her land—and Hercules."

Derringer stared at him for a long moment and then said, "I think you'd better start from the beginning."

It took Jason less than ten minutes to tell Derringer everything, basically because his cousin stood there and listened without asking any questions. But once he'd finished the questions had begun...as well as the observations.

Derringer was certain Bella loved him because he claimed she looked at Jason the way Lucia looked at him, the way Chloe looked at Ramsey and the way Pam looked at Dillon—when they thought no one was supposed to be watching.

Then Derringer claimed that given the fact Jason and Bella were still sharing the same bed—although no hanky-panky had been going on for almost a week now—had significant meaning.

Jason shook his head. "If Bella loves me the way you think she does then why hasn't she told me?"

Derringer crossed his arms over his chest. "And why haven't you told her?" When Jason couldn't answer Derringer smiled and said, "I think the two of you have a big communication problem. It happens and is something that can easily be corrected."

Jason couldn't help but smile. "Sounds like you've gotten to be a real expert on the subject of marriage."

Derringer chuckled. "I have to be. I plan on being a married man for life so I need to know what it takes to keep my woman happy and to understand that when wifey isn't happy, hubby's life can be a living hell."

Derringer then tapped his foot on the barn's wooden floor as if he was trying to make up his mind about something. "I really shouldn't be telling you this because it's something I overheard Chloe and Lucia discussing yesterday and if Lucia found out I was eavesdropping she—"

"What?"

"Maybe you already know but just hadn't mentioned anything."

"Dammit, Derringer, what the hell are you talking about?"

A sly smile eased across Derringer's lips. "The ladies in the family suspect Bella might be pregnant."

Bella walked out of the children's hospital with a smile on her face. She loved kids and being around them always made her forget her troubles, which was why she would come here a couple of days a week to spend time with them. She glanced at her watch. It was still early yet and she wasn't ready to go home.

Home.

She couldn't help but think of Jason's Place as her home. Although she'd made a stink with Jason about construction on her ranch, she didn't relish the thought of going back there to live. She had gotten accustomed to her home with Jason.

She was more confused than ever and the phone call from her mother hadn't helped. Now her parents were trying to work out a bargain with her—another proposal of a sort. They would have their attorney draw up a legal document that stated if she returned home they would give her the space she needed. Of course they wanted her to move back onto their estate, although she would be given the entire east wing as her own. They claimed they no longer wanted to control her life, but just wanted to make sure she was living the kind of life she was entitled to live.

Their proposal sounded good but she had gotten into enough trouble accepting proposals already. Besides, even if things didn't work out between her and Jason, he deserved to be around his child. When they divorced, at least his son or daughter would be a stone's throw away.

She was crossing the parking lot to her car when she heard someone call her name. She turned and cringed when she saw it was her uncle Kenneth's daughter, who was the mother of the twins. Although Uncle Kenneth had had an outburst at the trial, Elyse Bostwick Thomas had not. She'd been too busy crying.

Drawing in a deep breath Bella waited for the woman to catch up with her. "Elyse."

"Bella. I just wanted to say how sorry I was for what Mark and Michael did. I know Dad is still bitter and I've tried talking to him about it but he refuses to discuss it. He's always spoiled the boys and there was nothing I could do about it, mainly because my husband and I are divorced. My ex moved away, but I wanted a father figure in their lives."

Elyse didn't say anything for a moment. "I hope Dad will eventually realize his part in all this, and although I miss my sons, they were getting too out of hand. I've been assured the place they are going will teach them discipline. I just wanted you to know I was wrong for listening to everything Dad said about you and when I found out you even offered to help pay for my sons' attorney I thought that was generous of you."

Bella nodded. "Uncle Kenneth turned down my offer."

"Yes, but just the thought touched me deeply considering everything. You and I are family and I hope that one day we can be friends."

A smile touched Bella's lips. "I'd like that, Elyse. I really would."

"Bella, are you sure you're okay? You might want to go see the doctor about that stomach virus."

Bella glanced over at Chloe. On her way home she had dropped by to visit with her cousin-in-law and little Susan. Bella had grown fond of the baby who was a replica of both of her parents. The little girl had Ramsey's eyes and skin tone and Chloe's mouth and nose. "Yes, Chloe, I'm fine."

She decided not to say anything about her pregnancy just yet until after she figured out how and when she would tell Jason. Evidently Chloe had gotten suspicious because Bella had thrown up the other day when Chloe had come to deliver a package to Jason from Ramsey.

Bella knew from the bits and pieces of the stories she'd heard from the ladies that Chloe was pregnant when she and Ramsey had married. However, Bella doubted that was the reason Ramsey had married her. Anyone around the pair for any period of time could tell how in love they were.

Bella never had a best friend, no other woman to share her innermost feminine secrets with. That was one of the reasons she appreciated the bond she felt toward all the Westmoreland women. They were all friendly, understanding and supportive. But she was hoping that because Chloe had been pregnant when she'd married Ramsey, her in-law could help her understand a few things. She had decisions to make that would impact her baby's future.

"Chloe, can I ask you something?"

Chloe smiled over at her. "Sure."

"When you found out you were pregnant were you afraid to tell Ramsey for fear of how he would react?"

Chloe placed her teacup down on the table and her smile brightened as if she was recalling that time. "I didn't discover I was pregnant until Ramsey and I broke up. But the one thing I knew was that I was going to tell him because he had every right to know. The one thing that I wasn't sure about was when I was going to tell him. One time I thought of taking the coward's way out and waiting until I returned to Florida and calling him from there."

Chloe paused for a moment and then said, "Ramsey made things easy for me when he came to me. We patched up things between us, found it had been nothing more than a huge misunderstanding and got back together. It was then that I told him about my pregnancy and he was happy about it."

Bella took a sip of her tea and then asked, "When the two of you broke up did you stay apart for long?"

"For over three weeks and they were the unhappiest three weeks of my life." Chloe smiled again when she added, "A Westmoreland man has a tendency to grow on you, Bella. They become habit-forming. And when it comes to babies, they love them."

There was no doubt in Bella's mind that Jason loved children; that wasn't what worried her. The big question was if he'd want to father any with her considering the nature of their marriage. Would he see that as a noose around his neck? For all she knew he might be counting the days until their year would be up so he could go his way and she go hers. A baby would definitely change things.

She glanced back over at Chloe. "Ramsey is a wonderful father."

Chloe smiled. "Yes, and Jason would be a wonderful father, as well. When their parents died all the Westmorelands had to pitch in and raise the younger ones. It was a team effort and it wasn't easy. Jason is wonderful with children and would make any child a fantastic father."

Chloe chuckled. "I can see him with a son while teaching him to ride his first pony, or a daughter who will wrap him around her finger the way Susan does

Ramsey. I can see you and Jason having a houseful of kids."

Bella nodded. Chloe could only see that because she thought she and Jason had a normal marriage.

"Don't ever underestimate a Westmoreland man, Bella."

Chloe's words interrupted her thoughts. "What do you mean?"

"I mean that from what I've discovered in talking with all the other wives, even those spread out in Montana, Texas, Atlanta and Charlotte, a Westmoreland man is loyal and dedicated to a fault to the woman he's chosen as a mate. The woman he loves. And although they can be overly protective at times, you can't find a man more loving and supportive. But the one thing they don't care too much for is when we hold secrets from them. Secrets that need to be shared with them. Jason is special, and I believe the longer you and he are married, the more you will see just how special he is."

Chloe reached out and gently touched Bella's hand. "I hope what I've said has helped in some way."

Bella returned her smile. "It has." Bella knew that she needed to tell Jason about the baby. And whatever decision he made regarding their future, she would have to live with it.

Chapter 10

Jason didn't bother riding his horse back home after his discussion with Derringer. Instead he borrowed Zane's truck and drove home like a madman only to discover Bella wasn't there. She hadn't mentioned anything at breakfast about going out, so where was she? But then they hadn't been real chatty lately, so he wasn't really surprised she hadn't told him anything.

He glanced around his home—their home—and took in the changes she'd made. Subtle changes but changes he liked. If she were to leave his house—their house—it wouldn't be the same. He wouldn't be the same.

He drew in a deep breath. What if the ladies' suspicions were true and she was pregnant? What if Derringer's suspicions were true and she loved him? Hell, if both suspicions were true then they had one hell of a major communication problem between them, and it was one he intended to remedy today as soon as she returned.

He walked into the kitchen and began making of all things, a cup of tea. Jeez, Bella had definitely rubbed off on him but he wouldn't have it any other way. And what if she was really pregnant? The thought of her stomach growing big while she carried his child almost left him breathless. And he could recall when it happened.

It had to have been their wedding night spent in the honeymoon suite of the Four Seasons. He had awakened to find her mouth on him and she had driven him to more passion than he'd ever felt in his entire life. He'd ended up flipping her on her back and taking her without wearing a condom. He had exploded the moment he'd gotten inside her body. Evidently she had been good and fertile that night.

He certainly hoped so. The thought of her having his baby was his most fervent desire. And no matter what she thought, he would provide both her and his child with a loving home.

He heard the sound of the front door opening and paused a moment not to rush out and greet her. They needed to talk and he needed to create a comfortable environment for them to do so. He was determined that before they went to bed tonight there would be a greater degree of understanding between them. With that resolution, he placed the teacup on the counter to go greet his wife.

Bella's grooming and social training skills had prepared her to handle just about anything, but now that she was back at Jason's Place she was no longer sure of her capabilities. So much for all the money her parents had poured into those private schools.

She placed her purse on the table thinking at least she'd had one bright spot in her day other than the time spent with the kids. And that was her discussion with Elyse. They had made plans to get together for tea later in the week. She could just imagine how her uncle would handle it when he found out she and Elyse had decided to be friends.

And then there had been her conversation with Chloe. It had definitely been an eye-opener and made her realize she couldn't keep her secret from Jason any longer. He deserved to know about the baby and she would tell him tonight.

"Bella. You're home."

She was pulled from her reverie by the pure masculine tone of Jason's voice when he walked out of the kitchen. Her pulse hammered in the center of her throat and she wondered if he would always have this kind of effect on her. She took a second or two to compose herself, before she responded to him. "Yes, I'm home. I see you have company."

He lifted a brow. "Company?"

"Yes. Zane's truck is parked outside," she replied, allowing her gaze to roam over her husband, unable to stop herself from doing so. He was such a hunk and no matter what he wore it only enhanced his masculinity. Even the jeans and chambray shirt he was wearing now made him look sexy as hell.

"I borrowed it. He's not here."

"Oh." That meant they were alone. Under the same roof. And hadn't made love in almost a week. So it stood to reason that the deep vibrations of his voice would stir across her skin and that turn-you-on mouth of his would make her panties start to feel damp.

She met his gaze and something akin to potent sexual awareness passed between them, charging the air, electrifying the moment. She felt it and was sure he felt it, as well. She studied his features and knew she wanted a son or daughter who looked just like him.

She knew she needed to break into the sensual vibe surrounding them and go up the stairs, or else she would be tempted to do something crazy like cross the room and throw herself in his arms and beg him to want her, to love her, to want the child they had conceived together.

"Well, I guess I'll go upstairs a moment and—"

"Do you have a moment so we can talk, Bella?"

She swallowed deeply. "Talk?"

"Yes."

That meant she was going to have to sit across from him and watch that sensual mouth of his move, see his tongue work and remember what it felt like dueling nonstop with hers and—

"Bella, could we talk?"

She swallowed again. "Now?"

"Yes."

"Sure," she murmured and then she followed him toward the kitchen. Studying his backside she could only think that the man she had married was such a hottie.

Jason wasn't sure where they needed to begin but he did know they needed to begin somewhere.

"I was about to have a cup of tea. Would you like a cup, as well?"

He wondered if she recalled those were the exact words she had spoken to him that first time she had invited him inside her house. They were words he still remembered to this day. And from the trace of amusement that touched her lips, he knew that she had recalled them.

"Yes, I'd love a cup. Thank you," she said, sitting down at the table, unintentionally flashing a bit of thigh.

He stepped back and quickly moved to the counter, trying to fight for control and to not remember this is the woman whom he'd given her first orgasm, the woman who'd awakened him one morning with her mouth on him, the first woman he'd had unprotected sex with, the only woman he'd wanted to shoot his release inside of, but more than anything, this was the woman he loved so very much.

Moments later when he turned back to her with cups of tea in his hands, he could tell she was nervous, was probably wondering what he wanted to talk about and was hoping he would hurry and get it over with.

"So, how was your day today?" he asked, sitting across from her at the table.

She shrugged those delicate shoulders he liked running his tongue over. She looked so sinfully sexy in the sundress she was wearing. "It was nice. I spent a lot of it at the children's hospital. Today was 'read-a-story' day and I entertained a bunch of them. I had so much fun."

"I'm glad."

"I also ran into Uncle Kenneth's daughter, Elyse."

"The mother of the twins, right?"

"Yes."

"And how did that go?" Jason asked.

"Better than I expected. Unlike Uncle Kenneth, she's not holding me responsible for what happened to her sons. She says they were getting out of hand anyway and is hoping the two years will teach them discipline," Bella said.

"We can all hope for that" was Jason's response.

"Yes, but in a way I feel sorry for her. I can only imagine how things were for her having Kenneth for a father. My dad wouldn't get a 'Father of the Year' trophy, either, but at least I had friends I met at all those schools they shipped me off to. It never bothered me when I didn't go home for the holidays. It helped when I went home with friends and saw how parents were supposed to act. Not as business partners but as human beings."

Bella realized after she'd said it that in a way Jason was her business partner, but she'd never thought of him that way. From the time he'd slipped a ring on her finger she had thought of him as her husband—for better or worse.

The kitchen got silent as they sipped tea.

"So what do you want to talk about, Jason?"

Good question, Jason thought. "I want to talk about us."

He saw her swallow. "Us?"

"Yes, us. Lately, I haven't been feeling an 'us' and I want to ask you a question."

She glanced over at him. "What?"

"Do you not want to be married to me anymore?"

She broke eye contact with him to study the pattern design on her teacup. "What gave you that idea?"

"Want a list?"

She shot her gaze back to him. "I didn't think you'd notice."

"Is that what this is about, Bella, me not noticing you, giving you attention?"

She quickly shook her head. Heaven help her or him if he were to notice her any more or give her more attention than she was already getting. To say Jason Westmoreland was all into her was an understatement. Unfortunately he was all into her, literally. And all for the wrong reasons. Sex was great but it couldn't hold a marriage together. It couldn't replace love no matter how many orgasms you had a night.

"Bella?"

"No, that's not it," she said, nervously biting her bottom lip.

"Then what is it, sweetheart? What do you need that I'm not giving you? What can I do to make you happy? I need to know because your leaving me is not an option. I love you too much to let you go."

The teacup froze midway to her lips. She stared over at him in shock. "What did you just say?"

"A number of things. Do I need to repeat it all?"

She shook her head, putting her cup down. "No, just the last part."

"About me loving you?"

"Yes."

"I said I loved you too much to let you go. Lately you've been reminding me about the year I mentioned in my proposal, but there isn't a year time frame, Bella. I threw that in as an adjustment period to not scare you off. I never intended to end things between us."

He saw the single tear flow from her eyes. "You didn't?"

"No. I love you too much to let you go. There, I've said it again and I will keep saying it until you finally hear it. Believe it. Accept it."

"I didn't know you loved me, Jason. I love you, too. I think I fell in love with you the first time I saw you at your family's charity ball."

"And that's when I believe I fell in love with you, as well," he said, pushing the chair back to get up from the table. "I knew there was a reason every time we touched a part of my soul would stir, my heart would melt and my desire for you would increase."

"I thought it was all about sex."

"No. I believe the reason the sex between us was so good, so damn hot, was that it was fueled by love of the most intense kind. More than once I wanted to tell you I loved you but I wasn't sure you were ready to hear it. I didn't want to run you off."

"And knowing you loved me is what I needed to hear," she said, standing. "I've never thought I could be loved and I wanted so much for you to love me."

"Sweetheart, I do. I love every single thing about you."

"Oh, Jason."

She went to him and was immediately swept up into his arms, held tight. And when he lowered his head to kiss her, her mouth was ready, willing and hungry. That was evident in the way her tongue mated with his with such intensity.

Moments later he pulled back and swept her off her feet and into his arms then walked out of the kitchen.

Somehow they made it upstairs to the bedroom. And there in the middle of the room, he kissed Bella again with a hunger that she greedily returned. He finally released her mouth to draw in a deep breath, but before she could draw in one of her own, he flipped her dress up to her waist and was pulling a pair of wet panties down her thighs. She barely had time to react before he moved to her hips to bury his head between her legs.

"Jason!"

She came the moment his tongue whipped inside of her and began stroking her labia, but she quickly saw that wouldn't be enough for him. He sharpened the tip of his tongue and literally stabbed deep inside of her and proceeded to lick circles around her clitoris before drawing it in between his lips.

Her eyes fluttered closed as he then began suckling her senseless as desire, more potent than any she'd ever felt, started consuming her, racing through every part of her body and pushing her toward a orgasm.

"Jason!"

And he still didn't let up. She reached for him but couldn't get a firm hold as his tongue began thrusting inside her again. His tongue, she thought, should be patented with a warning sign. Whenever he parted this life it should be donated to the Smithsonian.

And when she came yet again, he spread her thighs wide to lap her up. She moaned deep in her throat as his tongue and lips made a plaything of her clitoris, driving her demented, crazy with lust, when sensations after earth-shattering sensations rammed through her.

And then suddenly he pulled back and through glazed eyes she watched as he stood and quickly undressed himself and then proceeded to undress her, as well. Her gaze went to his erection.

Without further ado, he carried her over to the bed,

placed her on her back, slid over her and settled between her legs and aimed his shaft straight toward the damp folds of her labia.

"Yes!" she almost screamed out, and then she felt him, pushing inside her, desperate to be joined with her.

He stopped moving. Dropped his head down near hers and said in a sensual growl, "No condom tonight."

Bella gazed up at him. "No condom tonight or any other night for a while," she whispered. "I'll tell you why later. It's something I planned to tell you tonight anyway." And before she could dwell too much on just what she had to tell him, he began thrusting inside of her.

And when he pushed all the way to the hilt she gasped for breath at the fullness of having him buried so deep inside her. Her muscles clung to him, she was holding him tight and she began massaging him, milking his shaft for everything she had and thought she could get, while thinking a week had been too long.

He widened her legs farther with his hands and lifted her hips to drive deeper still and she almost cried when he began a steady thrusting inside of her, with relentless precision. This was the kind of ecstasy she'd missed. She hadn't known such degrees of pleasure existed until him and when he lifted her legs onto his shoulders while thrusting back and forth inside her, their gazes met through dazed lashes.

"Come for me, baby," he whispered. "Come for me now."

Her body complied and began to shudder in a climax so gigantic she felt the house shaking. She screamed. There was no way she could not, and when he began coming inside her, his hot release thickened by the intensity of their lovemaking, she could only cry out as she was swept away yet again.

And then he leaned up and kissed her, but not before whispering that he loved her and that he planned to spend the rest of his life making her happy, making her feel loved. And she believed him.

With all the strength she could muster, she leaned up to meet him.

"And I love you so very much, too."

And she meant it.

"Why don't I have to wear a condom for a while?" Jason asked moments later with her entwined in his arms, their limbs tangled as they enjoyed the aftermath of their lovemaking together. He knew the reason, but he wanted her to confirm it.

She lifted her head slightly, met his gaze and whispered, "I'm having your baby."

Her announcement did something to him. Being given confirmation that a life they had created together was growing inside her made him shudder. He knew she was waiting for him to say something.

He planned to show her he had taken it well. She needed to know just how happy her announcement had made him. "Knowing that you are pregnant with my child, Bella, is the greatest gift I could ever hope to receive."

"Oh, Jason."

And then she was there, closer into his arms with her arms wrapped around his neck. "I was afraid you wouldn't be happy."

"You were afraid for nothing. I am ecstatic, overjoyed at the prospect of being a father. Thank you for everything you've done, all the happiness you've brought me."

She shook her head. "No, it's I who needs to thank you for sharing your family with me, for giving me your support when my own family tried to break me down. And for loving me."

And then she leaned toward his lips and he gave her what she wanted, what he wanted. He knew at that moment the proposal had worked. It had brought them together in a way they thought wasn't possible. And he would always appreciate and be forever thankful that Bella had come into his life.

Two days later the Westmorelands met at Dillon's for breakfast to celebrate. It seemed everyone had announcements to make and Dillon felt it was best that they were all made at the same time so they could all rejoice and celebrate.

First Dillon announced he'd received word from Bane that he would be graduating from the naval academy in a few months with honors. Dillon almost choked up when he'd said it, which let everyone know the magnitude of Bane's accomplishments in the eyes of his family. They knew Bane's first year in the navy had been hard since he hadn't known the meaning of discipline. But he'd finally straightened up and had dreams of becoming a SEAL. He'd worked hard and found favor with one of the high-ranking chief petty officers who'd recognized his potential and recommended him for the academy.

Zane then announced that Hercules had done his duty and had impregnated Silver Fly and everyone could only anticipate the beauty of the foal she would one day deliver.

Ramsey followed and said he'd received word from Storm Westmoreland that his wife, Jayla, was expecting and so were Durango and his wife, Savannah. Reggie and Libby's twins were now crawling all over the place. And then with a huge smile on his face Ramsey announced that he and Chloe were having another baby. That sent out loud cheers and it seemed the loudest had come from Chloe's father, Senator Jamison Burton of Florida, who along with Chloe's stepmother, had arrived the day before to visit with his daughter, son-in-law and granddaughter.

Everyone got quiet when Jason stood to announce that he and Bella would be having a baby in the spring, as well. Bella's eyes were glued to Jason as he spoke and she could feel the love radiating from his every word.

"Bella and I are converting her grandfather's ranch into a guest house and combining our lands for our future children to enjoy one day," he ended by saying.

"Does that mean the two of you want more than one child?" Zane asked with a sly chuckle.

Jason glanced over at Bella. "Yes, I want as many children as my wife wants to give me. We can handle it, can't we, sweetheart?"

Bella smiled. "Yes, we can handle it." And they would because what had started out as a proposal had ended up being a whole lot more and she was filled with overflowing joy at how Jason and his family had enriched her life.

He reached out his hand to her and she took it. Hers felt comforting in his and she could only be thankful for her Westmoreland man.

Epilogue

"When I first heard you'd gotten married I wondered about the quickness of it, Jason, but after meeting Bella I understand why," Micah said to his brother. "She's beautiful."

"Thanks." Jason smiled as he glanced around the huge guest house on his and Bella's property. The weather had cooperated and the construction workers had been able to transform what had once been a ranch house into a huge fifteen room guest house for family, friends and business associates of the Westmorelands. Combining the old with the new, the builder and his crew had done a fantastic job and Jason and Bella couldn't be more pleased.

He glanced across the way and saw Dillon was talking to Bane who'd surprised everyone by showing up. It was the first time he'd returned home since he had left nearly three years ago. Jason had gotten the chance to have a long conversation with his youngest brother. He was not the bad-assed kid of yesteryears but standing beside Dillon in his naval officer's uniform, the family couldn't be more proud of the man he had become. But there still was that pain behind the sharpness of Bane's eyes. Although he hadn't mentioned Crystal's name, everyone in the family knew the young woman who'd been Bane's first love, his fixation probably since puberty, was still in his thoughts and probably had a permanent place in his heart. He could only imagine the conversation Dillon was having with Bane since they both had intense expressions on their faces.

"So you've not given up on Crystal?" Dillon asked his youngest brother.

Bane shook his head. "No. A man can never give up on the woman he loves. She's in my blood and I believe that no matter where she is, I'm in hers." Bane paused a moment. "But that's the crux of my problem. I have no idea where she is."

Bane then studied Dillon's features. "And you're sure that you don't?"

Dillon inhaled deeply. "Yes, I'm being honest with you, Bane. When the Newsomes moved away they didn't leave anyone a forwarding address. I just think they wanted to put as much distance between you and them as possible. But I'll still go on record and say that I think the time apart for you and Crystal was a good thing. She was young and so were you. The two of you were headed for trouble and both of you needed to grow up. I am proud of the man you've become."

"Thanks, but one day when I have a lot of time I'm

going to find her, Dillon, and nobody, her parents or anyone, will keep me from claiming what's mine."

Dillon saw the intense look in Bane's face and only hoped that wherever Crystal Newsome was that she loved Bane just as much as Bane still loved her.

Jason glanced over at Bella who was talking to her parents. The Bostwicks had surprised everyone by flying in for the reception. So far they'd been on their good behavior, probably because they were still in awe by the fact that Jason was related to Thorn Westmoreland—racing legend; Stone Westmoreland—aka Rock Mason, *New York Times* bestselling author; Jared Westmoreland, whose reputation as a divorce attorney was renowned; Senator Reggie Westmoreland, and that Dillon was the CEO of Blue Ridge. Hell, they were even speechless when they learned there was even a sheikh in the family.

He saw that Bella was pretending to hang on to her parents' every word. He had discovered she knew how to handle them and refused to let them treat her like a child. He hadn't had to step in once to put them in their place. Bella had managed to do that rather nicely on her own. They had opted to stay at a hotel in town, which had been fine with both him and Bella. There was only so much of her parents that either of them could take.

He inwardly smiled as he studied Bella's features and could tell she was ready to be rescued. "Excuse me a minute, Micah, I need to go claim my wife for a second." Jason moved across the yard to her and as if she felt his impending presence, she glanced his way and smiled. She then excused herself from her parents and headed to meet him.

The dress she was wearing was beautiful and the style hid the little pooch of her stomach. The doctor had warned them that because of the way her stomach was growing they shouldn't be surprised if she was having twins. It would be a couple of months before they knew for sure.

"Do you want to go somewhere for tea…and me," Jason leaned over to whisper close to her ear.

Bella smiled up at him. "Think we'll be missed?"

Jason chuckled. "With all these Westmorelands around, I doubt it. I don't even think your parents will miss us. Now they're standing over there hanging on to Sheikh Jamal Yasir's every word."

"I noticed."

Jason then took his wife's hand in his. "Come on. Let's take a stroll around our land."

And their land was beautiful, with the valley, the mountains, the blooming flowers and the lakes. Already he could envision a younger slew of Westmorelands that he and Bella would produce who would help take care of their land. They would love it as much as their parents did. Not for the first time he felt as if he was a blessed man, his riches abundant not in money or jewelry but in the woman walking by his side. His Southern Bella, his southern beauty, the woman that was everything to him and then some.

"I was thinking," he said.

She glanced over at him. "About what?"

He stopped walking and reached out and placed a hand on her stomach. "You, me and our baby."

She chuckled. "Our babies. Don't forget there is that possibility."

He smiled at the thought of that. "Yes, our babies. But mainly about the proposal."

She nodded. "What about it?"

"I suggest we do another."

She threw her head back and laughed. "I don't have any more land or another horse to bargain with."

"A moot point, Mrs. Westmoreland. This time the stakes will be higher."

"Mmm, what do you want?"

"Another baby pretty soon after this one."

She chuckled again. "Don't you know you never mention having more babies to a pregnant woman? But I'm glad to hear that you want a house filled with children because I do, too. You'll make a wonderful father."

"And you a beautiful mother."

And then he kissed her with all the love in his heart, sealing yet another proposal and knowing the woman he held in his arms would be the love of his life for always.

* * * * *

We hope you enjoyed reading

Impetuous

by *New York Times* bestselling author

LORI FOSTER

and

Surrender

by *New York Times* bestselling author

BRENDA JACKSON

Both were originally Harlequin® series stories!

From passionate, suspenseful and dramatic
love stories to inspirational or historical,
Harlequin offers different lines to
satisfy every romance reader.

New books in each line are available every month.

**Luxury, scandal, desire—welcome to the lives
of the American elite.**

Harlequin.com

♦ HARLEQUIN

DESIRE

Luxury, scandal, desire—welcome to the lives of the American elite.

Save $1.00

on the purchase of ANY Harlequin Desire book.

Available wherever books are sold, including most bookstores, supermarkets, drugstores and discount stores.

Save $1.00

on the purchase of ANY Harlequin Desire book.

Coupon valid until September 30, 2020.
Redeemable at participating outlets in the US and Canada only.
Not redeemable at Barnes & Noble stores. Limit one coupon per customer.

52616730

5 65373 00076 2 (8100)0 12459

BACCOUP54263